THE
FRONTIERS SAGA
EPISODE 5

RISE OF THE
CORINARI

D1738832

Ryk Brown

The Frontiers Saga Episode #5: Rise of the Corinari
Copyright © 2012 by Ryk Brown All rights reserved.

First Print Edition:
ISBN-13: 978-1480121157
ISBN-10: 1480121150

Cover and formatting: Streetlight Graphics

This is a work of fiction. Names, characters, places, and incidents either are the product of the author's imagination or are used fictitiously, and any resemblance to locales, events, business establishments, or actual persons—living or dead—is entirely coincidental.

CHAPTER ONE

Nathan stared at the large display screen on the forward bulkhead of his ready room as he flipped through page after page of damage reports generated by the Aurora's newly installed automated diagnostic systems. The list of malfunctions was daunting. The jump drive was offline, only one antimatter reactor was working, gravity plating on half the ship was fluctuating, and half their rail gun turrets were down as well. Of course, they only had about two seconds worth of rail gun ammo left, so a lack of functioning turrets was the least of their problems. At least they had maneuvering, so they could crawl around the system if necessary.

His concentration was broken by the sound of the entry buzzer. The hatch opened to reveal Tug standing in the hatchway with his usual stern, yet friendly, expression.

"May I enter, Captain?" Tug asked with unusual formality.

Nathan waved him in as he continued scanning the reports on the wall display. "Of course."

"Interesting data?" Tug asked, glancing at the display.

"Damage reports," Nathan responded with obvious disdain. He sat back up in his chair and turned toward Tug, switching off the wall display. "Corinair seemed like a nice place, didn't it?" he began. "Find a little piece of land, build a home, do a little farming, lead a quiet, peaceful life…"

"Until the Ta'Akar return and occupy the system," Tug interrupted, "or worse."

"What can I do for you, Tug?" Nathan asked, his daydream now fully dissipated.

"There is something that I wish to discuss with you, Captain," Tug began, again with a more formal tone than usual.

"That's twice you've called me captain in the last two minutes. It must be serious."

"Forgive me if what I am about to say seems…" Tug paused a moment, searching for the appropriate Earth expression. "…Out of line?"

Nathan's expression changed, a faint look of surprise registering. "Speak your mind, Tug," Nathan said, trying to assure the leader of the Karuzari that he was free to say whatever he wished.

"Well, it is about the tone of your command." Tug took a seat across from Nathan on the other side of his desk.

"Really?"

"Do not misinterpret my meaning," Tug quickly added. "I find your approachable demeanor and your trustworthiness quite pleasant. However, I am not sure that it will serve you well under the current circumstances."

"How so?" Nathan had a feeling Tug was leading somewhere. However, he was a bit surprised that Tug was treading so gingerly around his point.

"The Corinari are highly trained, highly disciplined combatants. They are also fiercely loyal. But that loyalty must be earned."

"And you think my *friendly manner* will not earn their loyalty."

"Actually, I suspect you have already earned it through your actions," Tug explained. "Keeping that loyalty, however, is another matter. The Corinari do not tolerate weakness in their leaders."

"You find me weak?" Nathan asked, feigning insult.

"Not at all, Captain. Quite the opposite, actually. But your *friendly manner* as you put it—it *could* easily be misunderstood by the Corinari."

"I see." Nathan couldn't help but be amused by how uncomfortable the subject seemed to make Tug. "I'll take that under advisement, and I'll try not to be so *friendly* in the future." Nathan smiled, then noticed that Tug still seemed somewhat pensive. "Was there something else?"

"I am afraid so... your crew. They seem to be a bit on edge."

Nathan had noticed a change in the few surviving crew he had left. They had become more segmented than before, limiting their associations to small select groups and avoiding the other groups altogether whenever possible. It was like two teams at a sporting match, neither one talking to the other. "Yes, I did notice that," Nathan admitted.

"I believe that the most recent Ta'Akar incursion is the cause of the unrest," Tug asserted. "I have overheard several conversations in passing. It seems your crew is trying to decide who should be blamed for the failure of security that led to the attacks. I believe that their debate is the result of the accusations being tossed about by Jessica and Vladimir. Each appears to be blaming the other, at least indirectly."

"I'm not sure any one person is to blame," Nathan defended.

"You are mistaken, Captain. The blame lies with one person and one person alone."

Nathan stared at Tug for a moment, waiting for a response. When it did not come, he shrugged and gestured for the answer from Tug.

"I am afraid the blame is yours, Captain."

"Tug, I wasn't even on board at the..."

"Precisely," Tug interrupted, his frustration building. "You were *not* on board, and you should have been."

"I was only trying to secure..."

"Captain, I comprehend what you were doing and I commend you for your devotion to your friends. But you have to understand something; you can no longer afford to *be* their friends. At least not in public. You are their captain now. Be *that* first, be their friend second. They need a leader more than they need a friend, as do the Corinari. Lead them, and they will follow you. If you do not, they will turn on you faster than you might imagine."

"What are you saying, that the Corinari might mutiny?" Nathan asked, somewhat shocked. "If that's the case, then maybe we should reconsider taking them on as crew."

"Captain, do not overreact to what I am saying," Tug warned. "You need to look at the situation from their perspective. The Corinari may be loyal, but their entire world is at stake. All of them might not see you as the legendary Na-Tan, but they all understand that your ship and its jump drive are the best hope they have to secure their world. If they believe that you are not up to the challenge, they will do what they must to save themselves, no matter how distasteful they might find it to be."

"What is it you suggest I do differently?" Nathan

asked in a tone that was perhaps more of a challenge than he had intended.

"Captain," Tug began with a sigh, "ever since we met, you have been in survival mode. You have been scrambling to keep your ship and your crew alive and intact; to meet each challenge as it is thrown your way. Despite your lack of experience, you and your crew have done a remarkable job thus far."

"But?" Nathan asked, fully aware that Tug's compliments were meant to soften the sting of the criticism that was to follow.

"But much of your success to date has been nothing more than amazingly good fortune," Tug warned.

Nathan was not surprised by Tug's statements. Nathan had been blessed throughout his life with such favorable luck. Whenever he appeared to be in unavoidable trouble, something would come along and provide him a way out. Tug was not the first to notice this, but Nathan had practically become reliant on his reoccurring good fortune over the years. His parents, his sisters, even his Fleet Academy roommate, Luis, had warned him that someday his luck would run out. "Yeah, I've always been pretty lucky," Nathan admitted.

"Do you ever ask yourself what you will do if your luck fails you?" Tug asked.

"Not really," Nathan admitted with some degree of embarrassment.

"Captain, I have known my share of men such as yourself. Call it luck. Call it fate. Call it instinct; the name by which it goes is of no matter. Sooner or later, it no longer works; their luck abandons them. Unfortunately, they are usually not the only ones who are affected by their dire change of fortune."

Tug looked Nathan straight in the eyes. "Are you willing to risk the fortunes of everyone, our worlds' as well as your own, on your good luck?"

"Tug," Nathan began hesitantly, "we both know that I'm not really qualified for this job."

After an abnormally long pause, Tug asked, "How did you end up as captain, Nathan?"

"You already know..."

"Yes, but tell me once more," Tug interrupted.

"I was the last one standing," Nathan summarized.

"Was not Commander Taylor standing as well?"

"I was the most senior officer left standing," Nathan said, somewhat annoyed that he was having to retell the story.

"Because your captain had promoted you over Commander—then Ensign—Taylor."

"Correct."

"And why do you think he chose to promote you over her?"

"He thought I had natural leadership abilities," Nathan admitted, although he had never shared his late captain's belief. "But I doubt that he expected me to be sitting in his chair so soon," Nathan added.

"But he was aware that the possibility existed," Tug insisted, "and that one of you had to be of higher rank than the other."

"But that was for the purpose of running the flight teams," Nathan argued, "not commanding the entire ship."

"Possibly," Tug conceded. "However, I suspect that he also made his selection because he felt that you were a better choice, should the unthinkable happen." Nathan was about to disagree, but Tug did not give him the chance. "You said that Captain Roberts was conscious and alert when he formally handed you command of the Aurora. Had he felt that you were not the right man for the job—or more specifically, had he thought that Ensign Taylor had been better suited for the position, I expect he would have said as much."

Nathan sat back in his chair, staring at Tug and remembering some of the things Captain Roberts—whom he had buried only a day ago on the world below—had said to him only a few weeks ago. He had also liked to lead Nathan to his conclusions rather than just presenting them outright. "You know, you remind me of him at times."

"Excuse me?"

"Captain Roberts," Nathan explained.

"I will take that as a compliment," Tug said as he looked curiously at Nathan. "My point is that you have the training required to perform your duties, even if you do not yet have the experience. The situation is difficult, yes, but not impossible." Tug noticed that Nathan was still staring at him. "I hope I have not been imprudent," Tug asked.

"Not at all, Mister Tugwell," Nathan assured him. "And I will try to be more *captain-like* in the future."

"Very well," Tug announced as he rose. "Then I will see you at the briefing," he added as he turned and headed for the exit.

"Where did you learn so much about command, Mister Tugwell?" Nathan wondered aloud. "Certainly not as the leader of a rebellion, and definitely not as a molo farmer."

"I have a rich and colorful past, Captain," Tug told him as he turned back and smiled. "Even before my days in the Palee militia. I hope that I can share it with you someday."

Nathan smiled back. He had no doubt that there

was far more to Redmond Tugwell than met the
eye—even more than Jalea, Tug's subordinate in
the Karuzari, already knew. He seriously doubted
anyone would ever learn of it all.

* * *

Nathan paused at the entrance to the briefing
room when he saw two Corinari guards escorting
Ensign Willard of the Yamaro's crew. They had
just reached the top of the ramp that led from the
Aurora's main deck up to her command deck, and
were moving down the corridor toward him.

"Gentlemen," Nathan greeted. The two Corinari
guards stopped a few steps from the captain,
snapping simultaneous salutes which Nathan
awkwardly returned. The Corinari salute was
somewhat different, with their forearms at a forty-
five degree angle to their torso and the palm of their
hand turned directly toward their faces, thumb
tucked in tight. Nathan couldn't help but think that
if they just moved their salute hands a little more
toward their noses, they would look like they were
trying to cover one eye.

"Thank you for coming," Nathan said to Ensign
Willard.

"I am honored to be asked," Ensign Willard
responded.

Nathan glanced down at the restraints on the
ensign's wrists, the same type that had been on the
wrists of the Takaran soldier they had interrogated
several days ago. It was an ugly episode that Nathan
wished he could forget. "Are the restraints really
necessary?" he asked one of the guards.

The guard glanced at his partner briefly before

responding. "Orders, sir," the guard responded with a heavy Corinairan accent. "Your security chief..."

"Remove them." Nathan interrupted.

"Yes, sir," the guard responded, immediately removing the restraints from Ensign Willard and placing them in the pouch on his utility belt. "Shall we continue to guard him, sir?"

"From out here," Nathan instructed in no uncertain terms.

"Thank you, Captain," Ensign Willard said as they entered the briefing room.

"Not at all," Nathan told him. "I expect your experience in the service of the Ta'Akar will provide us with some valuable intelligence."

"I will help in any way I can."

"Your Angla is quite good," Nathan commended as they walked the few meters from the hatchway to the briefing room table.

"My mother was a strong follower of the legends," he explained. "She taught us the language so that we would know the truth."

"I see." Nathan kept walking along the row of chairs, leaving Ensign Willard to take his seat at the only other chair that was left empty, which was at the opposite end of the table from where he, as the captain, usually sat. Everyone else was already seated and waiting for Nathan to arrive, still chatting amongst themselves as he worked his way around to his seat. It occurred to him that Tug, who was currently sitting at the chair to the left of the captain's chair, was right. If Captain Roberts had walked into this room, everyone would have snapped to a position of attention out of respect for his position; at least the fleet personnel would have done so. Maybe he *was* being their friend more than their captain. "As you were, everyone," he said sarcastically as he took his seat.

Jessica looked from side to side as she grasped his subtle hint, but it was already too late, as Nathan had taken his seat and was about to start the briefing.

Nathan paused for a moment before speaking, making sure he had everyone's attention. "For the last two weeks, we have been operating in a state of occasionally controlled chaos. Obviously, events left us very little choice in the matter, but this in and of itself has led to a breakdown in communication between departments, as well as a breakdown in the general chain of command. This has to end, now."

"Nathan," Jessica started. Nathan glared at her. "My apologies, sir. I meant Captain." She paused for a moment, checking Nathan's expression to be sure it was safe for her to continue. "It's a little hard to have a proper chain of command when we're down to a crew of twenty-three."

"Perhaps, but we'll soon have considerably more crew joining us from Corinair. If we don't set a proper example, how can we expect them to follow us?" Nathan looked at Jessica, who nodded her concession to his point. Nathan turned to Tug. "Speaking of volunteers, how are we doing on that front, Mister Tugwell?"

"So far, we have nearly four thousand volunteers. According to the last communiqué from Chief Montrose, it has yet to show any signs of letting up."

"What kind of people are volunteering?" Nathan asked.

"All types, it appears. Everything from simple laborers to physicists."

"Anyone with experience in space?"

"A few," Tug said, "but you have to remember, Captain; most of the young men that are forced to serve in the ranks of the Ta'Akar never make it back to their home worlds. Less than ten percent, I would imagine."

"Are you saying that ninety percent of them die in combat?"

"If I may?" Ensign Willard interrupted. Nathan nodded for him to continue. "Yes, some do die in the service of the Ta'Akar, but most of them just end up somewhere else. You see, when your time has been served, the Ta'Akar tend to just let you off on the nearest world for you to find your own way home, which is not an easy task."

"Nice folks," Jessica mumbled.

"Precisely," Tug agreed. "This is why there are so few on Corinair with experience on a combat space vessel. Since most of their tours end in the Takaran home system, the majority of them end up stranded there. It also serves to provide the Takarans with a low-income worker-class to do the jobs that Takarans themselves do not wish to do."

"There are at least twenty of them still amongst the Yamaro's crew, Captain, and probably many more from other worlds that might be willing to serve your cause in exchange for a promise to be returned to their homes. And they do have experience aboard a combat space vessel."

"Yeah, a *Takaran* combat space vessel," Jessica chimed in. It was obvious to all that she was not in favor of the idea.

"Exactly my point," Ensign Willard stated in response to Jessica's snide remark. "With you, it would be their choice. With the Ta'Akar, it was not."

"I'll take the idea under advisement," Nathan

told Ensign Willard. Out of the corner of his eye, he could see Jessica's disapproving glare, but chose to ignore it. "Doctor," he began, looking to Doctor Chen next, "how is Commander Taylor doing?"

"Remarkably well," Doctor Chen admitted with obvious astonishment. "The nanites they used did incredible work. It will take several weeks for them to finish, and then a few weeks more before they are all flushed from her system. She is looking at about a month of recovery time, at least according to her Corinairan doctors. On Earth, if she had survived, it would've taken nearly a year of therapy and even then there would probably have been permanent motor and cognitive deficits."

"Is she well enough to do some interviews?" Nathan asked.

"As long as they are done close to the hospital, so she can easily return to her room if she tires, which I suspect she will quite easily, at least for a few more weeks."

"Very well. Tug, forward your application lists to Cameron for review. She's still the XO on this ship, and I want her to pick the crew."

"As you wish."

"How are your other patients, Doctor?"

"What other patients?" Doctor Chen stated. "The Corinairans took care of all of them. The worst cases were taken down to the surface, and the rest were treated on board by Corinairan medical staff. The ones on the surface may be out of action for awhile, but the twelve treated on board will be ready to return to duty in a few days."

"What about Josh?"

"He was treated on board as well. He'll be ready to rub everyone the wrong way again in another day or two."

"That's good to hear, Doc." Nathan turned his attention to Jalea, the next person seated on that side of the table. "Jalea?"

"Six Karuzari have reported in so far."

"How many do you think are on Corinair?" Nathan inquired.

"There is no way of knowing," she warned. "I know of at least that many who escaped the attack on Taroa. There were at least a dozen more that were already on Corinair at the time of the Yamaro's attack. If they survived, we may yet hear from them. The situation on Corinair is still somewhat chaotic in most places. I should also point out, Captain, that one of the Karuzari that reported in stated that he heard there may be a dozen more in the Savoy system. Apparently one of our recruiters passed through this system on his way to Savoy several months ago. If he made it to Ancot, the Savoy system's only inhabited world, then there could be additional volunteers there as well."

"Understood."

"Captain," Ensign Willard interrupted again, "the Yamaro was due to arrive in the Savoy system in about forty standard days. We were scheduled to pick up a batch of inductees before we returned to Takara to complete our patrol."

"And if the Yamaro doesn't show up as scheduled?" Nathan asked.

"Once the Yamaro is at least a few days overdue, the local military commander will either send out a patrol in search of the Yamaro, if any are available, or send word to the home world that they are overdue, which would also result in some type of action."

"What's the flight time between Savoy and

Darvano?" Nathan wondered.

"About thirty of your days, if I am making the conversion properly. I still do not fully understand your method of time measurement," Ensign Willard admitted.

"So if there *is* a ship in the Savoy system when the Yamaro becomes overdue," Nathan said, "it would take them a month to reach us, *if* they had reason to fly directly here."

"Correct. As our standard patrol route took us quite close to the Darvano system, it would be logical to look here, in case we had problems and had to make port in the Darvano system."

"So, we've got about seventy days before another Takaran ship comes snooping around," Nathan concluded.

"I would be more worried about the comm-drone on its way to Takara, Captain," Ensign Willard reminded.

"What comm-drone?" Jessica asked.

"I told Ensign Mendez about all of this," Ensign Willard assured them. "Sergeant Weatherly was there as well."

"Why am I only hearing about this now?" Nathan asked as he shot a glare Jessica's way.

"I'm sorry, Captain," Jessica said. "Sergeant Weatherly was pretty shaken up by what happened. Those were some ugly firefights, and he and Enrique had gotten pretty chummy in the last couple of weeks. I hadn't gotten around to debriefing him yet."

"Not good enough, Ensign," Nathan told her. "Tell the sergeant to suck it up. Nobody sits on intel, understood?"

"Yes, sir."

"Tell me more about the comm-drone," Nathan

told Ensign Willard. "We intercepted it as we were passing the system. It was carrying word of your presence in the Darvano system back to Takara. When the message reaches command, they will dispatch a battle group."

"And how long will it take for the battle group to reach us?" Nathan asked. He didn't much care for the direction the conversation was headed.

"It depends on where the battle group is located," he explained. "Command keeps a battle group wandering the cluster at all times. Only the admiralty knows its route. If the battle group is nearby, it could take as little as thirty days. If not, it could take much longer. If the battle group is too distant, they will send ships directly from Takara, which would take about one hundred and sixty days."

"Ensign Nash, I want this man fully debriefed as soon as this meeting is over. I want us to know everything he knows."

"Yes, sir," Jessica answered.

"I'm assuming we can count on your cooperation, Ensign Willard?"

"Of course, Captain."

"Sir, if I may?" Jessica interrupted.

It was not like Jessica to ask permission to speak. Nathan knew that his own more formal demeanor was the cause of her behavior. "Go ahead."

"No offense to Ensign Willard," she began, nodding politely at him, "but I would advise not taking information from *any* source without independent verification."

"A wise precaution," Nathan admitted, turning to Tug. "How much help can you provide in that area, Mister Tugwell?"

"Some," Tug admitted, "such as travel times, ship

strengths, common patrol routes; all these things we have known for some time now. However, much of the information that Ensign Willard provides will be unverifiable by any means currently available to us."

"Very well. Do what you can."

"Of course."

"Ensign Kamenetskiy," Nathan said, turning to Vladimir sitting to his right, "how bad off are we?"

"It is not so good, I am afraid. We have one good reactor. The other three will be online within a few days. So power is no problem. Maneuvering is online, but many systems are not at one hundred percent. Response will be sluggish, and she will fly, but like a turtle. We also have problems with life support, gravity plating, and the hangar bay is a mess from the firefight—not to mention the burn by that crazy medevac pilot. He nearly melted the bulkheads."

"What's wrong with life support?" Nathan inquired.

"I do not yet know. Some intermittent problem with CO_2 scrubbers. I have not yet checked. The worst news is that we cannot jump, as there are at least six emitters that are damaged or gone. And of course, do not forget about the big hole in our bow."

"But this is all repairable, is it not?" Nathan wondered.

"Mostly, yes, but it will take time. And I do not know about the emitters. I do not think I have the parts to assemble replacements. Our fabrication facilities were not yet installed when we left Earth."

"How much time are we talking?"

"If I can replace or repair all parts, maybe two to three months, if we have more technicians. With what we have now, maybe a year or more."

"Captain," Ensign Willard interrupted, "you could use the Yamaro's fabricators."

"Come again?" Nathan said. Ensign Willard just stared at him, confused. "What fabricators?" Nathan added, prompting the confused Ensign for a more detailed explanation.

"All Ta'Akar ships carry fabricators in order to create replacement parts while on patrol. We are usually a long way from support and have to be very self-sufficient. If given the correct specifications and raw materials, the fabricators can produce just about any component you might need."

"How many of them does the Yamaro have?"

"Four. Two for large components, and two for smaller ones."

"Can you operate them?"

"Unfortunately, no. The officer in charge of the fabricators was one of the nobles that assaulted the Yamaro. He was killed. However, I'm sure the Corinairans could figure out how to use them in no time."

"I thought their technology was less advanced than the Ta'Akar," Nathan said.

"Their technology, yes," Tug explained, "but not their knowledge. There were restrictions on what technologies they could possess, but there were no restrictions on what they could know or understand. I am sure that Ensign Willard is correct in his assertions. The Corinairans should be able to utilize the Takaran fabricators quite easily. In fact, if they can be used to build additional fabricators, then it could greatly diminish the time needed to complete your repairs. Furthermore, all the raw materials you might need are available throughout the Darvano system, especially in the asteroid belt. That is why it was so heavily mined. It is also one of the reasons the Ta'Akar seized control of this system in the first place."

Nathan thought for a moment before speaking. "Ensign Willard, earlier you stated that the Yamaro intercepted a comm-drone from the Darvano system on its way to Takara. How exactly did you intercept it?"

"Whenever a Ta'Akar warship is going to cross a known comm-drone route, it first broadcasts a signal to alert any drones in their area that they wish to exchange messages. When a comm-drone detects this signal, it drops out of FTL and decelerates enough to allow the exchange of messages. By piggybacking our own messages onto the inter-system drones, we reduce the use of our own drones."

"Then it's possible to intercept that drone," Nathan exclaimed, "to stop it from reaching Takara."

"Theoretically, yes."

"No one has ever tried," Tug interrupted, obviously intrigued.

"Why not?" Nathan couldn't help but ask.

"Comm-drones are the fastest thing in space," Tug explained. "At least they were until you came along."

"Then it is possible for us to catch it. We could jump ahead of it and broadcast that signal."

"Actually, you would have to jump behind it first," Abby interjected. "You can't see an object traveling faster than light when it is coming toward you. The object would arrive before its light, until the very last second that is. By that time it would be too late. Once it passes you, it would already be traveling faster than the stop signal, so you would then have to jump ahead of it in order to transmit a stop signal."

"But once it passes us, we could see it," Nathan said, seeking clarification.

"Yes. Its light would be red-shifted, of course, but we would see it."

"So we find it, calculate its exact course and speed, then jump just ahead of it. Then we transmit the stop signal so we can target it and kill it." Nathan looked at everyone in the room, expecting them to be as excited about the idea as he was. "It could work, right?"

"Theoretically, yes," Abby conceded.

"You're talking about a really small target traveling extremely fast," Jessica warned. "I don't think the rail guns could track it accurately enough."

"Can we tell it to slow down?"

"Once the drone drops out of FTL, it will automatically reduce its subluminal velocity by at least ten percent in order to facilitate signal exchange. If it had to reduce its velocity much more than that, it would expend too much energy during re-acceleration and would be unable to decelerate once it arrived at its final destination," Ensign Willard explained.

"Shoot at it head on," Abby suggested.

"What?" Jessica asked.

"If you take your shot from head on, the target's only motion is toward you, which means it's essentially no longer a moving target."

"Oh yes it is," Jessica objected. "It's moving toward you at ninety percent the speed of light!"

"You just have to be ready to move out of the way in case you miss," Abby told them.

"Problem is, at that velocity, there wouldn't be enough time to fire and maneuver out of its path,"

Nathan explained. "And the accuracy of our rail guns drops significantly as the range to target increases, so firing from behind won't work either. Besides, we don't have any ammo for them. We'd get about a two second burst, which would only be a few hundred rounds, *and* we'd have to fire blind."

"We could use my interceptor," Tug suggested. "It has energy weapons, it is more maneuverable, and it is faster. Also, as the interceptor uses energy weapons, I could fire continuously without fear of running out of ammunition. It would just be a matter of slipping into position behind the drone just after it passes by and opening fire."

"You would only have a limited window of opportunity, Captain," Ensign Willard warned. "The drone will automatically return to FTL and continue on at top speed after five minutes."

"So," Nathan stated, "we've got five minutes to hit a drone the size of a bus, traveling at nearly the speed of light, with a laser cannon mounted on an interceptor." Nathan shrugged his shoulders. "Piece of cake. Question is: is it worth the risk?"

"What risk?" Jessica wondered. "It's not like the drone will be shooting back at us."

"Three spacecraft traveling at near relativistic speeds, all within close proximity to each other," Nathan said. "Trust me, there's risk."

"Destroying the drone would keep the Ta'Akar from becoming aware that anything is amiss in the Darvano system," Ensign Willard pointed out. "It could provide you with weeks or even months of additional time in which to prepare a defense."

"We will need the help of the Corinairans," Tug reminded him.

"Leave that to me," Nathan assured him. "They

love me down there."

"As you wish, Captain."

"Does anyone else have any immediate concerns to discuss?" Nathan looked around the table. "Very well. Doctor Sorenson, I will need to meet with you later. I have some questions regarding physics and relativity I need answered."

"Whenever you like, Captain," Abby responded.

"Nash, Kamenetskiy, you two remain seated. Ensign Willard, if you'll wait outside with the guards, Ensign Nash will be out to take you for your debriefing shortly."

"Of course."

"Everyone else, thank you. You're dismissed."

Nathan leaned back in his chair, watching the others exit, waiting until the room was clear before speaking. He couldn't help but feel like a secondary school administrator about to punish a couple of unruly teens. It was an amusing thought, as in the past he was usually the one doing the misbehaving.

Although he wasn't looking directly at them, he could see Jessica and Vladimir exchange glances. Neither of them appeared to have any idea why they had been asked to stay behind. Jessica, however, appeared as calm as ever, confident that she could do no wrong. That was her strength, and Nathan knew it. But at times it was also her weakness, and he wondered if she was aware of that side of her personality.

Vladimir was a different story altogether: excitable, emotional, outspoken, but generally a nice, dependable guy. On Haven, in fact, he had also proven himself quite reliable under fire. If he had any real fault, it was that he worked too hard. The man refused to sleep unless everything was working, sometimes falling asleep on his console in engineering with a tool in his hand. The Aurora had been in need of repair since they first jumped away from Earth, so it was reasonable to assume that Vladimir had gotten very little sleep over the last two weeks.

Two weeks, Nathan thought. It seemed like only a few days ago. Everything had been happening so fast. At other times it felt like months since he had looked down on the familiar sight of the Earth slowly rotating below them. That view had been comforting, but he hadn't realized just how comforting it had been until now.

Tug was the last to exit the briefing room, casting a knowing look Nathan's way as he closed the hatch behind him. Nathan stared at the hatch as he thought about how to best proceed. He didn't relish the idea of having to admonish his friends. They had been through a lot together. The events of the last two weeks had been hard on everyone, but they had also brought them closer together. They were rapidly becoming comrades in arms, family. Unfortunately, the behavior of his friends was disrupting the operations of his ship, and as captain he could not tolerate it.

"It has come to my attention that the two of you have been casting blame on one another for the most recent attempted assault on this ship. Is that correct?"

"I never said it was his fault," Jessica began.

"Oh, please. Why do you lie?" Vladimir objected.

"I didn't say it was your fault. I said that you should have..."

"Enough!" Nathan warned sternly, his earlier soft spoken tone having vanished. "Listen to you two.

You're like a couple of teenagers..."

"If he had just taken the time to check..."

"Time? What time? If she had done her job to begin with..."

"Zip it!" Nathan said even louder. "It's not your fault," he told Vladimir, "and it's not yours either, Jess. The fault is mine. I'm the captain. I should have made damned sure that the ship was secure before I went down to the surface. Hell, I probably shouldn't have gone down to the surface at all, for that matter. But I was more worried about my injured friend than my ship. I should have given clear instructions to both of you. So the fault is mine and mine alone, got it?"

"Yes, sir."

"*Da.*"

"I've got to stop being everyone's friend and start being the captain of this ship," he said, more to himself than to his friends. He turned to look at them again. "And that also means you two have to start treating me like the captain as well. No more 'Nathan this' or 'Nathan that'. It's either 'Captain' or 'sir'. Is that understood?"

"Yes, sir," Jessica answered.

Nathan looked at Vladimir. His lips were pursed as if he were about to explode into laughter. Nathan swung out his foot under the table and kicked Vladimir in the shin.

"*Oy!*"

"I said, is that clear?" Nathan asked again, also trying to hold back a grin of his own.

"*Da, da, da,*" Vladimir responded, holding his bruised shin.

"There's going to be a hundred or so Corinairan volunteers joining our crew; many of them will be members of the Corinari. We need an obvious chain of command for *everyone* to follow if we expect them to do the same. As command ranked officers, we have to lead by example. We have to..." Nathan paused mid sentence, noticing that Jessica was hesitantly raising her hand for permission to speak. "What is it?"

"Beg your pardon, sir, but we're not command ranked officers. We're ensigns." Jessica looked at Vladimir. "Right?"

"Yes, she is correct... uh... sir," Vladimir agreed.

Nathan looked at the two of them, finally acquiescing. "Good point. Go down to the quartermaster's office and dig up some new rank insignias. You're both lieutenant commanders now."

Smiles crept across both their faces as they exchanged looks.

"Do we get a pay raise as well?" Jessica asked.

"We'll see how it goes," Nathan told her. "Dismissed."

Jessica and Vladimir quickly rose and headed for the exit, afraid Nathan might change his mind.

"The two of you had better earn your new ranks, or I'll take them away just as quickly."

Jessica exited the briefing room first, with Vladimir only a step behind her. The big Russian paused in the hatchway for a moment, checking to make sure no one in the corridor would hear him before turning back toward Nathan. "I am still not saluting you," he joked.

"If you don't, I'll cut off your hand and have the Corinairan surgeons reattach it."

"Maybe just this once then," he said. He snapped to attention in proper military fashion, issuing a perfect salute which Nathan promptly returned.

"Go, get your new rank pins," he ordered.

* * *

Compared to how it had been before, the Aurora's hangar bay seemed busy. There were four Corinari shuttles on board, as well as a medevac shuttle and a cargo shuttle that came every day with meals for the Aurora's crew as well as the Corinari troops that were currently providing security for the ship. A maintenance team from Corinair had set up shop in a corner of the bay in order to take care of the various shuttles the Corinari were flying between the Aurora and the surface. For the first time since they left Earth, the hangar bay actually felt alive.

After nearly losing both the Aurora and the captured Takaran vessel, the Yamaro, the Corinari were taking security quite seriously. The automatic doors for the transfer airlocks had been deactivated, and inbound shuttles were held on the landing apron while Corinari technicians in full pressure suits inspected their exteriors for suspicious devices. Once cleared by exterior inspectors, the inbound shuttle was allowed to enter the transfer airlock where their interiors were also searched, and the crew and any passengers had their identities thoroughly checked. With the Corinari on duty, no one was getting on board the Aurora who did not belong there.

Similar measures had been taken on board the Yamaro, although activity in her hangars was almost nothing. The remaining crew on board the Yamaro had made their way off the ship using the escape pods a few days ago, when they feared that Captain de Winter would scuttle the Yamaro to keep her out of the hands of the Corinairans. Most of them had either been picked up on the surface or had voluntarily turned themselves in and were being detained until arrangements could be made to get them back to their home worlds. However, given the current circumstances, getting them home might take considerable time.

Nathan strode out across the flight deck toward the shuttle that appeared to be preparing for departure. A group of four Corinari were standing near the shuttle's boarding hatch, apparently waiting to board. As he continued toward the shuttle, Tug, Jessica, and Sergeant Weatherly appeared from the starboard entrance to the hangar and came toward him. Jessica said something to the sergeant as they approached, and he left them and headed toward the four Corinari guards standing by the shuttle.

"Captain," Tug greeted as he approached.

"The sergeant's going with us?" Nathan asked Jessica as he nodded to acknowledge Tug's greeting.

"I figured he needed an assignment to keep his mind off things," Jessica answered. "So I gave him one."

"Doing what?"

"He's in charge of your security detail."

"Do I really need a security detail?"

"Regulations state that, while out of the Sol system, the captain of the ship doesn't leave without a security detail." Jessica flashed a grin. "Just doing my job, sir," she added, tapping the new lieutenant commander rank insignia pin on her collar.

"You're really trying to earn that pay raise, aren't you?" Nathan said.

"You bet."

"I really don't think I need..."

"Actually, you do," Tug interrupted. "There are

still people on Corinair who oppose you. In fact, you would be a high value target for a Takaran assassin."

"Thanks, I feel so much better." Nathan looked back at Jessica. "You sure five guys are enough?" He was only half joking.

"These five will stick to you two like glue. And I've already contacted the security office at the Aitkenna spaceport. They'll provide additional personnel for you when you arrive."

"Wouldn't it be safer for us to fly straight to the meeting?" Tug asked.

"All of Aitkenna is a no-fly zone right now. Only Corinari traffic is allowed. All traffic to and from orbit goes directly to Aitkenna, or else."

"Or else what?" Nathan asked.

"Or else they get shot down," she told him as they continued toward the shuttle.

"I guess they're taking security just as seriously down there as you are up here," Nathan commented.

"Actually, yeah," Jessica agreed. "Now that the dust has settled, there are armed troops everywhere in Aitkenna. It's like a police state down there. From what I hear from the Corinari on board, you can't go a hundred meters without being asked to show ID."

Red lights on the underside of the shuttle started flashing in unison as the shuttle began to spin up her power plant. Nathan could see the flight crew through the cockpit windows as they prepared for departure.

"Ready to go, Sergeant?" Nathan asked as he approached the shuttle.

"Yes, sir," the sergeant responded, snapping a salute.

Nathan returned the salute in similar fashion. Although constant saluting aboard ship was not normally required, marines tended to be a little more formal about such matters. He also felt that the orderly routine and familiar behaviors would help the sergeant overcome his recent traumatic events. "Very well," Nathan told the sergeant as he stepped up onto the shuttle's boarding steps. "Let's get going."

Nathan disappeared into the hatch, followed by Tug, the four Corinari guards, and Sergeant Weatherly. The flight technician on board the shuttle closed the hatch, and the shuttle began to slowly roll backward toward the transfer airlock. Jessica watched as the shuttle passed into the starboard transfer airlock, the door beginning to descend from overhead even before the shuttle was completely across the threshold. In a few minutes, after the airlock cycled and the outer door opened, the shuttle would roll out onto the flight apron, where its lower gravity would require only a small amount of thrust for the Corinari shuttle to move away from the Aurora and begin her short trip down to the surface of Corinair.

* * *

"Good afternoon, Prime Minister, Mister Briden," Nathan greeted as he and Tug took their seats in the Corinairan Prime Minister's office, across from the Prime Minister and his translator. Although the Hakai Nation's capitol complex had been heavily damaged by the strikes a few days ago, the primary government complex for the city of Aitkenna had suffered little damage. With much of the city government's staff either killed or otherwise missing, unoccupied offices were quickly allocated for the national government's use.

The Prime Minister sat behind a stately desk that had obviously been moved from another office, as it neither matched the other furniture in the room nor was sized properly for the smaller space. The Prime Minister's translator, Mister Briden, stood at the Prime Minister's right. Although the Prime Minister did speak some Angla, the nature of his position required precise, as well as documented, translations.

"Thank you for seeing us," Nathan began. "I apologize for the urgency of our request, but we have become aware of some new intelligence that requires rather immediate action on both our parts in order to be dealt with before it is too late."

"Please, Captain, go ahead," Mister Briden urged.

"Apparently, there is a Takaran communications drone headed for the Takaran home world. It is expected to reach its destination in approximately ten days," Nathan explained.

"And how did you come about this information?" Mister Briden asked before he even translated the captain's words to his superior.

"One of the communications officers from the Yamaro revealed this to us during his debriefing this morning," Nathan explained.

"And you believe what he is telling you? After all, he is a member of the Ta'Akar."

"Actually, sir, he is not," Tug explained. "The man is actually of Corinairan ancestry, born and raised on Corinair and inducted into service approximately two years ago. He was serving as a common officer, without any of the rights and privileges bestowed upon the regular officers of Ta'Akar nobility. Such officers are usually chosen based on their unique and valuable skill sets. In this case it was for his skills in communications and cryptology."

"Have you been able to verify this information?" It was obvious that Mister Briden was not convinced that the provider of the intelligence should be trusted.

"That would be difficult to do, given the circumstances," Nathan assured them. "But I have no reason to doubt the veracity of this man's claims."

"Just because he is of Corinairan descent?" said Mister Briden.

"And because he led the mutiny aboard the Yamaro, and because he led the volunteers that defeated the boarding parties on both the Yamaro and the Aurora. In fact, it's quite possible that his actions saved the world of his birth, your world, from complete destruction."

Mister Briden offered no rebuttal, instead taking a moment to thoroughly translate the conversation for the Prime Minister. The two spent several minutes discussing the matter, which to Nathan seemed a curious thing to occur between a Prime Minister and a mere translator. Finally, Mister Briden offered a response. "You spoke of a need to take action, Captain. To what action do you refer?"

"We believe that the interception of this comm-drone is critical. Doing so would prevent word of our presence in your system from reaching the Ta'Akar and could possibly buy us weeks if not months of additional time in which to prepare."

Mister Briden looked confused. "Captain, the weekly comm-drone was not due to be launched until tomorrow. We are preparing false reports to mask recent events as we speak. Exactly where did this drone come from?"

"It is our understanding that it was sent by a Ta'Akar officer stationed on your world," Nathan explained. "He received an anonymous tip and immediately dispatched a priority message to his command. The Yamaro intercepted the message as she was passing. That's why they came here. They were looking for us, and my Karuzari friend here."

"Then there is no word of our involvement in this message," the translator pointed out.

"Maybe not," Nathan conceded, "but when the Ta'Akar come to investigate and they find the disabled Yamaro orbiting your recently bombarded world, what do you think they're going to do? Do you really think you can put that genie back in its bottle?"

Again, Mister Briden exchanged words with the Prime Minister, this time for nearly a full minute before responding. "How much time are we discussing?"

"There are too many unknown parameters to be sure, but our best estimates indicate anywhere from a few weeks to several months. It all depends on the position of the Takaran ships at the time their home world sends out orders to respond."

"I see." Mister Briden again exchanged words with his superior in their native Corinairan language. With some understanding of the language, Tug concentrated to covertly overhear their whispers, hoping to gain some insight into their position. "Captain," Mister Briden began, "has it occurred to you that this could be a trap?"

"Excuse me?"

"While it may not have occurred to Captain Scott," Tug interrupted, "it has to me, as I have a better understanding of the ways of the Ta'Akar."

"Yes, as the leader of the infamous Karuzari rebels, I would expect that you might."

Tug ignored the translator's obvious disdain for the Karuzari and continued. "While it might seem like a way to lure the Aurora into an ambush, such a plan would have required considerable forethought and planning, as well as more rapid communications capabilities than the Ta'Akar currently possess. To be more direct, sir, it would be logistically impossible."

Nathan fought back a smile, realizing that while Mister Briden had inferred that the Karuzari were undesirable, Tug had just accused the translator of being stupid. "I assure you, Mister Prime Minister," Nathan began, subtly reminding Mister Briden that the conversation was between them and the Prime Minister, not his translator, "we have analyzed the logistics and motivations of this information and are quite convinced that it is accurate and should be acted upon with great haste."

After another moment of discussion with the Prime Minister, Mister Briden asked, "And what do you require of the Corinairan people?"

"Do you know anything about the fabrication systems used by the Ta'Akar?" Nathan asked.

"Yes, we have heard of them, but while we understand the technology we do not have any of our own. They are a closely kept secret of the Ta'Akar."

"Well, apparently the Yamaro has four of them. We believe that they could be used to quickly repair the damaged components that are preventing us from intercepting the drone. Unfortunately, we do not know how to use them."

"Cannot your informant explain them to you?"

"He cannot. Apparently, they were controlled by one of the noblemen who died attempting to retake the Yamaro. The common crewmen were not versed in their operations. But our informant seems convinced that your people could easily figure them out."

"I see," Mister Briden said. "I am sure he is correct in that assumption. However, I have to wonder, Captain, should we provide you with what you need to repair your jump drive, what is to prevent you from simply jumping away and leaving the entire Darvano system to its untimely demise?"

Nathan locked eyes with the translator. At that moment, he was quite sure that not only was Mister Briden more than a simple translator, but that he was also not speaking solely on behalf of the Prime Minister. There was undoubtedly another agenda in play, and it was not necessarily the Prime Minister's.

"My honor, sir," Nathan answered without missing a beat. "The very same honor that forced me to risk myself, my ship, and my world in order to defend yours." While maintaining his steely gaze, Nathan added, "You be sure to translate that for your superior... word for word."

Their eyes remained locked for another moment before Mister Briden turned to the Prime Minister and translated Nathan's words, speaking loud enough for Tug to easily understand his translation. Nathan continued watching him until he finished his translation, then turned slightly toward Tug for confirmation.

"It was not word for word, Captain," Tug told him, "but I believe he delivered both your message and intent accurately enough for our purposes." Tug's words were also spoken loud enough for Mister Briden to understand.

The Prime Minister began speaking in a more

official tone to his subordinate, as if he were stating an official position. After a moment, Mister Briden began his translation. "The Prime Minister states that while the people of Corinair are free to join you in your fight against the Ta'Akar, committing the scientific, technological, and possibly even natural resources of this world to your cause, thereby forcing such support upon the already overburdened people of Corinair, might not be possible, unless..."

Ah, here it comes, Nathan thought. All his years of listening to his father's political speeches and public statements, as well as the summers he had spent as his intern, had taught him two things; a politician always wants something, and a politician never gives anything away without getting something in return. Nathan waited without any change in his expression as the Prime Minister continued speaking.

"...the Corinairan people are offered something with which to protect themselves. Perhaps something that would give them a significant technological advantage over the Ta'Akar," Mister Briden added.

"And that would be?" Nathan asked, already knowing the answer.

"The specifications of your jump drive technology," Mister Briden stated.

Nathan took in a deep breath before continuing, thinking—in rather uncharacteristic fashion—carefully about how he would respond. "You ask a lot, sir."

"I do not believe so, Captain," Mister Briden disagreed. "The Prime Minister believes that a mission to intercept this drone poses significant risk. Should your vessel be destroyed, or worse yet captured, the loss would be catastrophic to the people of Corinair, as we would be left with no means of defense."

Nathan realized he had been played, and quite expertly. The Prime Minister was no fool; that much was clear. "Point taken," Nathan admitted. "However, I am not sure that it is within my authority to grant your request. I would need to consult my legal officer." Nathan rose smartly from his seat, Tug doing the same. "I'll try to return with an answer shortly," he added.

"Of course, Captain," Mister Briden agreed.

The Prime Minister stood, offering his hand to Nathan. For a moment Nathan thought he saw a look of satisfaction creeping into the old politician's friendly smile. "Thank you, Captain Scott," the Prime Minister struggled to say in Angla, the words nearly smothered by his heavy Corinairan accent.

"Good day, sir," Nathan told him as he shook the Minister's hand before turning and exiting the room.

Nathan and Tug walked down the corridor and out into the main lobby of the bustling capital building, all without speaking a word. Tug followed Nathan out the main doors into the afternoon sun.

"Well, that went well," Nathan commented as he took in the fresh air and sunlight. The smell of rubble and burnt buildings still tinted the breeze in Aitkenna.

"I was not aware that you had a legal officer on board the Aurora, Captain," Tug commented.

"We don't," Nathan admitted, "but we have Cameron, and that's just as good."

* * *

Sergeant Weatherly entered Commander Taylor's hospital room, making a visual inspection to be sure it was clear of any threats before allowing the captain and Tug to enter the room. Cameron was sitting on her bed, dressed in a thick hospital robe and reading a data pad when the sergeant entered.

"Sergeant," she commented with surprise as he slowly eyeballed the room, "can I help you with something?"

"No, ma'am, just checking the room," the sergeant informed her. He turned and nodded to Captain Scott, who was still waiting outside the door in the corridor. "It's all clear, sir," he reported, stepping aside to assume a watchful position just inside the door.

"What the hell..." Cameron began.

"Security detail," Nathan interrupted. "Lieutenant Commander Nash insisted," he explained. "There's four more outside in the corridor." Nathan turned to the sergeant. "Thank you, Sergeant. You can wait outside."

"Yes, sir."

"Oh, and ask the Corinari to arrange a similar security detail for Commander Taylor as well," Nathan added.

"Yes, sir," the sergeant promised as he exited the room.

"Lieutenant Commander Nash?" Cameron inquired.

"Don't worry, you still out rank her," Nathan told her.

"Who else did you promote?"

"So far, just her and Vlad. But I'm thinking of adding Ensign Willard to our roster as well."

"The guy from the Yamaro?"

"Yeah," Nathan said.

"You want to put the mutineer on our crew?" she

said with disbelief. "You really think that's a good idea?"

"Sure. I was thinking of making him a lieutenant and putting him on comms and crypto."

"What, are you XO now as well as captain?"

"You're right," Nathan agreed. "You decide where to put him."

"Well thanks," she said, a hint of sarcasm in her voice.

"Wait... how did you know about him already?"

Cameron held up the data pad she was holding. "Jessica transmitted a report to my data pad less than an hour ago, along with the intel from his debriefing."

Nathan shrugged it off as unimportant. "Anyway, that's not why I'm here," he told her, changing the subject. "We have a bit of a dilemma."

"The comm-drone," Cameron surmised, having already read the report.

"Sort of," Nathan said, scratching the side of his neck.

"Uh oh," Cameron began, noticing his scratching. "What are you thinking of doing now?"

"What?"

"You always scratch your neck when you have to say something you don't want to say, or when you're unsure about something."

"Really?" he said, surprised by the revelation. He immediately stopped scratching and took a seat next to her bed. "Remind me never to play cards with you."

"Spit it out, Nathan," she insisted.

"With our jump emitters down, we can't jump. If we can't jump, we can't catch that drone, which means we have less time to fix the ship..."

"What do the Corinairans want?" she asked, interrupting him. Nathan looked at her quizzically. "The report," she reminded him, again holding up the data pad. "She included the stuff about the Yamaro's fabricators."

Nathan took a deep breath before continuing. "They want our jump drive technology." Nathan braced himself for her response, expecting a flurry of opposition.

"You do realize how incredibly classified that technology is?" she asked calmly.

"Yes, of course."

"And you also realize that if you shared it with them, you'd probably end up being the first officer executed in the brief history of the Earth Defense Force."

"The thought did cross my mind."

"You already did it, didn't you?" she accused, her tone becoming sharper.

"No," Nathan defended, "of course not."

"Look me in the eyes and tell me you didn't already promise them you'd share it!" she insisted.

"I didn't!" he said, making bug-eyes at her.

Cameron looked at Tug, who was still standing by the door.

"I promise you, Commander, he did not promise them anything. In fact, he told them that he did not believe he had the authority to do so. He told them he needed to consult his legal officer first."

"Really?" she asked in disbelief.

"Yes," Tug assured her. "I believe you call it a 'bluff'."

"Wow," Cameron said, stunned. "I guess you're not as dumb as I thought you were."

"Gee, thanks," Nathan replied.

"So, I'm your legal officer now?"

"Close enough. I was hoping you might know something in the regs that would help."

Cameron thought for a moment. "Well, I don't know that they were thinking about something like this, but there is a section about alliances. It says that a duly appointed captain of an EDF ship may enter into an agreement or alliance with the government of an extrasolar system under certain conditions."

"What conditions?" Nathan asked.

"Well, first the captain must be reasonably unable to make contact with fleet command, or with a superior officer of flag rank, or that making such contact would result in the loss of the opportunity. Second, the agreement or alliance must be of benefit to the Earth and must enhance the security of the Earth or improve its ability to defend itself against aggressors."

"Any other conditions?" Nathan asked.

"Yes, it also has to be a balanced agreement. In other words we can't be giving up more than we're getting, or vice versa I suppose."

"Then we're good then," he concluded.

"Whoa, not so fast there," she warned. "I admit that it *sounds* like you're covered, but you have two really big gray areas here. First, is the agreement balanced?"

"That's pretty much a judgment call, isn't it?"

"Yes, but you might want to run the terms past a few of your senior staff first, just for the record. Although admittedly, none of your staff is very senior so I don't know how much weight any of our testimonies would carry in a court-martial."

"And the other one?"

"The circumstances of your assumption of the role of captain may come into question—the whole 'duly appointed' part. Did anyone witness the captain handing over command to you before he died?"

"I don't know. I could ask Doctor Chen. I know she was nearby as it only took her a moment to respond when he died."

"It might be worth asking her," Cameron suggested.

"You really think it would go that far?" Nathan asked. "A court-martial, I mean."

"I don't know, Nathan. I really don't know. But as your executive officer, I have to advise you to take some time and think it over—a lot of time. Maybe there's a way we can fix the emitters ourselves, without having to share the jump drive with them."

Nathan leaned back in his chair and sighed. Such decisions were exactly why he was never interested in command. "Unfortunately, I think this is one of those 'loss of opportunity' situations," he confessed. Nathan looked Cameron in the eyes. "Are you going to back me if it comes to that?"

Cameron kept her eyes on Nathan as she thought about it. "I honestly do not know, Nathan. I'm sorry."

"Fair enough," Nathan said.

* * *

There was very little discussion on the way back to the Aitkenna spaceport. Nathan stared silently out the window of their airship as it streaked along over the tops of the buildings, occasionally altering course just enough to avoid the tallest buildings that were still standing. At least it wasn't the wild ride they had experienced their first day on Corinair. Of course, the situation in Aitkenna had been far more volatile at the time.

Nathan's instincts were telling him that making an alliance with the Corinairans was the right choice. But sharing the jump drive technology with them, or with anyone, was an incredible risk. Although he was certain that it would not have any immediate negative impacts, the long-term consequences seemed incalculable.

"What would you do?" Nathan finally said to Tug.

"I may be the wrong person to ask," Tug admitted, "as I too have a stake in your decision. My people would benefit just as much as the people of Corinair, should you choose to share the jump drive technology."

"Yeah, that occurred to me as well," Nathan admitted. "In fact, no offense, but I think my superiors would be more upset if I shared it with the Karuzari than with the Corinairans."

"No offense taken, of course, but the statement does surprise me. Surely you do not find the Karuzari a threat to Earth."

"Not at all," Nathan assured him. "But in the eyes of some, you could be seen as an illegal rebellion that is trying to overthrow an established multi-system government. An admittedly brutal one, yes, but to be honest I don't really know enough about the Ta'Akar to make that call."

"I understand your position, Captain, and I do not envy it. Perhaps it would be better for you to base your decision on what you do know, rather than what you do not."

Nathan nodded his agreement, turning to look out the window once again. The Ta'Akar were definitely ruthless, and their leader, 'Caius the Great' as he liked to be called, was indeed a megalomaniac. If there ever were an empire that needed to be taken down it was the Ta'Akar, and as best he could tell, that was exactly what the Karuzari were trying to do.

"What will the Karuzari do if Caius is removed from power?" Nathan asked without preamble.

Tug appeared to be caught slightly off-guard by the question. "I suppose the logical thing to do would be to let each world within the empire decide its own fate." A chuckle rolled out of his mouth. "To be honest, Captain, in over thirty years of fighting the Ta'Akar, I have never really given it much thought. The Karuzari have only ever sought freedom from his tyranny, nothing more."

That was exactly what Nathan wanted to hear, and for a moment, he wondered if that was why Tug had said it.

"However," Tug continued, "I do not believe that the goals of the Karuzari or the fate of the Corinairans are what is troubling you. If it were, your decision would be easy. You fear the possible repercussions of your actions."

"Is that wrong?" Nathan asked.

"Not at all," Tug assured him. "Stupid men have no fear. Brave men have fear, but they do *not* allow it to prevent them from doing what they feel is right."

"But how do I know what the *right* thing is?"

Tug could see the angst in Nathan's eyes. "Nathan, as a member of your military, what is your ultimate purpose?"

"To defend my world to the best of my abilities against any and all aggressors," Nathan stated, quoting directly from the oath he had taken when he first enlisted in the Earth Defense Force.

Nathan stared at Tug as the old man began to grin. "You just answered your own question, Captain."

Nathan's demeanor suddenly became more confident. "Tell the pilot to change course. We're going back to see the Prime Minister again."

Tug smiled wryly. "As you wish, Captain."

* * *

"I apologize for returning unannounced," Nathan told the Prime Minister, "but I believe every minute counts right now."

"Have you already spoken with your legal officer?" Mister Briden asked.

Nathan was pretty sure that both Mister Briden and the Prime Minister knew exactly where they had been every moment since they last spoke, and that they were well aware that his only contact had been with his executive officer, Commander Cameron Taylor. "In a manner of speaking, yes."

"And what news do you bring us, Captain?" Mister Briden asked smugly.

"In order for me to properly exercise my authority in this matter, I must propose a military and trade alliance between our people."

"I see. And what does such an alliance entail?"

"First, all parties must agree to provide any and all military aid as is reasonably necessary to protect and defend the sovereignty of a member from any and all aggressors." Nathan paused for a moment before continuing, allowing Mister Briden to make his translation for the Prime Minister. "Second, all parties will share all knowledge, history, and technology, both military and otherwise with any and all members." Again, Nathan paused for translation. "Finally, all parties will provide reasonable humanitarian aid when needed to any and all members."

Mister Briden finished his translation and then responded. "You spoke of 'all' parties, Captain. Other than your people and ours, to whom else do you refer?"

Nathan wasn't surprised by the question. "I refer to the Karuzari, of course."

Mister Briden was surprised, or at least he was doing a good job of appearing to be. "Captain, I find it hard to believe that your government would be willing to enter into an alliance with the Karuzari. After all, they are not even a legitimate government."

"You are correct; they would not. However, that is easily solved. All you have to do is grant them sovereignty within the Darvano system."

"You are not serious," Mister Briden stated grimly.

"There are other sovereign worlds other than Corinair within the Darvano system, are there not?" Nathan said.

"They are more colonies than worlds, but at least they have physical worlds to which they lay claim. What world would the Karuzari lay claim to?"

Nathan realized that Mister Briden was not actually expecting an answer, which made it all the more enjoyable. "There is an asteroid within the belt of the Darvano system in which the Karuzari have already established a covert base of operations. All you have to do is grant them sovereign rights to that asteroid." Nathan glanced at Tug. The old man had a face of stone, despite the fact that Nathan had just told the highest living government official within the

Darvano system about the Karuzari's secret base. He then looked back at Mister Briden who, despite his best efforts, was not hiding his outrage at this new revelation anywhere near as well.

"Captain," Mister Briden began, his demeanor suddenly becoming deadly serious, "you do realize that I could have Mister Tugwell arrested on the spot based solely on your statements here. I could have you arrested as well, I might add."

"And I am sure you also realize," Nathan countered, "that doing so would surely doom your world to annihilation at the hands of the Ta'Akar." Nathan was equally steely-eyed at the moment. "And I believe the pronoun you meant to use was 'we' or 'he', not 'I'. After all, you *are* only a translator."

Mister Briden was silent for a moment, staring at Nathan as he considered his accusation. Before he could respond, the Prime Minister spoke to him. The two Corinairans exchanged words for several minutes, apparently debating the issue, thereby confirming Nathan's accusation that Mister Briden was more than just a translator. At the very least he was an aide or special consultant. It was even possible that he was a member of their security forces or even their intelligence services.

"The Prime Minister," Mister Briden began, putting emphasis on the point that it was the Prime Minister's statement and not his own, "is not sure that what you offer in trade is enough to sway the hearts and minds of all the people of the Darvano system. After all, other than your jump drive, we have not seen any other technology that is more advanced than what we currently have at our disposal. As well, it is our understanding that your world is in just as much peril as our own, perhaps even more so."

"When I said that we would share all science, history, and technology, I was not only speaking of what we carry with us on the Aurora, which I admit is comparatively limited. I was also referring to all the information contained within the Data Ark back on Earth."

That was enough to break Tug's stone-cold expression, causing him to shoot a concerned glance Nathan's way.

"Although I am not privy to all the information contained within the Ark," Nathan told him, "I can tell you that what we carry with us now is only the tip of the iceberg. Our people have only scratched the surface of the knowledge contained therein." Nathan could see that the Prime Minister was intrigued. "My world had only begun to industrialize once more a mere two hundred years ago. The Data Ark was discovered about a century ago, and in that short time span, we have advanced technologically nearly three hundred years. By our best estimates, we are still another two hundred years behind what the Ark has to offer, and that is a conservative estimate, I promise you."

"That still may not be enough, Captain," Mister Briden warned.

"Mister Prime Minister," Nathan continued, "imagine the consequences of exposing the truth about the origins of humanity and how your people came to be in the Pentaurus cluster. Imagine the impact on your people when they discover their ancestry, their cultural roots, their original religions." Nathan looked at Mister Briden, who was not translating what he was saying to the Prime Minister. "Tug, tell the Prime Minister what I said."

Tug began translating Nathan's previous statements.

"I am the official translator for..."

"Then do your job, Mister Briden!" Nathan insisted.

"Captain! I demand that you..."

Tug was already raising his voice in order for his translations to be heard and understood by the Prime Minister over the objections of Mister Briden.

A moment later, Sergeant Weatherly burst into the room, his hand on his sidearm. He looked around quickly, expecting trouble but finding only a room full of four men, all of which appeared angry. "Sir, I heard yelling." Behind the sergeant were two of the four Corinari guards. Mister Briden took notice of the three men, each of them ready to draw their weapons in an instant. While Mister Briden knew nothing of the Aurora's sergeant, he was well aware of the Corinari's reputation for accuracy.

"Mister Briden," Nathan began in a calm tone, "if you would be so kind as to speak in a volume and manner that Mister Tugwell can hear and understand, we can avoid such misunderstandings in the future."

Mister Briden did not respond until urged to do so by his superior. "Of course, Captain. I apologize for speaking outside of my position," he added, clearing his throat as he regained his composure. "These are difficult times for all of us, and I was only trying to do what is best for my people."

"As are we all," Nathan agreed. He turned his head back toward Sergeant Weatherly who was standing in the open doorway behind him. "Thank you, Sergeant. That will be all."

"Yes, sir," the sergeant answered as he backed

out of the room and closed the door behind him.

After a moment, Nathan spoke. "Now, where were we?" he said, a smile forming on his face.

* * *

The Corinairan shuttle rolled slowly into the Aurora's main hangar bay, coming to a stop in the middle. It had taken longer than normal for the shuttle to clear the secondary security inspection due to the number of first-time visitors carried by the shuttle, despite the Captain's presence among the shuttle's passengers.

As soon as the ramp came down, Sergeant Weatherly was out the door and on the deck, checking the security of the area before his charge disembarked the shuttle. As soon as he saw Jessica and Abby coming toward him, his demeanor relaxed slightly.

"Any problems, Sergeant?" Jessica asked as she approached.

"We had a few interesting moments," the sergeant confessed.

"Yeah, there usually are whenever our captain goes to the surface," she mumbled. "Any idea why he asked you here?" she asked Abby.

"None at all."

Jessica snapped to attention along with everyone else as Nathan came down the shuttle's boarding ramp with Tug following behind him.

"*Attention, all hands,*" a voice said over the loudspeakers. "*Aurora, returning.*"

As soon as the captain approached, Jessica snapped a salute which he promptly returned. Her brow furrowed slightly as she noticed a string of scholarly looking men emerge from the shuttle.

"Nice touch," Nathan commented as he finished his salute. "You'll need to get comm-units registered and distributed to all these men, ASAP."

"Yes, sir," Jessica responded, her smile turning into a look of curiosity. "Who are they?"

"They are the brightest scientific and technical minds from the city of Aitkenna—at least the ones that could be rounded up on short notice. They're on loan to us from our new allies."

"Our what?" Jessica stumbled.

"Group A will need a ride over to the Yamaro. Send Ensign Willard with them to show them the fabricators," Nathan ordered.

"Yes, sir," Jessica responded, a look of confusion on her face.

"Doctor Sorenson," Nathan continued, turning his attention toward Abby as they walked, "group B will be with you. I want you to show them everything they need to see about the jump drive, including full specs. I want you to give them a complete copy of all data about the project, understood?"

"Captain, you're talking about highly classified information."

"Not anymore, Doctor. I've exercised my rights under article what-ever-the-hell-it-was in the EDF regulations to enter into a formal Alliance with the Corinairans and the Karuzari. They now get to know everything we know, and vice versa. Is that clear?"

"Yes, sir," Abby answered, looking somewhat concerned.

"Captain," Jessica interrupted, "the Karuzari aren't a government. Hell, they don't even have a world."

"They do now," Nathan told her as he reached

the forward exit. "And I suspect that Mister Tugwell is going to need a ride there."

"A ride where?" Jessica asked.

Nathan stopped at the hatchway leading from the forward end of the main hangar bay into the main central corridor and turned around momentarily. "To their asteroid," he said with a smile. "Where else?"

"Captain," Abby called after him as she followed him into the corridor, "may I have a word?"

"Of course, Doctor," he answered as he continued down the corridor.

"With all due respect, Captain, I'm not sure that I can follow your orders."

"I assure you, Doctor, regulations do grant me the authority to make such decisions."

"I am sure they do, Captain. However, we were told never to reveal anything about the project to anyone without the express consent of the director."

"Well, I'm sure if the director were here he would agree with my decision."

"Perhaps, but he is *not* here and our instructions on the matter were quite clear."

Nathan stopped at the base of the ramp that led up to the command deck. "Doctor Sorenson, we are standing on a vessel that is one thousand light years away from home, and our jump drive is damaged. The most powerful empire in the area is hunting for us, and there are armed Corinari troops guarding this ship. If they decided to take the jump drive from us, we probably couldn't stop them. I don't think they realize that just yet, so I'd prefer not to give them a reason to consider that option. Better to make a new friend than another enemy. If we offer the technology to them as a condition of the alliance, we get the help we need right here, right now, and we get back to Earth sooner rather than later—maybe even soon enough for the jump drive to make a difference back home." Nathan stared at her as she contemplated his words. "So what's it going to be, Doc?"

"Can I get something in writing?" she asked half-heartedly. "I don't want to end up rotting in some cell for the rest of my days."

"Write up whatever you like; I'll sign it," Nathan promised.

Abby sighed in resignation. "Very well, Captain. I'll do as you asked."

"Great," Nathan said, "because I sure didn't want to go behind your back," he added with a smile.

"You couldn't have," she reminded him. "The files are all encrypted. They would have deleted themselves." Abby smiled right back at him.

"All right then," Nathan said as he started up the ramp.

"Does this mean I can have the suicide implant removed from my tooth?" she asked.

CHAPTER TWO

"Attention all hands. Aurora, returning," the loudspeakers blared in the background over the noise in the hangar bay. The cavernous main bay was bustling with activity now that shuttles were constantly coming and going as they ferried technicians, materials, and supplies between the Aurora, the Yamaro, and the surface of Corinair below. Between the Aurora and the Yamaro, there were a few hundred people aboard them at all times, at least a third of which were working as security forces under Lieutenant Commander Nash. Jessica had even gone as far as to keep the ship compartmentalized, with the main pressure doors constantly closed and locked and a pair of armed guards on each side. If anyone did sneak on board, they wouldn't get very far.

Nathan came down the boarding ramp of Corinari shuttle two-two-five, which had become known as 'the captain's shuttle' over the last few days as it constantly flew him back and forth between the Aurora and Aitkenna for negotiations over the terms of the proposed alliance. He was tired, hungry, and had not slept well in days. To make matters worse, he seemed to be spending all his time in negotiations, which to him was just as bad as politics.

"Captain," Vladimir called out as he jogged across the main hangar bay to catch up to him.

"Cheng," Nathan answered as he continued walking. Now that his friend was the official Chief Engineer of the Aurora, Nathan had taken to addressing him by the commonly used acronym. It was one of many military acronyms that had carried over into the Earth Defense Force over the years. "How go the repairs?"

"Very good, sir. Life support, artificial gravity, and inertial dampeners are all working normally again. Propulsion and maneuvering are not quite one hundred percent, but they are functioning well enough."

"That's promising. How about the reactors?"

"The containment bottle on number four still will not stabilize," Vladimir admitted, "but I managed to convince Doctor Sorenson to loan me one of her Corinairan scientists to help us solve the problem. I am hoping he can figure it out."

"Let's hope," Nathan agreed as they exited the hangar bay through the forward main doors, returning salutes from the Corinari guards as they passed them by and headed down the corridor for the main ramp.

"We are also taking advantage of the down time to run new power and control lines to all emitter points. The Corinairans have this wonderful cabling that has almost zero resistance, so it generates very little heat and has almost no power loss in the transfer. It may even increase our jump range a little."

"Did you run this past Abby first?" Nathan wondered aloud. He didn't imagine that she had been too receptive to the idea.

"Yes, and it was not easy to convince her, but I won her over with my devastating charm."

Nathan smiled for what was possibly the first time in days. "Yes, I'm sure that's what did the trick."

"And how are the negotiations going?" Vladimir asked.

Nathan's smiled instantly disappeared. "Awful. Well, that's not really true, I guess. They're going fine; I just hate the process. Endless discussions about the smallest of details. I swear, the Corinairan politicians want to discuss every possible eventuality, regardless of how unlikely it actually is. It's mind numbing, and it feels like it will never end."

"Come, have lunch with me. You will feel better," Vladimir promised.

"I can't. I have a meeting with Abby in fifteen minutes. Another time," he offered as he started up the ramp to the command deck.

Vladimir turned and started down the opposite ramp, heading for the lower deck in order to return to engineering. *I am glad I am not the captain*, he thought as he descended the ramp.

* * *

"Captain?" Abby inquired as she entered his ready room. She held up two clear containers that held lunches prepared by the Corinari mess on Aitkenna, who had taken it upon themselves to feed the crew of the Aurora as well as the Corinari on board.

"Come in, Abby," Nathan told her, noticing the containers. "What do you have there?"

"Corinairan root salads," she told him as she approached his desk. "Vladimir told me to feed you."

"He did, huh?" Nathan was hungry, but in his hurry to wash up before the meeting, he had forgotten to stop by the mess. "Is it the marinated kind?" he wondered. "I love those," he added as he accepted a container from her. He immediately opened the box, picked up one of the slices of deep red root , and popped it into his mouth. It was slightly sweet, with a contrasting bitterness when bitten into that was delightful. He also suspected that it was far healthier than the emergency survival meals they had been consuming up until a week ago.

Nathan chewed his slice of root and swallowed before talking. "How is it going with the emitters?"

"More quickly than I expected," she told him as she opened her meal container. "We have already finished fabricating all the components. We just have to finish assembling them. I suspect we will begin installation tomorrow, after they have all been bench tested."

"So quickly? It seems like you only started on them yesterday."

"Actually, it was four days ago," she corrected.

"Really?" he asked in disbelief as he tossed another slice of root into his mouth. "Guess I lost track of time."

"I do have some concerns, however," she admitted as she began to eat. "There are some minor differences in the materials used for replication. It may affect the output of the new emitters."

"Will that be a problem?" Nathan asked between bites.

"I hope not. If the variances are minor, then the other emitters in the array should be able to automatically compensate. However, if the variances are too great, we will have to recalibrate the entire array, which would also require that we rewrite all the transition algorithms."

"Is that difficult?"

"No, it is mostly automated. It is just time consuming, as the algorithms are quite complex. It would take at least a day or two to rewrite them, and then several more days to complete validation."

"Let's hope it doesn't come to that," Nathan said. "We only have five days left before that comm-drone reaches Takara and begins transmitting."

"So, is that why you asked to speak with me, Captain?" Abby asked. "To get an update on the jump drive repairs?"

"Not exactly," he admitted as he finished the last of his root salad. "I meant to speak with you a couple days ago, after our status briefing, but I've been busy."

"How can I help you?"

"Have you had much time to examine the Takaran FTL comm-drones?" he asked.

"Not really," she admitted, "but they appear to use the same mass-canceling fields that this ship was originally designed to utilize. Why do you ask?"

"Well, I was wondering just how much kinetic energy one of those comm-drones would have if it struck another object while at FTL velocities."

"I'm not entirely sure, Captain, but it would definitely be more than this ship could withstand, if that's what you were thinking."

"I wasn't thinking about this ship, Doctor. I was thinking about Takaran targets."

"You mean, like a faster-than-light missile?" she asked, a bit surprised by the concept.

"In a manner of speaking, except it would be more like a projectile, as there wouldn't be any way to significantly alter its course while at FTL speeds. I'm just wondering if the mass-canceling fields would rob the projectile of its kinetic energy as well."

"I do not know," she admitted, "but I would expect that at the moment of impact, the mass-canceling fields would collapse, and the drone's original kinetic energy would be conserved."

"And that would be enough to take out an enemy ship?"

"It would be enough to take out an entire planet, Captain," she corrected, shocked at his understatement. "However, you do not need FTL velocities in order to accomplish your goal. Any significant fraction of the speed of light would provide more than enough kinetic energy to do the job. In fact, the only advantage the FTL velocity gives you is that the target cannot see it coming. The problem is in the timing. To intercept a moving target using an FTL drone would require extreme precision."

"Not if they were flying directly toward the incoming drones. You said so yourself in the meeting a few days ago," he reminded her. "That's where I got the idea. If we launched the drones toward the target, then jumped in and engaged the target, getting him to chase us, we could lead him directly into the path of the incoming drones. All we have to do is jump clear at the last second. Hell, we could even put a small explosive device in the drones to blow them apart a few seconds before impact, so the debris would spread out and be more likely to hit the target."

Nathan looked at Abby, noticing that she seemed apprehensive about his idea. "What's wrong? You don't think it would work?"

"No, it probably would, as long as the timing was correct," she admitted.

"Then what is it?"

"Nothing really. I just do not believe this was what my father meant when he said the jump drive would change everything." Abby looked down at her hands which now lay in her lap, remembering her father. "He was never a fan of weapons research," she added in a soft tone. "He felt that such efforts usually resulted in a subversion of science."

"Well, if it makes you feel any better, we're not actually using it as a weapon, just as a means to utilize another weapon. Besides, I'm sure your father knew that the technology would be used in such fashion, sooner or later."

"Yes, of course," she admitted. "But he had such dreams for it. Exploration, colonization, communications—he imagined humanity colonizing the entire galaxy, maybe even the universe someday. He would spend hours theorizing on its myriad applications, none of which ever involved death or destruction."

Nathan felt a little guilty over his enthusiasm. "I'm sure that will all come in time, Abby. But for now, we have allies to defend and a war to fight, and we have to use everything at our disposal in order to do so. Right now, you and that jump drive are our biggest assets. In fact, that and surprise are the only two things we have going for us right now. And I'm not entirely sure the surprise factor is still with us. So as much as it pains me to do so, I have to ask you to start thinking of ways that we can utilize the jump drive to our tactical and strategic advantage."

"I know very little about such things, Captain."

"Maybe, but you do know about the jump drive and what it can and cannot do. I'm confident that if you, Tug, and Jessica put your heads together, you'll come up with a few ideas."

"I'll do my best, Captain," she promised.

* * *

Nathan made his way down the main corridor of the command deck, heading aft toward the ramp. The command deck had been one of the first decks to get a good scrub-down thanks to the first group of unskilled Corinairan volunteers. The Aurora's dwindling crew had not had time to keep their ship clean during the preceding weeks. Nathan hadn't even noticed the buildup of dirt, as he had been too busy trying to survive, but now that it was clean he could certainly see the difference. They had even replaced damaged lighting panels in order to rid the corridors of its gloomy shadows, which had given the ship a dismal ambiance.

Nathan overheard the Corinari guard as he informed his partner at the bottom of the ramp over his comm-set that the captain was on his way down. The four main ramps that connected the different levels of the ship had also been turned into checkpoints on Lieutenant Commander Nash's orders. Not a single pair of boots hit one of those ramps without the guards at the top and bottom knowing about it.

Although most of the ship was either cramped or strategically used space, each deck had a wide main corridor that ran its length. The ramps allowed for movement of large equipment between decks, which had been necessary during her construction back at the Orbital Assembly Platform above the Earth. Nathan knew that soon those ramps would become heavily used once again, as much of their secondary systems and equipment were still stored in the cargo holds, as well as in the fighter bays on either side of the main hangar deck. They had been forced to depart from Earth before their build-out was complete, and Nathan was bound and determined to finish the job as best they could during their down time, assuming it continued long enough.

Lieutenant Commander Nash met him at the bottom of the ramp. "You wanted to see me, Captain?"

"Yes, I want you and Tug to get together with Abby. Do a little brainstorming and see if you can come up with ways to use the jump drive to our advantage against the Ta'Akar."

"Sounds interesting."

"I think it would be a good idea if you included Ensign Willard as well."

"Sir?"

"There are ten FTL comm-drones stored on the Yamaro that I think we could make use of."

"You wanna send the Takarans a message?" Jessica quipped.

Nathan grinned. "Yeah, something like that. Abby will fill you in."

They rounded the corner and passed the guards at the entrance to the main hangar bay, entering the massive bay and heading out across its deck toward the captain's shuttle. Nathan looked ahead and saw Josh and Ensign Kaylah Yosef looking a bit friendlier than he would have expected.

"Josh and Kaylah?" he asked Jessica as they continued walking. "When did that happen?"

"That's a recent development," Jessica told him. "I guess taking a blast in the shoulder to protect her made an impression."

"I didn't see any of that in the after action reports," Nathan commented.

"Yeah, well, the details of what happened on the bridge are still kind of fuzzy."

Ensign Yosef noticed the captain approaching and immediately straightened up, stepping back an appropriate distance from Josh, who seemed none too pleased about the sudden change in her behavior.

"Sir," Ensign Yosef greeted as she snapped a salute.

"Ensign, how are you doing?" Nathan asked as he returned her salute.

"Fine, thank you, sir. We've finished repairing the damaged screen on the port auxiliary station on the bridge. The Corinairans are going to be tearing out the fried comm-stations and the two damaged starboard stations later today. Those should be replaced within a week or so."

"Very good, Ensign. Carry on." Nathan smiled at Jessica, noticing a slight blush on Ensign Yosef's cheeks as she glanced at Josh.

"Sirs," she said as she moved away to return to her duties.

"So, Josh," Nathan said, "how's the shoulder?"

"A little stiff, Captain, but healing up nicely, thanks."

"Good. Are you ready to go?"

"Yes, sir," Josh answered as he headed up the ramp.

"Lieutenant Commander," Nathan said, bidding Jessica farewell as he headed up the ramp, followed by Sergeant Weatherly and his team of four Corinari guards.

Jessica tapped her comm-set. "Captain's leaving."

"*Attention all hands,*" the loudspeakers announced. "*Aurora, departing.*"

Nathan followed Josh up the ramp and into the shuttle. Josh, having never been aboard a Corinari passenger shuttle, was taken aback slightly as he entered the main cabin. The shuttle was one of the diplomatic ships used to ferry government officials between worlds within the Darvano system. It was a bit opulent for Captain Scott's needs, but considering the amount of time he spent shuttling back and forth between the Aurora and Aitkenna, he didn't mind the extra comfort.

"Nice," Josh exclaimed as they entered the cabin, "very nice."

The main passenger cabin was five rows deep, with two high-backed overstuffed seats on either side of the center aisle. The windows were larger than on most passenger shuttles, giving those inside a better view. Forward was the cockpit, and at the back of the cabin was a restroom and a steward's station. The interior color scheme was deep and luxurious, and the cabin was so heavily insulated that once the main hatch was closed, you could barely hear the whine of the engines.

Nathan took his seat in the middle of the cabin, just as Sergeant Weatherly had originally requested on their first ride days earlier. With a pair of Corinari guards at either end of the cabin and the sergeant seated directly behind the captain, he was effectively surrounded by armed guards. The sergeant even had the inboard seats at the forward and aft ends of the cabin removed, as well as the one next to his position just behind and to the left of the Captain, in order to make it easier for his men to maneuver while carrying weapons and wearing armor. This had lowered the seating capacity of the shuttle by five passengers, but as the shuttle had become dedicated to the captain's personal needs, it had not been an issue.

To Nathan's surprise, seated one row in front of him was Jalea. He had not seen her for several days as he had been quite busy negotiating the terms of the alliance.

"Going on a trip?" Nathan asked, noticing that she had a packed duffel bag in the seat next to her.

"Tug has asked me to round up the all the Karuzari who have reported in on Corinair and take them to the asteroid base to begin preparations," she explained. "The Corinairans have been kind enough to provide us with a transport for our needs."

"How many Karuzari have reported in?" Nathan asked.

"A total of fifteen. I do not expect many more are on Corinair."

"That's still pretty good. You should be able to get your base spun up in short order, especially if the Corinairans help."

"I do not expect the Karuzari will receive the same enthusiastic support that the Aurora has received."

"I'll see what I can do about that," Nathan promised as he continued on to his seat.

The steward closed the main hatch and made his way down the aisle, checking that everyone was secure before moving to the back of the cabin and signaling the pilot that they were ready for departure.

The shuttle began to roll backward before turning slightly to maneuver itself into the center transfer airlock used by larger spacecraft. Josh watched out the window as the shuttle rolled into the airlock and the inner door descended. After a quick depressurization cycle, the outer door raised allowing the light reflected from the planet below to spill into the airlock, altering the colors inside the cabin.

Nathan paid little attention to the vista outside his window as the shuttle backed out onto the landing apron, having already made this trip more than a dozen times in the last few days. Instead, he began reviewing his notes from the last negotiating session on his data pad.

"Man, the pilot sure takes his time about it, doesn't he?" Josh commented.

"Sometimes that's a good thing, Josh," Nathan told him.

"Yeah, good and boring."

"So, you and Ensign Yosef, huh?" Nathan said, testing Josh's reaction.

"Huh? Oh, yeah. She's a nice one, she is."

"Yes, she is," Nathan agreed. "Isn't she a few years older than you?"

"Could be. I don't really know, to be honest," Josh admitted.

"What, you don't know how old you are?" Nathan wondered, his attention diverted from his data pad.

"Well, I know my twentieth birthday is coming up. But I was born on Palee. We moved to Haven when I was four or five, I think. Haven's years are all screwy because it orbits a gas giant instead of a star. After my mom passed, Marcus tried to do the math to figure out when each of my birthdays were, but I'm not so sure he got it right."

Nathan was amused, having never considered such a conundrum. "Well, since we have all the navigational data for the Pentaurus cluster and the surrounding systems, including Palee, I'm sure if we asked Abby she could figure it out for you. Since you're serving on an Earth ship, I guess we should figure out your birthday based on the Earth calendar."

"Sounds good enough," Josh agreed as the shuttle fired its thrusters and ascended off the Aurora's landing apron and began to drift to starboard. "Jeez, is he gonna fly this slow the whole way down?"

"Patience, Josh. I'm sure Tug won't take off until you get there."

"I'm just dying to get in that thing. I've never flown anything into FTL."

"Neither have I," Nathan told him.

"Really?" Josh said, somewhat surprised. "But how the..."

"We jumped here, remember?"

"Yeah, I guess you did at that," Josh realized as he sat back in his seat, watching the planet below as it slowly moved closer to them.

* * *

After a rather lengthy clearance process, Josh was finally allowed into the heavily guarded portion of the Aitkenna spaceport that was reserved for the Corinari combat air and space operations. Although the various interceptors and tactical shuttles operated by the Corinari were significantly inferior to those used by the Ta'Akar, they were still decades ahead of what Josh had flown back in the Haven system. Nothing he had flown had been armed, except for a few side arms stored in a locker on board.

Josh had to walk all the way across the compound, asking several Corinari technicians—most of whom spoke little to no Angla—where to find Tug and his Takaran interceptor. Finally, after wandering about in frustration, he was directed to a back corner where an unmarked maintenance hangar stood. Its main door open, Josh could see the forty-year-old interceptor standing in the middle of the hangar. Tug stood next to the spacecraft in a black Corinari flight suit speaking with Marcus. The relationship between the Corinari and the Karuzari was tenuous at best. Because of this, Tug had asked Marcus to personally oversee the maintenance on his interceptor while Tug continued to represent the Karuzari at the alliance negotiations.

"Man, they sure stuck you way back in a corner, didn't they?" Josh commented as he walked in the front of the small hangar.

"Yeah, I get the feeling the Corinari are none too fond of you Karuzari types," Marcus commented.

"Yes, there is still a great amount of distrust and suspicion yet to be overcome," Tug agreed.

"She all good to go, Marcus?" Josh asked. Although Marcus was a gruff old guy, he had been taking care of spacecraft for as long as Josh had known him. The man had practically raised him after his mother had died, so he was one of the few men that Josh actually trusted. Even though Marcus always rode him, Josh was glad that Marcus had also ended up marooned on the Aurora after the events back on Haven.

"Good as new," Marcus boasted. "The Corinairans may not be as advanced as the Ta'Akar, but they sure know their way around forty-year-old technology. Those boys can fix just about anything."

"They have had to make do with a reduced production capacity for several decades now," Tug explained. "They have been forced to keep what they have in good repair."

"I know how that goes," Marcus reminded Tug. "I'm from Haven, remember?"

"Of course," Tug remembered, having lived there off and on for the last thirty years himself, until recent events had forced them all from their homes. "There is a flight suit in the locker on the back wall," he told Josh. "It should fit you well enough."

"Great," Josh exclaimed as he headed toward the back of the hangar. "I can't wait to hit FTL for the first time."

Marcus waited until Josh was out of earshot before speaking. "You sure you want to let him fly this thing? He's a bit of a wild stick, you know."

"Yes, I am well aware of his unorthodox piloting style," Tug assured Marcus.

"Don't know that I'd rightly call it a 'style'," Marcus observed.

"Well, perhaps I can smooth out some of the rough edges," Tug said as he started up the boarding ladder.

"Save yourself some time," Marcus sneered. "Skip the smoothing and go straight for the cutting."

Tug smiled at Marcus's remarks as he climbed into the rear seat of the cockpit. It had been over thirty years since he had sat in the rear seat. That had been when he trained his last wingman back in his days with the Palee militia. "I will keep that strategy in mind," he promised as he strapped himself into his flight seat.

Marcus turned around to see Josh coming toward him wearing a baggy black Corinari flight suit and carrying a flight helmet. "I do believe the previous owner of that suit stood a bit taller than you," he teased. "Probably had more meat on him as well."

"What are you talking about?" Josh said. "It fits

fine. A little loose, maybe."

"As long as it seals up properly it will serve its purpose," Tug assured him.

Josh bounded up the boarding ladder, noticing that Tug had taken the back seat in the cockpit as he crested the top of the ladder. "I'm sitting first seat?" he asked, stunned.

"If you are to fly this ship, that is the seat to do it from."

"Oh hell yes," Josh stated excitedly.

"I will get us airborne first," Tug warned. "For now, you become acclimated to the controls and the flight displays."

"No problem."

Tug looked to Marcus as he handed Tug his flight helmet. "How are you getting back to the ship?"

"I'll be catching a ride up with the captain later," he told him.

"Very well," Tug said, extending his hand. "Thank you for looking after my ship, my friend. It was greatly appreciated."

Marcus took Tug's hand, shaking it for the first time since they had met in the galley over a week ago. "You're welcome," Tug answered, feeling guilty that he had called him a terrorist during that first meeting. "Just don't let junior crash it."

"I will make certain he does not," Tug promised as he donned his helmet and sealed it against the collar of his flight suit.

Marcus picked up Josh's helmet from beside the front seat and plopped it down over Josh's head, sealing it up as well. "Do what the old guy tells you, kid," he instructed. "I have a feeling he knows a bit more about flying than you do."

"No worries, Pops," Josh promised as he examined

the displays on the console in front of him.

Marcus climbed down off the boarding ladder, released its brakes, and rolled it back away from the wedge-shaped spacecraft. After a second, the interceptor's two reactor plants lit up and hummed to life, her engines turning over moments later. He eyeballed the floor of the hangar around the small ship, checking for any obstacles. When he was satisfied it was clear, he gave a thumbs up signal to Tug.

The interceptor's engines began to increase their pitch slightly and the warning lights on her underside began to flash, telling anyone who might be around that the spacecraft was now under her own power and was about to roll out of the hangar.

Marcus grabbed the ear muffs that were hanging around his neck and put them on to protect his ears from the sound of the spacecraft's engines as their pitch and volume continued to increase. He looked up at the cockpit of the interceptor as it began to roll slowly forward, the canopies automatically lowering as they left the hangar. Josh looked over at Marcus, a monstrous grin stretching from ear to ear. Marcus noticed that Tug had already closed his helmet visor and Josh had not, so Marcus gestured wildly at Josh to lower his own visor as well. Josh, oblivious to the true meaning of Marcus's gestures simply waved back at him. Marcus repeated the gesture and finally Josh got the hint and closed his own visor.

Marcus watched the interceptor roll out onto the tarmac as it headed out to the nearest launch point, the canopies finally coming down and locking into position as it rolled away.

"Dumb kid," Marcus mumbled to himself as he

turned and headed for the washroom.

Tug increased the thrust levels on the main turbines used while operating in the atmosphere, causing the interceptor to lift slowly off the ground. "While unloaded, this ship can take-off vertically using only five percent thrust," he told Josh. "Fully loaded with maximum weapons and fuel, she needs at least twenty-five percent to get off the ground."

"Got it," Josh answered over the comms built into their flight helmets.

"The ships that you have flown all used separate engines for lift and forward propulsion, did they not?"

"Yeah, the harvester did. The shuttle had a separate engine for everything," Josh commented.

"This ship has four basic flight systems," Tug explained. "There is a single turbine system used for atmospheric flight. As the body is a flying wing, once at speed it generates its own lift. You will find it a bit different than flying a ship that uses powered lift systems to maintain altitude."

"You use the same engine for lift as you do for forward thrust?"

"Yes. The turbine has a series of thrust ports along either side of the ship. Each thrust port is gimbaled and can move twenty degrees in all directions from its vertical centerline. It makes the ship quite maneuverable at speeds that are insufficient to provide adequate aerodynamic lift."

"How do you control the amount of thrust that generates your lift?"

"You do not," Tug told him. "You simply indicate with your flight control stick that you wish to go up, and the system decides how much thrust to create, and how much of it needs to be diverted to the lift systems. As your forward velocity increases, so does the aerodynamic lift generated by the ship's lifting body design. As the aerodynamic lift increases, the amount of thrust being diverted to the vertical lift thrusters decreases. By the time you reach a minimum lifting velocity, the vertical lift thrusters have disengaged."

"But it's all automatic, right?" Josh asked. "I mean, you don't have to think about all that, you just tell it to go and it goes, right?"

"True, but you really should understand how it all works."

"Yeah, I understand. The thrusters point down, spit out some thrust to keep us in the air until we get up to speed and the lifting body does its thing. I got it."

"Very well," Tug conceded. "Since you already know so, put your hands on the controls."

"Seriously?"

"Of course."

Josh placed his right hand on the control stick along his right side and his left hand on the throttle along his left side. "Okay, I'm ready," he announced.

Tug flipped a switch on the control stick and then hovered his hands just off the controls. "The ship is yours."

"Thrusting forward," Josh announced, manipulating his flight controls. The interceptor began sliding forward as it continued to slowly climb. Josh adjusted his rate of ascent until the ship stopped climbing, continuing its forward motion about thirty meters above the ground. He looked out the port side of the interceptor at the spaceport below him as they continued slowly picking up forward velocity.

"Very good," Tug praised. "As soon as we clear the fence line, you can pitch up and accelerate until we achieve aerodynamic flight velocity."

"Copy," Josh reported. "Fence line coming up. Hold on to your lunch; here we go," Josh announced as he pulled the nose up slightly and pushed the throttles forward.

The interceptor leapt forward much faster than anything Josh had ever flown, pushing him back hard in his seat. "Whoa! This thing's got some power! Are the inertial dampeners on?"

"Easy on that throttle, Josh," Tug warned. "She is more powerful than you realize."

Josh looked down at his instruments. "Holy crap! We're already doing a thousand K's, and we're only at ten percent forward thrust! I guess the dampeners are working. But how come I'm getting pushed back in my seat?"

"The dampeners allow some of the feeling of acceleration to get through in order to give you a better sensation of the flight. As you increase your rate of acceleration, the dampeners will also increase their power to compensate so that we are not crushed."

"Oh yeah? Let's see." Josh pushed the throttles to fifty percent, getting pushed back yet again as the interceptor accelerated further. "Shit!" he yelled. "We are hauling ass! We're already passing five thousand K's and accelerating."

"You might want to pitch up a little more, Josh. We do not want to run into any low-flying aircraft."

"Right, pitching up." Josh pulled the nose up a bit more, peeking out the side of his canopy as the blurry ground began to rapidly fall away from them. "How long does it take this thing to reach orbit?" Josh asked.

"Every world is different," Tug explained. "Different mass, gravity, atmospheric pressure. At full power it can escape the average human-hospitable planet's gravity in a few minutes. I have yet to calculate it for this world," Tug admitted.

"We might as well find out," Josh insisted as he began pushing the throttles forward.

"Josh?" Tug's hands were ready to take control away from the young pilot, fearing that his reaction time would not be sufficient to handle the spacecraft at its top atmospheric speeds.

Josh snapped the ship into a roll to port, rolling it completely over and then stopping, exactly centered again. He then repeated the roll to starboard. "Man, she is really responsive!"

Tug relaxed, putting his hands at his sides and grasping the hand rails on either side of his seat cushion to brace himself for what was coming. "Very well, Josh. Take us up."

Josh pulled the stick back, bringing the nose up even more, and slammed the throttles all the way forward, applying full thrust. The interceptor streaked upward with alarming acceleration, the surface of Corinair falling away behind them.

Josh watched the instruments as the velocity and altitude indicators scrolled so quickly he could barely keep track of the numbers. He looked forward out the front section of the canopy at the sky above as it quickly darkened. To his sides, he could see the planet's horizon drop lower and lower until the blue sky above finally gave way to blackness.

"Transition," Tug announced calmly. "Throttle

back to thirty percent."

"Throttling back," Josh responded, not asking why. A moment later, the turbines died out and the main drive kicked in, lurching them forward again.

The instruments on his console blinked, the numbers all dropping by huge factors. "What just happened?" Josh asked.

"Your displays have changed their increments," Tug explained. "Look at your velocity indicator. It is now reading in kilometers per second instead of per hour as they were in the atmosphere."

"Oh, I get it."

"They will continue to change their increments as we accelerate further."

"So that would be the second flight system."

"Correct. In a few moments we will have achieved orbital velocity for this world."

"How do we know the correct velocity?" Josh wondered.

"The ship knows. On your main display, do you see the circle around the image of the planet? It represents the optimal orbital path. As your current trajectory approaches that circle, it will begin to flash. At that point you should start throttling back gradually so that you are at zero acceleration when you reach the optimal orbital path."

"Got it," Josh answered.

"Once you have achieved orbit, the orbital path will turn green."

Josh kept glancing down at the main display. Just as Tug had predicted, the line indicating their trajectory began to flash. "Throttling back," Josh announced as he began to slowly pull the throttles back. The constant drone of the main engines slowly faded as their output was dialed back. Thirty seconds later, Josh felt the throttles come to a stop at their zero position and the orbital path on his display turned from white to green. "Orbit achieved," he reported calmly. "Do we get to go to FTL now?"

"Patience," Tug urged, after which he muttered something in Takaran.

"What was that?" Josh asked. Having lived on Haven for most of his young life, he had never learned the Takaran language, as their forces had abandoned the system when he was still a child.

"It is an old training adage," Tug explained. "It means 'crawl, walk, run'."

"Okay," Josh answered, not really getting the meaning. "So what do we do now?"

"The third system," Tug said, "maneuvering. When we were in atmospheric flight, your control stick had three directions of movement available: angled front or back, twisting left or right, and angled left or right. This gave you control over pitch, yaw, and roll. Now that you are in space flight, two additional directions of movement have been enabled. Your stick can now slide forward or backward to apply forward or reverse thrust, and it can slide right or left to provide lateral thrust."

"So it works the same as in most other spacecraft," Josh observed, "except it's all combined into one stick instead of two."

"Correct."

"What about thrusting up or down?" Josh wondered.

"The little slider on the top of the stick on the side facing aft. Slide it up or down to thrust upward or downward."

"Slick. I like it," Josh concluded.

"Practice reorienting the ship to different points

around your coordinate sphere. For example, try pointing the ship forty-five degrees to starboard so that your attitude is directly parallel to your flight path."

Josh twisted his control stick slightly to the right, causing the ship to rotate on its center axis to starboard. A split second later, he twisted the stick back to the left to stop his rotation. "Done," he announced, boredom evident in his expression.

"Very good," Tug admitted. "Now bring it one hundred and eighty degrees to port so that..."

Josh didn't wait for Tug to finish his instructions, spinning the ship to port even more quickly than he had spun it to starboard.

"Very well," Tug said. "I can see you are ready for something a little more challenging." Tug began entering commands into the ship's computer.

"Like what?" Josh asked.

"A maneuvering drill," Tug explained.

A set of pale blue lines forming a sphere flickered to life in the space directly in front of Josh's face. It appeared to be floating in mid-air. "Whoa, what the hell?" Josh exclaimed as he reached up and passed his left hand through the floating image.

"This is a training prompter," Tug told him. "See the small flashing dots? When one of them appears, you point the ship toward that dot."

"Got it. When do I start?"

"One moment."

The sphere began to quickly expand until it went beyond the canopy and out into the vacuum around them. Once it stopped, Josh noticed that his head was now at the center of the sphere. He looked about outside the cockpit at the blue lines that now encircled his cockpit from outside. A replica of the sphere was also displayed on one of his small display screens on his forward console.

"Okay, that was impressive."

"Prepare to begin the exercise," Tug warned, "in three......two......one......begin."

A red light appeared on the projected sphere outside the cockpit at a point forty-five degrees to port. Josh swung the ship's nose over to point it at the dot which then turned green. A second later, the green dot disappeared and another red dot appeared forty-five degrees to starboard. Josh swung the nose back to starboard, again lining up with the red dot and causing it to turn green. The process repeated, the dot showing up slightly above and slightly below the ship's horizontal plane, each time forty-five degrees from the previous dot. Josh swung the interceptor's nose back and forth, up and down, with considerable precision. Josh and Tug rocked slightly back and forth as the interceptor swung about.

"Very good," Tug admitted. "You are not over-maneuvering at all. Would you like me to increase the difficulty level?"

"You mean I beat level one?" Josh joked.

"Yes, you could say that." Tug entered some more commands into the ship's computer. "Let us expand the range of the maneuvers a bit," Tug suggested. "I will vary the range of degrees between each maneuver as well."

The next red dot appeared about sixty degrees from the previous dot and considerably farther off the ship's horizontal plane than before. Josh still had no problem bringing the interceptor's nose onto the dot, but the next dot was only thirty degrees away, and he slightly overshot the mark. However, within a few more maneuvers he was again hitting his marks with precision, having forced himself out of the previous pattern in order to treat each maneuver separately.

"Hey, this is kind of fun," Josh exclaimed.

Tug realized that Josh was not even having to concentrate, and decided to raise the challenge once again. "Switching to adaptive mode, full range and variance."

"What?" Josh asked. The dots began coming at more random locations, on all points around him. Above, below, fore and aft, they even began coming more frequently, forcing him to maneuver faster. "Okay, okay... I got this," Josh proclaimed, swinging the interceptor's nose about wildly as he chased the red dots flashing all around him. Soon, the red dots were no longer turning green before the next red dot appeared, as Josh was no longer getting his nose on target before the next target came into view in its place. "All right, all right!" Josh declared. The sphere outside his cockpit disappeared in an instant as Tug discontinued the drill. Josh breathed out a sigh of relief. "That was insane!" He adjusted the attitude of his ship so that his nose was again pointed along his flight path, and his ship was level in relation to the planet's surface below.

"But very good practice," Tug added. "You did quite well for you first time. There is another exercise I would like you to try."

"Sure. Why not?"

"This time, the red dots will be coming at you, as if they are objects in space that you are flying toward. Your goal is to maneuver the ship up or down, and side to side, in order to avoid colliding with the dots as you pass them."

Josh adjusted himself in his seat and slid his right thumb onto the vertical thrust slider on his control stick in preparation for the next drill. "Sounds easy enough."

"Prepare to begin the exercise," Tug warned again, "in three......two......one......begin."

A red dot appeared in space a distance ahead of them. It rapidly grew in size, giving the appearance that it was coming directly toward them. Josh pushed the vertical thrust slider upward for a split second, then immediately slid it downward to counter the upward thrust and stop the ship's upward movement in relation to its original flight path. The red dot began to stretch out slightly as it appeared to pass under them. Just as soon as the first dot passed by, another dot appeared in their path. Doing the opposite, Josh slid the ship downward slightly, allowing the dot to pass above them. The drill repeated several times. Josh moved the ship up, down, left, and right in order to avoid colliding with the dots as they passed.

Josh quickly became bored. "Is this the beginner's level, or what?"

"Very well," Tug answered, adjusting the parameters of the exercise.

This time, the dots came in groups, forcing Josh to maneuver the ship in certain directions in order to avoid being struck by any of the dots as they passed. Again, his maneuvers became more aggressive as he instructed the interceptor to slide around at his whim. With each few waves that were successfully avoided, the following waves began to come in faster. Josh became quiet as he concentrated on keeping the ship out of the path of the onrushing clusters of red dots. As the waves of dots came faster and faster, alerts started sounding, indicating that a few of the dots had made contact with the interceptor's outer edges. Just as Josh was about to give up, the waves went back to single dots coming more slowly.

"Now," Tug began, "as you maneuver the ship to avoid colliding with the dots, try to keep your nose pointed toward the dots as they pass."

"Got it," Josh answered, recollecting himself.

"As soon as the dots pass, swing the nose back to forward in order to track the next oncoming dot."

"Understood." Josh slid the interceptor slightly to starboard while keeping his nose pointed at the dot as it passed to port. As soon as it passed, he swung the nose back around to face forward, but barely had enough time to slide the ship back to port in order to avoid the next dot. Over the next few passes, he continued to have the same problem.

"Keep your head on a swivel," Tug advised him. "Do not restrict your visual tracking to your forward quarter. If your ship is tracking a dot to starboard, keep glancing to your left along your flight path in order to locate the next dot before you swing around. You can then maneuver the ship out of the dot's path before you even swing your nose back around to track it."

"Got it," Josh answered. Most of Josh's flying in the past had been straight forward, with the nose of his ship usually pointed in the direction he was flying. The automated flight systems maintained such attitude orientations automatically. Now he was being asked to fly sideways, upside down, backward—it would take some time to get used to the new technique.

Tug watched as Josh struggled with the maneuvers, fighting the urge to call out every mistake the young pilot was making. However, Josh was quickly figuring it out for himself. Within a few minutes, he was beginning to get the hang of it, and was slipping the ship in between the dots, spinning about one way or another in order to track them with his nose. If this had been target practice, Tug was pretty sure Josh would have scored highly.

After about ten minutes of practice, the dots disappeared. "That should be enough for now," Tug told him.

"That was a lot of maneuvering," Josh admitted. "And I thought scooping up debris from the rings was tricky. I hope I didn't burn up all our maneuvering propellant."

"Doubtful," Tug assured him. "The maneuvering engines in this ship are extremely efficient. We have not even used one percent of their capacity."

"Wow," Josh exclaimed. "Are the mains that efficient as well?"

"Indeed they are," Tug told him. "This ship was designed as a deep-space interceptor. Back in its day, it was taken on long patrols between star systems. We would use the FTL drive to quickly get out into the patrol corridors, then dart around at half-light as we scanned for red-shifted FTL trails."

"What are those?" Josh wondered.

"You cannot see something that is traveling toward you at speeds faster than light, as they would arrive before their own light reached you. You would only see them for a millisecond as they passed you by. Instead, we would search for their visual trails as they traveled away from us. Their light would be red-shifted since they were traveling away from us, and the rate of shift would tell us if they were at FTL speeds."

"So then you would chase them down and attack?"

"No. It is quite impossible to target a ship traveling at FTL speeds," Tug told him. "But this ship is still faster than most larger spacecraft, so we could get ahead of them and warn of their impending arrival, thus providing time to prepare a defense."

"Then why is this called an 'interceptor'?" Josh asked.

"If the targets were traveling at subluminal speeds, we could easily intercept them while they were still some distance away from their final target and engage them."

"Nice," Josh said.

"There was nothing 'nice' about such engagements, Josh," Tug corrected. "There is very little separating us from the icy vacuum of space in this interceptor, and our suits would only keep us alive for a few hours at best. At the distances from base these ships would operate, rescue was extremely unlikely. You were more likely to get picked up by the enemy, or picked off by the opponent that bested you."

Josh thought about that for a moment before speaking. "So now what?" he finally asked.

"Set a course for the asteroid base. When you are ready, engage at fifty percent thrust."

"Copy that." Josh fidgeted with the navigation computer, as he figured out how to plot a course. After a few moments, he had it figured out. "Okay, course plotted and locked," Josh announced. "Coming to new heading." Josh turned the interceptor slightly to starboard, rolling the ship over as he did so in order to put the planet beside him. It wasn't entirely necessary, but using the Darvano system's ecliptic helped him keep his orientation. After changing his artificial horizon to use that same ecliptic as its reference, he checked that the ship was on course before engaging the auto-flight system. "Auto-flight locked on course for Karuzara," he announced.

"For what?" Tug inquired.

"Well, you've got to call it something," Josh insisted. "What were you going to call it, Rebel Rock?"

Tug laughed. "Karuzara it is, then."

"Throttling up," Josh announced as he inched the throttles forward again.

* * *

Commander Taylor sat next to Chief Montrose at the conference table in one of the hospital's many meeting rooms. As the Aurora's executive officer, she had insisted on conducting the final interviews of all the prospective candidates volunteering for duty aboard her ship. It was a long and painstaking process which tired her out more than she would have thought, as she was not yet fully recovered from the critical injuries she had sustained during the battle against the Yamaro. Had it not been for Chief Montrose, who had convinced the commander's physicians to allow them to conduct the interviews in the hospital where Cameron's condition could be monitored, she would not have been able to participate in the selection.

Cameron had insisted on having a uniform brought down to her so that she could present herself properly during the interviews. The last thing she wanted was for people she would eventually command to see her in a hospital robe looking weak and frail. Despite the fact that she was recovering nicely, she was still many weeks away from returning to full active duty.

Nathan had resisted her participation, mainly because he feared that she would over exert herself and delay her recovery. He wanted to be sure that she was well enough to oversee training of the new crew. In the end, her desire to make sure the best crew was selected from the start had won—that and her stubborn side, to which Nathan still had the bad habit of yielding.

"That makes fifty interviews on this day," Chief Montrose stated in less than perfect Angla.

"*Today*," Cameron corrected, "the expression is *today* not *on this day*."

"Too-day," the Chief repeated. "That makes fifty interviews *too-day*," he repeated, more to himself than to Cameron.

"Let's do one more."

"It is late," the chief protested. "You now should rest."

"Don't ever tell me to rest, Chief," she warned. "Besides, I hate even numbers. Let's interview one more before we call it quits for the day."

"As you wish, Commander," the chief acquiesced. "I will carry you back to room when you are not conscious," he added with a laugh as he activated his comm-set and called for another volunteer.

Cameron leaned back in her chair and closed her eyes for a moment. Perhaps the chief was right; she was tired. In addition, she was lightheaded and at times—despite assurances by the Corinairan doctors that at this stage of her recuperation it was highly unlikely—she felt as if she could feel the nanites inside her, scurrying about mending her insides. It was just a vague tingling sensation, intermittent at most but annoying nonetheless. It was only the second day of interviews and, by her calculations, they had at least a month's worth of primary and secondary interviews before they whittled the thousands of applicants down to a full crew of three hundred. Lieutenant Commander Nash would conduct another set of interviews after that, along with Sergeant Weatherly and members of the Corinari, in order to select another hundred men to serve as ground assault force. They had no plans to use such a force as of yet, but it was agreed that it would be best to have one ready, just in case.

Cameron's eyes popped open when she heard the door open. A confident and rather distinguished looking man of average height and build entered the room. His hair was dark and full with graying at the temples and streaks of the same throughout. He had the same piercing confidence that she had always seen in Captain Roberts, the Aurora's original captain. In fact, in many ways his appearance reminded her of the captain, although this man lacked the contented look that had made Captain Roberts so approachable as a commanding officer. This man appeared far more serious, more like Commander Montero, her predecessor.

He walked the short distance from the doorway to the table, extending his hand to Commander Taylor. "Thank you for this opportunity, miss."

"In our military, an officer is referred to as 'sir', regardless of gender."

"A sensible tradition," the man agreed in perfect Angla. "However, as I am not yet in your service, Corinairan custom dictates that I refer to you as 'miss' or 'ma'am'. If selected, I will be more than happy to follow your fine traditions."

Cameron released his hand, satisfied with his

answer, as it was both honest and respectful. "I'm Commander Taylor, the Aurora's Executive Officer. This is Chief Montrose of the Corinari."

"It is a pleasure to meet you both," the man offered graciously. "My name is Dumar. Travon Dumar."

CHAPTER THREE

Nathan sat in the command chair at the center of the Aurora's bridge, watching as Josh and Loki performed the tasks that he and Cameron had been responsible for only a few weeks ago. It still felt unusual to be watching someone else perform his old job, especially from the command chair. He had only been the ship's official pilot for about a week, and had only actually flown her for one mission—technically it was only half a mission—before circumstances threw him into his new role as de facto captain of the Aurora and the figurehead of an interstellar revolution. As a student of history, Nathan had read of many men and women who had not set out to become leaders. They too had been thrown into dire situations, some of which did not go well. He only hoped that he did not end up as one of history's greatest failures.

He rose and slowly walked the perimeter of the bridge, checking on the work being performed by what were mostly Corinairan technicians. Lieutenant Commander Kamenetskiy, his chief engineer and friend, had formed work teams that consisted of four Corinairan technicians and one member of the Aurora's crew in order to help the Corinairans better understand the systems they were attempting to repair. In many cases, the crewmen had little to no training on the particular system being repaired, but at the very least they could translate any labels or manuals relating to the systems themselves. That in itself made it easier for the Corinairans to do their work. When all else failed—which it often did—they could always call Vladimir.

The damaged consoles on the starboard side of the ship were slowly being rebuilt. The two communications stations at the rear of the bridge would take considerably longer, as they had been more heavily damaged by electrical fires within. For now, they were forced to operate without a dedicated electronic countermeasures operator or a sensor operator. The few electronic countermeasures systems that still functioned could be handled from the tactical station behind the command chair, and the role of sensor operator had been assumed by Ensign Yosef, the Aurora's only science officer. She had performed the role admirably over the last few weeks, and Nathan knew she was dying to get back to her normal duties. Unfortunately, it would be several weeks before that might happen, if at all.

After the initial damage to the bridge, communications had been transferred to the port-side auxiliary console. After their acting comm-officer had been executed by Captain de Winter during the attempted siege of the Aurora, the Volonese translator, Naralena, who had been stranded on board since their hasty departure from Haven, had kindly offered to assume the role. Since she already knew how to speak many of the native languages of the region, including both Takaran and Corinairan, she seemed a natural choice. She had picked up the use of the comm-systems easily enough and was already making herself at home in her new role, although she was still learning fleet communications procedures.

"Captain," Naralena called, "Lieutenant Commander Nash reports that the Prime Minister and his party have finished their tour and are on their way to the bridge now, sir."

Nathan checked his watch. "Two hours. That was a long tour. Very well, alert the bridge guard detail."

"Yes, sir."

"Sir," the crewman leading the repair team working on the starboard consoles began, "should we break for now and come back afterward?"

"Thank you, no, Ensign," the captain answered. "Carry on with your repairs."

"Yes, sir."

Nathan walked over to the aft starboard console, the one they referred to as 'jump control' since Abby still controlled the process from that station. "Are we ready, Doctor?"

"Yes, I believe so."

"How are those variances?"

"Worrisome, but not enough to delay testing. I was planning to jump a relatively short distance and to a wide open area, so I do not anticipate any problems."

Nathan smiled at her comment. "I don't believe we anticipated *any* of the problems that we've encountered thus far," he reminded her. She did not answer, only nodded her head in agreement.

Nathan moved back down to the helm, standing between Josh to his right and Loki to his left. "Josh, how are we looking?"

"All systems show ready to go, Captain," Josh answered.

Nathan's expression changed as a thought occurred to him. "Josh, what's your last name?"

"My last name?" Josh asked, not sure he understood the captain's question.

"Your family name," Nathan explained, "the one you were born with. For example, my family name is Scott, as in Nathan Scott."

"Oh, you mean my surname," Josh realized. "I'm not sure what my father's surname was, as my mum passed before I was old enough to be curious about such things. But her surname was Hayes. I guess I could use that one."

"Very well, Joshua Hayes it is." Nathan turned to Loki. "And you?"

"Sheehan, sir. Loki Sheehan."

"Captain, why do I need a last name?" Josh asked.

"I need something to call you by," Nathan explained. "I can't call you Josh, as it wouldn't be proper, especially in front of the Prime Minister and his party. And I can't call you by your rank because you don't have one. So I'll call you by your surname, Mister Hayes."

"If you say so, Captain," Josh agreed. "I just hope I can remember that you're talking to me," he added under his breath as the captain turned and headed toward the back of the bridge.

A few moments later, Jessica entered the bridge from the port entrance with the Prime Minister, his translator Mister Briden, a Corinari general, and a few members of the general's staff. Behind them was a team of four armed Corinari guards. Nathan wasn't sure if they were personal guards of the Corinairan party or Corinari guards working as Aurora security personnel. Jessica had ordered that all unassigned visitors were to be escorted by an armed squad, regardless of their identity. After nearly losing the

Aurora to sloppy security procedures and insufficient security staff, she wasn't taking any chances.

"And this, gentlemen, is the bridge," Jessica announced to the entourage as they followed her onto the bridge. Mister Briden interpreted for the Prime Minister as well as the general and the members of his staff.

"Such as it is," Nathan added. "Good to see you again, gentlemen."

"The Prime Minister is excited to finally witness firsthand the miraculous ability of your ship to jump between the stars," Mister Briden interpreted.

"Well, I'm afraid we won't be jumping quite that far this time," Nathan explained. "Until we are sure that the emitters are fully calibrated, we don't want to risk anything more than a short hop. But the effect will be the same."

"Where will we be 'hopping' to?" Mister Briden asked.

"To a point about two light hours away," Nathan explained, glancing at Abby as she looked his way. "The point is just above your ecliptic in order to stay away from any orbital debris—another precaution until we are sure everything is working properly."

"Wonderful," Mister Briden interpreted without the same enthusiasm as was expressed by the Prime Minister himself.

"If you'll give us a few minutes to prepare. Lieutenant Commander, maybe you can show them around the bridge while we prepare to get underway?"

"Of course, sir," Jessica responded. "Gentlemen, perhaps you'd like to see jump control?" Jessica led the party toward Abby at the aft-most starboard console while Nathan stepped over to Naralena.

"Let all hands know we're about to get underway,"

Nathan told her as he continued around and back down to the helm. "Gentlemen, let's review our flight plan."

"We take her out slow and easy, break orbit, and put her on the course and speed Doctor Sorenson gave us," Josh recounted. "Then it's hands off until she jumps us. After that, we make a slow, easy turn and put her back on a reciprocal heading home, and she jumps us back again. After that, we settle back into orbit."

"No problem, Captain," Loki assured him under his breath. "We've got this."

Nathan looked at the two young pilots that only weeks ago had been flying a rickety old harvesting spacecraft around the rings of Haven. They had spent every spare moment in the very same simulator Nathan and Cameron had first practiced in a month earlier. Unlike them, Josh and Loki did not have the benefit of years of flight training at the Fleet Academy back on Earth. Then again, he and Cameron didn't have the years of actual spaceflight experience that Josh and Loki had. Furthermore, Josh and Loki had first flown the Aurora under fire and had proven their worthiness; of that he had no doubt. Still, Nathan couldn't seem to let go of all the things that could go wrong. Vladimir had assured him that the ship's propulsion and maneuvering were working properly, and Abby was confident that the jump drive was equally ready.

Nathan wondered if Captain Roberts had experienced similar misgivings the first time he and Cameron had taken the Aurora out of the Orbital Assembly Platform on her first test flight. Had he been worried that something would go wrong? Had he been worried that his new pilot and navigator would make a mistake and send them hurtling into the system's sun? He had certainly had enough reason to be concerned, considering all the problems that Nathan and Cameron had experienced trying to work together.

As Naralena instructed the entire ship to prepare to get underway, Nathan tried to console himself in the knowledge that nothing had gone wrong with his first flight. He and Cameron had performed their duties correctly. Then he remembered that despite having done everything correctly, the unforeseen events that had followed had gotten them into this mess. Suddenly, he felt nervous once again.

"We're ready whenever you are, Captain," Josh urged.

"Right." Nathan straightened up and turned around to face his guests. "Gentlemen, we're about to get underway."

Nathan took his seat in the command chair at the center of the bridge. The chair was on a slightly raised platform and was located directly under the dome-shaped main view screen that encircled the front section of the bridge in a quarter sphere. The effect was like sitting in a glass dome, looking forward, upward, and to either side of the ship. At first, Nathan had found the view hypnotizing, but recently he had begun to wonder if it wasn't more distracting than anything else. The Aurora was flown by looking at data displays and graphical interfaces, not by looking out the front window like when driving a car.

At the moment, their visitors also found the view impressive. The Aurora's current attitude had the planet of Corinair above them. Since their topside was facing the planet, it gave their guests a wonderful view of their world as it hovered above their heads. As a space-faring civilization themselves, it was probably not the first time they had seen their world from orbit. However, it might have been the first time they had seen it in such fashion, and the effect it was having on them was obvious. The panoramic view gave you a real sense of being out there, in the vacuum of space. It was a sensation that mere display screens could not convey.

"Mister Hayes, are all systems ready for departure?" Nathan asked. He already knew the answer, but decided to run down the list as a show for their visitors.

"Yes, sir. Maneuvering and propulsion are online," Josh reported.

"Mister Sheehan?"

"Navigational systems are online as well, Captain," Loki answered.

"Ensign Yosef?" Nathan inquired, turning toward the sensor operator to the left of Loki's navigation console.

"All sensor packages are operational, sir."

"Comms?"

"All departments report ready for departure, Captain," Naralena reported.

"Tactical?"

"All contacts are identified and are being tracked, sir," Jessica reported. "The threat board is clear."

"Doctor?"

"Jump drive is ready," Abby reported.

"Very well." Nathan took in a deep breath and exhaled slightly. "Helm, break orbit and proceed on course for the first test jump waypoint."

"Aye, sir. Climbing out of orbit and proceeding to first waypoint," Josh reported. As much as he wanted to grab the manual flight stick and the throttles and fly the Aurora just as he had flown his old harvester around the rings of Haven, Josh followed the teachings of the Aurora's executive officer. He simply told the ship where he wanted to go and let the flight computers decide how to manipulate the ship's various systems in order to get there. A moment later the ship's main engines engaged and the ship began to accelerate, climbing into a higher orbit as she circled the planet below. "Climbing out of orbit," Josh reported. "Orbital departure point in three minutes."

"Understood," Nathan answered as he rotated his chair to the right to address his guests. "Gentlemen, for this test, we will climb out of orbit and accelerate on course toward the point we wish to jump to. Once we reach the first waypoint, we'll execute the jump and arrive at our target destination a split second later. At that point, we'll come about on a return course and jump back to our original point of departure."

"Will we feel anything?" Mister Briden asked, presumably on the behalf of the Prime Minister.

"Nothing at all," Nathan assured them. "There is a bright flash of light that is translated inside through the main viewer at the moment we jump, but we have programmed the viewer to reduce its intensity whenever we jump to avoid momentary blindness."

"I see. And how will we know that the jump was successful?"

"Verifying our position is easy enough," Nathan assured him.

"Perhaps," Mister Briden responded. There was a touch of disbelief in his voice that did not go unnoticed by Nathan. One of the Corinari generals then asked a question, which Mister Briden promptly translated. "The general asked how many times you have performed such jumps."

"I'm not sure," Nathan admitted. "I stopped counting after about a dozen."

"And what is the range of your jump drive?" Mister Briden asked.

"The maximum range of the jump drive is ten light years," Nathan reported, knowing full well that Mister Briden and the others were already aware of the system's capabilities. "However, we prefer to limit our jumps to slightly less than that in order to allow us enough reserve energy to make an emergency escape jump should we find unexpected trouble upon arrival."

"A wise precaution," Mister Briden admitted. "We were told that its range can be greatly increased, if given enough power."

"That's what we're hoping, yes," Nathan agreed.

"Leaving orbit now, Captain," Josh reported.

"Very good, Mister Hayes," Nathan answered. "Bring the ship on course to the first jump waypoint and accelerate to one tenth light."

"Aye, sir. On course to first waypoint. Accelerating to one-tenth the speed of light."

The image of the planet above them had been growing steadily smaller for the last few minutes as the Aurora's altitude had increased. Now that they had broken orbit, the planet slid quickly back over their heads and disappeared. The stars slid across the screen from starboard to port as the ship turned onto its new course, and Nathan could feel a slight sway as the ship accelerated rapidly.

"Velocity now at ten percent light, sir," Josh

reported. "Steady on course for the first waypoint."

"Very well," Nathan acknowledged.

"Ten seconds to jump point," Abby reported from the jump control console.

"Comms," Nathan said.

"Attention all hands. Stand by to jump," Naralena announced ship-wide.

"At this speed, it would take approximately twenty hours to reach our destination."

Abby counted down the last few seconds to the jump over the ship-wide loudspeakers. "Jumping in three......two......one......jump."

Everyone on the bridge stared out the forward section of the spherical view screen as pale blue-white light washed out from the emitters, spilling rapidly across the hull until it was completely covered. The light grew quickly in intensity, coming to a blinding flash a split second later. Had the viewing system not automatically compensated for the flash, they would all be seeing blue dots about now. Even with the filters, they still had to squint at the flash.

As quickly as it had come, the flash was gone and the hull was back to normal. The view outside seemed normal as well. In fact, it appeared as if they had not moved at all.

"Did it work?" Mister Briden wondered.

"Ensign?" Nathan inquired.

"We are exactly two light hours from our last position, Captain."

"The stars do not appear to have moved," Mister Briden commented.

"They would not," Abby interjected, "as the distance jumped was not enough to cause any noticeable change in the position of the stars themselves."

"How can we be sure that we are where you say we are?" Mister Briden challenged.

"Helm," Nathan began, still facing Mister Briden, "come about one hundred and eighty degrees, and put us on a course back to Corinair."

"Aye, sir," Josh answered. "Coming about."

"Ensign Yosef, after we come about, put the long-range optics on Corinair and find the Aurora."

"Yes, sir."

"Seeing is believing," Nathan announced to Mister Briden.

"Back on course for Corinair," Josh reported as the ship finished her turn.

"I have Corinair on long-range imaging, sir," Ensign Yosef reported.

"Put it up in a window on the forward viewer, Ensign," Nathan ordered.

A moment later a window appeared on the forward viewer covering most of the normal view of space. After a few seconds, a distant image of the planet Corinair appeared.

"Magnify and enlarge the window," Nathan ordered. The window grew to four times its original size, and the image filled the window itself. They were looking down at the planet's northern pole. "Can you zoom in and find the Aurora?" Nathan asked.

"One moment, sir." Ensign Yosef worked her controls for a moment, zooming in further and sliding the image of the planet around in the window as she searched for the image of the Aurora orbiting the Corinairan home world. "Got it," she announced, zooming in even farther.

"Zoom in on the Aurora only, Ensign."

Ensign Yosef continued to zoom in until the image of the Aurora filled the window. The image was surprisingly clear, considering they were two light hours away. From the left side of the window, a small ship came into view as it approached the Aurora from aft.

"You came on board a couple hours ago," Nathan explained. "That's the image of your shuttle landing on this ship two hours in the past."

Gasps were heard from the Prime Minister, as well as from the general and the members of his staff. Mister Briden, however, offered no such response, remaining calm and unaffected.

"Anytime you're ready, Doctor," Nathan said, confident that he had made his point.

Abby nodded then looked at Naralena. Naralena repeated her warning to the crew, after which Abby again counted down the last three seconds before they jumped. The window on the forward view screen disappeared, and once more the bridge was filled with the subdued blue-white flash as the ship jumped back to her previous position just above Corinair. The planet filled the entire bottom half of the viewer, its sudden appearance catching the Prime Minister and the rest of the party, including Mister Briden, somewhat off-guard.

Their voices filled the bridge as the visitors chattered excitedly amongst themselves in their native tongue. In their excitement, they did not notice Josh and Loki scrambling to reduce speed and quickly maneuver the ship into orbit after jumping in considerably closer to the planet than expected.

Everyone else on the bridge did notice, as did Nathan. A quick glance at the helm displays told him that they were going way too fast to stay in orbit. "Flip her over and apply the mains," Nathan told Josh in a low voice.

Josh didn't need to be told twice and had already taken manual control of the ship. He began pitching her over before Nathan had even finished giving the order. Despite the amount of thrust being applied, it still took at least thirty seconds for the ship to finish pitching over and bring her main engines to face their direction of travel.

"Bring the mains up slow and steady, Mister Hayes," Nathan warned, remembering the way Josh had bounced them around in the harvester during their escape from Tug's farm on Haven. "Let's avoid knocking our guests off their feet."

"I'm not so sure we have time to worry about that, sir," Josh commented.

Nathan glanced at the displays again, checking their velocity, their angle of attack, and the recommended orbital insertion angles all painted on the helmsman's main display screen. Nathan quickly ran the math in his head, remembering similar numbers during a docking simulation that had gone wrong during one of his initial training sessions with Cameron. "You've got time," he added calmly.

Nearly a half-minute later Josh had the Aurora's main engines at full power. At one hundred percent, their main engines produced an incredible amount of thrust, and Nathan saw the velocity readout decreasing rapidly.

"Start taking them down slowly until you settle us into orbit," Nathan instructed.

"What altitude would you like, sir?" Josh asked, a mixture of sarcasm and overall relief in his voice.

"Any altitude will be fine for now, Mister Hayes,"

Nathan assured him. "We'll worry about re-parking her after our guests have departed."

"No prob... I mean, yes, sir." Josh looked over at Loki who looked as pale as Josh felt.

Nathan turned to face their guests, his eyes meeting Abby's concerned look from just beyond the group of chattering Corinairans.

"Captain," Mister Briden said, "I have to admit, that was an impressive display."

"Thank you," Nathan told him. "But we were slightly off target. I'm afraid that we will have to work hard to get the emitters recalibrated in time to intercept that comm-drone before it reaches the Ta'Akar home system."

"Yes, yes, of course," Mister Briden agreed. "We will leave you to your work, Captain."

"Thank you, gentlemen." Nathan looked at Jessica standing at the tactical station directly behind his command chair. "Lieutenant Commander, would you please escort our guests back to their shuttle?"

"Of course," Jessica answered. "Mister Briden, if you'll all follow me."

Nathan shook each of the visitors' hands as they exited the bridge, still chatting excitedly about what they had just witnessed. He had no idea what they were saying, but he was pretty sure they were contemplating the possibilities the jump drive presented. It was a subject that had weighed heavily on Nathan's mind since he had decided to share the technology with their new allies.

After the last visitor left the bridge, Nathan made his way over to Abby at the jump control station. "What the hell happened, Doctor?"

"The variances between the new emitters and the old ones had a more drastic effect than I had anticipated, Captain. We came out considerably off-target on both jumps."

"Yeah," Josh agreed, "especially that last one! That was some fun, huh?"

"Is there something wrong with the new emitters?" Nathan asked.

"No, sir. They just seem to be more efficient in their use of power. It's almost as if the sections of the jump field that are being generated by the new emitters are making the entire field take longer to decay to the point of collapse, causing us to come out of our jump slightly later than expected."

"Can they be recalibrated?" Nathan asked.

"Possibly."

"Can it be done in time to intercept that drone?"

"Doubtful," she admitted. "And certainly not with enough time to retest them."

"What if we purposefully jump short, just to be safe?" Nathan suggested.

"You're assuming that the effect will always be the same, and that it won't be compounded when we jump greater distances."

"Bad idea, huh?" Nathan admitted.

"Quite," Abby agreed. "The only way we could possibly intercept that drone now is if we replace all the emitters with replicated ones. That way they'd all put out a uniform amount of energy."

"Will that work?" Nathan wondered.

"It has a better chance of working than trying to calibrate them," Abby told him.

"How many emitters are we talking about?"

"Another thirty-seven emitters."

"Can we manufacture and install thirty-seven emitters in, what, twenty-eight and a half hours?" Nathan asked, looking at his watch.

"We never stopped producing them, sir," Abby told him. "In case any of them went bad or got damaged in combat, we thought it would be wise to have some spares. We have about a dozen spares already, and it only takes about an hour to make one emitter, and we have two micro-fabricators to work with. If we have installation teams working nonstop and have the new emitters brought out to them as they are made, we might make it."

"Let's get on it then," Nathan sighed. "Naralena, contact the Yamaro and tell them to pump out emitters as fast as they can."

"Yes, sir."

"Josh, as soon as the Prime Minister's party departs, adjust our orbit and rendezvous with the Yamaro again. I want us parked as close as possible to her."

"Yes, sir."

"Naralena, get Lieutenant Commander Kamenetskiy on the comm and put him through to me," he ordered as he headed into his ready room.

"Yes, sir."

By the time Nathan made it to his desk, Vladimir was already on the comms.

"How did the test go?" Vladimir asked over the comms.

"Fine, if you like nearly jumping into the planet's atmosphere at ten percent light."

"Shto?"

"Listen, Vlad, can your guys install thirty seven more emitters in twenty-eight hours?"

"Impossible. Why?"

"Abby didn't seem to think it was impossible."

"Of course she did not. She has no idea how difficult it is to do such things, or how dangerous."

"Dangerous? How is it dangerous?"

"You mean other than working in vacuum? The Darvano sun is different than ours. It is stronger, puts out more radiation. It limits the amount of time that workers can spend outside the ship to only a few hours per day. Any longer and they risk overexposure to radiation that could be fatal."

"What if we had more men?"

"The work requires two people to perform, and it takes them about two hours to replace one emitter. They can work three hours, maybe four. We would need maybe sixty people in order to complete the work so quickly."

"What if we kept the ship between the workers and the Darvano sun?" Nathan wondered.

"Da, that might help, I think. But it will be more difficult in the darkness."

"We're going to park up close to the Yamaro. Maybe she has some exterior lighting we can use."

"Maybe. But I only have twenty men that are qualified to do such work under such conditions."

"I'll get you more," Nathan promised, "as many as I can."

"You must do so quickly, Nathan," Vladimir urged. *"By the time they arrive and are ready to go to work, the men I have will probably have already reached their maximum exposure time."*

"Understood," Nathan told him. "Get your guys ready, Vlad. We'll rendezvous with the Yamaro in a few hours. I want you ready to go to work."

"We will begin installing the spare emitters we already have immediately," Vladimir promised. *"If you are able to rotate the ship to keep the work teams in the dark, it will help."*

"Will do. Thanks." Nathan switched off the

comm-set on his desk. His chief engineer and his band of volunteer Corinairan technicians had their work cut out for them, and it was dangerous work at that. Then again, stopping that comm-drone before it was able to deliver word of their presence in the Darvano system to the Ta'Akar command would probably buy them a few months to better prepare. Nathan was sure of that, and preparation was essential at this point. They couldn't continue reacting to events; doing so had nearly depleted the Aurora of ammunition, crew, and even spirit. They needed to take control, to go on the offensive.

Nathan switched the comm-set back on, pressing the button that hailed the comms-station. "Naralena, get me in touch with Commander Taylor on Corinair," he instructed, "and see to it that Chief Montrose is also on the line."

* * *

"Attention on deck," the guard at the door to the briefing room announced. Everyone in attendance stood at attention as Nathan walked briskly into the room.

"As you were," he ordered as he made his way to the head of the table and took his seat. "First, I want to thank you all for your tireless efforts over the last twenty-eight hours. Your dedication and that of your teams are why we were able to pull off the impossible and install all of the new emitters in time." Nathan paused and took a breath before continuing. "Unfortunately, as you all know, I cannot offer a break just yet, as we have a mission to perform. We need to locate and destroy the comm-drone that will be arriving in the Takaran home system in less than a day. If we are successful, we could gain at least two additional months before a Takaran battle group comes knocking at our door. That's time we desperately need to prepare." Nathan stopped and looked at the faces at the table. "Any questions?"

"How are we going to catch a drone moving at FTL speeds?" Josh asked.

"Good question, Mister Hayes," Nathan said. "Ensign Willard?"

Ensign Willard leaned forward in his chair as he spoke. "The drones accelerate up to between ninety and ninety-five percent the speed of light before they go into FTL. This is how they achieve FTL speeds of nearly one hundred times light. They are designed to drop out of FTL when they encounter a hail from a Takaran ship. Once they are out of FTL, they listen for a valid message exchange signal. If the signal passes authentication, the drone will decelerate and begin a message exchange with the hailing ship, returning to FTL once the exchange is complete."

"What if there is no valid message exchange signal?" Jessica asked.

"If no exchange request is authenticated within approximately five of your minutes, the drone will automatically accelerate and go back into FTL to continue its journey," Ensign Willard explained. "It is during this period that the drone will be vulnerable to attack."

"What if we miss?" Nathan wondered. "What will the drone do?"

"As far as I know, drones are not programmed to take any evasive maneuvers, Captain," Ensign Willard explained.

"That seems a bit hard to believe," Jessica stated with suspicion.

"FTL traffic within the Pentaurus cluster is restricted to either Ta'Akar warships or Ta'Akar controlled transports," Tug interjected. "They do not feel the need for such programming."

"I don't know," Jessica said. "One of the first things you go for in an armed conflict is the enemy's lines of communication."

"Yes, under normal circumstances I might agree," Tug granted, "but given the technologies available in the cluster, it is nearly impossible to target something moving at ninety percent the speed of light."

"He's right," Nathan stated. "Without the jump drive it would be impossible to intercept the drone."

"So, we just keep telling the drone to drop out of FTL and shoot at it until we get lucky. Is that the plan?" Jessica asked.

"Basically, yes," Nathan answered. "Sooner or later we have to hit something."

"I'm afraid it will have to be sooner, Captain," Ensign Willard insisted. "The drones are programmed to ignore all hails after the third interruption. It was necessary in order to avoid unusual delays in delivery due to malfunctions. There were several cases where a drone kept dropping out of FTL due to errant radio waves. A two week journey ended up taking two months, resulting in all manner of problems. They never figured out exactly how the errant emissions where causing the malfunction, but the three dropouts per flight subroutine effectively eliminated the problem and therefore was never removed from the standard programming package used in the drones."

"So," Nathan responded, "three strikes and we're out." Other than Jessica, Vladimir, Ensign Yosef,

Abby, and himself, everyone else in the room looked puzzled.

"If you mean three chances are all we get, then yes, Captain, you would be correct." Ensign Willard agreed.

"So we jump out to where we expect the drone to be, transmit a signal to get it to drop out of FTL, and then what?" Jessica asked. "We've got no rail gun ammo left to speak of."

"I can engage the drone using my interceptor," Tug explained. "The energy cannons do not require ammunition, only energy, of which there will be an ample supply, thanks to the new reactors installed by the Corinari."

"How will we locate this drone?" Vladimir asked. "It will be traveling faster than light. By the time we see it, it will already be gone."

"We jump just ahead of it and off its course slightly," Nathan explained. "As soon as it passes us, we'll be able to see it."

"Our optical and radar suites are sophisticated enough to track the drone as it passes us by," Ensign Yosef explained. "It will measure the range of the drone while in close proximity, and the optics will track the bearing to the drone as well as measure the Doppler component of the signal. All of this information combined will yield enough data to predict the drone's position even over extended ranges."

"Very good," Nathan remarked. "Then all we have to do is jump in ahead of it and transmit the dropout signal using the codes and frequencies provided by Ensign Willard. The drone drops out of FTL and Tug chases it down in his interceptor and destroys it. Sounds easy enough to me," Nathan stated enthusiastically. As he looked around the table at each of their faces, it quickly became apparent that they did not share in his enthusiasm.

"Captain," Abby interrupted, "may I remind you that we have yet to test the new emitters?"

"Sorry, Doc," Nathan said. "Your first test is going to have to be en route. We're out of time."

"I wouldn't recommend that, Captain."

"Is there any reason to think that they will not work?" Nathan asked.

"No, but..."

"Then I'll give you one short jump on our way out," Nathan interrupted. "If it works, the next jump will be about four light years."

"Captain," Tug began, "I will need someone to feed me navigational information. I will be much too busy with piloting and targeting to do it myself."

"I could take second seat," Josh offered.

"No, it is much too dangerous," Tug insisted.

"It's not like the drone's gonna shoot back at us," Josh argued.

"I will be chasing a target at ninety percent the speed of light, firing high energy cannons. I can think of few things that are more dangerous," Tug told him.

"He's right, Mister Hayes," Nathan insisted. "Besides, I need you on the helm."

"Yes, sir," Josh answered.

"I could pilot the ship," Loki offered.

"No, you're going to be too busy calculating navigational tracks for both the Aurora and Tug."

"Oh yeah."

"Ensign Yosef, you'll be responsible for locating the drone and calculating its position as needed. Abby will be running jump plots and operating the jump drive."

"What am I doing?" Jessica wondered.

"You keep your eyes on that threat board, Jess," Nathan urged. "We're going to be coming awfully close to Takaran space, and we're essentially unarmed at the moment."

"What would you like me to do, Captain?" Vladimir asked.

"Same thing you always do, Cheng." A smiled crept across Nathan's face. "Hold her together so we can get the job done."

* * *

"Comms, alert all hands. We're about to get underway," Nathan ordered as he entered the bridge.

"Yes, sir," Naralena reported from the comm station.

"Mister Hayes," Nathan continued, "are we ready for departure?"

"Aye, sir. All systems show ready," Josh reported.

Nathan took his seat in the command chair at the center of the bridge. "Jess?"

"Threat board is clear, Captain," Jessica reported. "And Tug reports his interceptor is powered up and ready to go."

"Very well. Helm, take us out of orbit," Nathan ordered.

"Aye, sir. Breaking orbit." Josh fired the main engines, bringing them up sharply in order to quickly accelerate out of orbit over Corinair. Unlike the previous trip where he was trying to provide a smooth ride for the visiting dignitaries, this time they were on a mission and time was critical.

The Aurora surged forward as her engines roared

to life, sending a low rumble throughout the ship. The image of the planet below them fell away rapidly as they climbed up and away.

Nathan turned to Naralena, sitting at the comm station to his left and slightly behind him. "Comms, notify the Corinari that we are departing."

"Yes, sir."

"Ensign Willard," Nathan said, "I trust that your calculations have been fed to our navigator?"

"Yes, sir," Ensign Willard assured him, "both the standard comm-drone route between Darvano and Takara, as well as my estimate of the drone's current position along that route."

"Very good," Nathan responded. "Let's hope your estimations are accurate."

"I had your navigator check them, just to be sure," Ensign Willard assured him. "Even your physicist checked them over."

"I took the liberty of plotting some jumps at various points along the area of the route where we expect to find the drone," Abby explained.

"A wise precaution, as usual, Doctor."

"Breaking orbit, Captain," Josh reported.

"Bring us onto the intercept course, Mister Hayes, and bring her up to ten percent light," Nathan ordered.

"Coming to intercept course. Accelerating to ten percent light," Josh reported. Josh quickly accepted the course fed to him by Loki and instructed the Aurora to come to the new heading and accelerate. After pushing the execute button, the ship turned slightly to starboard and applied even more thrust.

"Doctor, run your test plot and initiate when ready," Nathan told her.

"Yes, Captain."

Tug sat patiently waiting in the cockpit of his interceptor, his flight helmet sitting atop the console in front of him.

"So where's your girlfriend been lately?" Marcus asked, trying to make small talk as he checked Tug's restraint system.

"Who?" Tug asked, his mind elsewhere.

"The rebel princess," Marcus said, "at least that's what Lieutenant Commander Nash calls her."

"Oh, you mean Jalea." Tug smiled, slightly amused by the reference. "She is supervising operations on Karuzara."

"Where?" Marcus asked, his face in a confused pinch.

"The asteroid base," Tug explained. "That's what Josh has named it."

"That boy shouldn't be allowed to name anything," Marcus insisted with a grumble.

"It seemed to fit well enough."

Marcus noticed Tug's distraction. "You sure you wanna do this? Chase a comm-drone across the cluster? Seems a bit crazy, if you ask me."

"If given a choice, a wise man would surely say no," Tug lamented.

"Guess you're not as wise as you thought, huh?"

"Sometimes life does not give us choices, my friend," Tug told him.

"Bullshit. It ain't life that left you no choice; it's honor."

Tug looked at Marcus's gruff old face. He was a bitter, sour man on a good day, but he was also wiser than he let on. "Perhaps you are correct."

"Listen, those new reactors the Corinari techs

put in are top notch. I'll bet you can push them up to at least a hundred and twenty percent if need be."

"I'll keep that in mind," Tug promised.

"Also, one of their computer guys programmed in some firing patterns for your main nose turret. I think he called them 'algorithms' or something. He said you might find them useful."

"I just might at that."

"Yeah, he said something about the old ones being geared for hunting forty-year-old ships or something. Couldn't hurt, right?"

"No, it couldn't."

"*Attention all hands. Prepare to jump,*" Abby's voice announced over the loudspeakers in the Aurora's main hangar bay.

"I hate this part," Marcus admitted.

Tug looked at Marcus with a puzzled look on his face, noticing how the old man was clenching his jaw as Abby counted down the last three seconds leading up to the jump.

"*Jump complete.*"

"Damn!"

"You can feel the jump?" Tug asked.

"Makes one of my fillings hurt," Marcus explained, "only for a second, mind you, but for that second it hurts like hell."

"Interesting."

"Not to me it ain't," Marcus exclaimed as he prepared to climb down from Tug's cockpit. "Good luck, Tug," he said, holding out his hand.

Tug took Marcus's hand and shook it. "Thanks."

"How are we looking, Abby?" Nathan asked.

Abby was busy looking over the reports from the

first test jump with all the new emitters installed. "That is unusual," she reported.

"What's unusual?" Nathan wondered.

"We're still on the correct course, Captain," Abby explained, "but we jumped approximately one point two five light hours instead of only one. Apparently, the new emitters are more efficient than the original ones. Less energy is lost in the initial generation of the fields."

"Is that good or bad?" Nathan asked.

"Well, it means we might have increased our potential range a bit," she told him. "I will need to do more calculations in order to determine exactly how much."

"Is that going to cause us any problems with this mission?"

"No, sir," she assured him. "I believe I can adjust the output parameters to compensate for the increased efficiency of the emitters, although it may take a few jumps to get it right."

"Very well," Nathan told her. "Plot the next jump to a point just ahead of the drone's current estimated position."

"Yes, sir."

"Helm, bring us up to maximum velocity, smartly if you will," Nathan ordered.

"Yes, sir," Josh answered, excited to have a chance to bring the Aurora to her maximum speed.

"Captain, is that really necessary?" Abby asked. "After all, the maximum jump ranges were all calculated on fifty percent light. Even at half that we would still have enough energy in the banks to complete the mission."

"Yes, I'm sure you're correct, Doctor," Nathan agreed. "But the faster we go, the easier it will be for

Tug to catch up to the drone and destroy it."

"Of course."

"Will that present a problem, Doctor?" Nathan asked.

"No, sir. It's just that we have never jumped at that velocity before."

"Yeah, firsts are becoming something of a habit on this ship," Nathan quipped.

"Passing twenty five percent light," Josh announced.

"Hold at fifty percent until we complete our next jump, Josh. Then continue accelerating after the jump is completed."

"Yes, sir."

"Thank you, Captain."

"Hey, I don't want to take any more chances than I have to, Doctor." Nathan turned his seat around to face Jessica at the tactical station directly behind him. "How are we looking, Jess?"

"Board is still clear, sir. Nothing but Corinairan traffic," Jessica told him.

"Sensors?" Nathan asked, rotating to port to face Ensign Yosef.

"All clear as well, Captain," the ensign reported.

"Ensign Willard," Nathan began, "if we're going to be following the same course as the drone, how are we going to keep from colliding with it? I mean, as I understand it, we don't actually jump past anything. We still go in a straight line."

"In order to avoid shipping traffic, the comm-drones have their own dedicated transit corridors," Ensign Willard explained. "These corridors run from the outer edges of the system, rather than from their centers, so their corridors, although parallel to the main transit corridors, are sufficiently offset in order to prevent collisions."

"So we'll be coming in at an angle," Nathan stated, "from outside the comm-drone corridor."

"Correct."

"Passing forty percent light," Josh reported.

"Jump plotted and locked in, Captain," Abby reported.

"Very good. As soon as we hold at half-light, make your jump."

"Understood."

"Comms?" Nathan called.

Naralena again activated the ship wide announcement system. "Attention all hands. Stand by for jump."

"Tug, be ready," Nathan called over the comms. "Hopefully we'll get lucky with the first jump."

"*I am ready to launch, Captain,*" Tug reported over the comms.

"Forty-five percent light," Josh announced.

"Sensors and tactical, keep your eyes peeled for threats after we jump," Nathan warned. "We'll be jumping to within a light year of Takara. There may be patrols."

"I think the odds are pretty slim that we'll actually run into a patrol," Ensign Willard insisted. "After all, we're talking about a pretty vast area, Captain."

"Yeah, you would think that," Nathan agreed, "but so far we've found space to be a lot more crowded than you might think."

"Velocity at half-light and holding, sir," Josh reported as he cut the main engines. The Aurora was now coasting silently through space at half the speed of light, and would continue to do so forever if left undisturbed.

"Abby," Nathan prompted.

Abby switched on the ship wide announcement system. "Jumping in three......two......one......jump." The blue-white light flashed through the bridge, subdued just enough by the filters on the main viewer to avoid blinding anyone looking at the screen.

"Jump complete," Abby announced.

"Starting sensor sweeps," Ensign Yosef announced.

"Continue acceleration, Josh," Nathan ordered.

"Aye, sir. Mains coming up again," Josh responded as he fired up the main engines once more and quickly brought them up to full power. There was no discernible lurch this time, as the ship was already traveling at two-thirds her designed maximum velocity. The rumble of the main engines returned, and the velocity readout again began to increase.

"Threat board is clear, sir," Jessica reported.

"Good," Nathan commented. He had half expected to come out of the jump right in front of another Takaran capital ship.

They waited patiently for several minutes while Ensign Yosef continued to scan the area ahead of them for the emission patterns that Ensign Willard had told her to look for.

"Nothing yet, Kaylah?" Nathan asked, becoming impatient.

"No, sir, just the usual background radiation and lots of extremely low power radio signals coming from other systems."

"Are you sure? Maybe it's there and you're just not seeing it?"

"No, sir. I'm sure," Ensign Yosef insisted.

"Sir," Ensign Willard interrupted, "we need to be patient."

"What if we jumped short of it?" Nathan speculated.

"We would still be able to detect it," Ensign Yosef added, "just not as accurately as if it flew past us."

"Very well, then we wait," Nathan decided.

"Passing fifty-five percent light," Josh reported.

The bridge remained quiet for what seemed like an eternity. The only thing punctuating the silence was Josh reporting their velocity every few minutes until they reached seventy-five percent the speed of light.

Now at three-quarters the speed of light, the main engines were again quiet as they coasted along through the vacuum of space, patiently waiting for their target to streak past them. Try as he might to think of nothing, Nathan couldn't help but contemplate all that was riding on the success of this single intercept. If successful, they would have several months in which to prepare the Darvano system to defend itself. It was even conceivable that several months might be enough time for them to wage some sort of guerrilla-style hit-and-run campaign to weaken the Ta'Akar enough that they could be completely overthrown. However, if they failed to intercept the drone, depending on the position of Takaran ships in the area, they could find themselves under attack within a month. That would barely be enough time to repair and rearm the Aurora, let alone establish any military capabilities within the Darvano system.

"Contact!" Ensign Yosef announced as her fingers danced across her consoles, quickly analyzing the incoming data streams. "The drone just blew past us, about a hundred thousand kilometers to port. Oh my God, it's traveling at ninety times the speed of light."

"That's what we expected," Nathan reminded her.

"Yes, sir. I know. I've just never seen anything traveling that fast before."

"Can you track it?" Nathan asked. "Can you verify its course?"

"Yes, sir. I just need a minute to collect enough data," she assured him.

"Comms," Nathan said, "tell Tug to get out onto the apron and get ready to launch."

"Yes, sir," Naralena answered.

"Abby, as soon as Kaylah has a plot, I need you to put us eight light hours ahead of that drone. That should give us just over five minutes to get Tug into position before the drone catches up to us."

"Understood," Abby replied.

"We'll be jumping even closer to Takara, Jess," Nathan warned.

"Don't worry, Skipper," she promised. "I'm not taking my eyes off the threat board."

"I've got the drone's true course and speed plotted, sir," Ensign Yosef announced. "I'm feeding it to navigation and jump control."

"Excellent. Whenever you guys are ready," Nathan told them.

"Tug reports he is on the apron and ready for departure, Captain," Naralena reported from the comms station.

"Remind him to close his eyes when we jump," Nathan instructed Naralena.

"Yes, sir."

"Jump plotted, Captain," Abby reported.

"Mister Sheehan?" Nathan inquired, wondering if he was ready.

"All set here, Captain."

"Let's do it."

"Attention all hands. Prepare to jump," Naralena announced.

"Jumping in three......two..."

Tug checked the mag-locks on his landing gear and put his hand on his flight control stick as Abby's voice finished counting down to the jump.

"...One......jump."

Tug closed his eyes tightly as the brilliant blue-white light of the Aurora's jump fields washed out over her surface, only to disappear a moment later.

"Jump complete," Abby reported over the comms.

Tug released his mag-locks and applied full upward thrust. The interceptor leapt up off the flight apron of the Aurora, quickly rising above the top of her main propulsion section just aft of the apron. Another thrust stopped his ascent and he fired his main engines at full thrust, angling to port as he quickly left the Aurora behind.

"Tug, Aurora. I'm away, moving into position."

"Start transmitting the dropout signal," Nathan ordered.

"Transmitting now, sir," Naralena reported. Ensign Willard watched over her shoulder, checking to see that the frequency and signal strength matched those used by warships of the Ta'Akar, which were the only ones authorized to order a comm-drone to drop out of FTL in order to exchange messages.

"Threat board is clear, Captain," Jessica reported. "Tug is moving into the slot. His current velocity is point eight light and accelerating."

Nathan said nothing, just stared straight ahead at the main view screen, wondering what good a view of the stars was at a time like this. "Jess, can you put your tactical view up on the main view screen?"

"Yes, sir," Jessica answered. A moment later a large window appeared on the forward section of the spherical view screen, superimposed over the view of the stars ahead of them. The window showed a three-dimensional view of the area, with an icon indicating the Aurora at the center, and another icon indicating Tug's interceptor moving away from them to port at a respectable rate. Sets of numbers indicating course and speed of both of the icons appeared just below them, moving along with them.

"Contact!" Ensign Yosef reported. "The drone just dropped out of FTL. Passing to port now, at point nine light."

Nathan looked back to the tactical display on the main viewer as the icon representing the drone appeared on the display. The icon was moving considerably faster than them and was already passing directly to port, but it was only moving a little faster than Tug's interceptor, which was now traveling at point eight seven light.

"Tug, Aurora," Nathan called out over the comms. "You got it?"

"I've got it, Captain. Moving into position."

Tug looked at his threat display, watching as the drone approached quickly from behind him and slightly to port. At the speeds they were both traveling he would only have a few seconds of targeting time to attempt to destroy the drone.

"Firing position in five seconds," Tug reported.

Tug watched as the drone caught up with him. He was only fifty meters to starboard of the drone's flight path. Although it seemed like a safe distance, the amount of kinetic energy carried by any object traveling at such velocity was sobering.

As his threat display showed the drone passing him, Tug applied thrust and started to slide his interceptor to port, slipping in behind the drone as it passed. A moment later, his nose turret targeting systems indicated that it had a lock on the drone. Tug depressed the trigger, sending a staccato stream of energy bursts stretching out ahead of him toward the target.

"What the hell?" Tug exclaimed as he stared at his weapons targeting display. The icon representing the drone was sliding randomly from side to side and up and down, and it was doing so both quickly and erratically. "Aurora, Tug," he called over comms. "The drone is maneuvering. It is taking evasive actions. I believe it knows it is being attacked."

"Can you hit it?" Nathan asked over the comms.

"I am trying, but it is moving away from me and I cannot accelerate further. How much time?"

"Thirty seconds," Nathan reported.

Tug continued firing his nose turret, struggling to try and track the erratic target, but it was no use. The drone was simply moving about faster than he could move the turret. "Switching to auto-track," Tug announced as he released control of the turret to the targeting systems. Suddenly, the icon representing the drone vanished from his display.

"The drone is gone!" Jessica reported.

"Did he hit it?" Nathan asked.

"No, sir," Ensign Yosef reported. "It went back into FTL."

"Can you plot its course again?" Nathan asked.

"Yes, sir. Give me a moment."

"Tug, Aurora," Nathan called over his comm set. "Get back on the deck and lock on. We'll jump ahead and give it another try."

"*Understood,*" Tug answered.

"Abby, new plot. Put us twenty light hours ahead this time,"

"Yes, sir," Abby responded.

"Cheng," Nathan called over the comms.

"*Yes, Captain?*" Vladimir answered.

"Could you possibly squeeze a little more power into the mains? I'd really like to try and get us up to point eight light."

"*I will try,*" Vladimir answered. "*Lieutenant Commander Patel originally believed we could do point eight.*"

"Great, let's see if we can prove he was right." Nathan switched off his comms and rose from his chair, stepping up between Josh and Loki at the flight consoles. "Josh, as soon as we come out of the jump, I want you to go to full power on the mains. The more speed we can get out of her the less Tug will have to accelerate to chase that thing."

"Yes, sir," Josh answered, a bit nervous considering that at zero point seven five light, he was already going faster than he had ever gone before.

"I've got an updated plot for the drone, sir," Ensign Yosef reported. "Feeding it to navigation and jump control."

After a few minutes of deceleration, Tug was

123

able to match his velocity to that of the Aurora's and began sliding his way to starboard to line up with her in order to land. He had never attempted to land on a ship traveling this fast, and although the procedure was relatively the same, he could not help but think about the incredible speeds at which they were traveling. The most deceptive part about space flight was that there was almost no sense of motion. Everything in space is moving at incredible speeds. Other than your own instrumentation, your only perception of motion is in relation to objects near you. In the case of the Aurora, they were both traveling at relatively the same speed, so the massive ship appeared to be moving quite slowly, despite the fact that they were both moving fast enough to experience a considerable amount of time dilation.

"*We're ready to jump as soon as you're down, Tug,*" Nathan informed him over the comms.

"I am on final approach now," Tug assured him. "I should be down and locked in sixty seconds."

"*Listen, after we jump, don't launch until we tell you. We're going to try and squeeze out a little more velocity first,*" Nathan explained.

"Understood. I am curious as to why Ensign Willard did not know about the drone's evasive capabilities," Tug added.

"My specialty was in communications systems and cryptology, Captain," Ensign Willard defended. "What I know about the drone's operational capabilities I learned from one of the technicians that maintained the drones carried on the Yamaro. I was not even aware they had a rear facing sensor package. I find it very odd, in fact, as their forward sensor suite is only for navigation and collision avoidance."

"It makes sense, sir," Jessica interjected. "Given the state of Takaran technology, I mean. They don't have jump drives; they haven't even conceived of one. The only way anyone could hope to shoot down a drone would be to chase after it when it's flying at subluminal velocity. Even then, the logistics are mind-numbing. I'm surprised they even bothered putting any kind of protective systems in it to begin with."

"They probably know how dependent they are on the drones as well," Nathan commented.

"I would expect so, sir," Jessica continued. "My guess is that the drone probably activates a threat detection system whenever it receives a command to drop out of FTL. Running that kind of evasive maneuvering system at all times would use a lot of power. I doubt that small drone could generate enough power to run both systems simultaneously."

"Tug is down and locked, Captain," Naralena reported.

"Jump us, Abby," Nathan ordered without hesitation.

"Jumping in three......two......one......jump."

Blue-white light splashed across the bridge once more as the ship jumped ahead.

"Jump complete," Abby reported.

"Full power, Mister Hayes," Nathan ordered.

"Aye, sir. Mains to full," Josh answered as he throttled up the main engines again.

"The drone should catch up to us in ten minutes and thirty-two seconds, sir," Ensign Yosef reported.

"Understood. Let me know when it's five minutes out," Nathan ordered.

"Yes, sir."

"Comms, relay everything we just discussed to Tug."

"Yes, sir," Naralena answered.

"Passing point seven six, Captain," Josh reported.

"Cheng, How are we doing down there?" Nathan called over the comms.

"*I'm running reactors one and two at one hundred and twenty percent, Captain. They seem to be tolerating the additional load nicely,*" Vladimir bragged.

"Good job. Keep me posted," Nathan answered, switching off his comm.

"Passing point seven, seven," Josh reported.

"Tug," Nathan hailed, "got any bright ideas?"

"*I do have one,*" Tug admitted, "*but it is extremely dangerous. I would prefer to save it as a final option, if you do not mind.*"

"Understood."

"Passing point seven eight," Josh reported.

"Seven minutes, Captain," Ensign Yosef reported.

"Start transmitting the dropout signal," Nathan ordered Naralena.

"Transmitting dropout signal," Naralena answered from the comm station.

Tug flipped through the various auto-fire patterns the Corinari programmers had entered into the fire control system on his nose turret. There were several new patterns added, a few of which appeared to cover a large area in an extremely random pattern. However, on his first attempt, the comm-drone had been so unpredictable in its evasive maneuvers that Tug seriously doubted that any of the firing patterns would be able to score a hit.

"*One minute to launch,*" Naralena's voice announced over his comms.

Tug switched off the auto-fire pattern selector and turned his attention back to his flight controls. A quick check showed everything was functioning normally. In fact, his interceptor was now performing better than he could ever remember, thanks to the highly skilled Corinari flight mechanics.

"*Thirty seconds,*" Naralena prompted.

"Passing point eight light, Captain," Josh exclaimed, trying to control his enthusiasm.

"Fifteen seconds," Ensign Yosef announced.

"Launch the interceptor," Nathan instructed calmly.

"Tug, Aurora," Naralena called. "Go for launch."

"*Understood,*" Tug's voice crackled over the comms. "*Launching.*"

Nathan watched the window on the forward display screen as the icon representing Tug's interceptor moved away from the Aurora and closer to the expected path of the drone.

"Passing point eight one," Josh said. "Acceleration is almost nonexistent now, Captain."

"Keep the throttles up, Mister Hayes," Nathan ordered. "Let's see if we can make point eight two."

"Contact!" Ensign Yosef announced. "Right on time; same course and speed, sir."

"Good work, Ensign." Nathan activated his comm set. "You got it, Tug?"

"*I have the contact on my screens,*" Tug announced. "*Moving into firing position.*"

Tug waited a few more seconds before he started his side slip to port, waiting for the drone to get a little closer. The Aurora's additional velocity at the time he had launched had helped him get up to eighty-nine percent the speed of light, a mere one percent less than the velocity of the drone. However, one percent the speed of light was still one percent; the drone was still going to pass him rather quickly. He figured he had maybe five seconds of firing time before the drone would be too far ahead of him for his targeting systems to effectively track.

Tug moved even closer to the drone's flight path than before, coming within thirty meters.

"You're awfully close there Tug," Nathan warned over the comms.

"I will be fine, Captain," Tug assured him, trying to convince himself it was true. A few seconds later the drone was passing him on his port side. Tug slid the ship hard over the last fifty meters, his nose cannon attempting to track the target as it streaked past. Tug fired continuously, but again he had no luck as the drone jinked left and right, up and down, just as erratically as the last time. Tug continued to fire after the nose turret lost its track on the drone. Even though the turret could not track it, the bolts of energy spewing forth from the turret's twin cannons had incredible range, and those bolts traveled at the speed of light. He even kicked in his wingtip lasers, firing continuous streams of energy as he swept his nose about wildly in nearly imperceptible increments in a frustrated attempt to score a hit. Then the contact disappeared again as it slipped back into FTL.

"Damn!"

"Tug, Aurora. Get back on deck. We've got one more chance at this," Nathan's voice ordered.

Tug reeled his emotions back in. "Copy. Returning."

"One more time, Abby," Nathan ordered. "Twenty light hours ahead again."

"Understood."

"Are we still accelerating, Josh?" Nathan asked.

"Barely, sir. We're mostly just burning propellant at this point."

"Shut down the mains."

"Yes, sir. Shutting down the mains," Josh answered as he throttled back the Aurora's main drive. "Velocity holding at point eight two light."

"Well, at least we know we can go point eight two now," Nathan commented.

Tug carefully brought his interceptor back down onto the deck of the Aurora as both ships hurtled along at over eighty percent the speed of light. Both attempts to intercept and destroy the drone had failed, and now they had but one chance remaining. If they failed, the drone would reach its destination in a few more days, and the Ta'Akar would immediately dispatch the nearest warship to the Darvano system. Within a month, the new alliance would have to defend itself against one or more aggressors, whether they were ready or not.

Tug closed his eyes as Abby's voice counted down to the next jump. Even with tightly closed lids, he could still see the flash—that miraculous flash that instantly propelled the Aurora across enormous stretches of space. The Aurora's jump drive was more powerful than any weapon he could ever dream of, and yet, if not given enough time to prepare, it might end up of little use.

Tug thought about the hundreds if not thousands of men and women who had died under his leadership fighting against the Ta'Akar Empire over the decades. They had gladly sacrificed their lives for what they believed. If he did not succeed this time, all of their deaths could be in vain.

Tug thought about his daughters, whom he had entrusted to Chief Montrose's family back on Corinair. They had lost their mother to his cause, and they might still lose their father as well. He could still see their faces as he bid them farewell. His youngest smiled and waved happily, as if he was off to the day's market on Haven. However, his oldest , Deliza, understood the gravity of the situation. After all, she had lived through the boarding attempt on the Aurora, hiding in the service tunnels with Vladimir as they struggled to find a way to stop the intruders.

"*Two minutes to launch,*" Naralena's voice announced, jarring him back to the present moment.

"Understood." Tug knew what he had to do, and it was no more than he had asked those who had served under him to do in the past.

"Transmitting dropout signal," Naralena acknowledged.

"Launch the interceptor," Nathan ordered calmly.

"Interceptor away," Naralena replied a moment later.

Nathan looked up one last time at the icon on the

forward viewer that represented Tug's interceptor as it moved quickly away from the Aurora toward its course parallel to that of the Takaran comm-drone.

"Contact!" Ensign Yosef announced. "Same course and velocity."

"*I have the contact*," Tug announced. "*Moving into firing position.*"

Nathan watched the track as Tug's fighter slipped into position, but something was different.

"Captain," Jessica called, "Tug has moved directly into the drone's flight path."

"Tug, Aurora," Nathan called out over the comms. "You're in the drones flight path!"

"*I know, Captain.*"

"You know? What the hell are you doing, Tug?"

"*Remember that bright idea I told you about, the one I was saving for last?*"

The collision alarm began sounding in the cockpit of Tug's interceptor. Tug killed his main drive and flipped his ship end over end, bringing his nose facing aft, directly toward the onrushing comm-drone. He was now flying backward at eighty-nine percent the speed of light. He immediately opened fire with both his nose turret and his wingtip lasers, piercing the blackness with their fiery intensity.

"*Tug, you've got about ten seconds before that thing hits you head on and turns you into dust!*" Nathan's voice yelled over the comms.

"Either way, that drone will be destroyed," Tug promised as he swung his nose back and forth. An idea hit him and he reached for the auto-fire pattern selector for his nose turret. He quickly scrolled through the selections until he found the one he was looking for—one of the wide, erratic patterns that the Corinari programmers had installed. He selected the firing pattern and activated it. His nose turret continued firing in rapid succession as it swung its barrels about in seemingly haphazard fashion. In fact, it was laying down a pinpoint firing pattern that placed a perfectly aimed shot in every square meter of space in front of him across an area of ten square meters in less than two seconds.

"Five seconds!" Nathan's voice called out.

The nose turret continued to fire, repeating the pattern as Tug braced himself for the inevitable collision that he probably would not even feel. Then it happened: a flash of light directly in front of him. Tug pulled his flight stick back hard, pitched his nose ninety degrees upward, and immediately fired his main engines at full thrust. As his interceptor continued to hurtle along the same path as the expanding debris field of the drone he had just blown apart, his powerful main engines caused his ship to leap upward.

"Target destroyed!" Jessica yelled. "He got it!"

"Tug, Aurora!" Nathan called over the comms. There was no answer. "Tug! Are you still with us?"

A few moments later, they received a crackled reply. *"Where else would I be?"*

Josh rose from his seat in excitement. "Now that's what I call playing chicken!"

"Captain, we're getting awfully close to Takara," Jessica reported.

"How close?"

"Coming up on half a light year from their heliopause, sir."

"Comms, tell Tug to get aboard as quick as he can. Abby, do we have enough energy left to jump back to Darvano?"

"Just barely," she warned.

"Captain," Loki interrupted, "at this speed, it will take us forever to come a hundred and eighty degrees about."

"We'll also be drawing a huge hot arc across the area," Ensign Yosef added. "Any ship with a half decent infrared suite will spot us."

"Maybe, but we'll be long gone before anyone even sees us, let alone comes to investigate," Nathan insisted.

"But you would be giving them another piece of the puzzle," Ensign Willard stated.

"He's right, Captain," Jessica agreed from her position at the tactical station. "Think about it. There are already a few hints about who and what we truly are. But the only solid explanation died with de Winter and his staff. As things stand, their focus is probably still on either the Korak or Haven systems. Those are the only two places that we've been where a Takaran ship saw us jump out and lived to send a message home."

"But Haven is too far out," Nathan argued. "There's no way they could've received word about the events there by now, not even at one hundred times light."

"True," Ensign Willard agreed, "but Korak is only four point four light years from Takara. If a message was dispatched immediately after your encounter there, which would be standard procedure, it has already reached Ta'Akar command."

"So a huge hot arc out here would be like a giant arrow pointing out the way we went," Nathan realized.

"Precisely," Ensign Willard agreed.

"Captain, I recommend we change course for Taroa," Jessica suggested.

"Taroa? Where we first arrived?"

"Yes, sir. My understanding is that there are still survivors of the Ta'Akar attack on that system's primary world. If we make ourselves seen in Taroa and word of our presence there gets back to the Ta'Akar, that would reinforce their perception that our interests are in that part of the Pentaurus cluster."

"Deception," Nathan stated, seeing the logic of her suggestion.

"It would also be a great opportunity to gather some more signals intelligence," Jessica added.

Nathan turned to Abby. "Can we make a jump to Taroa?"

"Again, barely. But we would arrive with insufficient energy to depart should we encounter yet another problem."

"Very well. Plot a jump to about halfway between Takara and Taroa. Then we'll sit and recharge the system before jumping into Taroa."

"It will take us longer to get back to Darvano," Abby warned.

"Seems worth it to me," Jessica added.

"Agreed. How long will it take us to get back to Darvano if we go to Taroa first?"

"Between twelve and twenty hours," Abby advised, "depending on how much charge we take on during our second layover."

"Well, the Corinari will certainly be worried," Nathan concluded.

"That's an understatement," Jessica mumbled.

"Helm, alter course for Taroa. Abby, as soon as you're ready, jump us to our first recharge layover. Just be sure Tug is aboard before we leave."

"Yes, sir," Abby answered.

"Changing course for Taroa," Josh announced.

* * *

Marcus came strolling up to Tug's fighter in the Aurora's main hangar bay, a dozen or more Corinari gathered behind him. "Hail the conquering hero!" he bellowed at Tug.

Tug climbed down the boarding ladder that had been rolled into place by two of the Corinari technicians assigned to the flight deck. He was grinning from ear to ear, which was a look that Marcus had never seen on the grim old man until now. As he set foot on the deck, he was greeted by several Corinari technicians offering congratulations.

"I am not the hero on this day," Tug exclaimed as he grabbed Marcus, hugged him, and then kissed him on the cheek. "It is you and your Corinari friends."

"Huh?" Marcus said as he wiped his cheek.

"Those firing patterns, they worked!"

"Oh, that," he replied, still wiping his cheek in disgust. "Jesus, I've been kissed by a terrorist. Does that mean I've been marked for death or something?" he asked, half-joking.

Tug finished accepting the congratulatory handshakes of the Corinari and then put his arm around Marcus's shoulder, leading him toward the exit. "If they served drinks on this ship I would surely buy you one, my friend."

Marcus shrugged off Tug's arm, not feeling too

comfortable being touched. "I'll take you up on that as soon as we get back to Corinair."

* * *

"Captain?" Tug called from the ready room hatch.

"Tug, come in," Nathan offered, happy to see him. "Nice shoot'n," he offered as he rose and shook Tug's hand.

"Thank you, Captain," Tug accepted, "but it was the new firing pattern provided by the Corinari technicians that did the job. All I did was fly the ship."

"Directly in the path of a drone rushing toward you at ninety percent the speed of light," Nathan added.

"Technically, as I was already doing eighty-nine percent light, it was only closing on me at one percent light."

"Oh, is that all?" Nathan joked. "So what, it was only doing about three million meters per second? So no big deal, huh?" Nathan sat back down in his seat. "So, I heard the Corinari threw you a little celebration. Must feel kind of strange."

"Indeed," Tug agreed as he took a seat across the desk from Nathan. "As you may have noticed, relations between the Karuzari and the people of Corinair have been somewhat strained as of late."

"Yes, I had noticed. But this should help, I suspect."

"Quite possibly, yes," Tug agreed. "However, I am not entirely sure that celebration is in order."

"How so?" Nathan asked, leaning forward again.

"The drone was not completely destroyed, Captain. There were many pieces, some the size

136

of a man's head, that although damaged, are still large enough to detect once they reach the Takaran system."

"You really think that's a problem?"

Tug leaned back in his chair, taking a deep breath before continuing. "If discovered, yes, possibly. It is possible to determine that the debris is from a destroyed comm-drone. It is also possible to determine the point of origin of that drone based on the flight path of the debris."

"That seems a bit unlikely, don't you think? I mean, that blast had to scatter the debris pretty widely. It would be difficult to figure out where it came from unless you had multiple pieces of debris on different trajectories."

"This is true. However, you should not discount the cleverness of the Ta'Akar, Captain. They are not stupid—arrogant, yes, but not stupid."

"Okay," Nathan said, becoming a little more concerned over the possibility. "Assuming that they did discover the debris, which would take at least six months..."

"Assuming a patrol ship does not discover the debris sooner," Tug interrupted.

"Assuming they don't," Nathan agreed, "after time spent figuring out what it was and where it came from, and then dispatching a response, we're still talking several months at the very least," Nathan insisted.

"I am sure you are correct, Captain. I only wish to point out that we still cannot afford to take our time. We must act decisively, and with great haste. Every moment we let slip by increases our chance of failure."

"But we need time to repair the ship, to rearm, to

prepare the Corinairans..."

"Yes, this is all true. But in the meantime, we need to devise a plan. We need to become the aggressor in this war. We cannot afford to let the Ta'Akar come to us. We must take the fight to them, at a time and place of our choosing, while they still have no idea where our base of operations is located. For once they discover our location, they will strike with everything they have. That is their favorite strategy, and it has served them well for many decades."

Nathan contemplated Tug's words for a moment. They had been reacting to everything thrown at them for so long, he had never stopped to seriously consider how to become the aggressor. However, his friend was correct; they had to do just that. "Any suggestions?"

"I have some thoughts on the subject, yes," Tug said with a smile. "But for now, I have an appointment with my bed. Perhaps we can talk later?"

"Of course." Nathan answered as Tug rose and headed toward the exit. "Tug?" he called after him. Tug stopped at the exit and turned back to face him. "It was still nice shoot'n."

Tug nodded and smiled, fatigue evident in his face now that the adrenaline of the events had finally subsided. "Goodnight, Captain," he said as he turned and stepped through the hatchway.

CHAPTER FOUR

"Jump complete," Abby announced.

"Threat board?" Nathan asked Jessica.

"All clear, sir," Jessica replied. "All normal traffic. No unidentified ships in the system. Everything looks pretty much as we left it."

"Great. How far are we from the asteroid base?" Nathan wondered.

"I took the liberty of jumping us relatively close by," Abby informed him.

"She did at that, Captain," Loki answered. "Karuzara is only an hour away at our current velocity."

"Karuzara?" Nathan asked.

"That's what Tug was calling it?" Loki defended.

"It was my idea," Josh bragged from the helm.

"Actually," Tug interrupted as he entered the bridge, "the official name is 'Do-Karuzara', which means 'home of the freedom fighters'."

"Technically, it means 'house of the warrior'," Naralena corrected, "at least in proper Palee, that is. I'm assuming that is where you got the term 'Karuzari'."

"Yes, you are correct," Tug confessed. "But I believe my translation is more fitting."

"Very well. Mister Hayes, take us to Do-Karuzara," Nathan ordered. "Will they be ready to receive us?" Nathan asked Tug.

"I believe so, Captain. I spoke with Jalea just before we departed, and she was confident that they were ready to begin repairs as soon as we returned. Since we have been gone considerably longer than expected, I expect they are ready and waiting for us."

"Very well. Naralena, please let Karuzara know our ETA. Also, contact the Corinari and transmit our mission report. I'm sure they're dying to know how things went."

* * *

"Look at that," Nathan said, his hand raised pointing at the view screen. "On either side. Are those doors?" he asked.

"I think you're right," Jessica agreed.

"Were those there last time?" Nathan asked.

"Hell no," Jessica insisted. "I was standing on the back ramp of the shuttle looking out as we flew in. I'm pretty sure I would've noticed a pair of massive doors."

"Many of the asteroids had pressurized interiors, as did this one. This is one of the reasons we originally chose this asteroid, as it would greatly facilitate repairing the exterior of our spacecraft. But the doors themselves, along with many other components, were taken by the original occupants. It took some time to obtain all the panels to make the doors themselves, but we never had the manpower to install them."

"Apparently Jalea has," Nathan commented.

"Yes," Tug observed, "she can be quite resourceful."

They watched as the ship passed the inner

threshold of the entrance tunnel, passing into the main central chamber. The interior of the asteroid was big enough to hold at least two ships the size of the Aurora if parked carefully.

"Captain, we're receiving docking instructions from Karuzara Port Control," Loki announced. "They want us to take up station on the starboard side of the main docking platform, as close in as we can put her."

"Very well, Mister Sheehan," Nathan answered. "You got this?" Nathan asked Josh.

"I got it, Captain. No worries."

Josh slowly maneuvered the Aurora into the main chamber, dropping her down toward the main docking platform that ran across the bottom half of the main chamber. Stopping all forward momentum, he continued drifting downward until he lined her up with the retractable mooring arms that the Karuzari technicians had recently installed.

Nathan was immediately reminded of the hydraulic mooring arms back at the Orbital Assembly Platform above the Earth, where the Aurora had been constructed. Her sister ship, the Celestia, was also being assembled there. She had been at least six months behind the Aurora in her build cycle. Nathan wondered if they had tried to pick up the pace of her build since the Aurora had disappeared. For the first time, he found himself wondering how his parents were doing. He wondered if they knew what had happened. His father undoubtedly knew something. At the very least, he knew that his son's ship was missing and presumed lost. But did his mother know? It wouldn't be unlike his father to hide such knowledge from her until he knew for sure what had happened. That had always been his style, making decisions for others as if they couldn't make decisions for themselves.

"We're in position," Josh announced.

"Mooring arms are extending," Loki added.

A moment later, there was a muffled thud and a mild vibration as the mooring clamps attached themselves to the Aurora's hard-points on the outside of her hull.

"We have capture," Loki announced.

"Kill all maneuvering systems, power down all flight controls, and signal engineering to bring the reactors down to minimal levels until further notice," Nathan instructed.

"Yes, sir," Josh answered.

"Comms, notify all hands; we are safely docked at Karuzara."

"Yes, Captain," Naralena answered.

"Lieutenant Commander, let's set up a security detail for the port boarding hatch. Everything and everyone gets checked both coming and going. No exceptions."

"Yes, sir."

Nathan looked at Tug. "Just playing it safe, for both our sakes," he assured him.

"A wise precaution, Captain," Tug responded.

"Finally, some time off," Josh exclaimed.

"Not so fast, Mister Hayes," Nathan warned. "You two get cleaned up and get some chow. Then report to the simulator for training."

"But Captain, we already know how to fly the ship," Josh objected.

"Not well enough to train new flight teams. Until Commander Taylor returns to active duty, you guys are going to be training officers. So you need to work your way through every simulation program in the database. And believe me, there are a lot of them, and they are not easy. In fact, some of them will make you cry. So I suggest you get to it."

"Yes, sir," Josh agreed sheepishly, heading for the exit with Loki hot on his heels.

Jessica watched them exit then turned back toward Nathan. "Some of them will make you cry? Really?" she said sarcastically.

"Too strong?" Nathan asked, remembering when Captain Roberts had said much the same.

* * *

Nathan, Tug, and Vladimir made their way through the tube that led from the Aurora's port boarding hatch to the Karuzara spaceport's docking platform. The platform was nothing more than a long, wide, single-story box that stuck out from the inside wall of the asteroid about fifty meters. Telescopic mooring arms with electrically actuated clamps reached out from the docking platform and were connected to the Aurora to hold her in place. The boarding tube was also telescopic and used inflatable seals to create an airtight inner chamber once the tube was fully extended and locked onto the side of the ship. Vladimir himself had helped modify the mating skirt on the boarding tube to seal up properly against the Aurora during their last stay inside what was then a secret rebel hideout deep within the Darvano system. Now, however, it was the sovereign territory of the newly formed Karuzari government of which Tug was the leader.

The four of them exited the boarding tube, followed by Sergeant Weatherly and the captain's security detail. As they walked out into the main docking hangar, they found Jalea and another man coming toward them. All around there were numerous technicians, some Karuzari and some Corinairans, all scurrying about doing their jobs as they prepared to begin their work on the Aurora.

"Jalea, a pleasure to see you again," Nathan greeted.

"Captain, Lieutenant Commander, sir," Jalea greeted. "May I present Mister Tonken," she said, gesturing to the man standing to her right. "He is the dock foreman. He is on loan to us from the Corinairans. He is quite experienced in spacecraft repairs and will be supervising the Corinairan technicians who will be working on the exterior of your ship. I thought Lieutenant Commander Kamenetskiy would like to meet him."

"Yes, of course," Vladimir said. "It is an honor, sir."

"The honor is all mine," Mister Tonken insisted. "Please, allow me to show you our facilities," he offered.

"Captain?"

"Enjoy yourself, Lieutenant Commander," Nathan insisted. He turned and looked at Jessica. She instantly gestured for two men from their security detail to follow Vladimir and Mister Tonken, after which Sergeant Weatherly radioed for two more troops to join their team from inside the Aurora in order to bring them back up to strength.

Jalea cast a suspicious look toward Jessica, which the Lieutenant Commander returned with a wry smile.

Nathan noticed the tension. "On my orders, all senior staff are to be escorted by armed security personnel when away from the ship," Nathan explained.

"A wise precaution," Jalea noted. "Did you also order everyone to wear side arms?" she added, taking note of the weapons worn on the hips of all of the Aurora's officers.

"My idea," Jessica stated.

"Yeah," Nathan agreed, "and there was far less resistance to that one."

Jalea turned and started slowly toward the far end of the docking platform, headed for the doors that led into the main facility attached to the walls of the asteroid itself. "I have received your mission report, Captain. It was most impressive."

"Tug did all the work," Nathan insisted. "We just kept putting him in front of the drone so he could do it."

"Nevertheless, heading deep into Takaran space carried its own risks."

"I thought there were only a dozen or so Karuzari on Corinair," Jessica said. "There's got to be at least fifty people on this dock alone."

"Yes. Most of them are on loan from Corinair. However I am happy to report that our own numbers have doubled in the last day and a half. Since word of the new Karuzari government was released, more members have come out of hiding. Some have been in hiding for years, from what I understand."

"Have these people been properly vetted?" Jessica asked.

"Of course," Jalea defended. "As much so as any of the Corinairans that are working here."

"Then I guess the Corinairans are making good on their promise of support," Nathan observed.

"Yes, in fact we have already received enough materials, equipment, and manpower to repair the structural damage and the hole in the bow of your ship, Captain."

"I'm sure that will make Vladimir quite happy," Nathan observed.

"And what of the Yamaro?" Tug inquired.

"The Corinairans have agreed to move the Yamaro into a nearby hollowed-out asteroid. It does not have the existing facilities inside as this one did, but it is big enough to hold the Yamaro. They have proposed that the Yamaro herself remain mostly intact to act as the inner shell, rather than tear her completely apart."

"Makes sense," Nathan agreed. "She still has working power plants, life support, crew accommodations, and a functioning flight deck."

"It would be easier to use the Yamaro's fabricators in their current environment, as it could take weeks to remove them and set them up elsewhere."

"Another advantage to their plan is that the inside of the asteroid still has a considerable amount of raw materials. Therefore, the additional structures and components needed to complete the conversion can be manufactured in situ, thus accelerating the process."

"Being in close proximity to Karuzara will make it easier to apply weapons and technology stripped from the Yamaro to the Aurora and other Corinairan spacecraft," Tug added.

"It all sounds like a reasonable plan," Nathan agreed. "Do they have a way to tow the Yamaro to this asteroid?"

"They are moving two cargo haulers in from one of the outer worlds now," Jalea advised. "They should be ready to start the towing process in a day or two."

"Well, it sounds like you've got things under

control here," Nathan decided. "Where are we headed now?"

"I thought I would show you around the complex until it is time for our departure."

"Departure?" Nathan asked. "Departure to where?"

"Back to Corinair, Captain," Jalea told him. "You and Tug have a treaty to sign."

* * *

The lobby of the largest building left standing had been decorated as lavishly as possible considering the stress the rebuilding of Aitkenna had placed on the city's available resources. There had been some controversy over the ceremony itself, as some felt the pomp and circumstance was inappropriate considering the many thousands of citizens still living in squalor in the hastily assembled survivor camps. In the end, it was decided that the ceremony would serve to inspire hope in the hearts and minds of the displaced citizens of not only Aitkenna, but the entire planet of Corinair, as well as the other minor worlds in the Darvano system.

With the help of Chief Montrose and a few Corinairan tailors, Nathan and Cameron had managed to put together something that resembled dress uniforms. Although their attire for the occasion would not have met fleet standards, it was sufficiently impressive for the evening's events.

Tug and Jalea had also put together uniforms of a sort befitting the minimalistic ways of the Karuzari. Since they were now officially a nation, their entire adult population of fifty-seven men and women also comprised their military. The Corinairans had

147

provided them with standard black uniform pants and shirts, to which the Karuzari had added stark white tunics to be worn as a simple dress uniform. As leaders of the new Karuzari nation, Tug and Jalea had added simple red baldrics hanging from their left shoulders down to the opposite hip where they fastened to their gun belts.

The Corinari officers in attendance were, of course, far more impressive in their understated black dress uniforms. Rather than the subdued gray trim and piping used on their basic duty wear, their dress wear used dazzling gold trim and piping, as well as bright red sashes around their waists that held ceremonial swords at their hips. By all accounts the appearance of the Corinari greatly belittled that of the Karuzari and of the two representatives of Earth, but the ceremony was more for the benefit of the previously oppressed people of Corinair than it was for their two new allies.

Despite his objections, Sergeant Weatherly had also been given a dress uniform similar to those worn by Nathan and Cameron. As the other four members of the captain's security detail were Corinari troops on loan to the Aurora, they wore the same dress uniforms as their Corinari brethren, the only difference being the fleet comm-sets hanging on their left ears as well as the heavier armaments they carried.

As they entered the decorated lobby, Nathan saw that Jessica would have been pleased by the security measures in place. They had undergone full retinal and ID checks upon entering, and there were armed Corinari guards positioned at every exit. In addition, he had noticed Corinari snipers on the mezzanine above and pairs of guards patrolling the crowd itself.

Getting past the main security checkpoint carrying weapons had been the difficult part, and in the end everyone except for their security detail had been forced to give up their side arms. Surprisingly, Nathan found himself feeling quite vulnerable without his sidearm, despite the fact that a few weeks ago he would've argued against carrying it at all. He shuddered at the thought of Jessica being ordered to give up her sidearm. It undoubtedly would have been an ugly scene.

The cavernous lobby appeared to be quite crowded, despite the fact that only a few hundred people had been allowed to attend. In addition, there were digi-cams set up at several key locations in order to broadcast the event to not only those watching through the system-wide communications network, but also for the thousands more gathered in the streets outside who were watching the ceremony via massive viewing screens erected on the sides of buildings. Those thousands outside, and the millions viewing online, all hoped to be part of a moment in history. It was an auspicious moment for the people of the Darvano system. Nathan only hoped it would eventually be considered as such by the people of Earth, as well.

Luckily, there were to be no speeches. The ceremony itself was kept relatively simple, despite all the tedium in its preparation. Each representative from the major nations of Corinair, as well as the lesser worlds within the Darvano system, stepped up to sign the document. As leader of the smallest and newest nation in the Darvano system, Tug was the last to sign. The Prime Minister was next, and finally Nathan himself signed the document, thus ending the ceremony. The announcement that the Earth-Darvano Alliance was now official raised applause from the crowds both inside and out.

It had taken more than two hours for all the dignitaries to arrive in addition to the hours of preparation that must have gone on prior. All for a ceremony that lasted less than thirty minutes. Nathan understood the purpose of the ceremony itself, as well as the positive effect the telecast might have on the people of the Darvano system. This had to be their most desperate time since the Ta'Akar first invaded their system over thirty years ago. Still, he found it all distasteful in the same way he had been irritated by all the 'fluff' around his father's many political campaigns. Only this time it was worse as he was no longer a spectator on the sidelines, he was center stage.

Eventually, it ended and the broadcast digi-cams shut down. The crowds outside began to disperse and the millions of people who had watched the ceremony through the system-wide communications network went back to the demands of their daily lives. Unfortunately for Nathan, the reception would last longer than the signing ceremony itself.

* * *

After an endless stream of handshakes and brief exchanges of translated pleasantries, Nathan finally found himself able to relax somewhat. After a few moments of searching, he spotted Cameron sitting at a side table with Chief Montrose. The chief had spent a lot of time with Commander Taylor over the last two weeks as they had interviewed thousands of Corinairan volunteers applying to serve on the

Aurora. As Nathan's presence had been required on the greeting line, the chief had taken it upon himself to attend to the commander's needs out of concern that she might over exert herself. Although she was making considerable progress in her recovery, her former drive and energy had still not returned.

"Chief," Nathan said as he took a seat at the table, "how is the family?"

"Fine, sir," Chief Montrose answered. "Deliza is very good. She is helping in the house and helping children with lessons."

"Lessons?" Nathan wondered.

"The neighborhood school was destroyed," Cameron explained. "A few of the parents started up their own little school in one of the larger homes. Deliza helps to teach the little ones."

"I had forgotten that Tug's daughters were staying with you and your family," Nathan told the chief.

"Not for much longer," the chief told him. "Soon she will join her father on Karuzara."

"Really?" Nathan wondered, somewhat surprised by the news.

"She's too smart to keep tucked away in some makeshift school," Cameron insisted. "She thinks she will be more useful on Karuzara helping with programming."

"She just might at that," Nathan agreed. "But what about his youngest daughter?"

"Nalaya? She will stay. She gets along very well with our girls," the chief explained. "Inside of rock in space is not place for little girl."

"You may be right, Chief," Nathan admitted. "You know, your Angla is getting better."

"Commander Taylor is most helpful with this," Chief Montrose explained. "She is always to be correcting me when I make mistakes."

"I'm sure she is," Nathan mused.

"Speaking of always to be corrected," the chief said, trying to make a joke as he looked at his watch, "it is time that I got home to my wife." The chief rose from his seat. "If you will excuse me, sirs?"

"Thank you, Chief," Cameron said. "I'll see you tomorrow."

Nathan waited for the chief to leave before speaking. "He's a good man."

"Yes, he is," Cameron agreed. "And he really believes in what we're doing."

"What about you?" Nathan asked. "Do you believe in what we're doing?"

"It's not as cut-and-dried as you think it is, Nathan. I still think we should have headed back for Earth the moment we got the jump drive back online back in the Korak system. We could have been halfway home by now."

"More like a quarter," Nathan joked. Cameron obviously wasn't laughing. "Okay, one-third maybe, but not half."

"You understand my point, Nathan. We didn't need to get involved in all of this."

"I was only trying to keep us alive," Nathan defended, "so that we *could* get home."

"I'll go along with that," Cameron agreed, "right up until you decided to take on the Yamaro."

"I couldn't let them destroy an entire world, Cam..."

"You don't know that they would have," she interrupted. "Besides, you were ignoring Captain Roberts' last orders and seriously jeopardizing our primary mission..."

"I was only doing what I thought was the right

thing."

"And you almost got me..." Cameron paused, correcting herself, "...got *us* killed."

Nathan could sense that the conversation was escalating and decided to back down for the moment. The reception for the signing of the Alliance treaty was not the place for this particular line of discussion. As the duly appointed captain of the Aurora, Nathan was not required to defend his actions to his executive officer, only to his superiors. He did, however, feel compelled to explain his reasons to his friend.

"However," Cameron continued, "in regards to this treaty, I've decided that I support your decision."

"Really?" Nathan wondered, not quite believing what he was hearing.

Cameron looked at him for a moment. "Are you really that surprised?"

"Actually, yes," he admitted. "May I ask why?"

"Well first, because you *do* have the authority according to regulations. Therefore, I don't have sufficient grounds to relieve you of command."

"Thanks, I feel so much better..."

"And second," she interrupted, "because I believe that allying with the Corinari and the Karuzari, and defeating the Ta'Akar, offers us the best chance of getting back to Earth and successfully defending her against the Jung."

Nathan leaned back in his chair, stunned at her sudden change of heart. "Wait, is this a trick? Is this one of those reverse-psychology things?"

"Just promise me you'll be smart about this," she said, looking deadly serious.

"What do you mean, Cam?"

"Promise me that we'll get this over with quickly.

We can't afford to be sucked into a long, drawn-out campaign here. The Earth needs us. Our people need us back there defending *them*, not out here playing cat and mouse with some other evil empire. Yes, it would be great if we picked up some advanced tech along the way, but they need our jump drive more than any cool tech the Ta'Akar might have."

"I understand all of that, Cam. Really I do," Nathan assured her.

"Promise me, no long campaigns," she declared, staring him in the eyes. "We get in, get it done, and get out."

"I promise," Nathan told her. "We jump in, slap a few people around, and jump out again." Nathan flashed his get-out-of-trouble smile again. Try as she might to resist, his stupid grin made her smile as well.

"Who are you planning to slap?" Tug asked as he and Jalea joined them.

"Caius," Nathan joked.

"That would be worth seeing," Tug mused as he took a seat. He looked over at Cameron, who appeared a bit pale. "Are you feeling all right, Commander?"

"Just a little tired, I guess," she admitted. "It has been a long day."

"Would you like me to send for the chief to see you back?"

"No, he's already on his way home. I'll have Sergeant Weatherly arrange an escort."

"Nonsense," Tug insisted, rising from his seat. "I'll see you back myself."

"What about Jalea?" Cameron asked.

"I'm quite capable of finding my own way back," Jalea calmly stated.

"I will meet you at the shuttle later," Tug told

Jalea as he offered his arm to Cameron, helping her up from her seat.

"Sergeant," Nathan called as he rose. Sergeant Weatherly nodded to his captain from his post nearby, signaling to one of his Corinari subordinates to arrange transportation for Tug and Commander Taylor.

"Get some rest, Cam," Nathan urged.

"Commander," Jalea bid in parting as Tug led Cameron away, two of the captain's security detail in tow.

"Captain Scott," Mister Briden called out as he approached, along with the Prime Minister of Corinair, "the Prime Minister was most impressed with your mission report."

"Thank the Prime Minister, Mister Briden," Nathan accepted graciously, "but it is not I that he should be impressed with, but rather with Mister Tugwell of the Karuzari. Were it not for his bravery and piloting skills, the mission might have had an entirely different outcome."

"Perhaps," Mister Briden agreed. "However, as the burden of responsibility rests upon the leader's shoulders, so do the fortunes of success."

"Yes, but I believe in giving credit where credit is due," Nathan countered.

"Yes, of course, Captain. I did not mean to belittle Mister Tugwell's contribution. It was indeed most spectacular. The Karuzari are nothing if not brave. However, the people came tonight to witness Na-Tan signing the treaty, not the Karuzari."

"Some might feel otherwise," Jalea protested politely, "and their numbers might be more than you realize."

"Perhaps," Mister Briden proclaimed, wishing to

Ryk Brown

avoid any confrontation. "I was merely pointing out that there is great political advantage in associating with a legend."

"Are you speaking for yourself, or for the Prime Minister, Mister Briden?" Nathan asked.

"I assure you, Captain, I am speaking for the Prime Minister. As you pointed out in an earlier meeting, it is not my place to comment otherwise."

There was a sinister smile behind Mister Briden's politically correct expression that made the hairs on the back of Nathan's neck stand up.

"If you'll excuse us, Captain, Miss Torren, the Prime Minister has other guests to visit before the night is over."

"Of course," Nathan nodded to the Prime Minister, purposefully forgetting to bid Mister Briden a polite farewell.

Nathan waited long enough for the Prime Minister and Mister Briden to get out of earshot before speaking. "He doesn't like the Karuzari much, does he?" he said, stating the obvious.

"The feeling is mutual, I assure you," Jalea answered as she took two drinks from a nearby tray and handed one to Nathan. "So, Captain," she continued as she turned and started making her way across the crowded lobby floor, "how does it feel to be a legend?"

"I am no legend," Nathan protested. "You know that as much as anyone."

"But you do use the leverage provided by your notoriety to your advantage, do you not?"

"Not by design."

"I see. You find the idea so distasteful?"

"Yes, very much so," Nathan insisted.

"More distasteful than not accomplishing your

156

goals?" she challenged.

"My goals?" Nathan wondered.

"Of returning to Earth and defending your world against its own enemies," Jalea reminded.

Nathan finished his drink, using the distraction as a means to avoid answering Jalea's question. The drink was fruity and sweet, with a slightly bitter aftertaste. It reminded him of the strawberry flavored spirits his sister Miri always served at dinner parties. He wondered if it had the same effects as he followed Jalea through the crowd.

"As distasteful as I find the whole Na-Tan hype, I do recognize its usefulness to our cause," Nathan admitted. "To deny its value would be irresponsible on my part."

"Spoken like a true leader." Jalea smiled as she reached the exit, stopping to look around the room. The crowd had thinned out somewhat and the evening's events appeared to be winding down. Aitkenna as well as many other cities across Corinair were still in a state of chaos and disrepair, and most of the dignitaries in attendance had already departed to return to their endless responsibilities. "I believe we should be heading back to the spaceport, Captain. There is much to do back on Karuzara."

"Yes, of course," Nathan agreed, signaling the sergeant.

* * *

Tug had never spent much time with Cameron in the past, and he had never known her to be terribly talkative. However, she had said little during the ride back to the hospital thus far, which seemed odd even for her. He knew she was tired, as she was still expected to be in recovery and rehabilitation for several weeks, but there was more to it than just physical exhaustion, there was something bothering her.

"You are worried about him," Tug said, taking a shot in the dark.

"I'm worried about a lot of things," Cameron defended.

"As are we all," Tug agreed. "But you are mostly concerned with your captain."

"Well shouldn't I be? You saw him."

"To what do you refer?" Tug asked.

"His attitude... the whole 'gonna jump in and slap Caius around' bit."

"I do believe he was speaking in jest, Commander."

"Who jokes about slapping about the leader of an interstellar empire?" Cameron insisted.

"It is his way," Tug assured her. "He tends to diffuse stressful situations with humor or sarcasm."

"It was a reception," Cameron insisted. "How stressful could it be?"

"He has just promised to commit his ship and his crew to a battle that he may not survive. He also promised to commit his world to join forces with others in common defense. Even if he survives the events in this part of the galaxy, something worse may await him when you return to Earth." Tug laughed in exasperation. "Trust me, Commander; it is an extremely stressful time for Captain Scott."

Cameron turned to stare out the window again, watching the remains of the city pass by as they made their way down the main transportation corridor. "Captain Scott," she mumbled. "I don't know if I'll ever get used to that."

"Why is that?" Tug wondered aloud.

"If you had read his background files, you'd understand," she assured him.

"I am sure that was all in the past."

"It wasn't that far in the past."

"Tell me, Commander; do you believe that who we are is set at birth? Or do you believe that we are all the result of that which we experience along the way?"

"A little of both, I guess," she answered. "Well, maybe a little of the first and a lot of the second."

"Have the events of the last month changed you in any way?"

"Yes, of course," she admitted.

"Then is it not possible that they have changed your friend as well?"

"My friend?" Cameron questioned. "I'm not sure you could call us friends."

"I saw him toss all logic and reason aside to procure medical care for you," Tug told her. "And I watched him stay by your side every possible moment. Those are not the acts of mere coworkers."

Cameron was quiet for several minutes.

"What is it about him that worries you the most?" Tug asked, finally breaking the silence.

"I worry that he is so arrogant, so headstrong, that he will do something stupid that will get us all killed and leave the Earth to the mercy of the Jung."

"Do you think Nathan a bad person?"

"No, I just think he's irresponsible," she stated.

"The man I have come to know takes his responsibilities quite seriously," Tug argued, "perhaps even too much so." After another pause, Tug continued. "May I offer my perspective on the matter?"

"Do I have a choice?" Cameron retorted.

"Not really, no," Tug laughed. "Nathan's biggest problem is that he does not yet believe in himself, in his own ability to lead and to make the right decisions."

"Finally, we agree on something."

"Part of the reason for this," Tug said, "is that he does not yet feel that those he commands believe in him."

Cameron looked at Tug. "What you're really saying is that *I* don't believe in him."

"You are the only other person on the ship who could have taken on the role of captain, had it not fallen onto Nathan's shoulders, are you not?"

"Yes..."

"Then it is understandable that he might need your support, your *belief* that he can do the job, and that he is worthy of being followed."

The transport vehicle came to a stop outside the side entrance to the hospital in which Cameron had been recuperating for the last few weeks. Several Corinari guards and a few medical personnel came out to meet her, having been notified by comms of her arrival.

"Do me a favor, Tug," Cameron asked. "Keep an eye on him until I get back. Worthy or not, he still needs someone to keep him in line."

"I will do my best until your return," Tug assured her with a grin.

* * *

Nathan walked down the main corridor of the command deck on his way to the bridge. After changing back into a normal uniform, he felt much more himself. The ceremony for the signing of the

Alliance treaty had felt much like one of his father's political circus events back on Earth. He had grown to despise such events to such a degree that he had joined the fleet to get away from them. Yet here he was, more deeply embroiled in politics than ever before, committing his world to an interstellar alliance that might or might not save his world. It had not been what he had set out to do. All he had wanted was to get his ship and his crew back to Earth and turnover command of the Aurora to someone more qualified.

He wondered what would have happened had he followed Cameron's advice from the start and headed home immediately, slowly making their way back to Earth in a long series of jumps, ten light years at a time. Would he be halfway home by now? Who knew what dangers lay between the Pentaurus Cluster and the Sol system? It seemed entirely possible that they could have found themselves in an even worse position than they already were had they simply run home at their earliest opportunity.

Nathan knew that he had done the right thing by choosing to defend the Corinairans from the Ta'Akar. Whether or not it was for the right reasons was unimportant at this point. If he had allowed the bombardment to continue, the captain of the Yamaro might have destroyed the entire planet. Had he knowingly allowed the innocent people of Corinair to perish in such fashion, he would not have been worthy of his position.

Still, he couldn't help but review the events of the last few weeks in his mind, over and over again, wondering how a different decision at each step in their journey might have led to a different outcome.

One of the four surviving marines left on the

Aurora's crew stood guard at the main entrance to the bridge. As the most critical compartment on the ship, Jessica had insisted that the marines be solely responsible for its security. The Corinari could guard the rest of the ship. Nathan knew that while she did not actually expect any subterfuge from the Corinari, she also realized that they still knew too little about the politics and ways of their new allies to trust them completely. They had no choice but to accept their help, but there was no reason not to keep a watchful eye on them, at least until their loyalty had been proven beyond doubt.

The marine guard snapped to attention, raising his right hand in salute as the captain approached. "Sir."

Nathan returned the salute in a more casual fashion than it had been given. "Corporal," he greeted as he stepped through the hatchway. He stopped as he entered the bridge, surprised to find it both empty and dimly lit. He glanced at his watch and saw that it was only twenty-one hundred hours. "Where is everyone?" he asked the corporal at the entrance.

"In their racks, I expect, sir," the corporal surmised.

Nathan looked back at his watch, realizing it was still set to the local time for the city of Aitkenna back on Corinair. As preoccupied as he had been during their journey from Corinair to Karuzara, he had completely forgotten about the time difference. He expected they were going to have to come up with a way of dealing with such time issues in the future. Perhaps some sort of an 'Alliance Mean Time' would do the trick.

Nathan changed his watch back to shipboard

time and saw that it was four in the morning. "Ah, yes," he said to himself. That would explain the darkened, empty bridge. As shorthanded as they were, while safely docked within the Karuzara spaceport deep inside the asteroid, he had agreed to have only a duty officer and one guard on duty at night in order to allow their overworked crew some decent sleep for a change. They would be back to a normal routine soon enough.

"Where's the duty officer then?" Nathan asked the corporal, knowing that Jessica had been left in command during his absence. "No, wait; let me guess," he added, pointing toward his ready room at the back of the bridge. The corporal nodded.

Nathan entered his ready room and found Jessica right where he expected, sprawled out on the couch. She looked so peaceful that he hated to wake her, but he couldn't resist. He cupped his hands around his mouth and called out, "General quarters! General quarters! All hands, man your battle stations!"

Not taking the bait, Jessica opened one eye and peered at Nathan. "Nice try," she muttered.

"That's, 'Nice try, sir,'" he reminded as he took a seat behind his desk and turned on his display.

Jessica sat up. "Well at least you changed," she commented as she rubbed the sleep from her eyes. "That goofy dress-uniform you guys concocted made you look like a doorman at one of those overpriced European hotels."

"Please, don't remind me."

"I see you've got your sidearm back on," she commented, noticing his gun belt. "Good boy."

"They wouldn't let me wear it at the ceremony," Nathan explained. "I felt really uncomfortable without it."

"Yeah, the psych boys back home called it 'Persistent Readiness Syndrome'," she explained. "We're all going to have it for some time." Jessica laughed. "I can't imagine how the sergeant reacted when they tried to take *his* weapon away."

"He just looked at them and they backed down," Nathan said, chuckling at the memory.

"I'll bet," she said as she stretched. "So how was the party?"

"Pointless and boring," Nathan declared as he scrolled through reports.

"Worse than the last one?"

Nathan paused for a moment, trying to remember the last party he had attended. Then he remembered the party at his parents' estate the night before he had left Earth for his first assignment. He remembered getting fairly smashed, and he remembered that his father had announced his candidacy for the office of the North American Presidency. Mostly, however, he remembered his brief sexual encounter with a hot little brunette he had only just met. He had no way of knowing at the time that she was in the fleet, let alone that she would end up as his chief of security.

"No, this party was worse," he assured her, adding, "no hot, easy chicks in tight skimpy dresses at this one." Nathan flashed his usual charming smile, the same one that always got him out of trouble with his mother as a teenager.

Jessica smiled back as she stood and headed toward the exit, "Bite me, *sir*."

"Goodnight, Jess," Nathan said as she stepped through the hatch.

"Goodnight, Skipper," she answered from the empty bridge, knowing that he hated the term.

Nathan tapped away at his keyboard for several

minutes as he summarized the evening's events for his log. He noticed he had become more careful with his wording in recent weeks. He knew his logs would be carefully examined and picked apart by all manner of experts, both fleet and civilian. Perhaps, someday, even historians would peruse his account of the events in the Pentaurus cluster, passing judgment on his decisions based on the words he left behind.

CHAPTER FIVE

"We are up to eight work teams," Vladimir boasted as he placed his breakfast on the table across from Nathan and sat down to eat. Although still only at a fraction of its capacity, the mess hall seemed so much more alive now that there were at least one hundred Corinairan troops and technicians on board the Aurora.

"Half of them are working on repairs; the other half are concentrating on installing some of the original systems that were scheduled to be installed after our little 'test flight'."

"You mean all the crated stuff in the hangar bays?" Nathan asked.

"Da, and there is even more in the cargo holds," Vladimir added. "Most of it is not urgent, but if we are to have full crew soon, much of it will become important very soon."

"Possibly, but don't let it slow down repairs," Nathan reminded him.

"It will not," Vladimir assured him. "Many of the repairs must be done in certain order, so there is only so much we can do at once. That is why I have the other crews installing stuff; better than having them sit around doing nothing."

"What about the hull repairs?" Nathan asked. "Maybe they could help with that."

"Mister Tonken and the Corinairan technicians

are handling the repairs to the hull, and I get the impression that they do not wish to be disturbed any more than necessary," Vladimir explained between bites. "Once the hull repairs are completed and the inner hull has been pressure tested, we will open the forward compartments and begin repairs to the damaged interior sections."

"Did they give any indications as to how long it will take them?" Nathan asked.

"He would not commit to anything firm, but he indicated it could take several weeks. It depends on how much material they can get ready-made from the Corinairans, and how much they must process and fabricate themselves."

"They can do that?"

"Yes," Vladimir assured him, "they have the facilities already in place here. The Karuzari installed the heavy equipment long ago, when they first created this base. But the fabrication process is slow, as the ores must be mined and processed first."

"What about the Yamaro's fabricators?" Nathan wondered. "Can we use them to create hull plates?"

"Nyet, they are not designed to make such large components. They are limited to things no bigger than, say, this table."

"I thought they were supposed to be such wonderful devices."

"Oh, they are; they are most incredible. The speed and precision is amazing. They are far beyond anything we have on Earth."

"Then why aren't we using them?"

"As I said, they are not designed to make such large pieces," Vladimir reiterated. "Besides, hull plates are very simple in their construction, and

Mister Tonken seems confident that enough ready to use plating can be located." Vladimir quickly drank his tea and poured a second cup. "Anyway, the Yamaro's replicators are already busy."

"Doing what?" Nathan asked.

"Making more fabricators. What else?"

"When did that happen?"

"They started the moment they finished making our new emitters."

"Who made that decision?" Nathan wondered.

"Some scientist from Corinair," Vladimir told him. "He insisted they create at least two more before they did anything else. One to dedicate to making more fabricators, and another one for them to study."

"To study?"

"Yes, they plan to reverse engineer the fabricator and scale it up. They hope to use them to build ships."

"I don't think the Ta'Akar will give us that much time, Vlad."

"I don't think it matters," Vladimir laughed. "These Corinairans, they are like starving children. They have all this scientific knowledge they have been dying to utilize over the last thirty years. Now that they can, they want to build everything they can think of. It is actually quite entertaining to listen to them."

"Yeah, I'll bet," Nathan sighed.

"You sound disappointed."

"I was hoping we might use the fabricators to burn off a few million rounds for the rail guns."

"You do realize we are in port, yes?" Vladimir asked. "And *inside* an asteroid?"

"Yeah, I just hate being unarmed, even in port."

"Just ask the Corinairans to produce some slugs," Vladimir insisted.

"Slugs?"

"Da. Our rail guns have many different types of ammunition: explosive, radioactive tipped, fragmentation, even multilevel fragmentation; you know, the kind that breaks apart again and again," Vladimir elaborated. "But even simple metal slugs, when propelled to great velocities, carry great amounts of kinetic energy. They would be very destructive."

"They'd suck for point-defense," Nathan observed.

"This is true, but they would still be better than nothing at all," Vladimir insisted, "and they would be easy to mass produce. They are simple metal cylinders about the size of your fist, and solid, with no moving parts. Even a single factory should be able to fill all of our ammunition bunkers in a few weeks."

Nathan thought about the idea, and it did sound good. If Vladimir was right, they would have a few million rounds, enough to feed all their rail guns throughout a prolonged firefight. "I wouldn't mind that one bit," he admitted. "I'll put in a request to the Prime Minister."

"You do that," Vladimir insisted as he finished his food. "I must go."

"What about the briefing?" Nathan asked, checking his watch. "It starts in fifteen minutes."

"I have to meet with Mister Tonken. Besides, I already told you everything. Just call me if you have questions," he insisted as he rose and left the mess hall.

* * *

"Attention on deck," the guard at the hatch to the briefing room announced. Everyone in attendance stood as Nathan entered the room. "As you were," he insisted as he made his way to his seat at the head of the table. Despite the fact that the guard was only following standard procedures, Nathan still found it difficult to get used the formalities of command rank, especially at times like this. As he took his seat, it dawned on him that only half of the people in the briefing room, including himself, were members of the fleet. The others—Tug, Jalea, and Abby—stood out of courtesy, rather than by requirement.

"Doctor Chen," Nathan greeted, "nice to have you with us."

"Thank you, Captain," the doctor replied as she took her seat. "Hopefully my patient load will remain light enough in the future that I can always be present."

"Yes, hopefully," Nathan agreed. "Let's start with you; how are things in Medical?"

"The Corinairan medical staff has been extremely helpful, sir. Their understanding of the human body is far more advanced than ours," Doctor Chen explained. "At least five of my patients are ready to return to light duty because of the Corinairan treatment methods. They would've been out for at least another month had they been treated here using our technology."

"That's good news, Doctor," Nathan said. "We'll have them assigned to monitoring and consulting with the Corinairan work teams. What about the rest of your patients?"

"I only have a few still on medical leave recovering in their quarters. There are another ten more serious cases that are being cared for in the hospital in Aitkenna."

"Will they survive?"

"It's too soon to say," she admitted, "but I can assure you that, without the Corinairans, they would already have died."

"Thank you, Doctor," Nathan said. A wave of relief washed over him. At the very least, his decision to come to the aid of Corinair may have saved the lives of a dozen or more of his crew. That alone felt worth the risk.

"Captain," Jalea interjected, "the Corinairans have long been known for the quality of their medical care. The technological restrictions that the Ta'Akar have imposed on them over the decades has only enhanced their expertise."

"How so?" Nathan asked.

"I believe it forced them to find ways to be more effective with the technology at hand," Jalea said.

"There's one other thing," Doctor Chen added. "The Corinairans tend to look at the human body as a whole instead of a collection of related systems."

"Are you gaining any useful information from the Corinairan doctors?" Nathan wondered.

"Their biggest advantage over us is their diagnostic abilities. They have much more accurate testing and diagnostic methods, most of which are far less invasive as well. This not only speeds up the diagnostic process, it also makes it more accurate."

"Are they willing to share this technology with us?" Nathan wondered.

"So far, yes. They have promised to deliver various devices and training in the near future. But much of that may have to wait until the more immediate needs of the ship have been addressed."

"I'll see if I can keep it from being pushed too far down the list, Doctor," Nathan promised.

"Thank you, sir."

"Lieutenant Commander Kamenetskiy had to meet with the teams performing the work on the hull, so he could not be here. He reported to me this morning that the hull repairs could take several weeks."

"Captain," Jalea interrupted, "I spoke with Mister Tonken this morning, and he is confident that he can procure the necessary materials. Therefore the hull repairs should take approximately ten days."

"That's good news, Jalea," Nathan said. "Once the hull is repaired, damage repair teams will be concentrating on the forward compartments that have been inaccessible for the last few weeks. As you all know, with a full crew scheduled to come aboard in the coming weeks, the additional crew accommodations will be needed."

"If your forward compartments are not ready in time, we have plenty of room within Karuzara station," Tug offered.

"I'll keep that in mind. Meanwhile, our repair teams will be concentrating on repairing recent battle damage, as well as installing additional systems that were scheduled for installation upon our return to the Orbital Assembly Platform."

"Captain, might I suggest that we make installation of the remaining rail guns a priority?" Jessica suggested. "We are still unable to create a complete defense perimeter, even with all currently installed rail guns in full working order."

"I'll pass your concerns on to the Cheng," Nathan assured her. "My biggest concerns right now are the doors covering the backup heat exchangers. They took damage and will not open at the moment. If the primary exchangers failed, we'd be pretty screwed," he insisted. "How is security coming along?" Nathan asked, turning his attention to Jessica.

"While we're in port, we're maintaining two secure points of access to the ship: the port boarding airlock for foot traffic, and the number two hangar bay airlock for shuttles. As an extra precaution, we keep the port boarding airlock hatches closed, and only allow access in groups of four. I've got four armed Corinari in the boarding foyer and a quick response team of eight stationed halfway between the foyer and the hangar bay. I've also got two teams stationed in the hangar bay, and an inspection team in the number two airlock inspecting shuttles before they're allowed into the main hangar bay."

"Are four men enough?" Nathan asked, remembering that the last boarding attempt had brought twelve heavily armed men aboard in a medevac shuttle.

"If there's a firefight in the transfer airlock, the bridge has standing orders to open the outer doors and space everyone inside if it goes bad," Jessica explained.

"Seems a bit harsh," Nathan commented. "How do the Corinari feel about that?"

"It was their idea, Captain," Jessica insisted. "Those guys are just as hard-core as our marines."

"I guess so," Nathan agreed. "Anything else?"

"Just that everyone aboard is required to wear either bio-linked comm-sets, or guest badges that have tracking chips in them. Oh, and we've also got several pairs of guards roaming the ship at all times."

"Is there a chance we're going a bit overboard

here?" Nathan wondered.

"Well, sir, considering all that's happened, and that this ship is currently the best hope that the Corinairans have to survive, I'd say no. If anything, it's not enough. Don't forget, their world is still in a barely controlled state of chaos. There are still plenty of loyalist whack-jobs down there dreaming up ways to steal the ship and deliver it to Caius the Great. They can dream all they want, but they're not getting aboard this ship. Not again."

"Apparently not," Nathan agreed. "Doctor Sorenson," Nathan continued, turning to Abby, "how are things going with the Corinairan scientists?"

"All data regarding the jump drive has been translated into Angla, which as you know is very similar to English. Most of their scientists are old enough to have learned Angla in their youth. Eventually, they will translate the database from Angla to Corinairan."

"So they are understanding your research?"

"Indeed, sir," Abby exclaimed. "I expect that in a few months they will understand it better than we do. In fact, they are already talking about creating miniaturized versions and installing them into small shuttles. They plan on using them as some sort of early warning system."

"Is that possible?" Nathan asked.

"We would not be able to do it ourselves, at least not with our current technology. But with the help of the Yamaro's fabricators, it just might be possible. The biggest obstacle is that they would have to run the conduits for the emitters. According to the Corinairan engineers, retrofitting an existing ship in such fashion would be a time-consuming task."

"What if the ship already had the emitter network

and power sources installed?" Tug asked.

"You know of such a ship?" Abby inquired.

"My interceptor is capable of FTL travel, as well as two types of shielding. Its emitter network is quite similar to the Aurora's in design. And the Corinairans just installed two new fusion reactors."

"Where would we put the field generators?" Abby asked.

"We could remove the existing field generators for both the FTL fields and shields. That should provide ample space."

"It might work," Abby admitted as she contemplated the idea. "The range would be reduced, however, as there would be limited room to install energy storage banks."

"How much would the range be reduced?" Nathan asked. He, too, was intrigued by the idea.

"It depends on the efficiency of the Corinairan energy storage systems and the amount of space available for them on Tug's ship," she explained, "but if I had to guess, I would say possibly one light year."

"Captain," Jessica chimed in, "a small jump ship would be a huge asset."

"How so?" Nathan asked.

"Well, for starters the Corinari are correct; a network of small jump-enabled ships would make a great early warning system. You could place them a light month out and have them watch for inbound FTL traffic. If they detected something headed toward Corinair, they could jump back and alert command. That would give everyone at least a week to prepare."

"It would also be a great reconnaissance platform," Tug added.

"That's the other thing I was thinking," Jessica agreed.

"Or a weapons delivery platform," Tug added, getting a little excited at all the possibilities.

"I think you two are forgetting about the political ramifications," Nathan reminded them. They both looked at him, perplexed. "Giving the first jump drive to the Karuzari," he pointed out.

"I had not considered that," Tug admitted.

"You really think they'd make a stink?" Jessica asked.

"They might," Nathan stated.

"Captain," Abby interrupted, "it would take the Corinairans considerably longer to test their miniaturized version on one of their shuttles. And if the first one failed, it would likely destroy both the test shuttle and the prototype. They would have to start again from scratch. Tug's interceptor would offer such a significant shortcut that they would be fools to let politics stand in their way."

"Fools and politics," Nathan laughed, "two words that go hand in hand."

"We would gladly share ownership of the jump interceptor if that is what it takes, Captain," Tug offered.

"Thanks, Tug," Nathan said. "I agree the idea is worth pursuing, but let's not hand over your interceptor unless we have to." Tug nodded his agreement as Nathan turned to Abby. "Doctor Sorenson, speak with the Corinairan scientists and offer them the use of Tug's interceptor as a test craft. I wouldn't mind having another jump ship available to us," Nathan added, "even if it is short range."

"Yes, sir. I'll contact them immediately," Abby promised.

"Captain, I'll be heading to Corinair in about an hour," Jessica informed him. "Commander Taylor has asked me to participate in the final interviews for the short list of volunteers. Apparently she needs my 'suspicious eye' to check them over before she makes her final selection. I'll be bringing the most qualified and experienced volunteers back with me. Commander Taylor wants to get them trained as soon as possible so that they can help train the rest of the crew as they come in."

"Very well," Nathan agreed. "Who will be in charge of the ship's security in your absence?" he asked.

"Sergeant Weatherly, sir."

"You're leaving a marine in charge of security on a fleet ship?" Nathan smiled at the thought.

"No, I'm leaving a *kickass* marine in charge of security on a fleet ship," Jessica responded, smiling right back at him.

Nathan nodded his agreement. Sergeant Weatherly had proven himself as much if not more so than most, and he trusted the quiet, soft-spoken man without hesitation. It was a logical choice. "Agreed. Still, it will be another fleet first for the Aurora. Dismissed, everyone."

* * *

"You know, if they do manage to put a jump drive into Tug's interceptor, it would make a great recon platform," Jessica said to Nathan as they descended the ramp from the command deck down to the main deck.

"Yes, it would," Nathan agreed, "but I was thinking more offensively. It would be much easier for him to jump inside a target's shields and deliver a few nukes before jumping out."

"That it would," Jessica agreed, "and with his aerodynamics, he could jump into the atmosphere of a planet bypassing all their orbital defenses, launch his ordnance, and jump away, all before they even brought their surface defenses online."

The many different ways that Nathan could think of to utilize a fighter equipped with a jump drive seemed endless. "You know, ever since we got back from chasing down that drone, I've been thinking about all the different ways the jump drive can be used," Nathan explained as they entered the main hangar deck. "And I'm not just talking about military applications, either. Exploration, resource utilization and distribution, commerce, communications; it boggles the mind just thinking about it. Abby's father was right when he said it would change everything."

"All I care about is that it helps us knock Caius the Great off his throne and then gets us the hell out of the cluster and back to Earth," Jessica stated in no uncertain terms. "After that, it can *change everything* as much as it wants."

"*Attention all hands. Corinari Aerospace Command, arriving,*" came blaring over the loudspeakers. Four men in standard black and gray Corinari uniforms approached from a shuttle that had only just arrived. Two of them appeared to be older and of higher rank than the other two, both of which were at least ten years younger and obviously more fit. As they approached, Nathan found it amusing that even when separated by a thousand light years of space *and* a thousand years of time, pilots still wore wings on their uniforms.

"Captain," the Corinari guard escorting the

guests greeted as he snapped a salute, "may I present Generals Valachin and Senegora of the Corinari Aerospace Command."

Nathan returned the guard's salute and extended his hand to the visiting generals. "An honor, gentlemen. Welcome aboard the Aurora."

"Thank you, Captain," General Valachin greeted in a heavy Corinairan accent.

It was not surprising to Nathan that the general's Angla was perfect, as he had come to expect as much from the elders of Corinair. In fact, after finding so many that did speak Angla on Corinair, he found it surprising that the Prime Minister did not. "This is my chief of security, Lieutenant Commander Nash."

"Gentlemen," Jessica greeted as she politely shook their hands.

"Allow me to introduce Major Prechitt and Lieutenant Saren."

"Gentlemen," Nathan greeted, "welcome aboard."

"Thank you, Captain," Major Prechitt answered.

"I've heard your name before," Nathan said, trying to remember exactly where.

"Major Prechitt was one of the pilots that chased down the missiles that nearly destroyed your ship," General Senegora stated in slightly less perfect Angla.

"Then it is definitely good to have you aboard," Nathan stated. "As a pilot myself, I would love to hear the details of that engagement."

"I am sure there will be plenty of time for that, Captain," General Valachin announced. "Major Prechitt has been selected to command the fighter wing being assigned to the Aurora," the general explained. "Lieutenant Saren will be his second."

"Excellent," Nathan stated. "Then I suppose

179

you'd like to get started with the tour."

"Sir, if you'll excuse me," Jessica pleaded, "I have a shuttle to catch."

"Of course, Lieutenant Commander," Nathan granted.

"Sirs," Jessica stated as she stepped back and away, then turned and headed for the waiting shuttle.

After a moment, General Senegora spoke up. "A very confident young woman."

"Sir?" Nathan wondered.

"We have few women serving in our military," the general commented.

"Really?" Nathan stated. "I find that surprising."

"Oh, we have no rules against it, mind you," the general defended. "I suspect it is because the Ta'Akar do not allow women to serve in their military and have never inducted any from our population."

"We were much the same," Nathan admitted, "up until about a century ago. After the plague, women were revered as the bearers of children and therefore the only hope of repopulating our world. Over the centuries, as the population grew, those ways gradually faded."

"Some believe our women are too smart to waste their time rolling around in the muck playing soldier," General Valachin added.

"I think you'll find Lieutenant Commander Nash to be more qualified for her duties than most men," Nathan boasted as he turned to lead them to the starboard side of the main hangar.

"Of that, I have no doubt," General Senegora stated as they turned to follow Nathan.

"As you have probably all read in the ship's specs, this is the biggest of four bays. This main bay is used for most normal flight operations. On either side we have what we call 'fighter alleys'. This is where our fighters would normally be housed and launched through the forward launch tubes, of which there is a pair at the front of each fighter alley."

"How many fighters can each alley hold?" Major Prechitt inquired.

"They were designed to hold twenty-four of our fighters," Nathan explained as they approached the forward transfer airlock on the starboard side of the main hangar. "I'm not sure how many of yours might fit." As he reached the forward end of the hangar, he stopped and turned around to face aft. "On either side of the forward end of this hangar there is a transfer airlock. Inside is an elevator that can run from the auxiliary bay below us all the way up to the topside of the ship, where the elevator pad can then be used for launch or recovery operations. In addition, there are four smaller transfer airlocks located on either side at the middle and aft ends of the main hangar. Their elevators only go between this deck and the one below."

"I have to admit, Captain," General Valachin stated somewhat sheepishly, "that I did not have the time to read through all the details sent to us on your vessel. I was wondering why it is necessary to have the additional airlocks inside the ship."

"During prolonged combat operations, the main transfer airlocks to the flight apron outside can be lowered into the deck, opening the entire back end of this bay to space. This enables us to recover spacecraft without having to use the main airlocks, which take far more time. The combat configuration allows us to cycle spacecraft through the refueling and re-arming process more quickly so we can get them back into action."

"An interesting concept," the general admitted.

"If you'll follow me through the airlock, gentlemen," Nathan said as he turned to his left and headed through the airlock into the starboard fighter bay.

A minute later, the five of them strolled out of the airlock and into the starboard fighter bay. It was more dimly lit than the main hangar bay and was still packed with crates of equipment and components that had been there since they had first left Earth on their training flight almost a month ago.

"Is this a cargo bay?" General Senegora asked, somewhat confused at the sight of all the crates.

"As you may remember, gentlemen, we departed Earth before all of our systems and equipment were properly installed. In order to make room for the building of another ship, the plan was to make us space worthy and then continue installing the rest of the Aurora's internal systems and equipment while still in orbit. All of this would have been installed and this bay would have been clear long before our fighter wings came aboard. We are currently working on getting the higher priority items installed and the lower priority items moved to the cargo holds below this deck. But it may take some time before these bays are completely cleared. In the meantime, you should be able to operate your fighters from the main bay and use only the launch tubes here and on the port side to launch your fighters."

"Assuming that our fighters can be adapted to work in your launch tubes," General Valachin reminded him.

"Yes," Nathan agreed.

"My chief flight engineer feels confident that it

will not be a problem," Major Prechitt insisted.

"That's good to hear," Nathan stated as he headed forward to the launch tubes.

"The real challenge will be getting the fighters converted back to their original configurations," Lieutenant Saren added.

"Their original configurations?" Nathan asked.

"Our interceptors were once Takaran short-range space interceptors," Major Prechitt explained. "They were converted for atmospheric and orbital intercept before they were given to us by the Ta'Akar. In order to be used primarily as space-based fighters, we will have to change over the fuel systems, which primarily feed the atmospheric propulsions systems at this time. We will also have to install different targeting systems and navigational software."

"Navigational software?" Nathan wondered.

"In space, there is no horizon," the major said with a grin.

* * *

Jessica purposefully kept her eyes on her data pad as Travon Dumar entered the hospital meeting room where Commander Taylor and Chief Montrose had been interviewing candidates for over a week. The man's credentials were impressive, as was his experience, having participated in several actions during his mandatory service with the Ta'Akar.

"Thank you for coming in, Mister Dumar," Cameron began. "I hope you did not wait long."

"Not at all," Mister Dumar answered.

"As you are already aware," Cameron continued, "these are the final rounds for selection of the first group of volunteers to be trained for service aboard

Ryk Brown

the Aurora."

"Thank you for considering me," Mister Dumar said.

"You remember Chief Montrose from your first interview, and this is the Aurora's chief of security, Lieutenant Commander Nash."

"A pleasure to meet you, Lieutenant Commander," Mister Dumar stated.

Jessica looked up briefly from her data pad to meet Mister Dumar's eyes. They were steely and confident, and they spoke of a man who had seen and done things that most others had not. At first this worried Jessica. However, it was the kind of experience that the Aurora's crew was currently lacking. "Likewise," she mumbled as her gaze returned to her data pad. She also noticed that the candidate's composure seemed unaffected by her brisk manner of speaking. This too was a good indicator of the man's confidence and demeanor. The last thing Jessica needed in her intelligence unit was someone who was not confident in their own abilities, and so far her first impression was that this man appeared to fit the bill nicely.

"You worked in intelligence for the Ta'Akar?" Jessica asked, already knowing the answer from her data pad.

"Yes, that is correct," Mister Dumar answered, "but only as an analyst."

"Only?" Jessica wondered.

"Meaning I did not participate in field work."

"Were you trained for field work?"

"Yes, as were all those in my unit," Mister Dumar responded.

"What were your duties as an analyst?" Jessica asked.

"To predict likely strategies and tactics that might be used by the enemy, in order to develop defenses and take advantage of opportunities when presented."

"To take advantage of opportunities?" Jessica inquired further.

"There are generally three ways to win a battle:" Mister Dumar explained, "through the use of overwhelming force, superior tactics, or by taking advantage of opportunities as they arise. Such opportunities are quite often the deciding factor."

Jessica considered Mister Dumar's words for a moment. They were quite similar to the edicts she had been taught back in the Fleet Academy on Earth, although overwhelming force had never been an option for them. "It says here that you served an additional two years. Why is that?"

"At the time my service was fulfilled, the ship on which I was serving was in the Palee system, which is about as far from Corinair as one can get. The odds of finding a way back to Corinair on my own were unlikely at the time."

"Understandable, but two years?"

"I had not expected it to take that long. Unfortunately, there were some troubles in that region of space that occurred shortly after I agreed to stay on until we reached the Darvano system."

"You must have really wanted to get home," Jessica commented.

"Corinair was my home," he insisted. "I had no desire to live elsewhere. In addition, I had a fiancé waiting for my return. I felt obligated not to let her down."

Jessica had no comment in regards to his last statement, instead continuing to read his application

185

and background report from Corinari intelligence. "I see you have done well for yourself since your return," she commented. "What is it you do?"

"I forecast in commodities."

"Forecast?"

"Yes. I predict future changes in the availability and prices of valuable resources. My clients pay me for my opinions in such matters."

"Then it seems the skills you picked up during your service have been put to good use upon your return."

"Most men attempt to return to their original path upon returning from service," Dumar commented. "Some choose to utilize the training they obtained and put it to good use on their home world, as Chief Montrose has done."

"You have a family, correct?"

"Yes."

"You do realize a posting on the Aurora will undoubtedly put you in harm's way," Cameron warned.

"I believe we are all in harm's way at the moment, Commander. I simply have chosen to take an active part in the defense of my home."

"I understand that," Cameron continued, "but what of your family? Even if the Ta'Akar are defeated, there is no guarantee that any of us will return safely."

"My family is already well provided for," Mister Dumar assured them. "Should I perish in action, they have the means to carry on quite comfortably in my absence."

"How practical of you," Jessica mused.

"I believe in planning ahead," Mister Dumar insisted. "Another skill I picked up in the service of the Ta'Akar," he added with a smirk.

"Did you lose anyone in the bombardment?" Cameron asked. "Fortunately, no," Mister Dumar answered. "There were a few acquaintances, perhaps, but no one close to myself or my family. Even our home was spared. We were indeed fortunate in that regard."

Jessica continued scanning over the pages of electronic documents that had been gathered about the individual sitting across the table from her. While every detail seemed to be in order, she couldn't help but wonder why this man had volunteered for duty. He was older than most; by Jessica's math he was nearly sixty Earth years old. Most of the volunteers were at least half his age. But his stated reasons had been logical; everyone *was* in harm's way, whether they knew it or not.

In the end, Jessica decided that her lingering suspicions were simply because this man thought in a way a similar to her own, doubting and analyzing everything and everyone around him. She had met very few people in her life that had thought in such a manner. Hopefully, he would be an asset to the Aurora's mission.

Jessica placed her data pad on the table in front and looked straight ahead at the applicant. "One last question, Mister Dumar," she said. "Can you ship out this afternoon?"

* * *

"I will meet you at the spaceport, sir," Chief Montrose promised Jessica before he turned and exited Cameron's hospital room.

"Thank you, Chief," Cameron said as the door

closed behind him.

"He's an interesting type," Jessica commented as she plopped down on Cameron's couch. Corinairan hospitals were more like the hotel rooms back on Earth than the hospital rooms she had seen. The Corinairan medical community believed that healing was as much a psychological process as it was a physical one. To that end, most of the rooms were made to be as comfortable as possible. In fact, a lot of the long-term care on Corinair was done in the patient's home rather than in a hospital. But the nanites still coursing throughout Commander Taylor's body required periodic monitoring and reprogramming which, although not impossible, was difficult to accomplish away from advanced care facilities.

"The chief's a good man," Cameron insisted as she sat down and lay back against the inclined head of her bed.

"He sure keeps a close eye on you, that's for sure," Jessica commented.

"Yeah, sometimes he's worse than my father, but he's been a big help," Cameron admitted. "I doubt I could have gotten through all those interviews without him. He sorted through the weaker applicants all on his own, cutting thousands in a matter of days. He is very dedicated. The scary part is he really believes that we, or more specifically *Na-tan*, will defeat the Ta'Akar."

"What, you don't?"

"Let's just say I'm not as confident about Nathan's abilities as everyone else seems to be." Cameron sighed, relieved to finally be done with her responsibilities for the day and be able to relax. "These people don't know Nathan like we do."

"I don't know, Cam," Jessica argued. "He's changed a lot in the past week."

"How so?"

"Well, for one, he's acting all captain-like," Jessica said. "Hell, he's even got us saluting him—at least in public."

"Really?"

"Don't get me wrong; I mean, he's still Nathan, you know? He's just different."

"Different how?"

"I don't know," Jessica said. "It's like he's thinking about things more, instead of just making it up as he goes."

"You think he's finally taking things more seriously?" Cameron asked in disbelief.

"Maybe, or maybe it's just because nobody's tried to kill us for a while," Jessica admitted. "Either way, he's behaving more like a captain than *I* ever would have expected."

"Let's just hope it lasts," Cameron stated.

"So what about you?" Jessica asked. "When are you getting out of here?"

"Still a few weeks, as I understand it. As long as I've got these nanites swimming around inside of me, I can't be away from the hospital for more than a few hours at a time, or the buggers start doing something they're not supposed to do."

"What?"

"I don't know," she admitted in frustration. "All I *do* know is they have to check my progress and update the nanite programming every few hours."

"Well, when do they take those things out of you?"

"They're already coming out of me," Cameron explained. "When one of them finishes their assigned task or gets low on energy, they head for my kidneys to make their exit."

"Jeez, it's just creepy, the thought of having millions of those things inside of you, knitting away at your insides." Jessica shuddered at the thought. "What does it feel like, anyway?"

"Most of the time you don't feel it, at least not like before," Cameron explained. "When I first woke up, it was awful. It was like I was being poked with a million tiny needles from the inside. If it wasn't for the pain meds, I would've freaked. Now, it's just an occasional shooting pain here and there."

"Are you still on the pain meds?"

"No, not for a few days now."

"How are you sleeping?" Jessica asked. There was a pause, a long one. Jessica knew what it meant, as most of the crew had experienced some difficulty sleeping due to the events they had lived through, and Cameron had been through more than most.

"Not too bad," she said in a less than convincing fashion. "Some nights are better than others."

Another long pause told Jessica that it wasn't an issue to be pushed. "Well, just hurry up and get well," she told Cameron. "We've got a whole new crew to train, and if we leave it all up to Nathan and Vlad, we'll have a ship full of idiots."

Cameron smiled ever so slightly through her fatigued expression.

"I've got three hours until I've got to head back," Jessica stated, trying to change the subject. "How's the room service in this joint?"

* * *

Decades of training and experience had made it

impossible for Travon Dumar to sit in a confined space with anyone sitting behind him. From the back of the shuttle's main cabin, he felt more at ease, as he could easily keep an eye on everyone aboard.

He was on the first of two shuttles heading for Karuzara where the Aurora was docked. Between the two shuttles there were one hundred volunteers. When combined with the surviving members of the Aurora's original crew, the ship would have nearly two full shifts available. There were two more waves of volunteers due over the next two weeks as well, after which the ship would be fully staffed.

Training would undoubtedly be difficult, as time was short. Everyone knew that the Ta'Akar kept irregular patrol schedules so as to keep their subjects better in line. He looked over the rows of volunteers in front of him, noticing every type imaginable. They had come from all walks of life, with different skills and experience. Many of them had served aboard Ta'Akar ships during their mandatory service, but even more had not. He wondered if either had an advantage over the other, as he had no idea how different these people from Earth might run their military vessels.

The people of Corinair had a long history of being a proud, strong-willed people. Their strength and courage had earned them considerable respect from the field commanders of the Ta'Akar Empire during the invasion of the Darvano system over thirty years ago. However, nearly two generations and several decades of incessant brainwashing by Ta'Akar propagandists had bred much of the fight out of them. He could only wonder if these volunteers had what it took to stand up against the ruthless dictatorship that was the Ta'Akar.

Travon Dumar had no love for the empire. He had lost that long ago. He also had no expectations of returning safely to Corinair. He had sent his family away to the safety of a mountain retreat only he had known about. There was ample wealth to see to their needs, and from that location, they might even survive should the Ta'Akar achieve their goal and fully occupy the planet.

He had disbanded his unit and destroyed all evidence of its existence. The fires that had consumed it would be attributed to just another of the many conflagrations that had been burning in Aitkenna for days on end after the Yamaro had attacked the planet. He had even murdered the only other person who knew the secret he now carried with him. He had no plan, no idea, what he was going to do once he got to the Aurora, aside from one goal—find Redmond Tugwell.

The shuttle passed through the tunnel leading into the Karuzari asteroid with ease. The idea seemed so simple as to be considered genius. The belt was littered with such hollowed out shells, all waiting for their turn to be de-orbited and sent to a new orbit high above Corinair where their remains would be broken up and completely harvested once and for all. It was also somewhat embarrassing that the Karuzari had managed to establish this base under his very nose. He had searched his memory for days on end when he had heard the news of the secret Karuzari asteroid base, and he could not find a single clue he might have overlooked. These Karuzari were not stupid; of this he was sure. After all, they had managed to fight a guerrilla war for three decades and had reduced the strength of their enemy by more than half. It had been an accidental bit of intelligence that had led the Campaglia to the Taroa system, where they would have squashed the rebellion once and for all, had it not been for the Aurora.

Travon Dumar had taken his posting in the Darvano system in order to remove himself from the corruption and nepotism of the regime of Caius the Great. Yet here he was, about to be thrust into the middle of a struggle that could ultimately decide the very fate of the empire. He neither wanted to be here, nor could he walk away; that was the irony of the situation.

He looked out the window of the shuttle as the tunnel walls gave way, widening into a vast inner cavern. A minute later, he could barely make out the gray and white shape of the Aurora moored at the Karuzara docks in the middle of the lower half of the cavern. He looked in amazement at the ship as her back half, obviously the main propulsion section, passed beneath them and slid to their aft. The ship didn't look terribly different from any other he had seen. She had rather smooth lines, punctuated by various protuberances here and there, as well as the seams between outer hull plates.

The main propulsion section seemed to drop away suddenly and the shuttle fired her thrusters to initiate a rapid change in altitude in relation to the ship below her. Travon put his face to the small window, straining to look forward along the curve of the shuttle's hull to see the ship they were about to land on. A deck, an apron of some sort, with markings meant to assist the pilot in lining his ship up for a safe landing, were painted on the deck below. Lights inside the lines were flashing in a sequential pattern, moving from the aft end of the apron forward, shifting closer to the center line as they progressed. The shuttle fired more maneuvering thrusters, rolling slightly from side to side and yawing to starboard, then finally sliding laterally until she came to rest on the exterior landing apron of the Aurora. The shuttle shook slightly as the ship touched down. There was obviously a bit of gravity generated on the deck in order to make it easier for the pilots to keep their ships on the deck while rolling forward. As they rolled in under the aft canopy, he could feel the gravity increasing until it was at a level close to normal. He wondered what normal gravity was for the people of Earth. For that matter, had they chosen to use their normal level of gravity, or a level that was normal for the Corinairans who would be filling out the Aurora's crew roster?

The brightness of the lights outside the shuttle increased as it rolled inside the center transfer airlock. The lighting in the main cavern of Karuzara had been somewhat dim, but adequate for navigation. Here, however, they appeared to prefer much more light.

As the shuttle rolled to a stop inside the transfer airlock, Lieutenant Commander Nash stood at the front of the cabin and turned back toward the passengers. "May I have your attention," she ordered. A quiet quickly fell over the cabin, the sound of the ventilation fans inside the cabin being the only sound left. "As soon as the airlock pressurizes, a Corinari inspection team will come aboard and perform a security check. Please have all ID chips, bio-scan info cards, and personal belongings ready for inspection. If you do not cooperate you will be forcibly detained, and I do mean forcibly. Is that understood?" Before anyone in the cabin could answer incorrectly, the Lieutenant Commander continued. "The correct answer would be, 'Yes, sir.'" She looked them over again. "Is that understood?"

Everyone in the cabin responded with a resounding, "Yes, sir!"

"Very good," she told them. "Remain in your seats until your name is called. When you hear your name, remove your bag from under your seat and step forward. As the guards clear you, exit the shuttle and form up outside in the transfer airlock. Once the shuttle and passengers have been cleared, the inner doors will open. Is that understood?"

Again the group answered, "Yes, sir," together as one.

Travon Dumar smiled. He recognized Corinari security procedures when he saw them. He wondered how much of this was their idea and how much of it was on the orders of Lieutenant Commander Nash. Again, the idea amused him. He peered out his window again as the outer door of the transfer airlock slammed shut. The lighting in the transfer airlock suddenly became a pale blue, with green strobe lights flashing on the walls. A similar method was used on Ta'Akar ships to indicate that an airlock was currently re-pressurizing—yet another similarity between their peoples. As the pressure in the airlock increased, so did the audible hiss of the air being pumped into the room. At first, it was barely audible over the sound of the internal ventilation fans as well as the excited voices of the volunteers as they chatted amongst themselves in anticipation of what lay ahead. But within minutes the hiss was quite distinct, if one was listening for it.

A few minutes later, the hissing outside the shuttle stopped and the lighting changed from pale blue to a clean amber white light that was distributed evenly throughout the airlock. The green strobe lights had also stopped flashing. A small door opened in the main inner airlock door, and a column of ten heavily armed Corinari troops entered the airlock, followed by a sergeant carrying a data pad. The small door instantly closed after the sergeant entered. Moments later, two of the guards and the sergeant cracked open the hatch to the shuttle and stepped inside to begin the inspection.

* * *

"Attention on deck!" Jessica called out as she entered the room just behind the captain. Everyone in the room immediately stood at attention as Nathan stepped up onto the stage and took the podium. "At ease," he announced. He looked to his left at Chief Montrose who had entered behind him. "Good evening, everyone. I'm Captain Nathan Scott, commander of the UES Aurora. For those few of you who do not speak Angla, Chief Montrose will be translating."

Nathan paused for a moment as he looked around the room. The majority of the volunteers were male, by appearances between the ages of twenty-five and thirty-five, with a few older ones scattered about. There looked to be a handful of women as well, most of which seemed a bit younger. The average age of the volunteers surprised him, as most of the new cadets coming out of the three fleet academies back on Earth were in their mid twenties. He himself had been one of the oldest cadets in his class, having completed his graduate work before pursuing a commission in the Earth Defense Fleet.

"Before I begin," Nathan started, "I'd like to get a few things out of the way. First, by order of the Corinari Command Authority, Chief Doran Montrose is hereby promoted to Master Chief. Second, on the strong recommendation of my executive officer, Commander Taylor, I hereby appoint Master Chief Montrose as the Aurora's new chief of the boat. Congratulations, Master Chief," Nathan said extending his hand to Master Chief Montrose.

"Thank you, sir."

"I would like to begin by thanking all of you for volunteering to serve aboard this ship. Make no mistake; by doing so you are putting yourselves directly in harm's way. The Aurora will serve as the point of the Alliance spear. Many of us will not survive, but I have no doubt that all of us will be remembered, regardless of the outcome."

Nathan paused and looked around the room again as the chief of the boat caught up in his translations. "Why this ship? Why now? I can't answer the 'why now', but I can answer 'why this ship'. It's not because we're bigger, or stronger, or more heavily armed. This ship is unique because it is equipped with a system that can move her across vast distances of space in the blink of an eye. We call this system a jump drive, and it can jump us up to ten light years at a time. The jump drive provides a huge tactical advantage that we intend to use to defeat the Ta'Akar Empire and liberate not only the Darvano system, but all of the Pentaurus cluster. But this ship, as amazing as it might be, is only a tool. It is nothing without a crew that can use her properly. And that is where you, and the volunteers arriving over the next few weeks, come in. It will not be easy, as despite your various levels of expertise, many of you have no shipboard experience. The training will be endless and exhausting, but we have no choice, as the Ta'Akar could show up on our doorstep unannounced at any moment. We have to be ready to fight as soon as possible."

Nathan looked around the room one last time as the master chief continued translating. "As I said, I cannot tell you why we are here now. Call it chance; call it fate; call it legend; call it the will of whatever god you choose to believe in. The fact of the matter is that we *are* here now, and we have a job to do... together. For together we are one." After a moment's pause, Nathan realized he had nothing more to say. "I'll now turn over the room to Lieutenant Commander Nash who will go over the ship's basic rules and regulations, after which the chief... I'm sorry, the Master Chief, will pass out your berthing and duty assignments, as well as your training schedules. Thank you all again for volunteering."

The volunteers began to applaud as Nathan left the podium. He smiled slightly, a small wave escaping as he exited the briefing room.

"Attention on deck!" Master Chief Montrose barked, immediately ending the applause before it gained momentum, allowing Jessica to start her part of the briefing.

* * *

Nathan had been studying the training schedule Commander Taylor had sent back with Jessica for over an hour. As expected, the schedule was thorough and well organized. The only thing missing was training for flight operations, as she still had to meet with Major Prechitt and his deck chief in order to discuss operational issues.

Just as his eyes were beginning to cross, the entry buzzer sounded. "Yes?" he called.

"Ensign Willard to see you, sir," the guard who peeked in the hatchway stated.

"Send him in."

Ensign Willard stepped through the hatchway into the captain's ready room. "Thank you for seeing me, Captain. I hope I'm not interrupting."

"Not at all, Mister Willard," Nathan assured him. "Have a seat. How may I help you?"

"I was wondering," Ensign Willard began as he sat, "if you had considered allowing some of the Yamaro's crew to serve aboard the Aurora."

"The thought has crossed my mind, yes. But I haven't had a chance to discuss it at length with my XO. I also expect that my chief of security will have some issues."

"Understandable, Captain. However, at least twenty of the Yamaro's crew, most of them Corinairan born and raised, fought to protect this ship. Many of them gave their very lives."

"While that may be so," Nathan said, trying to remain respectful, "let's not forget, Mister Willard, they were fighting for their own lives just as much as they were fighting for this ship, perhaps even more so."

"Perhaps," Ensign Willard agreed, "but those men could just as easily have taken to the escape pods like the others, and they chose to stand and fight. And for what? So they could languish away in some internment camp on their own home world, watching as their people struggle to prepare for war?

Captain, if their skills are not to be utilized here, at least set them free to defend their own world, to be with their own families."

"Mister Willard," Nathan replied, leaning back in his chair, "has it occurred to you, that some of the people on Corinair might not make the distinction between those that ordered the attack on Corinair and those who carried it out?" He waited a moment for a reply, but saw that none was coming. "It's quite possible that they are safer right where they are, at least for the moment."

"I must admit, sir, I had not considered that possibility."

"Neither had I," Nathan admitted. "It was one of the Prime Minister's staff that raised the concern." Nathan studied Mister Willard for a moment. He was obviously concerned for the well-being of his shipmates. "Listen, make up a list of the names and qualifications of those among them that are from Corinair, and I'll take a look at it. I cannot promise anything, but I will give it serious consideration."

"Thank you, Captain," Ensign Willard said.

Nathan noticed that the ensign was not rising from his seat to depart. "Was there something else?"

"Yes, sir. I was wondering if you had any plans on how to deal with the Yamaro's eventual failure to show up in the Savoy system."

"There's not much we can do about that, I'm afraid. There is no way we can repair the Yamaro's damage. Her entire drive section is nearly gone. It would be impossible to get her into the Savoy system for her rendezvous."

"Then don't," Ensign Willard said. "Just send her transponder."

"Excuse me?"

"You could pull her transponder and go into the Savoy system yourself, transmitting her ID codes."

"This ship is nothing like the Yamaro; you'd have to be blind not to notice the differences."

"Of course, but no one will be looking at the Aurora. The Yamaro would not enter into a planetary orbit, Captain. Standard procedure for Ta'Akar warships is to park at a gravitationally stable point out of reach of the primary planet's defense systems."

"You're talking about Lagrange points," Nathan stated.

Ensign Willard continued, paying little attention to the captain's comment. "In order to conserve fuel, Captain de Winter normally parked at a gravity point even farther out, as it required much less deceleration than going deeper into the system. Granted, it is not much of a savings, but Ta'Akar ships are usually out on patrol for several years at a time. Their captains have this strange pride system. Showing up with empty tanks tells of a captain that did not plan well. It does make for more difficult transits for the shuttles, but they get refueled at their destination."

"But surely they have sensors that could determine we are not the Yamaro," Nathan pointed out.

"Savoy is not as advanced as Darvano, Captain. It's more of an agricultural system. They probably do have some deep-space sensors, but it is more than likely they will not bother looking. The Ta'Akar have been unopposed in the Savoy system for decades. As long as no other warships arrive while you are there, your masquerade should go undetected."

"What would we have to do while we are there," Nathan asked, becoming more curious about the idea, "for appearances sake?"

"We were scheduled to pick up inductees from the Savoy system and deliver them to Takara for training. You could use the Yamaro's shuttles to complete the mission. You would need a few Ta'Akar guards and at least one officer, a nobleman if possible."

"That sounds awfully risky," Nathan concluded.

"All you would have to do is land, load the inductees, and take off again. No one would be expecting you to stay in the system any longer than necessary to complete your task. As the Yamaro, you would be about to head home after a three year deployment. No one would become suspicious should you choose to depart as soon as your orders have been carried out. In fact, it would be expected. And if successful, you could be delaying your discovery by several months."

"And if not, we could be tipping our hand." Nathan sighed, "I admit, it is an interesting plan, but who would we get to dress up as Takaran troops? I would expect that there would be some measure of security, even on a backward farm planet."

"I suppose I could talk to the members of the Yamaro crew currently being detained on Corinair," Ensign Willard said. "They are all registered in the Yamaro's crew roster, so they would pass any identity scans at the spaceport. However, they might be more inclined to agree to such a dangerous mission if there were some offer of reward."

Nathan smiled. Ensign Willard obviously understood the concept of bargaining. "I'm sure something can be arranged. I'll run the idea past my staff. If they approve, I'll arrange for you to speak with your shipmates."

"Thank you, sir." Ensign Willard rose and left the ready room. On his way through the hatchway, he passed by Master Chief Montrose on his way in. "Master Chief," he said respectfully in passing.

Master Chief Montrose paused a moment, considering the man that had just passed him. He was wearing an Aurora jumpsuit; however, his accent was obviously Corinairan.

"Master Chief?" Nathan called from inside the ready room, stealing the Master Chief's attention away from the man that had just passed him.

"Captain," the master chief began, snapping a salute, "a moment of your time, sir?"

"How may I help you, Master Chief?"

"Permission to close the hatch, sir?"

"Of course," Nathan answered, somewhat surprised.

After closing the hatch, Master Chief Montrose turned back to face the captain, still standing rather formally.

Nathan noticed that the master chief seemed uncomfortable. "Is there a problem, Master Chief?"

"Yes, sir. I mean, I'm not sure, sir. This is not the Corinari, so I am not sure of the protocols involved, or if it is even my place to..."

"Would it be easier if I gave you permission to speak freely, Master Chief?" Nathan offered.

"Yes, sir."

"Then by all means, Master Chief, speak your mind."

"Well, sir, I'm not sure that I understand what my responsibilities are on your ship. I know what a master chief does in the Corinari, and I know what a deck chief does when in service of the empire, but I'm not sure if the roles are at all similar to your 'chief of the boat' position."

"How about you just do what you think is the right thing, and one of us will correct you if necessary."

"That seems like a rather dangerous way to start off, sir," Master Chief Montrose observed.

"I promise you, Master Chief, we'll grant you considerable leeway."

"Thank you, sir."

"Is that it? Was that the problem?" Nathan wondered.

"No, sir. The problem is you, sir."

"Me?"

"Yes, sir. Or more specifically, the way you behaved when you left the orientation briefing."

"I'm afraid I'm not following you, Master Chief," Nathan admitted.

"That little wave... like a politician leaving a campaign rally."

"That bad, huh?" Nathan said, not really taking the master chief's concerns seriously.

"That bad?" Master Chief Montrose was starting to get angry. "I do not know about captains on your world, but out here in the cluster, the captain of a warship is someone to be respected, to be feared, to be revered. When you are ready to start being that captain, I will be right at your side. The men are watching your every move. You need to start acting like somebody worth dying for, not somebody worth voting for."

Nathan watched the master chief as he went from being angry to being unsure again. "Is that all, Master Chief?" Nathan asked.

"Yes, sir," he answered. "And again, I apologize if my remarks were not in line with your expectations of my role as your chief of the boat."

"Well, I haven't known many COBs yet, but so far you seem to be doing just fine."

"Thank you, sir," Master Chief Montrose answered.

"Thank you, Master Chief," Nathan told him with all sincerity. "I will keep your words in mind."

"Very good, sir."

"Is there anything else, Master Chief?"

"No, sir," the master chief said, preparing to exit.

"Master Chief, have you eaten dinner?" Nathan asked.

"No, sir. I was just about to find your dining hall."

"We call it a galley," Nathan told him as he rose from his seat behind the desk. "I was headed there myself. I usually dine with Lieutenant Commander Kamenetskiy, our chief engineer. Perhaps you'd like to join us? The two of you should probably get acquainted."

"Thank you, sir. I would like that."

CHAPTER SIX

"Report," Nathan requested as he entered the bridge.

"Karuzara Command reports they just picked up a Ta'Akar frigate dropping out of FTL on the outer edge of the system," Jessica reported from the tactical console. "They're sending us the track now. Sending to main view screen."

The main view screen that surrounded the front half of the bridge in a quarter-sphere was currently displaying the view outside the Aurora, which was the inside of the Karuzari asteroid base commonly referred to as Karuzara. A rectangular chart of the Darvano system superimposed itself in the middle of the main view screen. The chart showed the positions of all planets and ships within the system, with a red triangle to indicate the new hostile contact. The triangle appeared to be just beyond the outermost planet in the Darvano system. Its speed indicator was counting down, indicating it was decelerating, as was usually the case when a ship dropped out of FTL on its way into a system.

"Karuzara Command confirms contact ID," Ensign Yosef announced from the sensor station. "Takaran Frigate."

"She's decelerating hard," Jessica announced.

"Course?"

"One moment," Jessica said. "She's headed for

Corinair, sir."

"Set general quarters," Nathan ordered, "and prepare to get under way." Nathan looked over at Master Chief Montrose standing in the corner of the bridge and nodded.

Naralena keyed up the ship-wide alert system. A moment later, the lighting in the corridors flashed red and the alert klaxon sounded, followed by a prerecorded voice announcing, "*General quarters! General quarters! All hands, man your battle stations! Prepare to get under way!*"

Less than a minute later, all the workstations on the bridge were manned and ready, and there were two armed guards at each of the hatchways. Nathan paced back and forth behind Jessica at the tactical station, glancing at her display that showed the current status of all the ship's departments. He knew that all over his ship, men and women were scurrying to get to their battle stations, and their department heads were waiting for all their people to become ready before they reported their department as ready for combat. Once every indicator on her display changed from red to green, he knew his ship was fully manned, buttoned down and ready for action.

"All battle stations report manned and ready, Captain," Jessica reported. "All four reactors are online and are running at fifty percent."

"Very good," Nathan answered, checking his watch. "Chief of the Boat, log the time."

"Minute thirty, Captain," the chief answered.

Nathan paid no attention to the chief's disappointment. "Comms, notify Karuzara Command; the Aurora is departing."

"Aye, sir," Naralena answered from the

207

comm-station.

"Helm, release all mooring clamps and thrust away from the dock."

"Aye, Captain," Josh answered. "Releasing mooring clamps and thrusting away." Josh released the clamps, and tilted his maneuvering joystick slightly to the right. The images of the cavern outside began sliding slowly to port as the Aurora slid to starboard, away from the docking platform inside the hollowed-out asteroid that held the Karuzari base. A moment later, he applied opposite thrust to stop the ship's sideways slide and started their ascent. "Clear of all moorings. Thrusting up," he announced.

"Any change on the frigate's track?" Nathan asked, watching the view of the cavern wall shift downward as the Aurora climbed.

"No, sir," Jessica reported. "Karuzari command reports no changes. Target is still decelerating and on course for Corinair."

"Thrusting forward," Josh announced.

Nathan watched somewhat nervously as the cavern walls on the view screen appeared to be moving toward them as they slid downward. He knew Josh was a natural pilot, but he couldn't help but look upward at the portion of the view screen above and slightly forward of his command chair. He could see the gaping entrance to the exit corridor that led from the central chamber out to the surface. The asteroid itself was three-quarters hollow, but her remaining crust was still half a kilometer thick.

"Mister Sheehan," Nathan called, "as soon as we come out into open space, I want to head for the far side of Cleo. We'll keep that gas giant between us and that frigate until she passes by."

"Yes, sir," Loki answered from the navigation console to the right of Josh's station at the helm.

"If we time it right, we'll never show up on her sensors," Nathan commented.

"Entering exit corridor," Josh announced confidently. "Engaging auto-flight." A moment later, Josh removed his hand from the maneuvering joystick as the Aurora's complex auto-flight computers began following the script Josh had written more than a week ago. The script told the Aurora how to maneuver the ship out the long curving corridor that snaked along a natural fissure in the crust of the asteroid. Although Josh would have preferred to fly the corridor manually, he had long since learned that the helm of the Aurora was no place to play flyboy. Their battle with the Yamaro had taught him that lesson, and it was not one he would soon forget.

"Three minutes to open space," Loki reported. "Course for the far side of Cleo is plotted and locked."

"Very good," Nathan confirmed.

"Doctor Sorenson, I trust you'll keep a short emergency jump plot ready at all times?"

"Of course, Captain," Abby answered in a matter-of-fact tone.

Nathan said nothing, just nodded approval as his eyes met the Danish physicist's brief glance.

"Let's keep our emissions and heat signature as low as possible, people," Nathan reminded everyone. "We'll be in the open for a few minutes when we first come out." Nathan turned his attention to the helm. "Mister Hayes, give us a good little burn just before we come out of the corridor, then use thrusters only until we're in Cleo's shadow."

"Yes, sir," Josh answered.

"Not too much though," Nathan warned. "We

don't want to melt the tunnel behind us."

"Yes, sir," Josh assured him, "I'll keep it cool."

"Two minutes to open space," Loki reported.

"Comms, ask Karuzara to keep feeding us their tracking telemetry via laser-link. We'll be blind once we put the gas giant between us and that frigate."

"Yes, sir," Naralena answered.

Nathan didn't notice that Master Chief Montrose was taking notes and grumbling to himself about something.

"Roll us ninety degrees to port, Mister Hayes," Nathan ordered. "We don't want to show them our heat exchangers as we come out into the open."

"Aye, sir, disengaging auto-flight. Rolling ninety degrees to port."

The image on the main view screen began to rotate to starboard as the Aurora rolled to port.

"Laser-link is online and tracking," Naralena reported. "Karuzara command confirms they will maintain the link for as long as possible."

"Very well," Nathan answered calmly. Up until recently, Naralena's duties had been pretty much restricted to basic internal communications and any external communications that required translation. Nathan was happy to see she had taken so easily to the more advanced tasks of managing all of the Aurora's sophisticated communications and telemetry systems.

"Roll complete," Josh reported.

"One minute to open space," Loki added.

"Disposition of contact?" Nathan asked Jessica at the tactical station behind him.

"Unchanged, sir. Contact is still on course for Corinair. Current speed is three-quarters light and decelerating."

"Stand by for main engine burn at one percent thrust," Loki reported. "In three......two......one...... ignition."

At one percent, there was no perceptible rumble or vibration on the bridge. It took at least ten percent before they could feel anything translating through the Aurora's primary frame.

"Ten seconds to open space," Loki reported.

Nathan watched the blackness of space rush toward them on the view screen as they accelerated out of the asteroid's exit corridor.

"Five seconds," Loki reported. "Four......three...... main engines off......one..."

The opening quickly grew until it encompassed the entire quarter-sphere viewing screen and disappeared behind them.

"Entering open space," Loki announced.

"Helm, come onto your new course, slow and easy," Nathan instructed.

"Aye, sir, changing course. Heading for orbital intercept with Cleo."

"Transit time, Mister Sheehan?" Nathan asked. He already knew the answer, as they had made this trip before. He just wanted to make sure his new navigator was keeping on top of the details, just as Cameron had always done.

"Twenty-two minutes at our current speed, sir," Loki reported. "Eight minutes until we're in Cleo's shadow."

"Very well," Nathan said. Loki was keeping on top of the details, just as a good navigator should.

"No change in the contact's course or rate of deceleration," Jessica reported, anticipating her captain's next question.

"No change in emissions from the target," Kaylah

added.

"Comms?" Nathan asked, pausing to see if Naralena would also anticipate his need for information.

"Laser array is locked on Karuzara's telemetry signal and tracking," she announced. "All feeds are strong and constant."

Chief Montrose grumbled to himself again.

"Very well." Nathan rotated in his chair to face Jessica at the tactical station behind him. "How long before that frigate reaches Corinair?"

"Assuming their rate of deceleration remains constant, eighty-seven minutes," Jessica answered.

"Put the plots up on the main screen for me," Nathan ordered.

"Aye, sir."

Nathan spun back around to face forward as the tracking plots showed up in a separate rectangle superimposed over the exterior forward view now showing on the screen. "Show me where the contact will be when we come around from behind Cleo and have line-of-sight on them again."

The icons on the forward view screen representing the Aurora and the enemy contact shifted to their new respective positions.

"Showing estimated positions fifty-two minutes from now," Jessica reported.

Nathan stood up, staring at the screen a moment before turning his head toward Ensign Yosef to his left. "Are their shields up?"

"From their emissions profile, I'd say no, sir," Ensign Yosef answered.

"Abby, can you plot a jump from that point to about a kilometer astern of that contact?"

"Yes, sir," Abby answered confidently.

"The planet's gravity well won't cause any problems?"

"No, sir, not since Deliza and I installed the computer cores from those shuttles into the jump drive's plotting system. With all that extra processing power, we can compensate for such things quite easily now."

"A thousand meters is a bit close, sir," Jessica warned.

"Not really," Nathan disagreed. "Look at his velocity at that point. It'll be just a little slower than our orbital velocity, since the gas giant is so much bigger than Corinair, and he won't be down to Corinair's orbital velocity yet. Our closure rate will be really low, so we'll have plenty of time to alter course enough to get a clear jump line before he can change his attitude and bring his guns on us."

"We're not going to do much damage with a few rail guns," Jessica commented. "It would be better if we had torpedoes... preferably nukes."

"If we show him our topside we could get all our rail guns on him. That would do some damage."

Jessica thought about it. "It might at that," she admitted. "At that angle, sir, I suggest we target his main propulsion ports. We're not going to get a shot at much else and we might get lucky and take out his main drive before he gets his shields up."

"Agreed," Nathan said.

"One minute until we enter Cleo's shadow, sir," Loki reported.

"All right then," Nathan announced. "Abby, get that jump plot ready..."

"Contact!" Ensign Yosef announced. "Dead ahead, transferring track to tactical."

"Got it!" Jessica announced. "Another frigate,

coming out from the back side of Cleo... She's firing!"

"Multiple contacts!" Ensign Yosef called out. "Three, four contacts, high-speed. They look like missiles, Captain! Transferring tracks to tactical."

"Helm, pitch down ninety, bring the mains up to full power. We've got to force those missiles to turn and burn out their fuel faster."

"Aye, Captain. Pitching down," Josh answered.

"Jess, all rail guns, point-defense mode."

"All we have are dumb slugs, Captain," Jessica reminded him.

"Damn. Then target the missiles as best you can. Put an equal number of guns on each inbound missile."

"Mains coming up to full power," Josh reported.

"Abby, get me an escape plot," Nathan ordered.

"Captain, the tracks aren't accurate!" Ensign Yosef warned.

"What?" Nathan asked.

Again, the chief of the boat grumbled and took notes.

"They're delayed. It takes nearly ten seconds for the track to reach Karuzara behind us, and then a few more seconds for them to relay the data forward to us. The targets are maybe fifteen seconds closer than they appear."

"Drop the feed and go active," Nathan ordered Ensign Yosef. "Time to impact?" Nathan asked Jessica.

"Twenty-two seconds, adjusted," she reported. "One missile down, three to go."

"Mains are at full power, sir," Josh reported.

"Abby?" Nathan called.

"Thirty seconds to a plot, Captain."

"Missiles are turning, sir," Jessica reported.

"They're trying to stay with us as we change course."

"Tracks are live through active sensors, Captain," Ensign Yosef reported.

"Two down!" Jessica reported, trying to control her excitement. "Two to go! Twenty seconds to impact!"

"Keep firing," Nathan urged. It was an unnecessary statement, as there was no way Jessica would stop firing until all four missiles were destroyed.

"Three down! One to go! Ten seconds!"

"Cease fire! Helm, snap roll one-eighty! Brace for impact!"

"Rolling one-eighty!" Josh answered, yanking his joystick hard to the left.

"All rail guns are cold! Five seconds!" Jessica reported.

"All hands, brace for impact!" Naralena called over the ship-wide call system, sounding the impact siren immediately afterward.

"Roll complete!" Josh reported.

"Two seconds......one......impact!"

The bridge vibrated and rumbled as the last remaining missile struck their reinforced underside.

"Damage report!" Nathan ordered.

"Stand by," Jessica answered.

"Ready to jump, Captain," Abby announced.

"Do it!" Nathan ordered.

"Jumping!"

The view screen dimmed as the blue-white flash of the jump drive filled the screen and lit the inside of the bridge for the split second it took for the jump to complete.

"Jump complete!" Abby reported.

"Position?" Nathan asked.

"Five light minutes down course," Abby reported.

"We're about four light minutes past Cleo," Ensign Yosef reported.

"Minor hull damage, Captain," Jessica reported. "If you hadn't rolled to show them our belly, it would've been worse. We're lucky they didn't use nukes," she added.

"I'm pretty sure they want us intact," Nathan observed. "Which ship is closer to Corinair?"

"Stand by," Jessica responded. "Damn it."

"What is it?" Nathan asked.

"I have to recalculate the positions of both contacts based on their last known positions. Give me a moment... Okay, got it. If the frigate by Cleo—the one that fired on us—if she changes course, she'll get there about ten minutes earlier than the first frigate."

"Not much of a difference," Nathan thought. "There's a chance that the first frigate still doesn't know about us or that the second frigate has fired on us. She may not even be at battle stations yet. What's the signal time between them?"

"About ten minutes," Jessica answered.

"Helm, new intercept course, on the first contact."

"Plotting," Loki answered.

"Coming about," Josh stated, starting his turn while waiting for Loki to give him an accurate heading.

"Same plan as before, Abby; we match his speed and jump in behind him. About five hundred meters, if you please."

"Yes, sir," Abby answered.

"New intercept course plotted and locked, Captain."

"Coming to new intercept heading," Josh answered.

"Match the speed of the target, Mister Hayes," Nathan ordered.

"Aye, sir. Decelerating to match target's speed."

"Be ready to pitch down to bring all guns to bear, Mister Hayes," Nathan reminded him, "just as soon as we come out of the jump."

"Yes, sir."

"All rail guns are pointed up and ready to fire, Captain," Jessica reported.

"Very well."

"Jump plotted, Captain."

"Whenever you're ready," Nathan granted.

"All hands, prepare to jump," Abby announced ship-wide, "in three......two......one......jump."

"Wait!" Jessica cried out as the blue-white flash filled the room.

"Jump complete," Abby announced, suddenly becoming aware of Jessica's last second warning. "Oh God."

Nathan looked up at the main view screen. Behind the rectangular display floating in the middle of the screen that showed the tactical plots, the view of space outside the ship was filled with the image of the tail end of the Ta'Akar frigate, coming at them fast.

"Helm! Full reverse!" Nathan ordered.

"Full reverse, aye!" Josh answered as he brought the deceleration thrusters up to full power.

"Ten seconds to impact!" Jessica announced.

"Captain, I can flip her over and use the mains!"

"No time!" Nathan cried. "Sound collision alert!"

"Collision Alert! Collision Alert!" Naralena announced ship-wide. "All hands brace for impact!"

The main view screen was now filled with the view of the frigate's stern as it rushed toward them.

Nathan noticed that, oddly enough, the tactical plot in the display in the middle of the view screen still showed them about five hundred meters astern of the frigate.

"Jesus!" Nathan swore, clutching the armrests on his command chair.

Josh and Loki grabbed the rails on the sides of their consoles, as did everyone else on the bridge, as they braced for the impact that was about to occur.

Suddenly, the main view screen went black for a moment. Then, the red-tinged lighting in the bridge switched back to its usual amber-white, and the image on the view screen switched back to the standard outside view facing forward, which was now the cavern wall inside the Karuzara asteroid base.

"*End simulation,*" Deliza stated over the comm-system.

"Saw that one coming," the master chief mumbled.

"And we just finished fixing the bow, too," Josh joked.

"What the hell happened?" Nathan asked as he turned toward Abby.

"I don't know, Captain. We jumped to the correct position..."

"Our closure rate was too high," Jessica interrupted.

"I think that was my fault, sir," Josh admitted. "I was trying to match the target speed indicated from real-time tracking."

"Karuzara's position was closer than our position after we jumped away from the second contact," Jessica explained. "Abby and I did our calculations based on that data, since it was more up to date. I guess our revised data never got pushed to the helm displays."

"So, you're saying it was a software glitch?" Nathan asked, somewhat surprised, as the Aurora's software was probably the most thoroughly tested software in existence—at least back home in the Sol system.

"Not a glitch, really," Abby explained. "The software was not written with jump drive tactics in mind, Captain. We have been manually compensating for such variations as we go."

"Well, that's obviously not going to work," Jessica surmised.

"Better we find that out now in a drill," Chief Montrose insisted.

"Captain," Deliza began as she came out of the captain's ready room and entered the bridge, her data pad in hand, "I believe we will need to develop a set of algorithms that will track both live sensor data, as well as data that was taken earlier from less distant locations, and then decide which one is more accurate and, thus, should be utilized."

"Sounds complicated," Nathan said, stating the obvious.

"Yes, considerably," Deliza agreed, "but not impossible. However, we will require assistance."

"Chief, contact the Corinairans," Nathan ordered. "I'm sure there are a few more programmers available on Corinair."

"Right away, sir," the chief promised.

"Nice job on the simulation, by the way," Nathan congratulated Deliza.

"Thank you, Captain," Deliza answered. "I try to make them as real as possible."

"Well, the vibrations from the main drive were a nice touch—oh, and the missile impact as well. How did you do that?"

"Sinusoidal waves through the gravity plating under the deck," she bragged. "Quite easy, really. In time, I can probably simulate the feeling of acceleration as well."

"That won't be necessary," Nathan insisted.

"Captain," Abby said, "what Deliza is suggesting is no small task. In fact, it may require the redesign of several interfaces."

"Well, we can't run the risk of slamming into the back of targets, now can we?" Nathan stated.

"Of course not," Abby agreed. "However, I would like to suggest that we take this opportunity to consider working the jump drive operations into the primary flight consoles instead of having them run by a separate operator."

"But I thought the jump plots where too complicated."

"They were," Abby agreed, "but ever since we installed the computer cores from that old mining shuttle from Haven, we have been able to refine the plotting process. Soon we will be upgrading those cores to ones provided by the Corinairans. We should be able to integrate the entire operation of the jump drive into the helm rather easily. And we are already working on such integration for use in Tug's interceptor, so we will have a prototype to work from and test prior to installing it in the Aurora."

"Then why bring it up now?" Nathan wondered.

"If Deliza's team is going to be upgrading the sensory data management and plotting algorithm, it might be easier for her to do so with the idea that the jump drive operations will eventually be integrated into the helm."

"I don't know, Doctor," Nathan said. "I have

to admit, I feel better knowing you're plotting the jumps. That system is your baby, after all."

"And should something happen to me?" she pointed out.

"Good point," Nathan admitted.

"Besides, I suspect the integration will not only decrease the potential for errors, but it will improve your overall flexibility of use, at least in combat situations."

"Then where will you be?"

"I will be down in the jump drive field generator control room, where I can keep a better eye on things. After all, I do not really belong on the bridge of a warship."

"Very well," Nathan agreed. "However, I would like you to remain on the bridge and monitor the jump plots for a while after the system is integrated, just to be sure."

"Of course."

"Would you like me to load up another simulation, Captain?" Deliza asked.

"Yes, please."

"Captain?" Naralena called from the comms station.

"Yes?"

"Lieutenant Commander Kamenetskiy is requesting you meet him down on the main deck, at the center hatch through the primary forward bulkhead, sir. They are about to crack open the forward section and he thought you might like to be present."

"Yes, of course. Tell him I'm on my way," Nathan told her. "Jess, break everyone for one hour. I should be back by then and we can pick it up again."

"Yes, sir," Jessica answered as Nathan exited the

bridge.

* * *

"Wow," Nathan commented as he approached the main hatch that led through the primary forward bulkhead into the bow of the ship. Vladimir and three of his repair teams were standing nearby, waiting for clearance to enter the forward compartment. "It's been awhile since that light was green," Nathan added, pointing to the pressure status light above the hatch. For more than a month, ever since they had first rammed the Ta'Akar battleship Campaglia and tore a hole in the Aurora's bow, that light had been red, indicating that the compartment on the other side of the hatch was unpressurized. For most of that time, there had been a temporary airlock setup around the hatch, allowing them to go into the compartment and conduct search and rescue operations, as well as to salvage needed equipment and supplies from the depressurized areas. "I see you removed the temporary airlock," Nathan commented.

"The forward compartment has been pressurized for nearly an hour now," Vladimir explained. "The Corinairan technicians outside are finishing their inspection, checking for leaks. We have also been watching the pressure inside the compartment. There have been no changes."

"Then what are we waiting for?" Nathan asked. "Let's go in and take a look around."

"It is still very cold in there," Vladimir warned, "maybe five degrees."

"I'll be fine," Nathan insisted. "You're not the only one who grew up with snow. Vancouver, remember?"

"Bah, that is the tropics compared to my village," Vladimir insisted.

"*Cheng, Comms,*" Naralena's voice called over the comm-set.

"Cheng. Go ahead," Vladimir answered.

"*Sir, Mister Tonken reports they have confirmed a good seal. You are cleared to enter.*"

"Copy," Vladimir answered. "We are opening the hatch now." Vladimir tapped his comm-set to kill the connection and signaled to the first repair team. "Open it."

The four-man repair team removed the metallic tape that had covered the hatch seal. The tape was designed to change color if the hatch seal was leaking, which it had not. They also removed the yellow caution strips that had been crisscrossed over the hatch, warning anyone who might have considered opening the hatch when the forward section had been sealed off. Although Nathan had seen pictures and video footage from the search and rescue teams, as well as the team that had gone in to salvage equipment and supplies, this would be the first live inspection that Nathan would be making of the damage that was caused when he rammed the Campaglia more than a month ago.

The technician pulled the locking lever open, breaking the seal on the hatch. There was a slight hiss of air, as the minor difference in pressure between the two compartments equalized.

"Check the mechanism and make sure the auto-close works properly before re-engaging the system," Vladimir instructed the repair team.

"Smells strange," Nathan commented. "Like burnt circuits and metal."

"Da," Vladimir agreed. "There were several fires

in there. They were extinguished when you backed out and the entire section vented to space. The smell will go away once everything is cleaned and repaired and the section has chance to ventilate properly."

"Is it going to stink up the rest of the ship?" Nathan asked.

"Nyet. Each main compartment has its own environmental system. They are all interconnected, in case one fails, but normally they do not mix the same air. This prevents contaminated air from spreading throughout the ship."

"Like the bridge?"

"Da. The entire command deck has its own system, as does the flight deck, main deck, lower deck, and engineering."

"Shall we?" Nathan asked.

"After you, Captain," Vladimir answered.

Nathan stepped through the hatchway into the forward compartment. The inside was unevenly lit, with a few of the lighting panels flickering off and on. The corridor stretched out in front of him, running forward all the way to the bow. However, the lights at the forward end were all off, having been damaged during the collision.

"Light?" Nathan asked the technician behind him.

"Most of this end has already been looked over by the SAR teams when we were still hiding in the Korak system," Vladimir reminded him.

"Yeah, I remember the videos," Nathan said as he took the flashlight being handed to him. He shined it down the corridor, lighting it up all the way to the end. "It doesn't look too bad down there."

"Most of the damage was on the port side," Vladimir commented as they moved forward.

They turned down a side corridor and headed to port until they reached the end, where it joined up with the perimeter corridor that curved inward as it led forward. As they passed the first escape pod hatch, he noticed some writing on the wall next to the hatch. "What's this?"

"When Commander Taylor had some people in pressure suits raid the food stores of the escape pods, she had them write down what they took from each pod on the wall."

"Why not just use a data pad and store it in the main frame?" Nathan asked.

"Everything was very hectic then. I think she just wanted to make sure the details didn't get lost."

"Makes sense, I guess," Nathan realized. "Don't let anyone paint over them until they've all been restocked."

"What are we going to restock them with?" Vladimir wondered.

"Cameron already thought of that," Nathan assured him. "She's planning on taking all the remaining emergency rations from all escape pods throughout the ship and redistributing them evenly."

Nathan stopped dead in his tracks as they neared the end of the corridor. The side bulkheads were smashed in and the overheads were crumpled and twisted down and inward. There were wires and conduits hanging like vines in some dense forest. "Those wires aren't live, right?" Nathan inquired.

"No, they have been powered down for weeks now," Vladimir assured him.

"You're probably going to have to gut most of this," he commented as he worked his way forward.

"The Karuzari technicians already removed a lot of the heavier stuff," Vladimir told him. "They had to in order to put in new bracing across the top quarter there," he explained, pointing upward to the port side. "You can see where they cut through some of the wreckage just to get it out of the way."

"We're not all the way forward yet, though, are we?" Nathan observed.

"No, not quite. There's still a little more beyond this, but it's probably all smashed in just like this."

Nathan climbed carefully through the debris, pushing wires and conduits aside and stepping over twisted ducting that had fallen to the floor. "There's no way the SAR teams could've gone beyond this," Nathan observed. "Not in full pressure suits, that's for sure."

Nathan continued forward with Vladimir following behind as they snaked their way forward.

"I think we might be better off to just gut all of this and turn it into a big storage area," Vladimir observed. "Most of these are just storage bays and maintenance lockers anyway."

They got past the forward-most point in the bow where the corridor cut back across to the starboard side. The central corridor was completely blocked off by a collapsed bulkhead, and more twisted wreckage blocked the starboard corridor. "We're never going to get through that," Nathan said. "We'll have to circle back around."

"Wait," Vladimir said, moving past Nathan. "This panel is just hanging by a thread..." He yanked on the large panel and it came crashing down to the deck. Behind it was more open corridor. Only this corridor had something else inside of it: the frozen, deformed bodies of several dead Ta'Akar soldiers. Their faces and hands were swollen and bluish, and their eyes had burst forth from their sockets, the swollen, ruptured eyeballs hanging by their optic nerves. Most of them had also suffered other trauma. Their limbs and torso had been snagged on jagged pieces of metal when they were being pulled down the corridor by the escaping atmosphere. One of the soldiers had his entire shoulder torn off by a twisted shard of a bulkhead that stuck out like a massive dagger. The bodies were beginning to smell a bit as well, as they had begun to thaw since the forward compartment had been pressurized. There were four of them altogether, all still dressed in their combat armor, except for one that looked more like an officer.

"Boarding party," Vladimir commented.

"Or what's left of them," Nathan added. "The rest probably got sucked out into space when we backed away."

"I'll get someone to start cleaning up the bodies," Vladimir said.

"Better notify Jessica first," Nathan cautioned. "She may want to go over them first."

"Nathan, they were fighting to survive and then died in a vacuum. I doubt they are booby trapped," Vladimir said.

"I was thinking more along the lines of intelligence, not booby-traps," Nathan told him. "Although, now that you mention it, it wouldn't hurt to check them for booby-traps first. You never know."

Nathan continued forward as Vladimir passed instructions on to one of his technicians to notify security and medical about the bodies. Beyond another bunch of wires dangling from the overhead, Nathan noticed something blinking. It was a red light of some type. He continued forward, pushing debris and dangling panels out of his way, trying to make it to the area from where the red light was flashing. "Vlad," Nathan called out as he moved closer to the source of the light. A sinking feeling began to form in his gut. "Vlad! I've got a SAR light flashing up ahead!"

Nathan continued to push through the debris, nearly getting tangled in the cabling himself as he rushed forward. Finally, he broke past the main bulk of the debris and reached a small part of the corridor that was clear. There, directly above the hatch to a maintenance compartment was the blinking red light that served to alert search and rescue teams that someone had taken refuge in the compartment and was waiting for help.

Nathan's mind swirled with the idea of a member of his crew trapped in that small compartment for over a month, waiting for rescue. As he wrestled with the door mechanism, trying to force it open, he could almost imagine someone in there, having long given up hope. He knew it was impossible, that no one could have survived in such a space for that long. Not even the cabins, which were designed to become emergency shelters in the case of sudden depressurization and could sustain someone for a month.

The latch finally gave and the door swung open. The smell hit him first—a mixture of spilled chemicals, burnt fabrics, and melted plastics... and the smell of rotting flesh. In the corner there were four bodies huddled together, buried under everything they could find in the compartment to try and insulate themselves from the freezing cold vacuum of space that had been just outside their hatch.

"Oh God," Nathan whispered as he peeled away

the pile of debris that covered the huddled bodies. There were three men and a woman. Two of the men and the woman were members of the fleet, all ensigns just as he had been at the time of the collision. The fourth man wasn't even in the fleet. He was a civilian technical specialist. Nathan imagined how they must have gotten cut off from the rest of the ship during the boarding attempt. The damage around them would've made it impossible to get further aft. This compartment had been the only place they could hide from the men with guns that had come aboard through the hole in the bow. It had to have been the absolute worst scenario anyone could have imagined, and they had lived it.

"*Oh, bozhe moi,*" Vladimir exclaimed as he came through the hatch. He looked at Nathan, who was reading something from a data pad he had taken off one of the dead crewmen.

"They were waiting for us to rescue them the whole time," Nathan mumbled. "They were in here for three days, Vlad. Three days, waiting and hoping... praying for help. They could probably hear the SAR teams searching..."

"It was a vacuum, Nathan," Vladimir interrupted. "They would not have heard..."

"They suffocated in here, alone and freezing. And where was I? Sitting in my ready room, eating lunch with some green-eyed alien woman, cozy and warm."

"Nathan," Vladimir began, trying to assuage his guilt, "you could not have known. The SAR teams could not have gotten this far. We barely made it this far now."

"I should have known," Nathan insisted. "I should have known what had happened to every member of my crew."

"There are still many of our original crew unaccounted for, Nathan."

"I need to take care of them," Nathan decided, rising to head for the hatch.

"Nathan," Vladimir said, putting out his hand to stop him, "go back to your drills. Let us take care of this."

"Get back to your repairs, Lieutenant Commander. That's an order," Nathan said as he pushed Vladimir's hand aside and headed out the hatch. "I'm going for some body bags."

Vladimir stood silently as Nathan stepped through the hatch and back into the corridor. He stared at the bodies, grotesquely deformed by the effects of hard vacuum and extreme temperatures, as he listened to Nathan make his way back through the debris. He reached up and tapped his comm-set, somberly speaking into the wire-thin microphone that hung down from his left ear along his cheek. "Comms, Cheng. Connect me to Karuzara command, please."

* * *

Other than his first two days, during which Lieutenant Commander Nash questioned him endlessly about his knowledge of Ta'Akar tactics, Travon Dumar had spent most of his first week on the Aurora cooped up in the intelligence shack. A large, dimly lit room, it was filled with workstations and displays that seemed constantly manned. Most of the work consisted of studying old communications traffic and past arrival and departure logs of Ta'Akar ships from both the Darvano system and her nearest neighbor, Savoy, only a light year away.

Other than the intel shack, his quarters, the galley, and the head were the only other spaces he regularly visited. So when Lieutenant Commander Nash asked him to inspect the dead Ta'Akar bodies found in the forward section of the ship, he welcomed the opportunity for a change of scenery. After ten days aboard the Aurora, he still had no idea if or when he might have an opportunity to get a good look at Redmond Tugwell in person, which had been his sole reason for volunteering in the first place.

The original hull breach had affected only the main deck, so his journey would be a short one. After traveling down the main ramp from the command deck on which the intel shack was located, to the main deck directly below, he made a U-turn and headed forward down the central corridor. As he approached the previously sealed off entrance to the forward section, he could see two men standing off to one side, talking. He recognized the man facing him as the Aurora's chief engineer, Lieutenant Commander Kamenetskiy, whom the crew normally referred to using the acronym 'Cheng'. However, the other man had his back to him. The second man was not wearing an Aurora uniform nor that of the Corinari, although the man's pants were of Corinari issue.

As he closed the distance between them, the unknown man's features became recognizable, even from behind. It was the same hair, the same build, the same mannerisms. It was the man he had been seeking, Redmond Tugwell, the leader of the Karuzari, the rebels who had plagued the Ta'Akar Empire for the last thirty years. He could not help but stare at the man's face as he walked by. He was older than Dumar remembered, much older, and his facial features had changed somewhat. It was possible they had been altered by whatever injuries he had sustained on that day thirty-seven years ago. The explosion Dumar had witnessed had been so immense, that there had never been any doubt that it had taken the life of this man. Yet here he stood, alive and talking.

"Gentlemen," Dumar greeted politely as he passed the two men in the corridor. Lieutenant Commander Kamenetskiy nodded acknowledgment of Dumar's greeting, but no reply was offered by the man going by the name of Redmond Tugwell. Their eyes did meet, however, even if only for a moment, before Dumar stepped through the hatch into the forward section.

Dumar kept his concentration, kept his composure, as he continued down the main corridor and to the left. The man he had just seen looked more like the father of the man he had once known. The father was deceased, of that he was sure. He had attended the father's funeral himself, as had countless others.

The man's eyes were what bothered him most. They were the same as he remembered, yet there was something unusual about them, something that he did not remember being present all those years ago. Dumar had seen it before in the eyes of men that had witnessed more pain and suffering than any one man should in his lifetime. It changed them. It took the magic and hope from their souls, replacing it with single minded purpose—usually survival.

Everything told Dumar that this man's name was not Redmond Tugwell. He was the man he had seen perish in a nuclear blast back in the Palee system nearly four decades ago. If he was that man, there was much that Travon Dumar was required to do, but he had to be sure. There was too much at stake now to risk making even the slightest of errors. The entire future of the Ta'Akar Empire and the worlds of the Pentaurus Cluster could rest on what Travon Dumar did in the very near future. He had to move carefully. He had to be cautious. Now was not the time to charge into action. Now was the time for careful planning, subtlety, and discretion. Action would come later, when he was certain beyond all doubt of the true identity of Redmond Tugwell.

* * *

Nathan had said nothing to the staff in medical when he came in to get the body bags; he had simply marched up to Doctor Chen and asked where they were stored. Everyone in the department had been smart enough not to inquire further. He expected they could all read it on his face, as could those he passed in the corridors on his return trip forward. They all simply assumed the appropriate position of attention as he passed and said nothing. Everyone except for Tug.

"Captain, a word?" Tug asked politely, cutting him off not ten meters from the entrance to the forward section.

"Can it wait, Tug?" Nathan asked. His tone of voice inferred that it was not a question, but more of a statement. "I'm a little busy right now."

"I am afraid it cannot," Tug insisted. He gestured to a nearby compartment, one of the empty offices that would eventually be used by the Corinari Aerospace Wing once it was officially assigned to the Aurora. Nathan glared defiantly at him. "I promise, it will not take long," Tug added.

Nathan knew enough about Tug to know that it would be hard to deny him his request. The man had a way about him, the ability to get others to do his bidding without having to issue direct orders. Nathan, however, was in no mood to be lectured, not by Tug or anyone else for that matter... not now.

Nathan turned and stepped into the compartment. Tug followed him through the hatch, closing it behind him to ensure privacy. When he did so, Nathan knew he was not going to like what the old man had to say.

"Is there something bothering you, Nathan?" Tug began.

"Yeah, you might say that," Nathan answered. "But you probably already know about the four half-frozen members of my crew lying in my bow right now. Otherwise you wouldn't be here."

"Yes, but I am not here about the four bodies you discovered," Tug explained, "I am here because of the way you are handling it."

"The way I'm handling it?" Nathan repeated, his irritation beginning to show. "I'm handling it by respectfully packaging up the bodies of my fallen crew. That's how I'm handling it!"

"You are handling it like a scrub ensign straight out of training!"

"I *am* a scrub ensign straight out of training! Remember?!" Nathan shouted back.

"Not anymore!" Tug shouted. "You are the captain of a warship, and on warships people die! You may not like it, and you certainly cannot change it, but you do have to deal with it."

"I didn't ask for any of this!" Nathan reminded him.

234

"Tough! Since when does life ask you what you want? Do you think I asked to lead a thirty-year rebellion? Do you think I asked to have my wife and my home taken from me? You arrogant little ass!" Tug spouted, finally losing his temper. "There are two hundred people on this ship and another hundred on their way, and they are all expecting *you* to lead them into battle. The captain of the ship does not carry out the wounded, and he does not cry over the dead, not even in private. He cannot afford to."

"Those people died waiting for rescue," Nathan pleaded, "a rescue that never came. That's my fault."

"Perhaps," Tug conceded, "but in the fog of war we make mistakes. That is why we train. That is why we drill, over and over again. So that when we are under fire, we do our jobs without thinking about the how, only the result. Your crew never had that training, Nathan, and neither did you. Just make sure that your new crew is as ready as you can make them."

Nathan stared at Tug for what seemed like an eternity to them both. Finally, Nathan picked up the body bags from the table and turned toward the exit. After two steps, he stopped and, without looking back, said, "My biggest regret is that those four did not get buried with the same honors as the rest of their shipmates."

As Nathan started for the exit again, Tug responded. "My biggest *fear* is that there will be many more opportunities to bury our bravely fallen, and much sooner than any of us would like."

Nathan paused and looked back at Tug. "Arrogant little ass, huh?" Nathan smiled. "That's what my sister, Miri, used to call me."

Nathan stepped through the hatch and continued the last ten meters to the entrance to the forward section. A team of four technicians were already in the compartment on the other side of the hatch. "Ensign," Nathan called to the one technician that was also a member of the Aurora's original crew, "take these bags forward and see to the bodies of our four crewmen," Nathan instructed, handing him the body bags.

"Yes, sir," the ensign answered.

"Take good care of them," Nathan added.

"Yes, sir, I will. I promise."

Nathan could tell by the look in the ensign's eyes that he would do just that. Satisfied by the ensign's response, he turned and started walking back toward the main ramps near the center of the ship, tapping his comm-set to open a channel. "Comms, Captain. Tell the COB break time's over. Have Deliza load up another simulation. I'll be there shortly."

* * *

"Mister Dumar," Jessica greeted as she entered the storage room, where he was going through the belongings collected from the dead Takaran soldiers earlier, "find anything interesting?"

"Possibly," he admitted. "Takaran boarding parties generally do not carry anything on them that would be of any use to the enemy. And most of the bodies were no exception. The body of the officer, however, might have provided something of use. I do not believe he was a member of the boarding party, at least not under normal circumstances. His unit patch was different than the others. He was a member of the support group, I believe you call them 'quartermasters'. I doubt he had any training in boarding actions. He was probably just the closest officer to the action at the time."

"Yeah, I helped fight them off," Jessica explained. "They didn't seem very organized. More like a 'Hey everybody, grab a gun and join us' kind of group."

"You may be right, Lieutenant Commander, and you should be thankful. Takaran boarding parties are not known for their failures."

"You see, that's useful intel. Why didn't you tell me that before?" she asked.

"You did not ask," Dumar responded.

Jessica grunted. "Yeah, you're an intelligence officer; that's for sure. So what *did* you find?"

"This," Dumar answered, holding up a small flat device not much bigger than the palm of his hand.

"What's this," she asked, "a data pad of some sort?"

"More of a communication pad. It is used for sending and receiving personal messages."

"You mean, like to friends and family?"

"Possibly, yes."

"But not for military messages?"

"Definitely not. The empire has a far more sophisticated messaging system than this. They use point-to-point messaging. These devices use broadcast topologies."

"Meaning they send it out to everyone, but only the person with the right address bothers to receive it."

"Precisely," Dumar confirmed.

"Yeah, not very secure. What do you make of it?"

Dumar studied the device for a moment. "My first concern was why he was carrying it on him. These are generally used while a ship is in port, and mostly only when they are in their home port of Takara to keep in touch with their families. Usually one would stow this in their personal locker for safe keeping. However, if he had only recently left port, he might have kept it on him for sentimental reasons, as they also store pictures and video clips to remind them of home. Many will do so for at least a few weeks, until they get over missing their families."

"But this happened in Taroa," Jessica pointed out. "That's, what, four light years from Takara? It would take months to make that journey."

"Three point nine light years, to be exact, and it would take approximately one hundred and forty-two days at top speed."

"So why was he carrying it on him?" Jessica wondered.

"The more important question would be: why was it encrypted?" Dumar asked. Jessica looked at him. "And not just any civilian encryption," Dumar added, "floating point, floating key, ten-thousand bit encryption."

"I'm not a crypto-geek," Jessica admitted, "but that sounds like some serious encryption to me."

"It is," Dumar assured her, "very much so."

Jessica continued studying the device as she spoke. "So why was a junior officer in a support unit, carrying around an encrypted personal messaging device while on a boarding action for which he was not trained, almost five months from home."

"My best guess is that he expected to send or receive a message from someone at any moment."

"But as I understood it, the Campaglia came out of FTL and went straight into her attack on the Karuzari encampment. That suggests that she was sent there from Takara for that express purpose."

"Agreed."

"The Karuzari?" Jessica wondered. "Maybe he was a mole, or a double agent."

"It is possible," Dumar agreed, "but it is also possible that he was planning on sending a message to friends or relatives, or even a mistress in the Taroa system. That is also a common practice among the nobles in Ta'Akar society."

"One in every port, huh?" Jessica joked.

"Excuse me?"

"An old Earth expression. Then you don't think it looks suspicious?"

"If it were not for the encryption, I would say no."

"Yeah, that makes you wonder, doesn't it? I'll have Ensign Willard take a crack at the encryption on this thing," she said. "Maybe there will be some messages still on it that will tell us something."

"Ensign Willard?" Dumar asked, trying to hide his curiosity. He remembered the late Captain de Winter mentioning the young mutineer before the captain had departed on his attempt to recapture his ship and take possession of the Aurora by force. "I do not remember seeing his name on the crew roster."

"He's not," Jessica explained. "He's the guy who led the mutiny on the Yamaro."

"A noble led a mutiny?" Dumar said, doing his best to sound surprised.

"Not a noble, a common officer. He's Corinairan, actually. He's been helping us out, providing us with intel and such."

"I see. What were his duties on the Yamaro?"

"Comms and crypto."

"Interesting, I can see how he might be of service. I would like to meet him someday and thank him for his brave actions. I am sure he saved countless Corinairan lives on that day—perhaps even my own."

"Listen," Jessica interrupted, suddenly having an idea, "you used to work in intel and mission planning and such, back when you served the Ta'Akar, right?"

"Yes, but that was many years ago."

"Tell me what you think of this idea. The Yamaro was due to stop in the Savoy system in a few weeks to pick up some inductees and ferry them back to Takara. Willard suggested that we use the Yamaro's transponders and pretend to be the Yamaro, go to the Savoy system and make the pick up using the Yamaro's shuttles. The captain thinks it could buy us some additional time to put together our little alliance before the Ta'Akar come a knockin'."

"Interesting idea," Dumar admitted.

"Do you think it'll work?"

"Yes, it might," Dumar agreed. "In Savoy it might. They are not as industrialized as the Darvano system."

"Yeah, that's what Willard said."

"But it is not without risk," Dumar warned. "If you *are* successful, it might buy you the extra time your captain seeks, but if unsuccessful, you could be losing time as well."

"Would you recommend it?" Jessica wondered as she picked up Mister Dumar's data pad and scanned the list of items found on the dead Takaran soldiers.

Dumar was very careful not to recommend Ensign Willard's plan with too much enthusiasm. A trip to the Savoy system might present him with a golden opportunity, but if he was too eager, the lieutenant commander might become suspicious of him as well. "The success of the mission hinges on two things. First, you must have a convincing officer and guards for the trip to Savoy. That will be key, as they will be speaking with the garrison staff directly when they pick up the conscripts. Second, if another Ta'Akar warship enters the system, you will be instantly exposed, as they *will* scan you to verify your identity, regardless of the ID codes your transponder is sending out."

"You didn't answer the question," Jessica said.

"I do not believe it is my place to make that call," Dumar defended. "However, the plan is sound and it could work. But, ultimately, it is up to the captain to decide if it is worth the risk."

"Nice. I like the way you worded your answer—again, like a true intelligence agent."

"It comes not from my work in intelligence," he assured her. "It is more from my work as a commodities speculator. It is never a good idea to tell a client where they should invest their money, but rather one should tell them the risks and rewards and let the client come to their own conclusions."

Jessica smiled. "Hey, I noticed that Takaran officer had an empty gun holster. They didn't find his weapon anywhere?"

"Not to my knowledge, no. I assumed it fell out of his hand as he was sucked out into space. As I said, he was not really trained for a boarding action."

"Right," Jessica remembered.

CHAPTER SEVEN

"Attention on deck," the guard called as Nathan entered the ready room.

"As you were," Nathan ordered as he made his way to his seat. "I trust you've all read Ensign Willard's proposal. I'd like to know if anyone has a problem with the idea."

"Sir, are you saying that we *are* going to do this?" Jessica asked.

"I'm seriously considering it," Nathan admitted. "Unless one of you can give me a good enough reason not to."

"How much more time do you really think it will give us?" Jessica wondered.

"Ensign Willard?" Nathan asked.

"It is impossible to say for sure, Captain. However, assuming that the Yamaro did not show up, and assuming another patrol ship arrived relatively soon afterward, it would only take that second ship one of your months to reach the Darvano system."

"Is there any way to know when the next patrol ship *will* show up in the Savoy system?" Nathan wondered.

"We've been monitoring communications from all over the cluster, sir," Jessica reported. "The Corinairans have also shared all their arrival and departure records. The Ta'Akar appear to keep at least one fairly regular patrol schedule. However, they also like to maintain a random patrol, surprising the systems within the cluster with irregular visits. They've even been known to double back a few days later just to check. Our best guess is that the Savoy system is due for a visit within the next month."

"Tug?" Nathan asked, wanting to get the opinion of the Karuzari leader.

"Lieutenant Commander Nash's assessment is accurate, at least as much as is possible."

"So, if the Yamaro doesn't show up, the worst-case scenario is that we get a visit one month later," Nathan surmised. "That would be about five to six weeks from now. What if a patrol ship doesn't show up, *and* they don't believe we're the Yamaro? How long do we have then?"

"It would take about two weeks for a message to reach Ta'Akar command," Ensign Willard stated. "At that point, they would either dispatch a ship from Takara—which would take about six months—or contact a ship that is already in the area which, again, could arrive within a month—even less if they happen to be close by."

"Sir, what bothers me is that we won't really know either way," Jessica pointed out. "Knowing we have to be ready to fight in a month requires a completely different build up than knowing we've got six months."

"I see your point," Nathan agreed, "but what can we do?"

"We could put a spy in the Savoy system," Jalea suggested. "We have been talking about trying to make contact with Karuzari that might be hiding out in the Savoy system. We just have not had a way to get anyone in place."

"What good would a spy be?" Jessica asked. "It

would take a year for a message to reach us."

"Not if you jumped into close proximity to the system," Jalea suggested.

"She may be right, Captain," Tug concluded. "We could set up regular contact appointments. We could jump in, wait for a broadcast from the agent on the surface, and then respond appropriately if a message is received."

"We don't know that the Aurora is always going to be available for such missions," Nathan warned.

"The Corinairans are making remarkable progress on the miniaturized version of the jump drive, Captain," Abby added. "They expect it will be ready for testing in another week or two."

"If it works, we could make regular contact jumps," Tug stated.

"Who would you send to the surface?" Nathan wondered.

"I would be the logical choice," Jalea offered.

"She does have extensive experience in covert intelligence," Tug pointed out. "And if there are still any Karuzari in the Savoy system, they will recognize Jalea and trust her."

Nathan looked at Jessica, well aware of her distrust for Jalea.

"As much as I hate to admit it," Jessica began, "it is a good idea. And it could turn out to be a really good idea, depending on what she learns."

"Are you sure you want to do this?" Nathan asked. "It sounds like it could be dangerous."

"No more so than before, Captain. I will be fine."

"How will we get you into the system?" Jessica asked.

"I can pose as an accountant for the Ta'Akar. They regularly send out investigators to keep their financial partners honest. I have used this ploy before with success."

"Such investigators are known to catch rides on warships, Captain," Ensign Willard pointed out. "It would not raise any suspicions if she were to accompany the team that would be going down to pick up the inductees from the garrison."

"In fact, it would probably serve to strengthen her credibility," Tug added.

"Ensign Willard," Nathan said, changing the direction of the conversation, "have you talked to your shipmates?"

"Yes, Captain. Although few were willing to take on such risk, there were enough that felt it was a worthwhile endeavor. I believe they will perform acceptably."

Nathan scanned the faces of everyone in attendance. "I have to admit that I was hesitant to take the risk before," he explained. "However, if we can get boots on the ground and get some real intel, especially an early warning of trouble headed our way, it makes the risk that much more acceptable." Nathan took one last look around the room, looking for any dissenting expressions. "Very well," he continued, sensing no opposition to the idea. "We've only got four days left to pull this off, and we've got a bit of work to do. If we're going to make this work, we need a plan. So let's get started."

* * *

Nathan's eyes widened as he entered one of the many rehabilitation suites in the Aitkenna hospital. There, in the middle of the room, was his executive officer, Cameron. She was dressed in an exercise suit and had some sort of virtual reality equipment strapped to her head, with a long cable running from the headgear to the ceiling above. She was reaching out and grabbing at the air, over and over again, as if trying to catch flies. Nathan watched for several seconds, trying to suppress his laughter, until finally he could no longer control himself. "Oh, God, please," he begged as he broke into semi-controlled laughter. "Tell me this is some kind of therapy, and that my XO hasn't lost it."

Cameron stopped the exercise cold, and placed her hands on her hips. "Drop dead... sir," she responded as she waited for the technician to come and remove the device from her head.

"What were you trying to catch?" Nathan asked.

"Little floating balls," Cameron answered.

"Why?"

"Hand-eye coordination testing, sir," the technician answered as he removed the apparatus from Cameron's head.

"Ah. Did she pass?"

"She always passes," the technician assured him.

Cameron flashed a sarcastic smile at him. "What are you doing here?"

"I brought the bodies of the four crewmen I found in the bow. The Corinairans are going to store them in their morgue until we have a chance to arrange a burial ceremony."

"You should have assigned that task to a junior officer, Nathan," Cameron scolded.

"And miss all this?" Nathan teased. "Actually, I did. I just hitched a ride. I needed to talk to you."

"About what?" Cameron inquired.

"Not here."

A few minutes later they were back in Cameron's room. As there was always a Corinari guard posted at the door, it was about as secure a location as they would find in the entire hospital on short notice.

"What's going on, Nathan? Why all the secrecy?"

Nathan handed her his data pad. She pressed her thumb to the biometric scanning window on the device to unlock it. Other than himself, Cameron, Jessica, and Vladimir were the only other people that had access to his data pad. "What's this, a mission brief?" she asked as she looked it over.

"Yeah, Jessica recommended we compartmentalize it—need to know and all that."

"Jessica thinks there are already spies on our new crew?"

"No, Jessica thinks there are spies everywhere."

Cameron's eyes widened as she read the mission brief. "You're going to masquerade as the Yamaro? Seriously?"

"It worked before," Nathan commented.

"We were pretending to be a Volonese cargo ship that no one had ever *seen* before, Nathan. This is not the same thing, not by a long shot, and you know it."

"Please, Commander, read on before you decide I'm a complete idiot," Nathan urged.

Cameron flashed another smirk at Nathan as she continued reading. "Do you really think we'll gain that much time if we pull this off?" she asked a few moments later.

"That's exactly what I thought, until Jalea suggested that she could remain there to gather intel and make contact with any Karuzari hiding in the system. If we're unsuccessful, at least she'll be able to warn us."

"That doesn't necessarily make it worth the risk, Nathan."

"No, you're right; it doesn't. But just putting Jalea on the ground there could be worth it. For all we know, word of what happened in the Darvano system may have already leaked out."

"I thought the Corinairans said that no other comm-drones had been dispatched."

"Yes, but in all the chaos, it *is* possible that they missed one. According to the logs that the Corinari gave Jessica, there were comm-drones leaving for various systems on a fairly regular basis. Most of them carried routine stuff: financial transactions, commodities reports, personal messages—that kind of thing. It would be nice to know if the closest system to Darvano still hasn't heard of the events here. It would make us all breathe a little easier."

"True, it might," Cameron agreed as she read on. "So you really think you can trust this Willard guy?"

"He's taking a bigger risk than any of us," Nathan pointed out. "He's guaranteed a swift execution as a mutineer if he's apprehended by the Ta'Akar. If he was smart, he'd find a hole somewhere and hide."

"Both Tug and Jessica are for this?"

"Yes, but more because it puts boots on the ground to gather intel. I'm not too sure Jessica's happy about Jalea being the one wearing those boots, but she is the best person for the job." Nathan noted the look of concern on Cameron's face. "What is it?"

"I just wish I could be there."

"Why? I wish I could stay here," Nathan joked.

"Every time you guys jump away, I'm sure I'm going to be stuck here forever, waiting for the

Ta'Akar to come and glass the planet."

"How much longer do they want to keep you here?" Nathan asked.

"A few weeks at least," she answered.

"Don't worry," Nathan assured her. "I'll make sure Abby's finger is on the jump button the entire time we're in the Savoy system." Nathan leaned back in his chair, taking a deep breath and changing the subject. "Now, enough about the Savoy mission. I've got a few other ideas I want to talk to you about."

* * *

The Corinairan sun had set an hour ago, and the air had already taken on a chill, made colder still by the winds sweeping across the open grounds of the spaceport. Winter, it seemed, was coming earlier than usual this year. The spaceport was poorly lit this night. Damage to the city's power generation facilities had made Aitkenna reliant on massive portable generators located throughout the city. Unfortunately, they were not enough to meet the normal demands of the burgeoning population of one of the planet's largest cities. The spaceport alone had four dedicated generators running, and even that was not enough to light all areas at once.

The poor lighting was to their advantage, however, as no one wanted to advertise their presence at the spaceport. Ensign Willard had been dressed in a standard uniform from the Aurora, while the eight Corinairan volunteers from the Yamaro's crew had been dressed in civilian attire prior to being smuggled out of the detention facility where the entire crew of the Takaran warship was being held. There were still those among the population of Aitkenna that might blame the crew of the Yamaro for the destruction rained down upon their city weeks ago. All had thought it best to avoid such problems.

"Attention on deck," Ensign Willard announced as the captain approached the waiting shuttle.

"Ensign," Nathan greeted as he approached, Sergeant Weatherly and his security detail following closely behind.

Ensign Willard snapped a salute, doing his best to keep up appearances as he tried to emulate the salute used by the crew of the Aurora. "The volunteers are ready for boarding, Captain."

"Very good. As you were, gentlemen." Nathan stopped and looked over the group of men, all members of the Yamaro's crew, all of them also having fought to liberate the Aurora from the hands of the Ta'Akar. "I want to thank you all for volunteering for this mission. Each of you has already done more than your part. Ironically, all of you fired the first retaliatory shots on behalf of your home world. Yet, here you all stand, unrewarded, imprisoned on the very same world you risked your lives to protect. I'm sure you've all been told time and time again how it's for your own safety." Nathan looked them over once more. "Yeah, I wouldn't have bought that either." He took a deep breath before continuing. "I cannot promise you your immediate freedom upon your return, nor the freedom of your shipmates. However, I can offer you a chance to work on the Yamaro as free men, or perhaps even on the Aurora as members of my crew. You will not be required to serve in either capacity, and you may choose to return to the detention center if you desire, until this conflict is over. The choice will be yours. But I promise you this much; you *will* have a choice, as will all of your shipmates. On this you have my word."

There was no response from the volunteers as they stood at ease in a precise line, just as they had been trained by their former leaders, the Ta'Akar. A few hopeful glances were exchanged among them, but no words were spoken.

"Load them up, Ensign," Nathan ordered. At the slightest of gestures from Sergeant Weatherly, two of his security detail went up the boarding ramp first, checking that the shuttle was secure.

"Gentlemen," Ensign Willard began, "pick up your gear and board the shuttle single file, and move briskly to the rear. Leave the last two rows empty. Move out."

The volunteers picked up the gear bags containing the Ta'Akar uniforms that had been taken from the Yamaro's supply lockers. The armor and weapons they would need to complete the masquerade would be waiting for them aboard the two shuttles that had been taken from the Yamaro and were now sitting in the main hangar deck of the Aurora.

Nathan stood fast against the chilling wind as he watched the volunteers file up the boarding ramp. Sergeant Weatherly moved next to the captain, also watching the men as they boarded. "Those men are either really brave, or they really hate that detention center," Nathan mused.

"They're brave, sir," the sergeant responded. "Trust me; I've fought alongside them."

* * *

"Open space in one minute," Loki reported.
"Threat board?" Nathan asked.

"Telemetry from Karuzara shows the system is clear, sir," Jessica reported. "All traffic has been identified. No tracks in the area of Karuzara or Cleo."

"Very good."

"Thirty seconds to open space," Loki updated.

Nathan watched the forward view screens as the last few hundred meters of the exit corridor from the Karuzara asteroid base slid past. It had been weeks since the Aurora had actually been out in space, and despite all the trouble they had run into since leaving Earth more than a month ago, it felt good to get underway again.

"Open space," Loki announced.

"Switching to live scans," Ensign Yosef reported.

"Helm, set course for Savoy and increase speed smoothly to ten percent light," Nathan ordered.

"Aye, Captain," Josh answered. "Changing course for Savoy. Coming up smoothly to ten percent light. Time to first jump point, ten minutes."

"Very well," Nathan confirmed. "Doctor Sorenson, our first jump will take us to just outside the Savoy system, correct?"

"Yes, sir. Twelve hours beyond the system's heliopause, to be exact."

"I'd like to linger there a bit before going in."

"Yes, sir," Abby answered.

"Captain?" Jessica started to question.

"I think it would be a good idea to take a series of long-range scans before heading into the system. Take a good, long look so we can verify that Ensign Willard's recommendations are sound."

Jessica looked quizzical. "You don't trust him?" she asked.

"It's not that I don't trust him," Nathan explained. "I just think it would be prudent to verify intelligence,

even from a reliable source, before acting upon it."
When he did not get a response from Jessica, he
turned his chair around to face her. "I'd expect that
you of all people would agree."

"Oh, I agree, sir," Jessica was quick to say. "I'm
just surprised to hear you say it."

"What can I say? I guess being captain has made
me more cautious."

"That'll be the day," Jessica mumbled to herself
as Nathan began to turn back around.

"Besides, Commander Taylor insisted on it," he
admitted. "Something about regulations."

"Yeah, that makes a little more sense," Jessica
stated.

"Ensign Yosef, how much time will it take to get a
detailed sweep of the system using passive sensors?"
Nathan asked.

"At least thirty minutes, sir," Ensign Yosef
responded. "An hour would be better."

"Very well," Nathan said. "An hour it is."

* * *

Tug paced up and down the line of eight men
in Ta'Akar security uniforms, checking them over
one by one as he spoke. "The Ta'Akar always look
polished and impressive when they arrive. This
helps promote a sense of order and efficiency, and
it serves to remind those that they have conquered
who is in charge. As a Ta'Akar soldier, you must
always appear confident and self-assured. Your
eyes must not shift about. Your expression must
not falter. You must at all times appear confident
in your knowledge that no one would be foolish
enough to oppose you and the mighty empire that

you represent."

Tug stopped pacing, standing front and center to face the line of men. "Remember the day that you were inducted. Remember standing on the tarmac as those fearless men marched out of the shuttles. Remember feeling as though your life were about to end. Those men never raised a weapon or even looked at you, yet you feared for your very lives. *That* is how the Ta'Akar operate. *That* is how they maintain discipline, through the knowledge that any and all disobedience will be met with extreme force."

"*Attention all hands*," Naralena's voice announced over the loudspeakers in the hangar bay. "*Prepare for jump.*" The volunteers from the Yamaro's crew glanced at one another. Thus far, the jump drive had been a rumor which many of them had begun to dismiss as another Corinairan legend.

"Now, we will go through the drills again and again, ensuring that you all move as one unit, the way that you were taught during your basic training on Takara."

"*Jumping in three......two......one......jump,*" Abby's voice announced.

Tug watched the faces of the men in the line, none of whom had ever experienced a jump before. To his knowledge, no one other than Marcus had ever described any sensation as a result of a jump. The men looked at each other, wondering if anyone had felt anything.

"*Jump complete,*" Abby announced.

"In case you're wondering, we are now positioned approximately twelve light hours outside the Savoy system," Tug told them. As he had anticipated, looks of disbelief spread across their faces. It was certainly not in keeping with their expected performance as

Ta'Akar security troops.

"Attention on the line!" Ensign Willard barked in perfect Ta'Akar. It was so perfect, in fact, that the men snapped to attention as if they were back aboard the Yamaro getting yelled at by a nobleman.

Tug looked at Ensign Willard, who had just arrived. He was wearing a Ta'Akar officer's uniform, complete with the sash of his house's lineage, just as any nobleman in the Takaran Imperial Forces would wear. "You're getting into character nicely," Tug said with a grin. "You wear the sash of your house well."

"Don't remind me," Ensign Willard stated with obvious disgust. "I was sincerely hoping to never wear such uniforms again."

"Hopefully this will be the last time," Tug agreed.

* * *

Jessica made her way briskly down the command deck's main corridor. It was a short distance to the office they had turned into the 'intel shack'. There was an actual intelligence section designed into the main deck, just forward of the primary bulkheads, but they had been inaccessible for the last month due to the rupture in the Aurora's bow. The office they had been using had actually been the XO's office, which Cameron had never gotten around to utilizing. Since Jessica also had to serve as the tactical officer on the bridge, the shack's close proximity made it quite convenient.

Jessica had spent so much of her time managing the security of the ship over the last few weeks that she had done little actual intelligence work. Although she lived for field operations, she did enjoy the analytical side of the intelligence world as well. Transmissions were perhaps the most common source of intelligence for the Aurora, and while flying through the Savoy system, they would have the perfect opportunity to gather more information about the state of things in this corner of the Pentaurus cluster. The Savoy system was only a light year from Darvano, which made it of particular interest, and until now all the signals intelligence they had gathered on this system was at least one year old.

With Jalea going to Ancot to gather intel on the ground and make contact with any Karuzari hiding out there, it was even more important for Jessica to better understand the state of affairs within the system. She still didn't trust Jalea, and Jessica wanted to be prepared to second guess any intel Jalea sent their way.

Jessica stepped through the hatch into the intel shack. It was a medium-sized office, with several desks against the walls and numerous monitors affixed to every vertical surface. There were always at least three people on duty, usually two signals technicians and an analyst. Until Travon Dumar had joined the crew, Jessica had been about the only analyst available. She hadn't minded the extra work, as she did enjoy it, but she was going on several weeks of insufficient sleep, and she could tell it was catching up to her. However, Mister Dumar was picking things up nicely. It may have been a long time since he was in the intelligence business with the Ta'Akar, but his post-service career as a commodities consultant seemed to have kept his analytic eye for details fairly sharp. She was sure that, given a few more weeks, he would be able to take over as the senior intelligence analyst for the Aurora. At least then she could start getting a good night's sleep for a change.

"Mister Dumar," she greeted as she entered the room, "any luck breaking the encryption on that messaging unit you found on our frozen bad guy?"

"Not yet, I am afraid. I am hoping that after this mission is completed, Ensign Willard will be able to assist."

"You might have Deliza take a look at it as well," Jessica suggested, "when we get back to Karuzara, of course."

"Deliza?"

"The young lady programming the bridge simulations, Tug's daughter."

"I did not realize she was Mister Tugwell's daughter," Dumar stated.

"Yeah, she's a whiz with computers and stuff, so she might be some help as well. So would the Cheng."

"He is also good with computers?"

"Yup," Jessica responded. "He hacked the Aurora's mainframe and turned her off during the last boarding attempt. Probably saved all our butts."

"I will be sure to enlist his assistance as well."

"Come to think of it, he might not have the time. There's still a lot of systems left to install to bring this ship as close to her original design specs as possible."

"I see."

"So," Jessica said, "anything else going on around here?"

"I was just about to deliver Miss Torren's ID papers and letter of authorization. She will need them to get past the guards at the Ancot spaceport.

I also thought I might go by the galley and pick up something to eat while I can, if that is acceptable?"

"Sure. I've got nothing to do on the bridge for another forty minutes. I might as well hang out here. Go ahead and take a break; I'll cover the shack until you return."

"Thank you, Lieutenant Commander." He picked up the documents and started for the hatch.

"Hey, pick me up a sandwich while you're there," Jessica told him.

"A sandwich?" Mister Dumar wondered, again finding himself unfamiliar with a word.

"It's like you guys dropped all the best words from the English language when you made Angla," she complained. "A sandwich. You know, two pieces of bread with some kind of dressing smeared on them, some meat and cheese in the middle, maybe some veggies shoved in there as well."

"I will ask the cook," Mister Dumar promised. "Surely he will know what you are referring to."

"Don't count on it," Jessica mumbled as he left the room. "The guy knows nothing about cooking Earth food."

* * *

Now that the Aurora was underway and there were no longer hordes of technicians coming and going all day, the number of Corinari security personnel roaming the corridors had been greatly reduced. Although all the guards were still on board, most were off duty during the mission. There were, however, still guards protecting the entrances to critical areas of the ship, such as the main hangar bay. If there were ever a time to make his move, this was it.

Dumar made his way aft through the hangar deck toward the two Takaran shuttles parked near the aft end of the bay. As he approached, he noticed Tug conducting another inspection of the team that was headed to Ancot under the guise of picking up inductees on behalf of the Yamaro. Dumar had been briefed on the details of the Savoy mission, and he knew that Mister Tugwell would be required on the bridge to conduct communications with the garrison on Ancot. Other than Ensign Willard and himself, Tug was the only male on board the Aurora who could speak Takaran well enough to be convincing as a communications officer from the Yamaro. Naralena did speak Takaran, but women were not allowed to serve in the Ta'Akar Empire's military, and Ensign Willard would be departing on the shuttles at the same time. So Tug was it, and that meant that soon, he would be heading for the bridge.

"Mister Dumar," Jalea greeted, catching him by surprise, "I was about to come see you."

"Ah, Miss Torren. I have the documents that you requested," Dumar stated politely, handing them over.

"Thank you, Mister Dumar. You saved me a trip."

"Your identity will be that of Analise Devonshire," Dumar explained to Jalea. "The details of your cover are on the data chip. You should memorize them during your flight and then securely delete them from the chip."

"I am well versed in field procedures, Mister Dumar," Jalea assured him.

"Of course. My apologies. You are employed by the Royal Bank of Takara as a senior field auditor. I trust you know your way around interstellar banking and accounting so as to be convincing."

"I believe so, yes," Jalea assured him.

"These are your ident cards and your data chip carrying your statement of authority and your power of audit as granted by your employers. It should be more than enough to convince the inspectors at the spaceport on Ancot. I would advise against using them any further than that, however."

Jalea looked over the ident cards, then inserted the data chip into her reader and inspected the statements stored on the chip. "Impressive work, Mister Dumar," she praised. "Did you create these yourself?"

"Yes," he assured her. "Documents of such a nature require individual attention to ensure no detail is overlooked."

"Most impressive," she repeated as she removed the chip and placed it in her ident card wallet, which went into the pocket of her long, flowing overcoat.

"Thank you. You are too kind."

"I will be sure to commit the details to memory before we arrive on Ancot," she promised. "You know, you would have made an excellent Karuzari, Mister Dumar," she added.

"Too dangerous a line of work for my tastes, I'm afraid."

"Yet here you are, in equal danger," Jalea added.

"Perhaps," Dumar admitted. "A safe journey to you, Miss Devonshire," he added with a wry smile.

"To us all, Mister Dumar," Jalea answered as she turned and headed for the shuttle.

Dumar watched Jalea exit. It was ironic that only a few weeks ago, he not only would have killed her on the spot without hesitation, but he would have been greatly honored for doing so.

Having confirmed Tug's location, Dumar made a discrete withdrawal from his vantage point, making his way back toward the front of the hangar bay. After a few moments, he was through the starboard hatch and was making his way down the corridor. He followed it around to the front of the main hangar bay, where the center hatchway leading into the bay was usually secured for security reasons and was rarely used. Fortunately, there were no guards in the short section of corridor that led from the starboard side of the hangar bay to the center corridor where the ramps were located. As soon as he turned the corner and was out of sight of the guards, he stepped quickly through an open hatch and into a darkened compartment. From there, tucked discretely behind a counter, he would be able to see when Tug rounded the same corner on his way to the bridge. Satisfied with his position, he settled in to wait.

* * *

Tug stepped away from the shuttles as their boarding ramps retracted and the warning lights on their undersides began to flash. The first shuttle rolled out into the over-sized center transfer airlock, pulling to its left to make room for the second shuttle following behind it. Tug watched as the second shuttle pulled in carefully to the right of the first and pulled to a stop. No sooner had it done so than the massive airlock door began to lower into its closed position.

After several days of repeated drills, Tug was satisfied that the volunteers were as convincing as Takaran soldiers as he could make them. At this point, he felt they would benefit more by a short break before their mission began than by continued practice. Soon enough they would receive their launch orders and their dangerous masquerade would begin.

As he stepped through the starboard hatch from the main hangar bay to the starboard corridor, he couldn't help but worry. However, he felt confident that they would fool the idiots at the garrison. A posting at the Ancot garrison in Savoy was not exactly a prestigious assignment for any noble. Hence, it was reasonable to assume that the officer in charge of the garrison would not be the most efficient commander in the empire. Additionally, Jalea's business suit was tight enough and sufficiently revealing in all the right places as to adequately distract the officer in charge at the spaceport on Ancot. Jalea had always been quite good at utilizing her charms in such a manner. It was one of the reasons she was such an effective field operative. Unfortunately, it also made her a dangerous ally, and Tug had come close to being cut by that double-edged sword on more than one occasion.

Tug turned the corner from the starboard corridor into the short passageway that led inward to the main central corridor. It was at that moment that he silently cursed himself for letting his own thoughts distract him to the extent that he hadn't noticed the movement behind him until it was too late; there was already a weapon pressing against his right flank.

"Step into the next compartment, Mister Tugwell... and do not make a sound," Dumar whispered from behind.

* * *

Jessica continued examining the sensor logs from the series of recon jumps the Aurora had nearly completed. So far, the interplanetary traffic within the system had been just as Ensign Willard had expected, all within the orbit of the Savoy system's most distant planet, Deikon. As he had indicated, it was a super-massive gas giant that would easily hide their jump flash upon arrival in the system.

Jessica looked at her watch again. She had about fifteen minutes until the Aurora reached her parking spot at one of Deikon's gravity points, and although there was not really much for her to do on the bridge when they did arrive, she still felt that she should be there, especially since Tug was going to be making a radio call to the garrison on Ancot.

Jessica tapped her comm-set to make a call. "Dumar, Nash." She waited a moment but got no response. "Dumar, Nash. Do you copy?"

One of the technicians noticed Jessica checking her watch for the third time in just as many minutes. "Worried about the mission, sir?"

"Hell no," Jessica responded without hesitation. "I just want my sandwich."

Her response was not one of bravado at all. In fact, she was not worried. She had been born into a large family filled with sons, eight of them in fact. She had been the only daughter, and the youngest of them all. They had lived in the everglades along the coast of the Floridian peninsula. As a child, it seemed that not a day had gone by that one of her brothers hadn't come home with some kind of injury. She had always been surprised that her mother hadn't worried more about what her brothers were up to that always seemed to result in injury. She remembered her mother once saying that if the day ever came that none of her boys came home injured, that would be the day that she would start to worry. 'Worrying' was simply something that a 'Nash' did not do.

Patience was also something that didn't come naturally to a Nash; at least not to Jessica. "Where the hell is that guy?" she mumbled as she looked at her watch a fourth time. She leaned forward and logged onto the workstation in front of her. As soon as she was online, she called up the crew tracking interface and requested the location of Travon Dumar. Much to her surprise, the system showed him not in the galley, but in one of the pilot's ready rooms—the very same room where Doctor Chen had nearly died during the attempt to capture the Aurora by the command staff of the Yamaro. "What the hell?" She noticed someone else in the room with Dumar and tapped on the other person's icon to display their identity. It was Tug... She suddenly had a bad feeling.

Jessica quickly logged out and rose to leave. "I'll be back in a few minutes," she announced on her way out.

"What do we do if we discover something in the scans?" the technician asked.

"That's what comm-sets are for," she answered as she stepped quickly through the hatchway.

* * *

Travon Dumar closed the hatch behind him, keeping his weapon trained on Tug the entire time.

"What is this about?" Tug asked. "Where did you get that weapon?"

"Security aboard this ship is not as tight as everyone seems to believe," Dumar explained as he relieved Tug of his sidearm. "But that is not germane to the matter at hand."

Tug circled to his right, maintaining his distance from Dumar as the man with the weapon moved to Tug's left, deeper into the dimly lit compartment. "What matter might that be?" Tug asked, trying to buy time. Sooner or later, someone would notice than one or both of them were not where they were supposed to be. If he could survive until then, he had a chance. He considered attacking the man, but Dumar was armed, and his movements spoke of considerably more training than his original resume had revealed.

"The matter of your true identity," Dumar explained.

"My true identity?" Tug repeated. "You mean the one that I announced to the entire population of Darvano? That is hardly a secret any longer."

"Remove your shirt," Dumar ordered.

"My shirt?" Tug asked, confused.

"Your shirt," Dumar repeated, "remove it, slowly if you please."

"I possess no other weapons, I assure you."

"Many years ago," Dumar began, gesturing for Tug to do as he asked, "there was a training flight. The lead pilot made an abrupt course change directly in front of his wingman. The two ships collided and both pilots had to eject."

"I'm afraid you have mistaken me for someone else," Tug said. He did not know the identity of this man, this Travon Dumar. Until he did, he dared not reveal anything more about his own past than necessary.

"It was a reckless, irresponsible maneuver on the lead pilot's part," Dumar continued, ignoring Tug's words, "but he was young and arrogant back then. His wingman suffered serious chest trauma that required emergency surgery. The lead pilot felt so guilty that he cut his own chest with his father's blade, the one that he carried with him for luck, so that he would never forget his arrogance."

Tug opened his shirt and revealed his chest. There, buried under the graying chest hair of an old man, was a thick scar that went from below his left clavicle down across his chest.

Dumar's eyes widened, his mouth falling agape at the sight of the scar.

"How do you know this?" Tug answered. "Do we know each other?"

"This is impossible," Dumar exclaimed in disbelief. "I saw your ship explode. You took a direct hit from a nuclear-tipped missile. No one could've escaped that."

Tug began to become concerned. There were only two people present all those decades ago when that mysterious spacecraft had appeared out of nowhere and killed his wingman and very nearly killed Tug. His wingman, who had himself just taken a devastating hit, and the pilot of the attacking craft, the one that had been waiting in ambush, the one that had known exactly when and where he and his wingman were to be...

The assassin.

Tug instinctively began to move to attack, but Dumar's hand was too quick, bringing his weapon up high and ready to fire. There was too much distance between them and there was no way Tug could close the gap and strike before Dumar could cut him down. There would be no escape for this assassin, but Tug was sure that his opponent was already aware of that. Such men were about the mission, nothing more.

"So, after more than thirty years," Tug stated, "you have finally come to finish the job."

Dumar ripped open his shirt. "I have come," Dumar began, emotion filling his voice, "to fulfill my obligation to protect my leader."

Tug looked in Dumar's eyes. They were full of emotion, of years of regret and torment. Then Tug's own eyes wandered down to Dumar's open shirt, where he found a surgical scar leading from the base of his neck down to his belly. Tug's mouth dropped open in disbelief. "Max?"

"Commander," Dumar responded, his weapon slowly lowering, "is it really you?"

"Yes, Maxwell, it is," Tug answered. He could not believe what he was hearing. The man standing before him had the eyes of his old friend and wingman, but not the face. "But you... your face..."

"But how, how could you possibly have survived?"

"I jumped into FTL at the last moment," Tug explained.

"But you never returned."

"I was injured, my ship damaged and adrift. To this very day I still do not know for how long. I ended up stranded on Haven. By the time I learned the truth about what had happened, it was too late. The empire had already conquered the core and most of the surrounding systems. There was nothing I could do," Tug pleaded.

"You could have contacted me," Dumar insisted. "I could have helped you."

"I thought you were dead as well," Tug explained.

Ryk Brown

"As far as I knew, the only man I could trust was dead. All others had betrayed me."

"But you lead the Karuzari..."

"Eventually I could no longer stand idly by and watch the empire subjugate the galaxy one system at a time."

"All this time, I thought I had failed you," Dumar confessed.

"You did not fail me, my friend. You were as equally betrayed as I," Tug insisted. "Surely you came to the same conclusions."

"Over time, yes," Dumar admitted, "but it was difficult to believe, and by then it was too late. I had already fought in so many campaigns in the name of Caius. The very thought of it sickens me now." Dumar paused, looking at Tug. "There is something you should know, Commander."

"Do not call me that," Tug warned. "My name is Redmond Tugwell."

"Hardly a name befitting a nobleman of your..."

"Enough!" Tug urged sternly. "The walls might have ears."

"Of course," Dumar promised, realizing his stupidity.

"What was it you wished to tell me?" Tug asked in a low voice.

"I was the leader of the Anti-Insurgency forces on Corinair. I was responsible for the attacks against this ship. But when I realized who you were, I aborted the attack and I destroyed all..."

"Do not speak further of it," Tug warned. "Not yet. There will come a time."

Dumar's gun hand fell to his side. Tug placed his left hand on Dumar's shoulder. "The time has come for us to fight together once again." Tug looked

Dumar in the eyes. "Are you with me, my old friend?"

"Need you ask?" Dumar responded.

"Drop the gun," Jessica's voice came from the half-opened hatch. "Do it now."

Neither man moved.

"Drop it... I'll drop you both if I have to."

"Do as she says," Tug whispered.

Dumar dropped the weapon to the deck.

"Hands behind your head and two steps backward," Jessica ordered. "You too, Tug."

"But..." Tug started to protest.

"I'm not asking twice," Jessica warned.

Tug knew better than to take a warning from Jessica Nash lightly. He had seen her in action on more than one occasion. He, too, raised his hands and placed them behind his head, stepping backward the same as Dumar.

Jessica stepped through the hatch, her gun held high, pushing the hatch closed with her foot afterward. "What the hell is going on here?"

"It is not what you think," Tug insisted.

"I sure as fuck hope not," she stated. "What do you have to say for yourself, Dumar?—which I'm pretty sure is *not* your real name."

"His name is Ridley," Tug stated. "Travon Ridley. He is a deep cover operative for the Karuzari."

"A deep cover operative," Jessica responded. "Bullshit."

"It is true," Dumar added.

"Then why didn't Tug recognize you when you first came on board?"

"His identity was changed after he departed to ensure his cover."

"I was waiting until the right moment to make contact," Dumar explained.

"He has intimate knowledge of the operations of the Ta'Akar," Tug insisted.

"Yeah? How is that?" Jessica asked, still not quite believing their story.

"My assignment was to infiltrate the Takaran Anti-Insurgency Command on Corinair. It was I that took them out and aborted the last missile moments before it would have destroyed your vessel," Dumar explained.

"Really?" Jessica said. "And why should I believe either of you?"

"You do not have to," Tug conceded. "You could simply shoot us both now. It would be the safest thing to do."

"Maybe," Jessica admitted. "But I actually *do* trust you," she said to Tug as she lowered her weapon. "And besides, *this* asshole still owes me a sandwich," she added, holstering her weapon.

* * *

"I've been looking at the scans, sir," Jessica reported. Nathan quickly returned to her side in order to view her display. "Just as Ensign Willard stated, there doesn't appear to be any traffic beyond Deikon. Not much reason for it, really. Nothing but ice and rock out there, and very little of that. However, Deikon's current position puts it uncomfortably close to Ancot, which means any ship near it would be more easily imaged than usual."

"What if we come in a little fast, right behind Deikon, and then shoot out past it? We could slow down and settle into stellar orbit just beyond Deikon."

"Captain," Ensign Yosef interjected, "I would

suggest an alignment that puts Deikon nearly between us and Ancot. If the alignment is just right, direct imaging of us would be nearly impossible due to interference from the gas giant."

"What about communications?"

"They might be somewhat garbled, but still possible," she answered. "Again the alignment must be just right."

"It will probably look like the Yamaro's navigator screwed up and came in off his mark," Loki commented.

"I guess we're going to have to ruin de Winter's reputation," Nathan joked. "Plot the course and prepare to jump."

"Yes, sir," Loki acknowledged.

"It makes it a bit farther for the shuttles to travel," Tug observed. "They will require refueling on Ancot before returning."

"Well, those shuttles look more the part than we do," Nathan observed. "I think the risk is lower this way."

"Agreed," Tug said.

"Comms," Nathan called, turning toward Naralena, "update the shuttle crews as to our change in plans, and make sure Ensign Willard knows they will have to refuel before returning."

"Yes, sir," Naralena answered.

"I have the course for a stellar orbit just beyond Deikon plotted and locked, Captain," Loki reported.

"Helm, change course and take us in," Nathan ordered.

"Altering course now, Captain," Josh reported.

"Abby?"

"Thirty seconds to a plot, Captain."

"Comms, activate the Yamaro's transponder

array," Nathan ordered. "And ask Lieutenant Commander Kamenetskiy to double-check that thing to be sure it's working properly *before* we jump."

"Yes, sir." Naralena called up the Yamaro's transponder array that had been recently installed by Ensign Willard and Lieutenant Commander Kamenetskiy.

"Jump plotted," Abby added.

"Cheng reports the transponder is working as expected," Naralena reported. "I also checked with the shuttle crews as well, Captain, and they are picking up the Yamaro's transponder signal.

"Good thinking." Nathan looked around the bridge, fighting the urge to make some witty remark, knowing that if he did so he would catch hell from Tug.

"Captain," Jessica called, "I suggest we set general quarters before jumping."

"I thought the scans showed no hostiles in the system?" Nathan asked.

"Yes, sir, but that data is twelve hours old. For all we know, a battleship could've arrived during that time," she explained. "Better safe than sorry."

"Very well," Nathan agreed. "Comms, set general quarters."

Naralena keyed up the ship-wide alert system. A moment later, the lighting in the bridge changed, taking on a red hue, and the alert klaxon sounded. Another moment later a prerecorded voice announced *"General quarters! General quarters! All hands, man your battle stations!"*

Nathan glanced at his watch and waited patiently, knowing that, throughout the ship, his new crew of Corinairan volunteers were rushing to their assigned stations. Weapons stations would be manned. Damage control parties would be positioned throughout key areas of the ship. Additional staff would report to the engineering, power generation, and life support compartments. Even medical would swing into action, sending quick response teams to strategic locations throughout the ship. In a few more weeks, they'd even have fighters preparing for quick-shot launches in the fighter alleys on either side of the main hangar bay. After operating with only thirty some odd crew for nearly a month, it felt good to have at least one full shift available.

"All compartments report manned and ready, Captain," Jessica reported. "All four reactors are online and are running at fifty percent. Chief of the boat is in Damage Control."

"Very well," Nathan answered. He looked at his watch. One minute even. Much better than their time on the last drill. "Doctor, jump the ship to Savoy."

"Attention all hands. Prepare to jump," Abby announced ship-wide. "Jumping in three......two......one......jump."

The bridge instantly filled with the blue-white flash of the jump, disappearing just as quickly. The reddish-orange gas giant, Deikon, suddenly filled the port side of the main view screen as the planet streaked past them at rather close range, momentarily filling the bridge with an eerie reddish-orange cast.

"Whoa," Dumar exclaimed with a start, flinching slightly as the massive planet slid past. His eyes were wide, having never witnessed a jump before. Until recently, he had only known linear faster-than-light propulsion, which required months to traverse the relatively short distances between the star systems of the empire. "Incredible," Dumar mumbled to himself.

"Yes, it is," Tug responded under his breath.

"Cutting it a little close, aren't you, Doctor?" Nathan stated.

"The new emitters are quite precise, Captain," Abby defended. "And we were trying to hide our jump flash, were we not?"

"Yes, but maybe a few more kilometers next time," Nathan said. "Or at least warn us first."

"Of course, sir."

"It's okay, sir," Loki reported. "We're plenty far away. Deikon is just a *really* big gas giant."

"Yeah, I can see that," Nathan agreed.

"Coming up on insertion point for stellar orbit," Josh reported. "Beginning deceleration."

"Remember, you're a Takaran warship, so try not to burn any more fuel than necessary, just in case anyone is watching. You have to protect Captain de Winter's reputation," Nathan mused.

"Uh, you mean the guy who shot me, right?" Josh remarked.

Nathan recognized the sarcasm in Josh's voice and patted him on the shoulder. "Yeah, that guy."

"What do we do if someone calls us?" Jessica asked.

"Ensign Willard assured me that no one in the system would hail the Yamaro first. They would only answer if the Yamaro called them," Nathan explained. "I guess the residents prefer not to call attention to themselves. We will have to contact the garrison on Ancot before we launch our shuttles, however."

"Ensign Willard has briefed me on the proper frequencies and protocols, sir," Naralena announced. "However, Mister Tugwell will handle the communications, as there would not be a female serving aboard a Ta'Akar warship."

"Understood," Nathan acknowledged. "Helm, time to orbit?"

"Five minutes, sir," Loki responded.

"Very well. Comms, tell the shuttles to prepare for launch."

"Yes, sir," Naralena answered.

"Tug, are you ready?" Nathan asked.

Tug stepped up next to Naralena at the comm station. "I am ready," he said confidently.

Naralena finished updating the shuttle pilots and Ensign Willard. She then set up the frequency and encryption according to the instructions given to her by Ensign Willard, who had been a communications technician aboard the Yamaro right up until the moment he had led the mutiny that resulted in her surrender. "Frequency selected; encryption activated. Opening channel," she stated in routine fashion. "Waiting for encryption lock."

Nathan looked at Tug, concern on his face. "For this deception to be successful," Tug explained, "the communications system at the garrison on Ancot must accept our encryption challenge and create a secure communications link. The Ta'Akar do not transmit anything in the clear."

"And if they don't?" Nathan asked.

"Then you have two choices," Tug continued. "You can send the shuttles down and hope the officer in charge at the spaceport will accept the shuttles into his airspace without proper clearance, or we can send a message stating that, if they fail to respond, we will depart without picking up the conscripts and they can answer to command for their failure."

"You think that would work?" Nathan asked.

"Which one?"

"Either one."

"Sending the shuttles down without clearance might still work, but sending a message threatening to leave would be a safer tactic, as it has less chance of repercussions," Tug observed. "However, it would fail to get our intelligence asset on the surface of Ancot."

"What's taking so long?" Josh said.

"The Savoy system may be small, Josh," Tug said, "but we are still a considerable distance from Ancot. It will take at least ten minutes for our request to reach the planet, and another ten minutes for their answer to reach us."

"That's an extra half hour with our butts hanging out just waiting for some backyard astronomer to find us with his telescope," Jessica complained.

"Possible, but highly unlikely," Tug commented.

"Captain," Mister Dumar said, "it would be acceptable practice to launch the shuttles before receiving confirmation back from the garrison. Such an action would not be abnormal for an arrogant nobleman in command of a warship. After all, they are not known for their patience."

"You're just telling me this now?" Nathan asked, somewhat annoyed.

"I was not included in the original planning of this mission, Captain," Mister Dumar stated.

"What do you think?" Nathan asked Tug.

"There is little risk," Tug agreed. "And it would reduce the amount of time that we are at risk of exposure. Besides, you can always recall them if necessary."

"Very well. Launch the shuttles," Nathan ordered Naralena.

* * *

Ensign Willard sat in his rear-facing seat at the front of the passenger area of one of the Yamaro's two shuttles. The shuttles were quite large, and could easily seat over one hundred men each. For now, there were only nine men in the passenger area, including himself. Soon, every seat would be full of fresh young inductees snatched from their lives on the farms of Ancot, forced to serve in the Ta'Akar military.

"Stand by for departure," the voice crackled over the loudspeakers.

Finally, he thought. They had been sitting on the flight apron outside of the Aurora's transfer airlocks for nearly thirty minutes. As dangerous as their mission was, he very much wanted to get it over and done with.

The shuttle jolted slightly as the pilot fired his ascent thrusters just enough to push away from the mild artificial gravity generated by the Aurora's flight apron. Firing again, the shuttle increased its rate of separation, climbing up above the height of the topside of the Aurora before thrusting forward.

Ensign Willard and his men all looked out the windows of the shuttle as it skimmed along the top of the Aurora. She was a sleek ship with graceful lines, far more graceful than Takaran ships which tended to pay more attention to function than aesthetics. He remembered his conversations with Lieutenant Commander Nash, who had explained that the Aurora and her sister ship, the Celestia, were intended to act as peace envoys first. He could see how her overall design would appear less threatening than the ships of the empire.

As they continued coasting forward, Ensign Willard could make out the various doors that covered the ship's numerous rail guns and other weapons emplacements. He noticed that the ship's light gray topsides seemed to have a shine to them, with little bits of light from the Savoyan Sun glistening off her finish.

Moments later, they passed forward of the Aurora, her gray image disappearing behind them quickly as the shuttle pilot fired their main engines and sped away. While larger interplanetary cargo ships might still use transfer orbits to navigate between worlds, ships with more power used brute force, acceleration and deceleration to traverse the vast distances of interplanetary space. Transfer orbits took time, too much time, and that was something they did not have.

* * *

"Encryption request acknowledge, Captain," Naralena announced. "We have an open channel with the Ancot garrison."

"Excellent," Nathan exclaimed, a wave of relief coming over the bridge.

"We are ready to transmit," she told Tug.

"Ancot garrison, Ancot garrison, this is the Imperial Warship Yamaro," Tug announced in Takaran over his comm-set. "We have dispatched shuttles to Ancot spaceport for scheduled pick up of inductees headed for training on Takara. You are instructed to have all passengers ready for boarding."

"That was straight to the point," Jessica

commented, "not that I understood any of it."

"It was very concise," Naralena assured Jessica.

"I thought it best not to give them any reason to doubt our veracity," Tug stated.

"So now we wait another twenty minutes to see if they believe us," Nathan stated.

"Unfortunately, yes," Tug admitted.

"Captain, if they don't, we're barely going to have enough time to send an abort message to those shuttles," Jessica warned.

"I'm well aware of that, thanks," Nathan replied.

* * *

The intercom next to Ensign Willard buzzed twice. He picked up the handset and listened for a moment. "Understood." After hanging the handset back up, he turned his attention to the eight men sitting in front of him. "Listen up!" he called out. "We just got our go signal, which means so far the garrison believes that the Yamaro is in the system and is sending her shuttles down for a pick up. It is up to us now. Remember, you are security troops of the Ta'Akar. Do as we rehearsed, and watch me for instructions."

Willard looked at the faces of his men, none of which appeared confident about the outcome of their mission. "Get it together!" he snapped. "We hit the atmosphere in five minutes!"

The men tightened their harnesses in preparation for the turbulent ride through the upper atmosphere of Ancot. In ten minutes, they would be landing at the spaceport, and they would either succeed or perish.

* * *

The Yamaro's two shuttles came in low over the spaceport, their engines screaming as they came to a hover just beyond the rows of inductees waiting on the tarmac. They rotated slowly, bringing their port sides to face their waiting passengers as they descended to the tarmac, settling gently onto their landing gear.

As their engines spun down, the boarding ramp on the first shuttle began to deploy and its boarding hatch swung open. Shortly after, the boarding ramp and hatch on the second shuttle also deployed and opened.

The eight volunteers, all clad in the uniforms and body armor of the Ta'Akar security division, came marching confidently down the ramp with their heavy weapons held close across their chests. Their helmets and chin straps were taut and their body armor glistened in the afternoon Savoyan sun as they split into two lines and fanned out, four men per side in either direction. Once in position, they turned to face the inductees lined up in eight rows of fifty. The volunteers stared straight ahead, their eyes locked on seemingly nothing.

Ensign Willard, now dressed as a lieutenant of the Ta'Akar and wearing the sash of a noble house, came down the boarding ramp with all the arrogance and charm expected of Takaran nobility. The two dozen guards from the Ancot garrison tasked with delivering the inductees to the Yamaro snapped to attention at the sight of a nobleman coming down the ramp. Reluctantly, so did the elder sergeant major in charge of the detail.

Other than the few officers in charge at the Ancot

garrison, very few nobles set foot on Ancot. Most considered the world a backward system with little to offer someone of noble blood. In fact, the sergeant major was surprised to see even a lower-ranking lieutenant of noble lineage setting foot on their dusty world. The officers of most ships that passed through the system sent down their functionaries to do their bidding on the surface of Ancot, not wanting their noses fouled by the smell of dirt and raw crops.

Willard strode confidently up to the sergeant major, returning the salute offered by the lower-ranked elder in the same irritated manner that most Ta'Akar officers displayed when returning the salutes of those they deemed inferior. "Sergeant Major," he addressed.

"Welcome to Ancot, sir," the Sergeant Major answered.

"Yes, thank you," Willard responded, maintaining his arrogant demeanor. "So," he began, looking over the rows of inductees, "these are Ancot's latest sacrifices, are they?" Willard strolled down the line a few steps before turning and coming back. "Not very impressive, are they?"

"No, sir, not yet. But I'm sure the drill instructors on Takara will shape them up in no time," the sergeant major assured him.

"Yes," Willard sighed. He looked up at the burning sun. "Dreadfully hot here, isn't it?"

"Yes, sir."

Jalea came strolling over from the second shuttle. She was beautifully attired in her tight-fitting business suit, and her feminine charms did not go unnoticed by the sergeant major, nor by his men.

"Lieutenant," Jalea said as she approached, "did

you forget about me?"

"No, of course not, Miss Devonshire. I was just about to arrange for your transportation into town, as a matter of fact." Willard turned back to the sergeant major. "Sergeant Major, allow me to introduce Miss Analise Devonshire of the Royal Bank of Takara."

"A pleasure, miss," the sergeant major stated, bowing his head respectfully. "To what do we owe the honor of your visit?"

"I am here on business," Jalea stated, "official business," she added, handing her documents and ident chip over to the sergeant major for inspection. "I am not at liberty to discuss it further."

The sergeant major understood her meaning. The Takaran banks loved to perform surprise audits of their business partners in other star systems. Something about being light years away seemed to make people think their inappropriate financial dealings would go unnoticed. Although it was not as heavily populated or industrialized as most worlds within the empire, the sheer volume of food shipped from Ancot made it a breeding ground for financial trickery.

"I assume you can provide transportation into the city for Miss Devonshire," Willard insisted.

"Yes, of course," the sergeant major promised. "Corporal!" he bellowed. A young corporal stepped forward in response to the sergeant major's call.

"Yes, sir, Sergeant Major."

"Transport Miss Devonshire into town and then meet us back at the garrison," the sergeant major instructed.

"Yes, sir," the corporal acknowledged. "Ma'am," he said to Jalea, offering to take her bag, "if you'll follow me."

"Thank you, Sergeant Major," Jalea said. "Pleasant journey, Lieutenant."

"To you as well, Miss Devonshire," Willard replied.

"Very well," Willard stated, "let's get on with it, then."

"Excuse me, Lieutenant," the sergeant major said, "but I will need your orders, sir."

"My orders?"

"The ones authorizing me to turn over two hundred inductees to your charge, sir."

"Oh, yes, of course," Willard said, reaching into the pouch on his belt. He pulled out a data chip and handed it to the sergeant major. "Here you are."

"Thank you, sir." The sergeant major inserted the data chip into his reader and looked over the electronic documents. He examined Willard, then returned his gaze to the reader, continuing to check that everything was in order. Willard waited, feigning impatience to cover his own nervousness. The orders he had given the sergeant major were indeed genuine. However, they had been tampered with by Mister Dumar in order to put Lieutenant Willard's image, credentials, and bio-scan data into the orders in place of the officer that should have been picking up the inductees. Such forgery was not an easy task, and the readers used by security personnel were quite good at picking up the slightest discrepancy.

As the seconds ticked away, Willard cursed himself for not reviewing Mister Dumar's methodology more carefully. How did an old man, a commodities consultant at that, know anything about forging Ta'Akar orders and digital security stamps? So he had once served the Ta'Akar in his youth, just as

Ensign Willard, but that was decades ago, and the technology had surely changed since then.

Just as Willard was sure he was going to have to try and shoot his way out, the sergeant major's reader beeped, startling him.

"Are you all right, sir?" the sergeant major asked, noticing Willard's start.

"Yes, of course," Willard insisted. "It is this foul air," he lied. "Most unpleasant."

"Yes, it does take some getting used to," the sergeant major agreed as he pulled the data chip from his reader and handed it back to the Lieutenant. "Everything appears to be in order, sir," the sergeant major stated respectfully. "You may proceed, sir."

"Thank you, Sergeant Major." Willard struggled to maintain control, feeling he would surely fall to his knees with relief at any moment. He just had to continue the charade for a few more minutes. "Sergeant of the guard!"

"Yes, Lieutenant," the volunteer dressed as a Takaran sergeant responded.

"You may load the inductees."

"Yes, sir!" the sergeant answered. "Attention on the line!" he bellowed at the group of inductees, causing the group to immediately come to attention. "You are about to board the shuttles. When you do so you will move to the back and be seated in an orderly fashion. The first group will board the shuttle on the left. The second group will board the shuttle on the right. If you are too stupid to know your right from your left, just follow the man in front of you. If you are too stupid to do that, then just drop dead right where you are, because you are a waste of air and will not be allowed aboard my shuttles. Now, single file, move out!"

The inductees began boarding as per the sergeant's orders. Within a few minutes, all two hundred of them were aboard and the guards divided into two groups, four to a shuttle, following the inductees on board.

"Sergeant Major," Willard began, "it has been a pleasure."

"Excuse me, Lieutenant, but will your captain be coming down? Our commanding officer claims to be an old friend and was hoping to visit with him."

"I am afraid not," Willard explained. "We are on the last leg of a three-year patrol, and Captain de Winter in quite a hurry to get home... as are we all, for that matter."

"I understand," the sergeant major said. "I am sure you are anxious to get the refit started."

"Yes, the refit, indeed," Willard responded, even though he had no idea what the sergeant major was speaking of.

"Please convey my commanding officer's greeting to your captain, and his regrets that duty prevented them from enjoying one another's company."

"I shall do so, Sergeant Major."

The sergeant major snapped a salute, which Willard quickly returned before spinning around in the same pompous manner as most noblemen.

The sergeant major watched as Willard marched away. "Arrogant nobles," he muttered to himself.

* * *

Though not as organized and efficient as the cities on Corinair, Ancot city, the planet's only major metropolis, had a character all its own. The city was situated along a large, nearly enclosed bay, and was built up along all its shores. Two-thirds of the planet's surface was covered with water, and most of the land was relatively flat with only a few mountainous areas in the upper latitudes.

On Ancot, the weather was almost always the same: morning showers, sunny afternoons, and partly cloudy evenings. It rained daily at least half the year, and weekly the other half. While a nuisance for planning outdoor events, it was perfect for agriculture. Nearly every stitch of arable land was used for growing crops, and any land that had not been cultivated was used to support the planets massive agricultural industry. Nearly ninety percent of the food grown on Ancot was eaten by people living elsewhere, and most of those lived in the Takaran system.

Ask any Ancotan and they'd tell you that the Ta'Akar didn't conquer their planet, they invested in it. The people of Ancot lived good, healthy lives because they produced what the Takarans needed most, food. For this reason, being a Karuzari on Ancot was not an easy task.

The military staff vehicle pulled up in front of one of the best hotels in the downtown area of Ancot city. An attendant immediately opened the passenger door to the vehicle and helped the lady out. Jalea stood and looked about.

"May I get your bag, miss?" the attendant asked politely.

"Yes, please," she answered, pointing to the back seat. She leaned into the front door of the vehicle. "Thank you, Corporal. I will be fine from here."

"Yes, ma'am," the corporal answered as she closed the door.

"Checking in, miss?" the attendant answered as

the vehicle pulled away. It was a logical assumption on the attendant's part, considering Jalea's attire.

"Yes, but I would like to use the restroom first," Jalea told him.

"Of course, miss. Across the lobby and to the right, near the side entrance," he directed.

"Thank you," Jalea answered, taking her bag from him and draping it over her shoulder. The attendant opened the door for her and she entered the lobby. Strolling across the open floor, she looked every bit the royal auditor her credentials claimed.

Jalea found the restrooms exactly where the attendant had indicated. After pausing for a moment to make sure no one was paying her undue attention, she entered the restroom.

The inside of the restroom was quite large, with rows of doors down each side. She continued down the length of the room until she found a door that showed 'available' and stepped inside. As the door clicked shut, the light in the little room came on. There was a sink, a toilet, a mirror, and several hooks on the wall. All the nicer hotels were equipped in this manner, with individual private rooms instead of rows of semi-private stalls. It was for this reason she had asked the corporal to take her to one of the nicer hotels. Besides maintaining her cover, she needed privacy for the next step of her mission.

Twenty minutes later, the door to her room opened and Jalea stepped out into the main foyer of the restroom again. This time, her brown hair and green eyes were gone, replaced with blonde hair and blue eyes, like so many of the Ancotans. Gone, also, was her fashionable business suit, replaced by attire more fitting a young Ancotan woman. She slung her bag—which had changed from black like

her business suit to pale blue to match her dress—
back over her shoulder as she headed across the
foyer. Her walk had changed as well. Instead of
her previous business-like stride, she now swung
her hips more subtly from side to side in the same
manner as most young women about the town in
Ancot city.

She exited the restroom foyer back into the lobby
and headed out the side entrance. The afternoon sun
was warm and bright. She donned her sunglasses
and continued down the street, blending into the
crowd. Jalea Torren was now undercover on Ancot.

* * *

The inductees stared out the windows of the
shuttle as it approached what they thought was the
Ta'Akar warship, Yamaro. None of them had ever
seen a warship. Most of them had never left their
home planet for that matter. However, more than a
few of them had seen images of many of the empire's
ships, and those that had seen such images were
quite sure that the ship they were about to land on
did not belong to the Ta'Akar.

The men began talking among themselves, first in
whispers. Soon, the whispers became louder. Then,
they began to escalate into shouts as they demanded
to know what was happening. Within minutes of the
first sighting of the Aurora, Ensign Willard had to
order his guards to shoot anyone who got out of their
seat. There were one hundred agitated young men
on board the shuttle, and there were only five armed
guards including Ensign Willard. In retrospect, it
might have been better to seal the windows shut.

Luckily, none of the young men wished to be
the first to die at the barrel of a Takaran energy

weapon, and they chose to remain in their seats. Ensign Willard promised them that they would not be harmed, that everything would be explained once they landed, and that they would all be kept safe until they could be returned to their homes. He could see in the eyes of most of the inductees that the thought of returning home without having to spend years in service of the empire was enough reason for them to be patient.

* * *

"Captain, the hangar deck reports the shuttles are in the transfer airlocks," Naralena reported.

"Very well," Nathan answered, relief washing over him. It had been a tense few hours as they waited in stellar orbit just beyond Savoy's fifth planet, Deikon. Finally it was over and they could return to Darvano. "Helm, set course for Takara and accelerate smartly to half-light."

"Aye, Captain," Josh answered. "Changing course for Takara. Accelerating smartly to half-light."

"Doctor," Nathan said, turning toward Abby, "as soon as we exit the system, jump us to a few light months along our course to Takara. Then we'll decelerate, change course for Darvano, and jump home."

"Yes, Captain," Abby answered.

Nathan rose from his seat and headed for the exit.

"Where are you going?" Jessica asked.

"To meet Tug in the hangar deck," Nathan told her. "There are a couple hundred farm boys from Ancot who need some answers."

"What are you going to tell them?" Jessica asked.

"Only what I have to, Jess. You have the bridge."

CHAPTER EIGHT

"Tug, Aurora. You are clear to launch," Naralena's voice came over the comms.

"Aurora, Tug. Launching." Tug fired a blast of his ascent thrusters, pushing his interceptor up and away from the flight apron of the Aurora. The jolt pressed him down in his seat for a moment as his ship leapt upward, quickly climbing above the Aurora's massive drive section. "Aurora, Tug. I'm clear."

"Copy, Tug. See you on the other side," Naralena answered.

Tug looked out his canopy as the Aurora fired her main engines and began to pull away from him. By the time her engine ports passed under him, she had already shut down her drive, having gained enough additional speed to pull away from them at an acceptable rate. Within a minute, the massive ship was no more than an abnormally large, irregularly shaped gray dot against the background of stars. There was a flash of blue-white light, and she was gone.

"That's what it looks like when you jump?" the man's voice asked.

"Yes, that's what it looks like, Mister Cauley," Tug responded.

"A little frightening, is it not?" Mister Cauley commented.

Tug could hear the nervousness in the scientist's voice. As much as Tug had urged for this to be a solo test flight of the new, miniature jump drive installed in his interceptor, the Corinairans had insisted that one of their team needed to be present to monitor the performance of the system during the tests. Unfortunately for Mister Cauley, he had been considered the most qualified for the ride.

The Karuzari had vehemently protested the idea of their leader conducting the test flight, but Tug had stood firm in his decision, stating that no one was more qualified to deal with whatever emergency might come about during the tests. He and Josh were currently the only two pilots in the system that were qualified to pilot the interceptor, and Josh had only flown it a few times. There were many pilots on Corinair, of course, all of which could be taught to pilot the interceptor, but time was short. Jalea had already been on Ancot for two weeks without any contact, as the Aurora did not want to risk exposure in the Savoy system again so soon after her mission masquerading as the Yamaro.

In the end, Tug had won the argument, and Mister Cauley had lost. The knowledge that he would be forever registered in Corinairan history as the first of his people to operate such a system didn't seem to ease the poor man's tension. Tug smiled to himself as he remembered how difficult it had been to get the terrified man into the cockpit of the interceptor. As they had walked across the Aurora's hangar bay toward the interceptor, he had feared the scientist's legs were about to give out. Fortunately in the end, the man had summoned up enough courage to climb into the cockpit. It was either courage or fear of looking silly in front of his fellow Corinairans, as most of them would've given anything to be the one climbing into the interceptor.

"Mister Cauley," Tug called over his helmet comm, "are you ready?"

"No," he responded. "Are they even in position yet? I mean, they have to go a whole light hour. That's about a billion kilometers."

"They arrived at the same instant they disappeared, Mister Cauley," Tug told him, "just like we will."

"Thanks. That last part really helped."

"How does everything look back there?" Tug asked. He could monitor the miniature jump drive from his position in the front seat as well, as the ship had been designed to be operated by one pilot. However, the scientist was there for a reason, and keeping his mind focused on the task at hand was likely to keep his thoughts away from what was about to take place.

"Everything appears normal," he reported. "The reactors are running at one hundred percent, the energy banks are fully charged, and the jump drive is ready. Jump algorithm is plotted, verified, and locked."

"Very well," Tug said. "Accelerating forward." Tug pushed his throttles forward, causing his main engines to ignite and come up to one percent thrust. They were already moving forward at considerable speed, as they had carried the Aurora's momentum with them when they had lifted off her deck. However, the first test jump had been calculated and recalculated by the Corinairans prior to this flight. It was to occur at an exact point in space on a precise trajectory at a predetermined speed. The Aurora had performed the exact same jump they were about to attempt, according to the exact same plot, in order to compare performance parameters and accuracy between the two ships.

Tug watched his flight display as he maneuvered the interceptor into the center of the indicated flight path. "Activating auto-flight system," he announced as he touched the screen to turn the auto-flight system on. The indicator turned green. "Auto-flight now has control," Tug announced. "Jump point in thirty seconds."

"Oh God," Mister Cauley mumbled as he frantically scanned every little parameter displayed from his consoles at the rear of the cockpit.

"Mister Cauley," Tug called, "you will have three choices when we jump. You can either drop your auto-visor first, close your eyes really tight, or be blinded for a few seconds and see a blue dot in your vision for an hour afterward."

"Huh?"

"I would strongly suggest you drop your auto-visor," Tug said. "Jump point in ten seconds." Tug pulled down his auto-visor, which was designed to adjust its light filtering qualities automatically to protect the wearer's eyes from the bright light often encountered during space flight.

"Oh God," Mister Cauley repeated, dropping his own auto-visor and locking it in place.

"Jumping in five..."

Mister Cauley scanned his instruments again, checking for any anomalies that would require a last moment abort.

"...four..."

Part of him hoped he would see such an anomaly.

"...three..."

Mister Cauley had no wish to go through with

the jump...

"...two..."

...but neither did he want his people's jump drive program to be set back.

"...one..."

There were no anomalies.

"...jump."

Blue-white light spilled out from the small emitters spread out across the interceptor. In a split second, the light from each emitter seemed to join into one, covering the entire surface of the ship. As the gaps in the field of light closed, the intensity of the blue-white light quickly rose. Although from Mister Cauley's perspective it seemed to take forever, it all happened in a fraction of a second. The light flashed, momentarily filling the cockpit with the eerie blue-white glow, and then all was normal again.

"Jump complete," Tug announced.

Mister Cauley looked around. "Are we there? Did we make it?"

"Checking position," Tug stated.

"*Tug, Aurora,*" Naralena's voice called across the comms. "*Report your status.*"

"Aurora, Tug. All systems are good."

"*Congratulations, Mister Tugwell,*" Naralena said. Tug could hear the voices of the Aurora's crew, as well as the Corinairan scientists from the jump drive program that were observing the test from the Aurora's bridge, all cheering triumphantly.

"You mean we did it?" Mister Cauley asked in amazement.

"We did it," Tug answered.

"Oh my God, that was incredible," Mister Cauley exclaimed.

"You see? I told you it was nothing to worry about," Tug told him.

"You were right. That was easy!"

Ten minutes later, when they climbed down from the interceptor and were greeted by several dozen Corinairan scientists all cheering and laughing, Tug noticed Mister Cauley had somehow developed a bit of a swagger in his walk. Tug couldn't help but smile.

* * *

Jalea went into the small home on the outskirts of Ancot city. As usual, it was raining outside. It had actually been raining for several days straight, which was not unusual for Ancot city. She shook off her umbrella and placed it in the corner, removing her poncho as well. She hung it on the wall and then made her way through the part in the heavy curtain that separated the entry foyer from the rest of the home. The video screen was flickering in the corner of the dimly lit room, playing some program that no one was watching.

She made her way across the room and down the short hallway, entering the bathroom at the end of the corridor. After closing the door, she stepped into the shower stall, swinging the stall door closed behind her. She pulled down on the shower head, causing the entire wall to slide forward nearly a meter, creating an opening through which she passed.

The hidden doorway was at the head of a long, narrow staircase that descended some four meters below the home. She could see the glow of light coming from the room at the bottom of the stairs and could hear men speaking in low, hushed tones as she descended the staircase.

The room was large, covering nearly the same area as the entire house above it. The ceilings were low and supported by preformed beams and columns that had been brought down in pieces and then fusion-bonded together in position. The bare dirt and rock had been walled over, and the gaps had been filled with a spray-on foam that provided insulation for both temperature and sound. All in all, the room had a very clean and professional appearance.

Unfortunately she could not say the same for the men and women that regularly occupied the room for days on end. They had to be careful about their comings and goings to avoid detection by both neighbors and the authorities in Ancot city, both of which were not supportive of the Karuzari. Ancot was considered one of the most difficult worlds on which to operate for the Karuzari for just this reason. Jalea had been surprised to make contact with six people claiming to be members of the rebellion. Unfortunately, she only recognized two of them, and therefore she had to be careful what she said around the other four. To be safe, she had chosen to speak to no one about her real mission, nor about the situation in the Darvano system, revealing only that she had been instructed to monitor all Ta'Akar activity in the system and log it, and that she would be contacted periodically to collect the information she had gathered.

So far, she had collected nothing of any importance. Crop yields, local crime reports, and some Takaran comm-drone traffic of little interest to their cause. After a few weeks of near daily rain, she was already growing tired of her assignment. Luckily, the man she had met up with and who pretended to be her husband was someone she knew and trusted well enough to feel comfortable letting her guard down without fear of being assassinated.

Still, she had hoped to at least establish a reliable cell on Ancot so that she could return to Karuzara, but this was not yet the case. She was beginning to wonder if it ever would be.

"Jalea," the man called Tomon said, "I have received word from Rena."

Jalea did not care for Rena. She was an attractive and intelligent woman who chose to engage in relations with her sources in order to retrieve information from them. Although Jalea had used similar methods in the past, she found much of the information obtained in such fashion to be suspect, as men seeking to impress their sexual partners often exaggerated to accomplish their goals.

"She reports that a Ta'Akar frigate will arrive here in a few days, a week at most."

It was exactly the type of news she had hoped to discover. "From where does it come?"

"Norwitt," Tomon added, "it comes from the Norwitt system."

"Then it will likely head for Darvano next," Jalea said, gesturing for Tomon to follow her into the corner, away from the others. "You must not speak of this to the others." She peered over his shoulder to make sure those in the room that she did not trust could not hear her words. "Instruct Rena to do the same. Do you understand?"

"Of course."

"I have another task for you, Tomon. Monitor this frequency," she told him, writing the number down on a small scrap of paper. "Only at the times indicated by this algorithm," she added as she continued to scribble on the paper. "Apply this algorithm from midnight of the Day of the Harvest. Each time, you must only monitor for one minute, no longer. Understood?"

"I know how this works, Jalea. I have worked comms before."

"Of course. When you make contact, transmit the information about the frigate," she instructed. "Call me the moment you make contact," she added, handing him a personal comm-unit. "Then dispose of this unit."

"Of course. But who will be contacting me?"

"I do not know, not for sure. All I *do* know is that it will be someone you can trust, and it will only be on this frequency and at the times indicated by the algorithm." Jalea put her hand on his neck. "Tell Rena she has done well and to continue to get more information from this person. If she discovers anything else relating to this frigate, include it in the message."

"Yes, Jalea, right away."

* * *

"Good morning people," Nathan greeted as he sat down at the head of the conference table in the command briefing room. "We'll start with you, Tug, since you've been having so much fun with your new jump interceptor."

"Thank you, Captain," Tug began. "As you are probably all aware, we have been putting the miniature jump drive through rigorous testing over the last few days. I am happy to report that it has performed exactly as expected."

"What's the official range?" Nathan wondered.

"Although we have not pushed it to its limits as of yet, it appears that the maximum safe range is one light year. The minimum range is one light minute."

"One light year?" Nathan said. "That's not very far."

"In order for the jump to occur," Abby explained, "the jump drive must dump massive amounts of energy into both the inner and outer fields at precisely the correct moment in order to cause the transition to occur. To do this on the Aurora, we use energy storage banks combined with the output from two anti-matter reactors. Tug's interceptor uses simple fusion reactors. They are extremely efficient, but they cannot generate enough energy at once to jump any farther than a single light year."

"Can't we install energy banks in the interceptor to increase her jump range?" Nathan asked.

"There simply is not any room for them," Tug said.

"Captain," Abby interrupted, "I should remind you that the use of storage banks is why the Aurora has to take the time to recharge between long jumps. The interceptor will not have this restriction, therefore it could jump considerable distances within a short period of time."

"We could send it all the way back to Earth," Nathan contemplated.

"It is a bit early to make such an assumption with any level of confidence, sir, but theoretically, yes. It could reach Earth in a matter of weeks."

"Still," Nathan said, "it does open up some interesting possibilities."

"That's an understatement," Jessica commented,

"we could send a message stating that we're alive, that the jump drive works."

"Exactly," Nathan agreed. "Tell them to start building more."

"Maybe include details of some of the weapons and shield technologies they have here as well," Jessica added. "That might give them an edge against the Jung."

"Let's not get ahead of ourselves, Captain," Abby warned. "We still have a lot of testing to conduct. I would not recommend making such a journey at this time. It is simply too risky."

"Can the interceptor be operated by a single pilot?" Nathan asked.

"Yes," Tug answered. "Although we have been conducting our tests with Mister Cauley as second seat, his job has been limited strictly to the monitoring of the system for scientific and developmental purposes. I have been piloting the ship as well as plotting and executing the jumps."

"The entire implementation was approached with the single pilot concept in mind, Captain," Abby explained. "Much of the interface was designed by Deliza and her team and will eventually be implemented aboard the Aurora, as we discussed."

"You should be proud of your daughter," Nathan said to Tug.

"I have always been proud of both of my daughters," Tug stated.

"So what's next for the new jump interceptor?" Nathan asked.

"I will be conducting a solo jump to the Savoy system in order to establish contact with Jalea. It has been three weeks since she was inserted into Ancot city. She may have something to report by now."

"Why solo?" Jessica wondered.

"The system was designed to be operated by a single pilot," Tug reminded her. "It is also possible that Jalea may already be in need of extraction, in which case I will need an empty seat."

"Well, let's hope that's not the case," Nathan stated. "Cheng, how are things coming along in your neck of the woods?"

"All ship's systems have been repaired, Captain, and we are nearly halfway through installing the systems that were still crated up and stored," Vladimir reported proudly. "The Corinairans have been most helpful. In fact, all crates that were stored in the fighter alleys have either been installed or moved into the cargo bays."

"Excellent, but don't let up," Nathan said. "We're going to need those cargo bays to store additional ammunition and consumables. How are things coming with the forward compartments?"

"I am happy to report that the forward section will be ready for habitation in a few days."

"That's good news," Nathan stated. "We still have two more shifts of volunteers waiting to come aboard. The flight crews have been bunking in the Karuzara dorms so they can take turns using our flight training simulators, but we really need to get the rest of the volunteers on board so they can get trained."

"Well, at least the galley is fully functional now," Jessica commented. "Maybe now we can start eating a normal meal once in a while."

"You know, Jess," Nathan started, "with most of the crew being Corinairan, we're probably going to be eating more like them from now on."

"Oh, are you kidding me?" Jessica protested. "They don't even know how to make a decent sandwich. They wrap the meat and cheese up in some dough and bake it. That's not a sandwich."

"Oh, da!" Vladimir exclaimed. "It is like perazhok! It is wonderful!"

"Wonderful my ass," Jessica disagreed, "there's no lettuce or tomato in it."

"Well, wonderful or not, you'd better get used to it," Nathan warned. "Maybe if you're nice to the cook, he'll let you make your own sandwich."

"Can't we just install a mini-fridge in my quarters and let me keep my own food in there?"

Nathan smiled. "Master Chief, how go things on the flight deck?"

"Nicely, Captain. As Cheng said, the fighter alleys are clear, so we finally have a chance to start getting organized in the main hangar bay. Since Marcus has been pretty much running that deck since you took him on board back in Haven, I have been allowing him continue to do so. He is not exactly Corinari issue, if you understand my meaning, but he is a good enough fellow, once you get past his gruffness. Besides, he has taken that hangar bay on as his own, which I believe is good."

"Do you anticipate any problems once the Corinari aerospace groups start moving in?"

"Maybe a few, Captain, I am not going to pretend otherwise. I expect it will be difficult for many of the Corinari to take orders from a civilian like Marcus, despite the fact he seems to know what he is doing."

"Would it help if we enlisted him and gave him a rank?"

"Captain..." Jessica interrupted.

"Perhaps," Master Chief Montrose agreed, "but

you would have to make him at least a chief. And since you people have the peculiar custom of assigning people to seemingly arbitrary ranks, why not just make him a senior chief so he will out rank most of the Corinari that might be working under him?"

"Oh come on," Jessica disagreed. "Marcus? A senior chief?" Jessica threw up her hands in resignation, leaning back in her chair and folding her arms to wait until someone decided what to do.

Vladimir smiled as he watched Jessica unravel before his eyes. "I think it is very good idea. I like Marcus. He is very reliable, in my opinion."

"Has everybody lost their minds?" Jessica wondered aloud. "Captain, you do realize that you're stepping way outside regs here. There's no way Cameron is going to go for this."

Nathan turned and looked hard at Jessica. "Commander Taylor will be fine with it, Lieutenant Commander."

Jessica straightened up slowly in her chair. Her captain's tone made her realize she had crossed a line.

"Ensign Willard," Nathan continued, purposefully leaving the topic of Marcus, as he considered it decided, "I hear you are leading your shipmates in their efforts to integrate the Yamaro into her new home within the asteroid," Nathan said. "How is that going?"

"Quite well, Captain. The men are happy to return to their familiar quarters. Many of them are still performing the same functions as they were when the Yamaro was a space-faring vessel. Those that cannot do so have taken on new roles, such as construction, fabrication, and even mining."

"Mining?" Nathan asked.

"Yes," Willard answered. "Although the asteroid was considered fully mined and ready to be de-orbited to Corinair for harvesting, there is still a considerable amount of material left within the asteroid. We expect to be able to harvest a few more metric tons without destabilizing the outer shell of the asteroid itself. That material will go a long way toward the expansion of our interior spaces within the asteroid, as well as the creation of additional fabricators."

"And how is the refit of the asteroid going?"

"Fine, sir. We have closed off the entrance to the inner chamber and now have a tunnel from the exterior that leads directly into the Yamaro's starboard hangar bay. We have also removed the bulkheads between the starboard and port bays, making it into one massive bay. We have sealed and pressurized the interior of the asteroid's main cavern, and have begun to assemble a construction platform that extends out into the inner chamber from the port hangar bay airlock."

"So you have a pressurized, micro-gravity shipyard?" Nathan asked.

"Yes, sir," Ensign Willard answered. "It will greatly speed up the refit of shuttles and other small spacecraft."

"Impressive," Vladimir stated. "I must visit this and see it for myself."

"How are things going with the fabricators?" Nathan asked.

"Rather than remove them from the Yamaro, we have been using them to construct new fabricators. Once the Yamaro's weapons systems have been removed, there will be room to create additional fabrication shops. We have created two more pairs of fabricators, both large and small, and another pair is nearly complete. One of the new pairs has been shipped to Corinair. I believe they have tasked it to continue making new pairs to increase their production capacity. The other one we have tasked to do the same, allowing us to start utilizing the existing pairs to begin the production of mini-jump drives at the request of both the Corinairans and the Karuzari."

"We feel it is imperative that we get an early warning system in place as soon as possible," Tug elaborated. "Advanced notification would greatly increase our chances of successfully defending this system against another attack."

"What about the third pair?" Vladimir asked.

"As soon as they are completed, they will be delivered to you, Lieutenant Commander," Ensign Willard promised.

"*Da!*" Vladimir exclaimed, slapping the table triumphantly. "*Harasho!*"

"How long will it take to fit these Corinairan shuttles with mini-jump drives?" Nathan asked.

"Using one pair of fabricators, it takes about one week to create the parts for a mini-jump drive," Ensign Willard explained, "and another week to assemble and install it. I would imagine that it would require another day or two for testing as well."

"Two weeks, huh?" Nathan wondered aloud. "So it will take some time to get a reliable early warning system in place."

"At least a few months," Tug stated. "However, even a single ship jumping about and taking scans can provide us with at least a few hours warning. It is not much, but it is better than being completely taken by surprise."

"Agreed," Nathan stated, wanting to wrap up the meeting. "We'll be taking the ship out of Karuzara in a few hours to conduct our first test launches of a Corinari interceptor using the launch tubes. If it works as expected, we'll have at least a wing or two of fighters on board within the week. Master Chief, round up Marcus and meet me in my ready room as soon as possible. Lieutenant Commander Nash, please remain. Everyone else is dismissed."

One by one the attendees filed out of the room, all off to begin their work for the day. Nathan waited until they had all left before speaking. The guard looked inside the room, and Nathan gestured for him to close the door.

Nathan looked at Jessica, who was leaning back in her seat, nice and relaxed. "What the hell is wrong with you?" he asked.

"With me? What the hell is wrong with you?" she retorted. "You can't just snap your fingers and make people members of the fleet. Come on. Marcus, a senior chief?"

"Straighten up, Lieutenant Commander," he barked. Jessica immediately sat up straight in her chair. "I'm the captain of this ship, and I'm the highest ranking member of the Earth Defense Fleet in this area of space. I'll enlist and or promote anyone I damn well choose. Hell, I signed an alliance between the Earth and a government nobody back home has ever heard of before. I even shared top-secret technology with them. You think I'm worried about the repercussions from a few questionable field promotions? Hell, if that had been an issue I wouldn't have promoted you or Lieutenant Commander Kamenetskiy."

"I was just trying to..."

"I don't give a rat's ass what you *thought* you were trying to do, Lieutenant Commander," Nathan interrupted angrily. "If you have a problem with my decisions, you are more than welcome to take it up with me... in private. Is that understood?"

"Yes, sir."

"Very well, Lieutenant Commander. Dismissed."

"Thank you, sir," Jessica responded in perfect military fashion. She rose from her chair, saluted, turned, and left the room. Inside she was fuming. It had been awhile since anyone had dressed her down in such a fashion. Coming from Nathan Scott, despite the fact that he was the captain, made it all the more difficult.

Her anger continued to boil as she left the briefing room and headed to her office. She couldn't stand the idea of Marcus becoming a member of the Earth Defense Force, let alone a senior chief. She had known a few chiefs in her short time in the fleet. Each of them had been incredible individuals to be feared, respected, and listened to. Those men had years of experience and unimpeachable honor and commitment. Marcus didn't deserve to wear the same rank as those men. He hadn't earned it, and she doubted he ever would.

Unfortunately, there was nothing she could do about it. Nathan had been right about one thing; he was the captain, and technically, he had the right to make such decisions. She had no doubt that command back home would highly disapprove of Captain Nathan Scott's actions, but that was of no matter now.

She had to admit one thing, however. She had been out of line arguing with her captain in front of others. For that, she felt embarrassed. She also felt grateful that he hadn't dressed her down in front of the others. It was sometimes hard for her to think of Nathan as the captain, but one thing was obvious; *the captain* was exactly who he was becoming.

* * *

Marcus looked nervous as he stood before the captain's desk. He had never been in the captain's ready room until now. In fact, the only time he had ever been on the bridge was just after they had stormed it to take the Aurora back from de Winter and his men. Since then, most of Marcus's time had been spent on the flight deck, in his quarters, or in the galley.

As he was standing next to Master Chief Montrose, Marcus was pretty sure he was in trouble. Exactly what kind of trouble, he wasn't certain. He and the master chief had gotten along pretty well considering the difference in their backgrounds. They had argued, surely, but they had also swapped a few stories and shared a few meals together as well, which was a sight more than he had done with most of the crew, short of Josh and Loki.

Marcus had seen it coming, though. He knew that soon the Corinari would be taking over the flight deck. He had run the deck for more than a month now—not because he was the most qualified, but because there had been no one else to do the job. So he had taken it upon himself to keep the deck in working order, and to tend to any spacecraft on his deck that needed attention. He had figured that, as long as he continued to do so, he might have himself a place to sleep and some food to eat. He had no delusions of ever getting back to Haven. To be honest, he had never really liked that place much to begin with. Even if he did find a way back, his old employer would probably blame him for the loss of two cargo shuttles and a ring harvester. It would take him the rest of his life to pay off that much debt. Besides, Josh was staying put. That much Marcus was sure of, and Josh was really the closest thing to kin that Marcus had, having taken the boy in and raised him since his mother was killed more than a decade ago.

"Marcus," Nathan began, "Master Chief Montrose has been telling me what fine care you've been taking of my hangar deck."

"Just trying to help out where I can, sir," Marcus stated.

"I've been talking to Josh and Loki about you as well," Nathan added.

"I wouldn't put too much stock in what Josh tells you, Captain," Marcus protested. "The boy's been bounced around the cockpit a bit too much, if you get my meaning. Some things have been shook loose up there."

"Josh tells me you can fix just about anything. He says you taught him everything he knows about fixing spaceships," Nathan said.

"Like I was saying, he's a bright boy that one. Very perceptive... like a son to me he is."

"As you are probably aware, the Corinari will be sending one of their aerospace groups over to fly off our decks. They should arrive in about a week."

Marcus felt his heart sinking. He seriously doubted there would be any place for him on the deck, not with the Corinari running things in the hangar bays. He suddenly had visions of himself back on Haven, working the mining crews again, but not as a foreman. He'd be back on the grunt line for sure. He could feel his expression change as his heart saddened further at the thought of leaving. He had been stranded aboard the Aurora for some time now. He had almost died several times along the way. Oddly enough, the ship had become home to him. Despite all the times he had sworn to jump ship at the first favorable system, Marcus had become attached to the Aurora and her crew... almost like they were family.

"Of course," Nathan continued, "we can't have a civilian running the deck. It just wouldn't work. The Corinari just wouldn't listen to the orders of a civilian, I'm afraid."

"I understand, Captain," Marcus admitted. "I pretty much saw this coming."

"That's why I've decided to offer you an enlistment in the Earth Defense Force, with the rank of senior chief," Nathan explained with a smile.

"Excuse me?"

"I want you to be my new 'Chief of the Deck'," Nathan told him.

"Did you just say you wanted to make me a senior chief?"

"Yes, I did," Nathan responded.

Marcus laughed. "Okay, I didn't see *that* coming!" Marcus's frown suddenly reversed as he let out a holler. "Hot damn! Oops, I mean, thank you, Captain." He laughed again. "Hell, I figured you were gonna toss me out an airlock or something."

"Not quite," Nathan said.

"Congratulations, Marcus," Master Chief Montrose said, reaching out to shake Marcus's hand.

"Does this mean I'm gonna be the same rank as you?" Marcus asked Master Chief Montrose.

"Not exactly," Master Chief Montrose replied.

"No, he's a master chief," Nathan explained.

"So you'll be my boss, then?"

"Only because I am also chief of the boat," Master Chief Montrose explained, "which as I understand, does give me authority over you. However, once the Corinari Aerospace Group moves in, I suspect you will be working for them."

"You'll probably be working under their equivalent to our air boss," Nathan explained.

"Hell, that's fine by me." Marcus laughed again, still not quite believing what had just happened. "I have to admit, Captain; I'm a bit surprised by all this. I mean, why me? There's got to be a hundred guys down on Corinair that are more qualified."

"I need someone that I know I can count on, Marcus. You've already put your life on the line on more than one occasion for this ship and her crew. And you may have to do it again real soon. I feel better knowing that you will."

"You bet your ass, Captain, sir. Oh crap, I did it again."

"I'll work on his decorum, Captain," Master Chief Montrose promised.

"Yes, of course," Nathan smiled. "Then I take it you accept my offer?"

"Yes, sir," Marcus agreed.

"Then congratulations, Senior Chief, uh..." Nathan paused, slightly embarrassed. "I just realized, I don't know your surname," Nathan said.

"It's Taggart, sir. Marcus Taggart."

"Then congratulations, Senior Chief Taggart," Nathan said, extending his hand.

"Thank you, Captain," Marcus said, "I won't let you down."

"I'm sure you won't, Senior Chief."

"I will get him some uniforms," Master Chief Montrose said. "There should still be a few in the quartermaster's compartment."

"Good idea," Nathan agreed.

"Captain," Marcus said as he was about to leave, "just one question, if I may?"

"Of course, Senior Chief."

"Do I get paid?" Marcus wondered.

"Technically, yes, but we'll have to get back to Earth before you can collect any wages. For now, you just keep my deck running smoothly."

"Yes, sir, I will," Marcus promised, grinning from ear to ear as he left the ready room.

* * *

"You know, I shot one of those down once," Marcus confessed, pointing at the Corinairan interceptor that was being loaded into the inboard launch tube at the front of the starboard fighter alley.

"Excuse me?" Master Chief Montrose asked.

"Yeah, when we were coming out of Aitkenna, just before the Yamaro attacked," Marcus explained. "Port Authority was trying to force us down, and we needed to get back to the ship. I had a laser cannon I took off Tug's interceptor—had mounted it in the back of an old cargo shuttle, the one that got fried on the Yamaro's hangar deck."

"Really?"

"I'm not bragging or nothing. I'm pretty sure it was just a lucky shot, caught him by surprise, I suspect. He probably wasn't expecting an old tub like that to have a gun in the back."

"I would not be so eager to share that story with anyone, Senior Chief, considering who your new shipmates are going to be."

"Oh yeah," Marcus said, realizing the implications. "It's not like the pilot died or anything. He bailed out. Saw the chute myself."

"Just the same, I would keep it to yourself."

"Yes, sir."

"Do not call me *sir*, Marcus. I am a master chief, not an officer."

"Sorry, I forgot."

"You should be overseeing all of this, you know," Master Chief Montrose told him.

"To be honest, I haven't spent much time in the fighter alleys. Had no use for them until now."

"Just the same, if you are going to run this deck, you had better do two things: know everything about this deck—and I mean everything—and make sure everybody on this deck knows that you are in charge."

"You think I should find something to yell at them about?"

Montrose shook his head. "That will not be necessary, Marcus. Not yet. For now it's enough that you're standing here, next to the chief of the boat, watching everything. Besides, I am sure these men know what they are doing. The Corinari would not have sent us any scrubs."

"Well, at least somebody knows what they're doing," Marcus said. "I feel like a complete dumbass standing here in this uniform."

"Stroll on over there and take a look around," the master chief urged, "like you are checking over their work."

"What?"

"You do not have to say anything, not unless of course you see something wrong."

"How am I going to spot something wrong? I've never even set foot in a launch tube."

"I have watched you work, Marcus. You figure things out quite quickly. I am sure you will do fine. You can study up on everything later. And believe me, you will be doing a lot of studying. For now, it is important that you establish your dominance over this deck."

"All right," Marcus said, uncrossing his arms and taking a step forward. He stopped a moment and turned back toward the master chief. "But if you're setting me up to look foolish, Chief of the Boat or not, I'm coming back here to kick your ass."

Master Chief Montrose smiled. "I will be waiting patiently for your return, Senior Chief."

Marcus strolled out of the transfer airlock from the forward end of main hangar bay into the starboard fighter alley. A team of five men were checking over the Corinairan interceptor in preparation for its test launch. Several more men were standing behind them, checking over their notes and pointing at the launch tube.

"Gentlemen," Marcus greeted as he walked past them and turned into the launch tube.

"Senior Chief," one of them answered back. Other than the captain and the master chief, this young man was the first Corinairan to call him by his new rank. It felt good.

As he came to the front of the interceptor, he squatted down to take a look at the nose gear. It was hooked to the catapult shuttle sticking out of the track in the launch tube's deck.

"How does it look, Senior Chief?" the Corinairan flight tech asked. "The engineers tried to duplicate the specs you sent us for the hook."

Marcus looked closer at the hook. "Just make sure you got tension on it before you close up for launch. The shuttle should be square up against the hook, so it can't jump when they charge the shuttle rails."

"Yes, Senior Chief."

Marcus stood up and looked forward down the dimly lit launch tube. "Did anybody walk the tube?"

"Senior Chief?"

"Did anybody inspect the tube?"

"We assumed you had, Senior Chief."

"Well of course I have," Marcus grumbled. "But the tube should be checked before every launch. You never know what might fall off of one of these birds when it gets shot outta here at a thousand clicks an hour!"

"Should we walk it, or can we just scan it?" the flight tech asked.

"Walk it before the first shot of the shift," Marcus explained, thinking quickly, "then scan it before each shot."

"I will get right on it, Senior Chief," the flight tech promised.

Marcus looked back at Master Chief Montrose standing in the airlock door, grinning from ear to ear. He looked up over his left shoulder at the cockpit. Major Prechitt looked down at him and smiled. Marcus snapped a slightly lazy salute at the Major. He returned it in similar fashion. "Have a good flight, sir."

"Thank you, Senior Chief," Major Prechitt responded.

Marcus headed out of the launch tube back into the fighter alley. As he did so, two junior flight techs went charging down the tube with bright handheld lights, scanning the deck as they moved forward. He couldn't help but smile.

"Bridge, starboard launch," the voice sounded over the Major's helmet comms. *"Bridge, go,"* Naralena's voice answered.

Major Prechitt checked his instruments one more time. The Aurora had already fed him its current course, speed, and location so that he could sync his navigation computers. The launch tube door had swung upward behind him and sealed him into the first chamber of the tube. The door in front of him had already closed, and the air in the tube beyond it had already been sucked out by the powerful vacuum pumps. Two seconds before launch, that door would drop into the floor. Immediately afterward, he would be shot out of the forward end of the tube, the catapult accelerating him another fifty meters per second above whatever speed the Aurora was traveling at the time of launch.

"Bridge, starboard launch. Requesting clearance for one shot."

"Starboard launch, you are cleared for one shot."

"Talon One, launch. You are cleared for forward launch."

"Talon One copies. Ready to launch." Major Prechitt placed his hands on the grab rails on either side of his cockpit walls, just below the lip where the canopy locked into the body of his interceptor. Even though his inertial dampeners would reduce the force of acceleration to tolerable levels, it was best to hold on to something during the shot so that his hands wouldn't flail about and slam into something by accident. During his launch, all his flight systems would be controlled by the auto-flight system until he was clear of the ship. At that point, he would be free to take control or continue on auto-flight for the first leg of his flight plan.

"Launching Talon One, cat three, in three..."

The interceptor's main engines began to spin up in preparation to fire once the ship was clear of the launch tube.

"...two..."

The door in front of the interceptor dropped into the deck in less than a second. The major could almost hear the air rushing past his canopy as it left the space around him, rushing forward down the launch tube and out the open end into the vacuum of space.

"...one..."

Major Prechitt tightened his grip on the hand holds and tensed up his body, pushing himself back into his flight seat.

"...launch."

The major grunted as the interceptor lurched forward, being sent hurtling down the launch tube by the force of the electromagnetic catapult system. The dim lights in the launch tube streaked past him, blurring into an almost solid amber line as he rolled down the tube. As he approached the exit, he could feel the gravity lessening around him as the adjustable gravity plating in the deck eased up to let go of the small spacecraft as it exited the long tunnel and shot out into space ahead of the Aurora.

Still a few hundred meters behind the bow of the ship, the gray colored starboard side of the Aurora streaked past the major as he coasted quickly out past the bow of the Aurora. Setup for the first test launch of a Corinairan interceptor adapted to launch from the Aurora's launch tubes had taken nearly a month to prepare for. The shot itself had taken two seconds.

"Wow!" the major exclaimed. "Aurora, Talon One, airborne!"

Nathan watched the main view screen as the small interceptor accelerated out past them. The ship was pulling away so fast that it was almost gone from view when it fired its main engines and began its turn to starboard.

"Copy that, Talon One," Naralena answered. "Congratulations, Major."

"*Aurora, Talon One. I am going to circle around you a few times just to test her out before I come back in for another launch cycle.*"

Naralena looked to Nathan for approval.

"Tell him to feel free to indulge himself," Nathan said, a smile on his face. He remembered the first time he had launched from the flight deck of the Reliant during his training. Although he had flown in orbit many times before that, the feeling of flying out in open space, free from the gravity of a nearby body, was an amazing experience.

"Talon One, Aurora. Captain says 'indulge yourself.'"

* * *

Tug had timed his arrival down to the perfect moment. His calculations had given him enough time to come in behind Deikon and use its gravity to slingshot him around and inward toward Ancot with only the slightest burn of his engines. It was extremely doubtful that anyone would have spotted his thermal signature. After his burn had completed, he shut down all systems and allowed his ship to grow cold in the icy depths of space in order to reduce his thermal signature even further. The portable environmental and life support systems within his suit would sustain him during the hours it would take to coast across the vast distance between the super-massive gas giant, Deikon, and the rocky, inhabited planet, Ancot.

As he coasted through the system, he thought about his late wife. She had died bravely on Haven, fighting like the warrior she was. She had been so different from his first wife, whom he had lost contact with after he was stranded on Haven. Somehow, despite the eventual repair of his ship, the new circumstances of his life made reconnecting with her an impossible task.

It had all been for the best, of course, for his second wife had given him two lovely daughters. Deliza, his oldest, was strong and determined like her mother. His youngest, Nalaya, was sweet and kindhearted, just as he had been at her tender age. Nalaya had taken her mother's death hard at first, becoming withdrawn and non-communicative for the most part. For weeks, the only person she would speak with was Deliza, and only then in private. That had rapidly changed once the Montrose family had taken her in. With all the other children around, Nalaya opened up again and became happier than he had ever remembered her to be. It only pained him that he was unable to spend as much time as he would like with her. Instead, he was floating through the Savoy system in the hopes of establishing contact with an undercover operative. It was not the place for a father of a young girl to be.

Tug checked his ship's clock, which he had set to count down to his contact window. He had timed his journey so that he would be at his closest proximity to Ancot during the one minute contact window indicated by the algorithm he and Jalea had worked out before her departure. Communications were the most dangerous part of an undercover operatives work, as it was at that moment when you were most discoverable. He was quite sure, however, that Jalea would take great precautions to ensure her own safety, even if it was at the expense of others.

Ancot grew larger in his canopy over the hours. Now, after nearly seven hours, he was close enough to make out the continents on the surface. There was little traffic in the Savoy system, and with most of his systems powered down for hours, his ship was nearly as cold as space itself. If his ship had been painted black, it would've been nearly invisible in both the infrared and visual spectrums. He made a mental note to have the ship repainted upon his return, as he anticipated more missions such as this in the near future.

Finally, the time had come. Tug switched on his focused laser communications array and locked it onto Ancot City below. It was late in the evening there, and he would still be in the shadows behind the planet as he attempted contact. If Jalea was still alive and had something to report, he would get a response, of that he was sure. He set the beam area to include the entire city of Ancot, as he knew not where she might be located. At the exact moment that contact was to begin, he fired three hailing pulses, each one containing the proper contact request codes. Moments later, he received an acknowledgment pulse. He quickly fixed his array on the exact location of the pulse and tightened his beam to be less than three meters. Someone would have to be within that three meter circle on the ground below in order to exchange messages with him.

Tug sent another hail pulse and got an immediate response. The communications system confirmed the authentication code of the sender and then began to receive the sender's burst transmission. Tug sent back a confirmation signal, followed by a message that indicated that they should continue following the same communication protocols. Once he received the final confirmation pulse, he shut down his array and continued to coast past Ancot.

Tug called up the data that had been sent to him via the burst transmission. The sender had used Jalea's transmission code. This meant that either the message was true, or the sender had somehow managed to get the authentication code from Jalea. The latter was impossible, for it, too, was based on an algorithm that they had concocted prior to her departure. The algorithm was written down and held in her possession. If captured, she would have swallowed it, and the algorithm was too complex to commit to memory. The information sent had to be from Jalea; Tug was sure of it. He punched in the encryption code and decrypted the message. As he read the message, his concern deepened.

Tug coasted along for another three hours until he was close enough to the Savoy sun that his heat signature and jump flash would be lost in its brilliance. He powered up his ship and jumped to the void just outside the Savoy system, where he changed course for Darvano and jumped home.

* * *

"Captain, Comms," Naralena's voice called over the intercom on the desk.

"Go ahead," Nathan answered.

"Sir, Karuzara Command reports Tug is inbound. He will be coming straight to our flight deck. He has urgent news and requests a meeting with you and Lieutenant Commander Nash. He also has requested that Mister Dumar be present as well."

"Understood." Nathan keyed off the intercom and rose from his seat. It had to be important for Tug to have called ahead, and that had Nathan worried.

"Naralena," Nathan said as he came out of his ready room, "call the COB and have him meet us in the intel shack. Direct Tug there when he arrives."

"Yes, sir."

"Ensign Yosef, you have the bridge."

Tug's interceptor rolled to an abrupt halt in the middle of the hangar bay. He wasted no time, jumping down from the cockpit before the Corinari deck hands could roll out a boarding ladder to him.

"What the hell's your hurry, Tug?" Marcus asked.

"Can you paint my ship black, Senior Chief?" Tug asked as he tossed his helmet to one of the deck hands.

"Sure, but why the hell do you want..."

"Then get started," Tug instructed, "and after that, please get her ready for launch as soon as possible."

Marcus watched as Tug quickly left the hangar deck, not even going to the pilot's dressing room to change first. "You heard the man," he hollered. "Find some black paint, damn it!"

Tug entered the intel shack and dropped his data chip on the table. "Intel from Jalea," he announced.

"What does it say?" Jessica asked as she picked it up and plugged it into a reader.

"A Ta'Akar frigate will arrive in Savoy sometime in the next few days. It is coming from the Norwitt system. Jalea expects its next logical destination would be Darvano, so she tasked her comm-operator to send me this information."

"So I guess she made contact with some hidden Karuzari on Ancot," Nathan observed.

"Yes," Tug acknowledged, "but there is more. Her suspicions were confirmed when a message from Takaran Command arrived in Ancot. Orders for the frigate that is due to arrive in Savoy, the Loranoi, to rendezvous with the battleship Wallach in the Darvano system."

"When?" Jessica asked.

"It does not say when, exactly," Dumar said as he read the data. "The transmission just says to 'make best speed to rendezvous with the Wallach in Darvano at the earliest'."

"Read on," Tug said.

"It says something about exchanging their comm-drones," Dumar said.

"Why would they need to exchange their comm-drones?" Nathan wondered. "Are they out or something?"

"No, that's not it," Jessica disagreed. "If that were the case, wouldn't they use the word 'replace'?"

"Yeah, or refurbish, or replenish—not exchange," Nathan agreed.

Mister Dumar's eyes squinted tighter for a moment. "Captain, I think I may know what is going on, and I am afraid it is not good."

"What is it, Mister Dumar?" Nathan asked.

"I have been wondering about something," Dumar began. "I could never figure out how news of the Ta'Akar attack on Taroa managed to reach the Darvano system so quickly. Taroa is nearly eight light years away, yet the footage of the attack arrived only three days later."

"How do you know the date of the attack?" Jessica wondered.

"On one of the videos, there was a woman clutching a boarding pass at the spaceport. It was probably overlooked as she was running away from danger so the image was only there for a moment." Dumar called up the video footage and played it back for them. "There." Dumar stopped the video and zoomed in on the date. "I was able to enhance the image and make out the date on the document. At eight light years away, it should have taken a comm-drone twenty-nine days to get from Taroa to Darvano, longer if it went through Takara first, which it normally does. These images got here in only three days."

"You're saying that the Ta'Akar have newer, faster comm-drones?" Nathan asked.

"It is the only explanation," Dumar insisted.

"But it would take far more energy than that provided by all four of the anti-matter reactors on this ship to travel at such speeds," Tug argued.

"Three days from Taroa to Darvano? That would require a speed of one thousand times that of light. For that you would need…"

"A zero-point energy device," Nathan said.

The room fell silent.

"You know, I wondered how those ships in Korak knew to look for us so soon," Nathan commented. "We weren't there more than a day when they came out into the asteroid field to find us. It should have taken five or six days for a message to travel from Taroa to Korak."

"That would also explain the message about exchanging the Wallach's comm-drones," Dumar explained. "Perhaps the Loranoi is carrying a surplus of the newer drones and is tasked with meeting up with warships still carrying the older versions."

"It makes sense, Captain," Tug agreed. "Upgrading the efficiency of their communications network, at least between warships and command, would be the highest priority. The drones used by the various systems can be replaced one drone at a time during normal comm runs."

"There is something else, Captain," Dumar warned.

"What, more good news?" Nathan quipped.

"Mister Willard's mission report from Savoy stated that the sergeant major at the spaceport said something unusual." Dumar picked up his data pad and started scanning through the reports. "Ah yes, here it is. He said 'I am sure you are anxious to get the refit started.'"

"He wasn't talking about comm-drones, was he?" Jessica observed.

"No, I suspect he wasn't," Nathan agreed.

"Captain," Tug said, "if they have managed to

create zero-point energy devices small enough to be installed in comm-drones, they must surely have created larger versions as well."

"But I thought the latest propaganda videos said those things were still months away." Jessica pointed out.

"I suspect they were a purposeful deception on the part of the Ta'Akar," Dumar stated. "It would be in keeping with their methods."

"Captain," Tug began in a considerably more serious tone, "if the Ta'Akar are allowed to install the zero-point energy devices in even half of their warships, we will not stand a chance against them."

"Why?" Nathan wondered. "We still have the jump drive."

"The shields on Ta'Akar warships are quite formidable, Captain," Tug told him. "With that much power available, it would take an army of ships to wear them down—not to mention their energy weapons. If powered by a zero-point energy device, I cannot begin to imagine the destruction their next generation of energy weapons might yield."

Nathan looked at Tug. "Then what do we do?"

Tug did not have an answer at hand, as he was just as worried about the new developments as Nathan. "I do not know," he admitted.

Nathan looked at Jessica, who shook her head in despair. He looked at Dumar, who looked equally dismayed. Nathan took a deep breath, letting it out slowly as he searched his mind for an answer. Finally one came.

"We have to attack," Nathan announced.

"Attack what?" Jessica asked.

"Anything and everything," Nathan said. "They have the zero-point thingy. I got that. They can blow us out of the sky. I got that as well. But they can't be everywhere at once, can they?"

"Of course not," Jessica said.

"Well, we can. We can jump in, attack, and jump out. We can take out comm-drone platforms, bombard ground installations, harass their warships, maybe even cripple a few. We just have to keep out of their cross-hairs and avoid taking a direct hit from a ship with a ZPED."

"It is a valiant idea, Captain, but just one good hit on the Aurora and the war would be over," Tug concluded. "It is just too risky."

"Then what do you suggest?" Nathan asked.

Tug looked at Dumar, his old friend. "The head of the dragon."

CHAPTER NINE

"Gentlemen, I'd like to thank you all for agreeing to meet with us on such short notice," Nathan began, taking well-placed pauses to allow the various interpreters in the room to catch up. He looked at the faces of the various generals, political and industrial leaders, and of course the Prime Minister and his interpreter, Mister Briden.

"I'm afraid I am the bearer of bad news," Nathan continued. "Our intelligence asset on Ancot has informed us that the Ta'Akar frigate Loranoi is due to arrive at Ancot sometime in the next few days. Furthermore, orders have been received by the garrison on Ancot for the Loranoi, instructing her to proceed with all due speed to a rendezvous with the battleship Wallach. This rendezvous is to take place here, in the Darvano system."

The room filled with a sudden burst of frantic discourse between attendees, most of which was in Corinairan. However, it was obvious to Nathan that the impact of his news was as expected.

"Has this intelligence been verified?" a translator for one of the generals inquired.

"No, sir, not as yet," Nathan admitted.

"Could this not be a ruse?" Mister Briden wondered aloud.

"We considered that possibility," Nathan said. "We are taking steps to confirm this information, but we thought it best to apprise you of the situation."

"How do you intend to make such a confirmation?" Mister Briden challenged.

"I will take the new jump interceptor out and attempt to locate the Loranoi," Tug explained.

"How can you possibly hope to find a single ship, traveling faster than light, over such a vast area of space?" another translator inquired.

"Our intelligence also indicated that the Loranoi was traveling to Savoy from the Norwitt system," Nathan said. "If this information is accurate, we should be able to locate the Loranoi along the route from Norwitt to Savoy."

"And the Wallach?" Mister Briden asked. "Can you locate her as well?"

"That may not be possible," Tug admitted. "We have no information as to her last port of call; therefore, we will have to search every imaginable route."

"Surely the mighty Aurora can handle a single frigate," a translator for one of the Corinari generals stated. "After all, did she not defeat the Yamaro?"

"The Yamaro was of an older design and was known to be underpowered," Tug asserted. "No offense to Captain Scott, but the Aurora did not defeat the Yamaro; the mutineers surrendered her."

"But the Campaglia," another translator spouted, "she was a battleship as well, and a formidable one at that."

"Yes," Nathan agreed, "but we were lucky. We had jumped inside her shields by accident. There was no time to take evasive action, and we were forced to ram her."

"But you also filled her with torpedoes, did you not?" the translator argued. "Were not they the cause of her ultimate destruction?"

"Yes, but…"

"The point is, Captain, that the mighty Campaglia was destroyed and the Aurora survived…"

"Barely!" Nathan interrupted. "The Campaglia was a powerful ship, yes, but she was caught by surprise by an unknown enemy. I'm not so sure we'll have the same advantage this time."

"Why not?" Mister Briden inquired indignantly.

"We have reason to believe that the Ta'Akar have already begun using the zero-point energy device in their comm-drones," Tug explained, "resulting in increased speeds, possibly as fast as one thousand times the speed of light."

Again the room filled with chatter as generals quickly recalculated the message transfer times resulting from comm-drones traveling a thousand times the speed of light. The looks on their faces revealed the depth of their concern.

"We believe this is why the Loranoi is to rendezvous with the Wallach, in order to exchange the Wallach's older, slower comm-drones for the newer, faster versions," Tug added.

"We also have cause to believe that they may have started to upgrade their warships, refitting them with the zero-point energy devices."

The reaction was explosive this time, and it took several minutes for the room to settle down to the point where discussion could continue.

Cameron watched in silence as she had since the beginning of the meeting. After witnessing the Corinairans argue and debate amongst themselves for several minutes, she finally had enough. "Nathan," she said, leaning closer to him in order to be heard. Tug also leaned in from Nathan's opposite side in order to hear her. "These people are never going to come to any consensus."

"How do you know?" Nathan wondered. "You can't even understand what they're saying."

"I don't need to," she insisted. "Just look at them; look at their body language. I doubt there are two people amongst the lot of them that are in agreement over anything you've presented."

"She is correct," Tug added. "The generals are screaming for action. The politicians are worried about global panic and the collapse of their governments. The industrialists are counting the profits to be made. And the civil security authority is worried about a resurgence of the anarchy that occurred after the Yamaro's attack."

"You have to say something," Cameron told him. "You have to pull them together somehow."

Nathan looked at her with surprise.

"Yeah, I know," she said. "I can't believe I said that either. But the fact is, it's time for Na-Tan to speak. These people need to act, not react."

Nathan looked at the men in the room. Their faces were reddened with anger as they shouted at one another about what to do, about what was to become of them. He surveyed those in attendance. There were numerous politicians, each representing either a major nation of Corinair or a minor world within the Darvano system. There were also several of the most influential industrialists, two Corinari generals, and the chief of civil security for all of Corinair. He was unsure how things would go if matters called for any kind of a vote, but he had little choice. The Aurora and the Karuzari could not defend the Darvano system against two warships without the help of the Corinairans, and the

Corinairans were practically helpless without the Aurora.

"Gentlemen," Nathan stated, but was not heard above the din. "Gentlemen! Please!" he shouted, standing up in the hopes of drawing their attention. He raised his hands and shouted again, but still it was of no use. "EVERYONE SHUT THE HELL UP!" Nathan roared, demanding their attention. He kicked his chair back and climbed over the top of the table, landing inside the circle of conference tables at which the attendees were arguing. He was not going to stand for any more mindless discourse. These people were going to listen.

"Gentlemen, now is not the time for debate. Now is the time for action. We have thirty days to prepare a defense."

"And what do we do if we are successful in defending ourselves?" Mister Briden asked. "The Ta'Akar will return, and most assuredly in greater numbers. Can you defend against an invasion as well?"

Nathan looked around the room, noting that each of the translators had communicated Mister Briden's words to their superiors, most of whom were nodding their agreement with Mister Briden's concerns. "We attack," Nathan stated calmly. "We take the fight to them. We hit them where they are most vulnerable."

"And where might such vulnerabilities be, Captain?" Mister Briden challenged. "The Ta'Akar are everywhere."

"They are?" Nathan asked. "I don't see them here now. Nor did I see them when we first arrived."

"They appear randomly, usually when you least expect them," Mister Briden warned.

"The Ta'Akar are not everywhere, sir," Tug stated emphatically. "They only wish you to believe as much. They control all interstellar travel and communications within the Pentaurus cluster, therefore they control all information as well. The Karuzari have weakened them over the decades, reduced their numbers by more than half. Because of this, they have abandoned the worlds they once held that lay beyond the cluster. They have gathered half their remaining fleet around their home system to protect themselves, while they shuffle the other half amongst their remaining systems."

"And what is the size of their remaining fleet?" Mister Briden asked.

"Our last estimates showed three battle groups, two of which are stationed in the Takaran home system. The third battle group is unaccounted for and is presumably roaming the cluster as we speak. In addition, there are seven more unattached vessels patrolling the cluster. Two cruisers and five frigates."

"That is eighteen ships," one of the general's translators declared. "We cannot possibly take on eighteen ships."

"We don't plan to," Nathan insisted. "We thin the herd. A series of strikes against isolated targets, combined with a series of comm-drones sent to deliver deceptive information to the enemy. If we can get the Ta'Akar to dispatch at least one of her two battle groups from the Takaran system, we could then conduct a surgical strike against their command and control, perhaps even against Caius himself."

"You are proposing that we attack the Royal Palace of the Ta'Akar?" Mister Briden sputtered.

"Are you mad?"

"It is not the dragon's claws you must fear," one of the general's translators began, "nor is it his tail..."

"It is the fire in his eyes and mouth," Tug finished.

"Gentlemen," Nathan stated calmly, "I propose we cut off the head of the dragon."

* * *

"I'll need you to represent our interests at the planning table with the Corinari generals," Nathan told Cameron as they walked quickly through the hospital corridors.

"I need to be back on the ship," Cameron protested. "We've got a new crew that needs to be trained, and in a really short amount of time I might add."

"Aren't you forgetting something, Commander?" Nathan said. "You're still a patient in this hospital."

"Oh, I can fix that real quick," Cameron insisted, stopping at the nearest nursing station. "Get me a doctor, now!" she ordered a nurse. The young woman behind the counter stared at her blankly, not understanding a word she was saying. "A doctor! Do you understand?"

Another woman, older than the first, stepped up. "Can I help you?"

"Yes, I need to speak with a doctor right away."

"Commander..." Nathan began.

"Don't even try, Nathan."

"I can order you, if you'd like."

"And I can ignore you, if I'd like."

"Cameron, I need you completely well and at full strength when the Ta'Akar come."

"And I will be, but you also need a crew that's as ready as they can be, and for that you also need me."

"Cam..."

"I'm fine, Nathan. I'm at full strength, I'm telling you. I don't even know why I'm still here."

"I'm sure that if the doctors thought..."

"Look, if the doctors say I can go, will that be good enough for you?"

"Of course, but..."

"Great." Cameron looked around. "Where the hell is a doctor when you need one?"

"Can I help you, miss?" the older woman in medical attire asked.

"I don't know; are you a doctor?"

"Yes, I am Doctor Marcella. What seems to be the problem?"

"I need someone to tell my captain here that I'm cleared to check out," Cameron insisted.

"You are the young woman from the Earth ship?"

"Yes."

"Your case was presented in conference the other day. Quite interesting."

"Great, I have an interesting case. Can I go back to my ship?"

"You should probably speak to your doctor about that," Doctor Marcella advised.

"Look, Doc," Cameron pleaded, "I just need to know if it's possible for me to return to my ship. I have work to do there, and I feel fine."

"It is my understanding that you still have nanites working inside you. If that is the case, then you still require periodic monitoring to ensure their proper operation, as well as their discharge from your body when their work is complete."

"Yeah, I know. I have to relieve myself in metal trays. Don't remind me," Cameron said, rolling her eyes. "Can't I do all that on the ship?"

"Well, there are portable nanite monitoring devices, but they are not routinely used as they..."

"Ah hah!" Cameron interrupted. "That's it! Get me a portable monitor!"

"Excuse me, Doctor, but is it at all possible that Commander Taylor could return to the ship using some kind of portable monitor setup?"

"It is possible," the doctor admitted hesitantly, "but you would need a doctor familiar with nanite therapy, as well as a nanite technician on board as well."

"Great," Cameron explained. "We're heading for combat in a month anyway. Seems to me having a few nanite specialists on board might be a good thing, right?"

"All right, I'll look into it."

"You'll look into it?" Cameron asked, not satisfied with his answer.

"I'll request it," Nathan promised, "but only if Doc Chen agrees. Meanwhile, you get busy with the Corinari generals and light a fire under their butts. We've got a month, tops."

* * *

"Good morning, everyone," Nathan greeted as he sat down for his morning briefing. "As you can see, we have a new member joining us. For those of you who have not met Major Prechitt, he will be joining us as the commander of the Corinari Aerospace Group being assigned to us. In other words, the major is our new CAG."

A round of, "Welcome aboard," greetings were tossed about the room.

"Excuse me, sir," Major Prechitt asked, "CAG?"

"Commander Air Group," Nathan explained. "It's the acronym we use to describe your position. It's left over from the days of surface navies back on Earth. I guess in your case, however, CAG would stand for 'Commander Aerospace Group.'"

"Yes, of course," Major Prechitt said. "Like Master Chief Montrose's title. 'Chief of the Boat' was it?"

"Yeah, something like that," Nathan agreed. "How are things shaping up with our new air group, Major?"

"The first group of twenty-four interceptors will be ready to begin flight operations from the Aurora within two weeks, Captain. In light of the new threat, efforts to get the second wing ready have been doubled. However, there is an additional problem in that the second wing is being formed using interceptors from multiple nations, so there will be some compatibility issues to be worked out, as well as some procedural ones."

"I can make it easy for you," Nathan said. "Normally, on an Earth ship, whatever the CAG says goes, at least in regards to the operation of the air group."

"It may not be that easy, sir. There are some cultural issues to deal with as well. However, I feel confident that they will not present too much of a problem. My biggest concern is the amount of time available for launch and recovery training. Our crews are trained for ground operations."

"We'll be able to provide some assistance in that area, Major. Both the XO and I are pilots rated for deck-ops, so we have some experience in that area. Plus, we have quite extensive policies and procedures manuals available in the mainframe for your people. If you like, we can have them translated into Corinairan as well."

"That will not be necessary," Major Prechitt assured him. "At least half of my pilots already speak Angla, and the rest are going through intensive language training as we speak. I would rather not give them an excuse to ignore their studies."

"Very well," Nathan responded.

"Sir, do you have any idea when we can begin training?"

"Both fighter alleys are clear and ready," Vladimir stated. "And the entire forward section is at least habitable now. There are still things to work on, but your people can move in whenever you are ready, Major."

"Excellent," Major Prechitt exclaimed. "We will begin setting up shop immediately. That way, I can get the ground, I mean, deck crews trained and ready before we fill your bays with fighters."

"I believe I like the sound of that," Jessica stated.

"We're getting some refits on our missile systems right now," Nathan stated, "but as soon as that's done, we'll be ready for open space again. I expect that'll happen well before your fighters start landing."

"That is good news, Captain. Eighty percent of our training has traditionally focused on atmospheric intercepts, with the other twenty percent spent on orbital. My pilots have almost no training in deep-space engagements."

"I suspect that will change rather soon, I'm afraid," Nathan admitted. "Commander Taylor and I will lend any of our limited knowledge and experience in that area as well."

"Thank you, sir. Anything you can share with us will be of use."

"Doctor Sorenson?" Nathan said, inviting Abby to begin her updates.

"The Corinairans have successfully tested their first mini-jump drive equipped shuttle. They are currently installing the necessary sensory and deep space navigational gear required for their new mission as early warning ships. They expect to be able to produce and deploy at least four of them before the Loranoi arrives."

"That will make Tug happy, I'm sure," Nathan commented.

"Where is Tug?" Jessica wondered.

"He and Josh are out in the interceptor searching for the Wallach."

"The Corinairans have expressed their displeasure at the fact that they have only one pair of fabricators available for the purpose of creating the mini-jump drives," Abby stated.

"Tough," Nathan answered. "We may be full up with rail gun ammo, but they're nothing but dumb slugs. That means our only defense against a missile attack is to jump away, which is great if the jump drive is working. But if it goes down, we're screwed. So until they can get some of their factories to agree to start producing fragmenting point-defense rounds for us, we're hogging those fabricators."

"Captain, even with all the fabricators running twenty-four hours a day, they will still not be able to produce enough frag-rounds to be of significant use," Vladimir pointed out.

"Yeah, I know that, and you know that," Nathan explained, "but the politicians on Corinair don't, and I don't have time to beg those industrialists to start stamping out ammo for us. This way, I get the politicians to put the pressure on them."

"*Da, konyeshna*," Vladimir agreed.

"They do realize there are two heavily armed Takaran warships on their way here, don't they?" Jessica asked.

"They believe the Loranoi is coming," Nathan admitted, "but I'm not so sure they believe that the Wallach is coming as well."

"What, one warship's not enough?"

"They seem convinced that we can handle the Loranoi all by ourselves," Nathan said.

"Then why are they even bothering with the early warning shuttles?" Jessica asked.

"I have no idea," Nathan admitted. "I suppose it makes them feel better."

"The Loranoi is a formidable ship," Mister Willard warned. "She is equipped with the most advanced missile batteries and target acquisition systems. She also has an advanced electronic countermeasures system, which makes it very difficult to lock weapons onto her during battle."

"Great," Jessica commented.

"How are things going with our EC suite?" Nathan asked Vladimir.

"Slowly I'm afraid. It was severely damaged, and the power surge that resulted fried most of it and the control runs, all the way back to the control console on the bridge. I do not think we can fix it, as we simply do not have the parts."

"Captain," Mister Willard interrupted, "I may have a solution for you."

"Yes, Ensign?"

"I am no longer an Ensign, Captain. My shipmates and I are now officially considered defectors from the empire. Therefore, we no longer carry a rank."

"Duly noted," Nathan said. "Congratulations, by the way."

"Thank you, Captain," Mister Willard said. "As I was saying, the electronic countermeasures equipment on the Yamaro was undamaged and is currently not scheduled for use. It is not as advanced as that on the Loranoi, but it might be possible to remove it from the Yamaro and install it on the Aurora."

"Do you think that would work?" Nathan asked.

"Their transponder array was pretty easy to adapt to our systems," Vladimir said. "If it works, it would be better than nothing."

"Very well. I'll put in a request to the Corinairans to allow you to get started on that, Mister Willard."

"Yes, sir," Mister Willard acknowledged.

"Excellent. Moving on then." Nathan turned to Doctor Chen. "Doc, how are things looking in Medical?"

"I'm happy to report that, for the first time since we left Earth, I have nothing but empty beds. Two more crewmen have returned from their rehabilitation down on Corinair. Those remaining will be there for at least another month. Also, along with more staff, we are also getting more diagnostic and laboratory equipment."

"More staff?" Nathan asked.

"Yes, sir. Somebody has to show us how to use the new equipment, and since we are expected to go into combat in the near future, they decided they might as well give us doctors. In fact, they gave us two trauma surgeons, as well as about eight nurses and technicians. We've almost got a full staff at this point."

"Well, with two more shifts coming on board in the next few days, we're going to need them." Nathan stated. "What about the nanite guys?"

"They're coming aboard with Commander Taylor later today," Doctor Chen stated.

"Cam's coming back?" Jessica asked.

"Yeah, I was saving that last," Nathan joked.

"Great," Jessica said, "now we can get our butts chewed on a daily basis."

"Well, she'll be touching down around fifteen hundred, so be ready," Nathan warned. "Very well, that about does it. We've all got lots of work to do, so let's get to it. Cheng, Abby, and Mister Willard, if you'll all please remain, everyone else is dismissed."

Once the others had left the briefing room, Nathan began speaking again. "Mister Willard, how many comm-drones are there remaining aboard the Yamaro?"

"I believe there were twelve when we arrived in the Darvano system, Captain. There are probably just as many on the comm-drone platform in the Darvano system, the one used by the local Ta'Akar communications office."

"How much do you know about their programming?"

"Enough, mostly about their communications code. Although I was primarily a communications technician, I also worked quite closely with the men responsible for maintenance and programming of the drones."

"Could those drones be reprogrammed to fly courses and speeds according to instructions transmitted to them on the fly?"

"The ones from the Yamaro, yes. They are already programmable, as they were designed to be used from anywhere. But the ones used by the Darvano system are fixed-destination drones, designed to travel between Darvano and Takara. They would need to be rewired."

"Could that be done?"

"I believe so," Mister Willard stated. "They are essentially the same, with just slightly different navigational packages. Even if they cannot be rewired, you could use the fabricators to create copies of the navigational packages in the Yamaro's drones and install them into the ones from the Darvano platform. May I inquire as to why?"

"I was thinking of using them as faster-than-light kinetic kill vehicles."

"Really?"

"If we could get a Takaran ship into a designated kill zone, we could send the jump interceptor out to a drone parked some distance away to issue launch orders. At FTL speeds, it would pack a hell of a wallop."

"*Bozhe moi,*" Vladimir exclaimed. "Do you realize how much of a 'wallop'?"

"I haven't tried to calculate that yet," Nathan admitted, "but I'm pretty sure it would be enough to penetrate the shields of a Ta'Akar battleship."

"And then some," Abby agreed.

"Forget nuclear weapons, Nathan," Vladimir exclaimed, "you are an evil genius."

"Captain, the odds of successfully striking a moving target in such a manner are astronomically small," Abby warned.

"I'm not so sure, Doctor," Nathan argued. "If we already know the speed and course of the target, and we can keep them on course and at that speed for even a short length of time, say five to ten minutes,

I think we have a very good chance of hitting it. Anyway, it's something that I do want to experiment with, and I'm hoping that you'll spearhead the development along with the Corinairans, Doctor."

"I'll do my best, Captain," Abby promised.

* * *

Cameron stared out the window of the shuttle as it made its way through the Karuzara entrance tunnel. She thought about the last time she had made this passage, and about the auto-flight script she had written to simplify the Aurora's transit through the long corridor. She hadn't really thought much about it at the time, but the tunnel had barely been big enough for use by a ship as large as the Aurora. Luckily, Nathan had been smart enough to send a shuttle in ahead of them, scanning and mapping the tunnel on their way in to be sure the Aurora really would fit. It had been tight, but they had made it through time and time again.

The tunnel looked bigger to her this time around. She wondered if the Karuzari had widened it, or if it was just an optical illusion since she was flying in a ship only a fraction of the size of the Aurora. In the end, she decided that it was a little bit of both, since she noticed a few spots that appeared to have been freshly excavated.

Cameron thought about all that had happened to her over the last three months, ever since she had first reported for duty aboard the Aurora back at the assembly platform orbiting the Earth. By this time, she had spent more than half of their mission in the hospital on Corinair. She was excited to get back to her ship, back to her people, but she was nervous as well. It was not the same crew that had left Earth. Three quarters of them were dead, most of them buried on Corinair. Those that remained no longer shared the same experiences as her. They had all been through a lot more on their own, without her. It was almost as if she were reporting to a new assignment, on a new ship.

At least she wouldn't have to prove herself to anyone this time around. She was reporting for duty as the executive officer, and with a full crew, her job would be a big one. She would no longer be just second-in-command, she would be running the day to day operations of the ship. That was, after all, the role of the XO, to make the ship and her crew do what her captain decided he wanted them to do. A good XO enabled the captain to think about what to do with his ship, instead of how to do it.

To think about what to do with the ship. The thought struck her as ironic to say the least. Nathan was not exactly the type to give something a lot of thought before acting. She had to admit that he had changed somewhat over the past month, but to her, he would always be Nathan Scott, the spoiled son of a rich politician whose daddy always bailed him out of trouble.

Not this time, she thought. He was going to have to get himself out of trouble. Funny thing was, he seemed to be doing all right without his father's help.

The interior of the shuttle filled with light as it left the tunnel and entered the main central cavern of the asteroid now officially known as Karuzara. *Karuzara. That's what you get for letting Josh pick a name,* she thought. She moved her face closer to the glass in order to look forward to get a better view of her ship. She hadn't seen the outside of her since she first walked through the windowed boarding tunnel from the assembly platform. It looked different somehow—more shiny, almost like she was wet. She remembered reading the notes about the special coating the Karuzari technicians had applied and concluded the glimmer must have been the result of the reflective elements in that coating. She decided she liked it, as it was far more interesting than the standard white and gray of most EDF ships. It looked more polished, more impressive.

Cameron could feel her pulse rate increase as she saw her ship for the first time in more than a month. As the shuttle descended toward the Aurora, she strained to try and see any evidence of the previous damage to her bow, but there was none. The Corinairan technicians had done a fine job of repairing her, a service for which she would forever be grateful.

The Corinari shuttle continued to descend in expert fashion, making only the slightest of adjustments to her flight path on the way in. Finally, it settled gently on the Aurora's flight apron, creating only the slightest bump within the cabin. *Now that's how you land a shuttle,* she thought. *Nothing like that little hotshot, Josh.* He was too undisciplined for her taste, much like her captain—at least how he used to be. Now, she wasn't too sure.

After the shuttle rolled into the transfer airlock and the chamber had pressurized, four heavily armored security guards in Corinari uniforms came through the personnel hatch into the bay and made their way to the shuttle. Two of them came on board while the other two began inspecting the exterior of the shuttle. One guard went forward into the cockpit to check the flight crew, while the other guard came into the passenger cabin and went straight to Cameron.

"Identification, ma'am," the guard said in a serious tone. Cameron handed him the ident chip that the Corinari had made for her before she left the hospital. After inserting the ident chip into his reader, he held it up and scanned Cameron's face. "Thank you, Commander." The guard then repeated the process for the doctor that had accompanied her and the nanite technician that would be monitoring and programming the remaining nanites in her body until they finally finished their work and left her system.

A message squawked in the guards comm-set. "Your shuttle has been cleared. If you'll remain seated, the ship will continue into the main hangar bay where you may disembark. Welcome aboard the Aurora."

The big inner airlock door began to rise, as did Cameron's pulse rate once more. As the shuttle began to roll forward, she could feel a queasiness building in her stomach.

"Are you all right, Commander?" the doctor asked. Apparently she looked like she felt.

"I'm fine, thank you."

The shuttle finally came to a stop. Cameron took a deep breath and stood. *Here we go*, she thought as she marched up the aisle toward the hatch.

The familiar flood lights of the main hangar bay filled her eyes as she stepped through the shuttle's boarding hatch and descended the ramp. There in front of her were the thirty-seven surviving members of the original crew, minus the ones still in the hospital on Corinair, lined up on either side of the boarding ramp, with Nathan, Jessica, and Vladimir all standing at the far end of the line.

"Attention on deck!" Jessica shouted. Everyone on the line snapped to attention simultaneously. Cameron felt her heart jump. Calling attention for her arrival wasn't in accordance with military procedures; it was being done as a tribute. At that moment, her nervousness, her fears, and her doubts, all seemed to fade away. She descended the ramp and marched down the row between the two lines of her shipmates, coming to a stop in front of Nathan at the end of the line.

"Commander Taylor, reporting for duty, sir," she stated, snapping a salute.

Nathan returned her salute with his usual smile, the one that always got him out of trouble with his mother, the same smile that always made Cameron want to smack him in the head. "Welcome aboard, Commander."

* * *

"Is there any type of flying that is more boring than this?" Josh wondered aloud as he entered the next destination into the interceptor's jump drive plotting computer. "Jump, sweep, flip, jump, sweep, flip, jump, sweep, flip. Hey, I know. Let's shake things up a bit. How about we flip, sweep, jump, just one time. What do you think?"

"I think you talk too much," Tug answered as he entered the time and results of the most recent sensor sweep. They had been jumping about in search of the Wallach for more than an hour now, concentrating on the three most likely routes that she would be traveling if indeed she was headed for the Darvano system. The problem was that, even if she were traveling along one of the three most likely routes, they had no idea what speed she was traveling. Therefore, they had no choice but to play it safe. Since they could not see a ship coming at them at speeds faster than light, they had to jump outward from Darvano a little at a time, pausing to look back for signs of the Wallach moving away from them toward Darvano. Since their sensor range was only a few light days, they had a lot of jumps ahead of them.

"We don't even know if the Wallach is going to be on any of these routes," Josh complained.

"Would you please stop whining and jump to the next sweep point?" Tug begged.

"Please, shoot me now and put me out of my misery," Josh said as he flipped the ship over to point the interceptor in the direction it was already traveling.

"If I had a weapon on me, I would," Tug stated, "for both our sakes."

"Ha ha," Josh replied as he lowered his helmet visor. "Jumping in three......two......one......jump."

The cockpit filled momentarily with the blue-white jump flash as the ship leapt ahead another light day along its course from Darvano toward the Juntor system.

"Jump complete," Josh reported, raising his visor. "We are now two hundred and ninety-eight light days out. Hey, see if you can guess what I'm going to do next."

"Flip?" Tug asked.

"You guessed it, boys and girls. It's time to flip the ship. Wee!" Josh flipped the ship end over end so that their nose was pointing back toward Darvano.

"Starting sensor sweep," Tug reported.

"Hey, doesn't this thing have any rear facing sensors?" Josh wondered. "At least that would cut out the flipping part. 'Cuz you know what? I'm pretty much an expert at flipping now. I really don't need more practice."

"I should have asked for Loki," Tug muttered.

"Yeah, you really should have. You know, Loki's always complaining that he doesn't get out much anymore. Let's jump back and swap pilots. Whattaya say? One jump and we're back at Karuzara. You'll be back out here flipping and sweeping in no time at all."

"Quiet," Tug ordered.

"I was just making a suggestion. No need to get all huffy..."

"Quiet!" Tug stared at the screen a moment. There was the tiniest of anomalies in his sensor sweep. "Reverse course and head for Darvano, then jump ahead eight light hours," Tug ordered.

"We're a lot farther from Darvano than eight light hours , Pops."

"I have a contact," Tug explained.

"Seriously?" Josh asked, straightening up in his seat.

"Yes! Turn around!"

"Outstanding!" Josh exclaimed as he flipped the interceptor back over and fired his engines. He pulled the interceptor into a tight left turn, kicking his tail out considerably in order to increase his turn rate. "Reversing course," he announced as he punched in the next jump destination into the interceptor's jump drive plotting computer. "Jumping ahead eight light hours in three......two......one......jump." Josh dropped his visor again on the word jump. Again the cockpit filled with the jump flash for a brief moment, after which he raised his visor again. "Do you see her?" Josh asked. "Is the Wallach out there?"

"Wow," Tug exclaimed.

"What?"

"According to these readings, she passed this point not more than a minute ago."

"That's cutting it kind of close, don't you think?" Josh exclaimed.

"Just get us home," Tug instructed.

"Now you're talking," Josh agreed as he set Darvano as the next jump point. Josh flipped down his visor. "Jumping in three......two......one...... jump."

* * *

"Helm, turn into the frigate," Nathan ordered. "Tactical, stand by all forward tubes."

"Coming to port. Bearing on the frigate, sir," the helmsman answered.

"That's it, just tell her where to go," Cameron instructed the helmsman. "You don't have to tell her *how* to make the turn, she already knows."

"Forward tubes loaded and ready, sir," the tactical officer answered.

"Prepare to snapshot all forward tubes," Nathan barked, "staggered launch."

"Aye, sir," the tactical officer replied.

"Say it back to him," Jessica instructed.

"Right," the tactical officer remembered. "Standing by to snapshot all forward tubes. Staggered launch. Aye, sir."

Nathan watched the forward view screen as the Aurora continued turning to port, bringing her nose to bear on the enemy frigate. The floor of the bridge shook under his feet as they received rail gun fire. Deliza's simulations were getting more realistic than ever. At any moment, Nathan was half expecting something on the bridge to burst into flames and send sparks flying across the room.

"Range?" Nathan asked.

"Five hundred meters and closing fast," the tactical officer responded.

"Helm, as soon as the torpedoes are away I want you to pitch down hard and dive under the frigate."

"Aye, sir."

Nathan continued to watch the forward view screen. "Bring all forward rail guns to bear on that frigate, simple slugs, and open fire."

"Firing forward rail guns, simple slugs," the tactical officer replied. He tapped his screen several times, and the rail guns began spewing forth fist-sized pellets of alloy at incredible velocity.

"Tactical, when the torpedoes hit their shields, you'll have a weak point. Concentrate all rail gun fire on that point and set the guns to auto-track on that point for as long as possible as we dive under her."

"Yes, sir."

At that moment, Nathan felt their turn end. The Aurora's nose was on her target. "Snapshot! Tubes one through four!"

"One through four away, sir!" the tactical officer replied.

"Dive under her now, Mister Chiles," Nathan ordered.

The Aurora's nose pitched down sharply. As the image of the frigate climbed up the forward view screen, there were four blinding flashes of light as the four torpedoes each struck the same point on the frigate's shields, each torpedo a split second after the one before it. The frigate's shields flashed several times as her emitters overloaded and failed. As they dove under her, Nathan looked up as the image of the frigate continued climbing up the view screen until it passed over his head and disappeared beyond the edge of the screen, the lines of fire from their rail guns tracking the frigate as it fell behind them.

The bridge shook violently beneath their feet, the vibrations translating up through the consoles.

"We're taking heavy fire aft!" the tactical officer declared.

"Helm, prepare to jump, one light minute out on present course," Nathan ordered.

"Jump one light minute out, aye," the helmsman answered.

"Scan ahead first," Cameron reminded the navigator, "make sure the path is clear. We can't jump through solid objects."

"Yes, ma'am, I mean, sir," the navigator answered.

"The frigate's losing emitters on her starboard side, Captain," the sensor officer reported.

"Give him an estimated time to shield failure," Ensign Yosef told the sensor operator.

"Estimate starboard shield failure in two minutes," the sensor operator added.

"Jump plotted and locked," the navigator reported.

"Jump!" Nathan ordered.

The bridge filled momentarily with the blue-white jump flash.

"Jump complete," the navigator announced.

Nathan waited a moment for the navigator to

report their position. Five seconds was too long. "Position?" he barked angrily.

"Uh," the navigator stumbled.

"Where are we Mister Riley?" Nathan asked impatiently.

"Position confirmed, sir," the Navigator finally reported. "We're one light minute out, the enemy is directly astern."

"Show me the current plot," Nathan ordered.

The tactical officer quickly sent the tactical plot to the main view screen, superimposing it over the current view of the stars.

"Helm, come to port. A hundred and ten degrees over and twenty degrees up relative."

"One ten to port, twenty up relative, aye," the helmsman answered as he frantically punched commands into the flight console. The Aurora began a hard turn to port as her flight path also came up relative to the system ecliptic.

"Mister Riley, as soon as the turn is complete, plot another jump. I want to end up along that frigate's flight path, about one light minute astern of her."

"Yes, sir," the navigator answered.

"Once we jump, we'll turn onto a pursuit heading, match the frigate's last known speed and course, and jump up next to her."

"Yes, sir," the navigator answered again.

Nathan sat back down in his command chair. It would take at least a minute for them to complete such a wide turn and get into position to jump again. He looked at Cameron who was kneeling on the deck slightly behind and between the navigator on the left and the helmsman on the right. This was the fifth such exercise in a row today, and the second time up for this bridge shift. And when they weren't in a simulation on the bridge, they were watching another shift run their simulation from the screen in the command briefing room.

"Tactical, when we come alongside that frigate, her starboard shields should already be down. If they are, I want you to put a spread of four missiles into her."

"And if her shields aren't down?"

"Then pound the crap out of her with the rail guns as we pass. Then we turn out and make another torpedo run at her starboard shields again. If that doesn't bring them down, I don't know what will," Nathan declared.

"Yes, sir."

Cameron turned her head back toward Nathan and smiled. She was becoming her old self again, confident and efficient as all hell, and always busy doing something. It had only been a week since she had returned, and she already had all the ship's departments organized and the department heads in place. To make life simple, she had granted each department head as much leeway as possible in figuring out how they wanted to run their department, promising to restrict her interference to only those times when it was necessary for the proper operation of the ship as a whole. She knew they had very little time, so she had accepted the fact that it would have to be enough to just get the ship running with a full crew. She could worry about making it run smoothly later.

"Finishing our turn, Captain," the helmsman announced.

"Jump plotted and locked, sir," the navigator reported.

"Jump," Nathan ordered. The bridge filled with the jump flash again. Nathan looked up at the plot on the forward view screen. They were exactly where he had asked, directly astern of the Takaran frigate, about a light minute behind her.

"Another turn to port, Mister Chiles. Put us on a pursuit course and change our altitude in relation to the ecliptic to match that of the target."

"Aye, sir. Turning to port, and adjusting relative altitude," Mister Chiles answered.

"Be sure to angle us outward just enough so that we end up about five hundred meters off her starboard side when we jump, and be sure to match her last known speed."

"Yes, sir."

"After we jump, I want you to immediately plot an escape jump, Mister Riley," Nathan instructed. "We don't know what shape her starboard guns are in. We may have to leave in a hurry."

"Yes, sir," the navigator answered.

Nathan spun his command chair around slowly, surveying his bridge staff. Every station that was working was manned, and the key stations had his regular staff watching over each of their respective trainees. While this normally would not be the case, Commander Taylor had felt it justified considering the limited time they had for training, hoping that it would get the new crews able to stand on their feet a bit quicker. It was, however, hard on the original staff, as they had to be present for every drill, while the crews they were training got to rest for nearly an hour after each session.

"Turn complete, Captain," the helmsman reported. "We're now on a pursuit course, same speed, same relative altitude, maintaining a one degree angle off the target's starboard side."

"Very good," Nathan stated. "Mister Riley?"

"Jump plotted and locked, sir."

"Tactical?"

"Port rail guns ready. Missile battery deployed and oriented to port, sir," the tactical officer reported.

"Very well, here we go. Jump."

"Jumping," Mister Riley reported.

The bridge flashed again, but the frigate was not on the port side of the view screen where they expected her.

"Where's the frigate?"

"We over shot!" the tactical officer reported. "She's just behind us off to port."

"She's running slower than expected, Captain," the sensor operator reported.

"Damn! Braking thrusters, Mister Chiles! Tactical, retarget, track and prepare to fire as she comes up alongside. Sensors, how are her starboard shields?"

"Target's starboard shields are gone, sir," the sensor operator reported.

"Firing braking thrusters!" Mister Chiles reported.

"She is firing rail guns!" the tactical officer reported.

Nathan looked to port as the ship began to shake from the impact of the enemy frigate's rail gun rounds. The nose of the frigate started easing into view from the aft edge of the port view screen. "Don't let her overshoot us, Mister Chiles." The image of the frigate started to roll away from them.

"Frigate is rolling to port!" the tactical officer reported.

"She's trying to protect her starboard side," Nathan said. "Helm, pitch up and apply power. Try to barrel roll around her to keep our guns on her unprotected starboard side.

"Captain," the tactical officer called, "I do not think she is trying to protect her starboard side. I believe she is trying to bring her last missile battery to bear on us!"

"Helm, move faster," Nathan ordered. "Tactical, fire when ready! Mister Riley, jump us as soon as that ship fires her missiles. Don't wait for my order!"

"Firing missiles!" the tactical officer reported. A few seconds later, there was a bright flash on the screen to their port side. "Direct hit!"

"Contacts!" the sensor operator announced. "Target fired just before she was hit!"

Nathan was about to order the jump when the bridge filled with the jump flash. Mister Riley had not waited.

"Nicely done, Mister Riley!" Nathan praised. "Position?"

"I only jumped us forward ten light seconds, sir," Mister Riley reported.

"Status of the frigate?" Nathan asked.

"Stand by, sir. We are still ten seconds out."

"Bet you my dessert we nailed him," Jessica challenged.

Nathan ignored her. She was standing next to the tactical board, so she knew better than anyone if their shot was likely to hit or not.

"Target is breaking up, Captain," the sensor operator reported.

"Outstanding," Nathan congratulated. "End simulation."

The lights on the bridge reverted from their red hue to the standard amber-white lighting and the main view screen returned to the view of the interior of Karuzara's main cavern.

"B-shift, stand down. Take a break, get some chow, then report to the command briefing room to watch your shipmates get put through the ringer," Commander Taylor announced. "A-shift, take fifteen. Then, we babysit C-shift."

The trainees from B-shift stood and headed off the bridge, happily congratulating one another on their simulated victory.

"You know, you almost screwed that one up," Cameron said to Nathan after the last of the B-shift trainees had moved beyond earshot.

"How?"

"You should have told the helmsman to set his speed slightly faster than the target, then had the navigator jump us just astern of him. Then he probably wouldn't have seen us in time to start his roll before we got our shots off."

"Yeah, you're probably right," Nathan admitted. "I guess we've all got some learning to do when it comes to using the jump drive in combat."

"Well, that's why the A-shift is sitting through every simulation."

"We should probably start each morning with a simulation of our own, with no trainees in the room. Have Deliza give us her worst," Nathan suggested.

"You really want to start your day being humiliated?" Cameron asked.

"Only if you promise that no one will be watching us from the briefing room," Nathan answered.

* * *

After more than a week straight of bridge simulations, Nathan was happy to get a couple days off. Mister Willard had managed to get the electronic countermeasures package pulled from the Yamaro and was currently installing it on the Aurora. It had necessitated the removal of all the arrays on the exterior of the ship in order to install the replacement gear. Unfortunately, none of the Yamaro's electronic countermeasures systems had been compatible with that of the Aurora. In the end, it was easier to rip it all out and start over. Therefore, Mister Willard and his teams needed the bridge for a few days. Since they were still in port, it seemed the ideal time to conduct the refit.

His flight teams were not so lucky. Commander Taylor continued to punish them in the flight simulator. He and Cameron had spent many grueling hours in that same simulator when they had first come aboard. He did not envy their punishment.

While Commander Taylor was running the simulations, Nathan had agreed to take over some of her duties in the interim, the first of which had been to answer a call from his security chief as to a recent shipment of ordnance from the Corinari.

The main hangar bay was a flurry of activity, as it had been for the last week, as Major Prechitt's teams moved into the flight deck and all the supportive compartments that surrounded the hangar bay and the fighter alleys. They had wisely begun by filling the areas on the lower decks with their supplies and ordnance before the main hangar deck became too congested.

Nathan made his way across the deck heading for Lieutenant Commander Nash and a group of very serious looking Corinari guards. "What have you got?" he asked as he approached, noticing the row of six carefully secured crates.

"You're not going to believe this," Jessica said. She gestured to one of the specialists that had accompanied the delivery. The technician unfastened the clamps on the lid covering one of the crates. He keyed in a code on the access panel, and the lid began to open, a slight hiss sounding as the hydraulics pressurized and lifted the heavy lid open.

Nathan leaned forward slightly and peeked inside. There were two pairs of what looked like some type of cruise missiles, one pair carefully stacked atop the other. The devices were nearly five meters long, more than a meter wide, and resembled flattened cigars. They appeared to have once had stubby wings on them as well, but those had since been removed and replaced with some sort of armatures located on all four sides near the front and rear of the device.

"What the hell are those?" Nathan wondered.

"Well, they were cruise missiles," Jessica stated. "Apparently, they're the same type the Corinari interceptors used to take out their own missile silos when the Takaran agents captured them. They've adapted them to be launched from our torpedo tubes."

Nathan noticed the symbol on the sides of the weapons. It was the same symbol that the Corinari had used as icons on their main tracking display when they were tracking the flight of nuclear weapons. "Are these nukes?" Nathan asked, his mouth nearly falling open.

"Yes, sir, they are," Jessica stated. "From what the tech boys here tell me, they're about twenty kilotons each."

"Holy crap," Nathan said.

"Don't get too excited," Jessica warned. "From what they're telling me, they've got no targeting systems. All they'll do is fly a straight line, and at less than impressive speeds. So it's going to be more like throwing a spear than firing a torpedo."

"A nuclear-armed spear," Nathan added.

"Yes, sir."

"We'll take them," Nathan insisted. "I guess the Corinairans are finally taking the threat more seriously."

"Yeah, well, Tug and Josh finding the Wallach on her way here probably helped push things along."

"You think we can get anymore?" Nathan wondered.

"These are all we could produce on short notice, Captain," the lead technician said. "We have many more, but they do not have nuclear warheads. These twenty were armed using warheads from our last remaining surface-to-orbit missiles."

"And there are twenty-four of them?"

"Yes, Captain."

"Well, be sure to tell your superiors that we're happy to receive them," Nathan insisted.

"Where should we put them?" Jessica asked.

"Don't ask me," Nathan smiled, knowing his answer was going to irritate Jessica. "Ask the chief of the deck, Senior Chief Taggart."

* * *

"Commander Taylor," Nathan announced, "fancy meeting you here."

"I'm a little busy right now, Captain," Cameron protested. She still had to report to medical every few hours to be scanned and have programming adjustments made to the remaining nanites that were still in her system.

"You don't look very busy to me," Nathan disagreed.

Cameron held up her data pad. "Performance reports," she said.

"Oh yeah? How's everyone performing?" he asked as he opened a food tray and handed it to Cameron.

"Pretty good, actually. What's this?"

"I brought you your favorite—rabbit food."

"They're vegetables, Nathan. They're good for you."

"If you're a rabbit."

"What are you eating?"

"Beef," Nathan stated proudly.

"There are no cows on Corinair, Nathan."

"Okay, it's more like a yak, I guess, but close enough," he insisted, taking a bite. "So what are they doing to you, anyway?"

"Altering the programming of my nanites," Cameron explained.

"Does it hurt?"

"Not in the slightest. All I have to do is sit here until the technician tells me I can go."

"When does the doctor see you?"

"To be honest, I haven't seen him since I came back on board."

"How does he know you're getting better?"

"I guess he reads the reports, just like I do."

"Oh yeah, the performance reports. So, have you figured out who our flight leaders are going to be?"

"That's a tough one. To be honest, at this point I'm leaning toward Josh and Loki."

Nathan choked on his food. "I think we need to get the doctor in here right away," he said in between coughs. "I think you're becoming delusional."

"Seriously, they've scored as high as anyone else for the most part," she explained. "They also work better together as a team than any of the others. Furthermore, we already know they can handle the stress of combat, as they have already proven themselves under fire. That is still an unknown factor with the other teams."

"I agree," Nathan said. "I just never thought I'd see you choose Josh over anyone."

"You know, Tug says he's gotten quite proficient at piloting the jump interceptor as well, despite the fact that he finds it rather boring to fly."

"Then I guess Josh and Loki are still our boys," Nathan agreed. "What about everyone else? Any problems I should know about?"

"Other than Jessica objecting to Marcus as a senior chief?"

"Yeah, that didn't go over so well."

"I understand why you did it, Nathan. I'm not sure I agree with it, but I do understand it."

"Marcus will do fine," Nathan insisted. "He's a smart guy—a bit gruff, I'll admit, but smart."

"Well, according to Master Chief Montrose, he *is* working hard to learn the ropes," Cameron admitted. "I just hope it will be enough to win her over."

"Jessica will get used to it eventually," Nathan dismissed as he continued eating. "There are going to be a lot of things that people just have to get used to," he added in between bites. "We're all just making it up as we go along at this point. The regs just weren't written for this situation."

Cameron thought about what he had just said. He was right, in a fashion. As complete as she had always found the fleet's extensive regulations to be, they just didn't cover everything, especially now. She had always been a stickler for the rules, confident that they would always guide her in making the correct decision under any circumstances. However, more and more, she was finding herself stepping just outside the very boundaries she had respected and adhered to her entire, albeit short, military career.

As much as she hated to admit it, she was beginning to wonder if Nathan wasn't the ideal captain for their situation after all.

* * *

"In position for spacecraft recovery operations, Captain," Loki responded.

"Very well," Nathan answered. "Comms, notify the XO; the ship is in position and is ready to receive spacecraft."

"Yes, sir," Naralena responded.

"Helm, maintain course and speed."

"Maintaining course and speed, aye," Josh acknowledged.

"Tactical, position of our fighters?" Nathan asked.

"Tracking twenty-four, in six groups of four. First four are inbound now, Captain. ETA five minutes," Jessica reported.

"Notify the air boss. He has control of the flight deck," Nathan ordered.

Commander Taylor looked at the row of view screens built into the overhang in front of her. The flight control center was just forward of the main hangar bay, one deck up. Its aft wall was a row of large windows that angled into the main hangar bay behind them, so that the air boss and his assistants could easily see into the bay. Although there were cameras everywhere, there was simply no substitute for being able to look out a window and see exactly what was going on below.

The center monitor was tracking the lead group, the one that Major Prechitt, the CAG, was leading in for a landing on the Aurora's flight deck. They were still a few minutes away and were barely visible on the screen, but that would all change soon enough. Unlike most shuttles, fighters didn't usually approach at low closure rates. They tended to come in fast and brake hard at the last minute, as if they were being chased. It was their way of practicing a quick landing in case they ever needed to use the skill under fire.

"Copy, air boss has the flight deck," she heard the air boss answer. She was only there as an observer. As the executive officer, she needed to understand how everyone aboard her ship did their job. She had chosen to allow the entire aerospace group to set their own procedures as much as possible. Out of respect for the Aurora's established procedures, the air boss, in turn, had requested a considerable amount of input from Commander Taylor. Until now, the Corinari had been operating from surface bases. This was *their* first time as much as it was the Aurora's.

"Talon Two, follow me to port. Three and four land to starboard," Major Prechitt instructed. One by one, the other three pilots acknowledged their instructions. "Remember, gentlemen, pass over the top of the main drive, then drop at a forty-degree angle of descent. You'll touch down just past the forward edge of the outer marker and have plenty of time to roll up smoothly and stop just before you reach the door. Don't forget, the deck has ten percent gravity at the outer marker, so it will pull you down the last half meter."

Major Prechitt thrusted downward, bringing his fighter just ten meters above the Aurora's main drive section. He waited patiently as it passed under him, glancing out to his right to see his wingman, slightly behind, following him in. As his ship passed the forward edge of the drive section, he fired a more intense burst of downward thrust, causing his ship to descend more rapidly. The single thrust had been just the right amount, and his angle of descent showed to be exactly forty degrees, just as he had hoped.

He watched as his range indicator counted down the diminishing distance between the bottom of his landing gear and the surface of the Aurora's flight apron. As the indicator changed to five meters, he applied upward thrust to further slow his descent. His closure rate dropped rapidly, reaching one hundred centimeters per second just as his altitude above the deck reached one meter. After another few seconds of coasting, the artificial gravity of the flight apron grabbed hold and pulled his spacecraft down the last half meter, his fighter bouncing slightly as his gear touched the deck, and he continued to roll forward along the Aurora's flight apron.

"One down," he announced as he applied braking thrust to stop his forward momentum and roll to a stop.

"Two down."

"Three down."

"Four down."

"First group is down," Jessica reported.

Nathan watched the view of the landing deck being displayed on the forward screen. "Nice landings," he commented. "The time they spent in those sims down on Corinair shows." He remembered his first landing on the flight deck of the Reliant where he had done his flight-deck training. He had done quite well on his first landing, but the approach to the Reliant was nearly a straight line, and he hadn't come in nearly as fast. The Aurora's flight deck was purposefully tucked in between her forward section and her main drive in order to protect it from a direct hit. Unfortunately, the placement required radical approaches from either above or beside the main drive section. She was not an easy ship to land on.

Nathan felt a sense of completeness filling him as the fighters continued to land in groups of four, each group five minutes apart so as to give their deck crews a chance to get accustomed to working the Aurora's hangar deck. By the time all fighters had been recovered, the Aurora had twenty-four combat spacecraft on board, twelve in each fighter alley. It was only half her designed load, but it was a good start.

Marcus watched from the forward edge of the hangar deck as the Corinari deck crews directed the four fighters out of the port and starboard transfer airlocks, sending each pair outward toward their respective fighter alleys as soon as they passed through the airlock doors. There were at least a dozen men, all moving about in different brightly colored shirts, each shirt identifying their function on the deck. *It's like watching one of those fancy dances*, Marcus thought, *but for men.*

"Nice work," Commander Taylor congratulated the major as he entered the flight command center. "Not a single bad landing in the entire group."

"Thank you, Commander," he answered as he pulled his flight suit down off his shoulders and refastened it so that the upper half would hang loosely from his waist.

"What's next?"

"First, a quick debrief of the flight in. After the deck crews refuel and clear the group for flight, we're going to launch all birds and do it again."

"Are you planning on launching them through the tubes?" Cameron asked.

"Is there any other way?" the major responded with a smile.

CHAPTER TEN

"Jump complete," Abby reported.

"We're back at our previous location, Captain," Loki reported. "One hundred thousand kilometers from the kill zone."

"Very well," Nathan answered. "Time to simulated impact of shot three?"

"One minute, sir," Ensign Yosef reported. "All perimeter sensors are online and transmitting."

"Hopefully this one is a little more accurate than the last two shots," Nathan stated.

"It is only a matter of finding a speed at which the drone can still make last moment adjustments to its course in order to hit the target zone," Mister Willard insisted.

"Well, I hope you're right," Nathan said. "Time to simulated impact?"

"Thirty seconds, sir," Ensign Yosef reported.

"Begin moving the target zone."

"Aye, sir. Moving target zone," Ensign Yosef answered.

Nathan watched the forward view screen as the tactical display showed eight markers representing the beacons out in space that, when working together, created a false image of a spacecraft on the sensors of the comm-drone. The drone's navigation software was originally designed to avoid objects in space, especially other spacecraft, despite the fact that the likelihood of such an impact was extremely remote. However, since the drones regularly flew into the heavily populated Takaran home system, such safeguards had been necessary to appease the concerns of the population.

For Vladimir and Mister Willard, it had simply been a matter of reprogramming the navigational software to tell the drone to steer *toward* an obstacle instead of away from it. So far, the drone seemed to be failing to make the last minute adjustments and had missed the target by a small amount on both test shots. They were hoping the third shot would be successful, as they only had one test drone left. Otherwise, they would have to go out and collect all four drones on the far side of the system and reload them onto the platform before they could try again. That would take time which they did not have, as the Ta'Akar frigate Loranoi was expected to arrive sometime over the next few days.

"Ten seconds," Ensign Yosef announced.

Nathan continued watching as the beacon icons on the tactical display began sliding to the right, indicating their movement through space.

"Five……four……three……two……one…… simulated impact," the ensign reported.

Nathan watched the red dot appear on the tactical display on the forward view screen, slightly behind the target area. "Damn," he cursed. "Any ideas?"

"I believe the problem may be that the simulated image is not strong enough for the drone's sensors to register until it is already too close to the target to maneuver."

"How can you be sure?" Nathan asked.

"I cannot," Mister Willard admitted. "But notice that the impact point was forward of the target area's original position. This would suggest that the drone was trying to maneuver. Since the rate at which it can turn does not change as long as the speed is constant, this would also suggest that the drone is not making the decision to turn until it is already too late."

"Well, if it's seeing the fake sensor image, why is it turning too late?" Nathan asked.

"I believe that the image is too weak when the drone is still at a distance that allows it enough time to turn."

"So we need to give it something real to aim at?"

"Or something with a stronger signal," Mister Willard suggested.

"We'll give it one last shot," Nathan said, "then we'll go pick the drones up and reload the launch platform before we call it a day. We can ask the Corinairans about boosting the signal strength on the decoy projectors."

"Yes, sir."

"Helm," Nathan began, "set course back to the launch platform. Abby, prepare to jump the ship."

"Contact!" Ensign Yosef reported.

"Belay that," Nathan said.

"Single contact, one thousand kilometers to port, sir."

"How the hell did it get so close?"

"It just appeared out of nowhere, Captain. Trying to ID..."

"Captain," Naralena interrupted, "I am getting a hail from Tug, sir."

"Confirmed, Captain. The contact is Tug's jump interceptor."

"Aurora, Tug. Do you copy?"

"Tug, Aurora. Go ahead," Naralena replied.

"Aurora, Early warning shuttle reports contact with the Loranoi. She is twelve hours away at current speed."

"Tug, Aurora. We copy message."

"Ask him if anyone has spotted the Wallach." Nathan ordered.

"Tug, Aurora. Has the Wallach been spotted as well?"

"Negative, no recent contact with the Wallach, although we expect her ETA to be the same. Major Prechitt requests you rendezvous with fighter group in orbit over Corinair so they can refuel and arm."

"Tug, Aurora copies," Naralena answered.

"Tug out."

"Contact is turning back toward the center of the Darvano system, Captain," Ensign Yosef reported.

"As are we," Nathan stated.

"Contact has jumped."

"Helm, new course. Head for Corinair."

"Aye, Captain. Turning toward Corinair," Josh reported.

"Abby, jump us to orbit over Corinair as soon as you're ready."

"Yes, sir," Abby answered.

"Comms, notify the XO and the COB of the situation, and let the air boss know he needs to prepare to recover his fighters."

"Yes, sir."

"All hands, prepare to jump," Abby announced ship-wide.

"On course for Corinair, Captain," Loki reported.

"Jump plotted, Captain," Abby reported.

"Jump."

* * *

"How much time do we have?" Major Prechitt asked as he entered the flight operations center. The air boss and his assistants were still managing the recovery of fighters and were too busy to talk.

"Just over eleven hours, sir," one of the flight controllers stated. He pointed at one of the mission clocks on the wall. "I set the red clock to the Loranoi's ETA."

"Good thinking," the major stated as he finished dropping his flight suit to his waist and donned his comm-set. "Comms, CAG," he called over his comm-set.

"*CAG, go for Comms,*" Naralena's voice answered.

"How long will we be in orbit over Corinair?"

"*Wait one.*"

A moment later Cameron's voice came on the comm-set. "*CAG, XO.*"

"Commander, how long are we going to be in orbit over Corinair?"

"*As long as possible, Major,*" Cameron answered. "*What do you need?*"

"The weapons yard at our airbase was supposed to be modifying some of our ordnance for use in space, specifically intercept missiles and ship-killers, sort of like the cruise missiles they rigged to work in your torpedo tubes but without the nukes. I do not know how many they managed to finish yet, but I would like to get whatever they have up here while we have a chance. I would also like to top off our fuel reserves while we are at it. We have been burning it up the last few days with all the round-the-clock training, and I do not wish to run low during combat."

"*Put your calls in ASAP, Major,*" Cameron told him.

"We're waiting for deliveries ourselves, primarily the point-defense frag rounds they've been making. We'll try not to pull out until we've received everything they can send us. Also, the captain wants a briefing in one hour."

"Copy that. CAG out." Major Prechitt killed the conversation with Commander Taylor and initiated a new call. "Comms, CAG."

"CAG, go for Comms," Naralena answered.

"Patch me through to Corinari Command."

"Right away, Major."

* * *

"Attention on deck!" the guard at the entrance barked as Nathan entered the command briefing room.

Before anyone had a chance to stand and come to attention, Nathan cut them short. "As you were." Nathan immediately crossed the short distance from the entrance to his seat at the head of the table, talking as he went. "Engineering?"

"All reactors are online and can come to one hundred percent in ten seconds. Main propulsion and maneuvering are ready," Vladimir reported.

"What about electronic countermeasures?" Nathan asked.

"Mister Willard has installed all the systems, but they have only been partially tested," Vladimir admitted.

"Let's test what we can while we have time," Nathan said. "The rest will just have to wait."

"Yes, sir."

"Weapons?"

"All sixteen quad rail gun turrets are online,

sir," Jessica reported. "The four double quads are operating as well, but we don't have any ammo for them yet."

"Why not?"

"It requires retooling their production line, sir," Jessica explained. "They already did it once to start making frag rounds for the quads to use for point-defense. They were going to retool to produce the larger rounds needed by the double quads after they finished up the frag rounds."

"Damn, we could really use the punch from the double quads right now," Nathan stated. "Don't those people have more than one factory down there?"

"In defense of my people, sir, we *are* still rebuilding after the Yamaro's bombardment," Major Prechitt pointed out. "It has only been a couple of months."

"Of course," Nathan said, "my apologies."

"We've still got the twenty-four nuclear torpedoes," Jessica reminded him. "That ought to pack a punch."

"What about missiles?"

"Total of sixty-four, sir. Long-range stuff mostly. But it wasn't easy getting the Yamaro's missile turret to work with our loading system. Don't expect to be able to reload at the normal rate."

"How long?"

"Figure at least a minute for each reload," Jessica warned. "If we go too fast they tend to jam. Then we have to send someone into the turret collar in a pressure suit. Not exactly a fun job, especially during combat."

"Understood," Nathan said. "Feel free to remind me of that during action."

"Yes, sir."

"Abby?"

"The jump drive is fully charged and ready. I've run diagnostics and rechecked the calibration of all emitters. The system is in better shape now than it's ever been. I've got Deliza and Loki calculating a series of likely jump points and entering them into a database. If we are anywhere near one of those points, it can reduce our plotting time by up to ten seconds by using the nearest pre-plotted jump point and adjusting for the difference in our position relative to that point."

"How is the navigator's jump drive control interface doing?" Nathan asked. "Is it ready to use?"

"I believe so, yes," Abby responded. "However, I'd like to remain at my post on the bridge for now in order to monitor the system in case there are any unforeseen problems in the new interface."

"Good idea, Doctor. I expect we'll be making quite a few short range combat jumps, so I'd appreciate it if you'd warn me ahead of time if our remaining charge becomes low."

"Of course, Captain," Abby promised. "However, I would not be too concerned if I were you. Based on the length of your previous combat jumps, you could make hundreds of such jumps without having to recharge the energy banks."

"That's good to know, Doctor, but I'd appreciate knowing that you're keeping an eye on the levels just the same."

"I shall," Abby promised.

"Doctor Chen, how is medical?"

"Fully staffed, sir," Doctor Chen responded, "fully stocked as well. The Corinairans are also sending up several combat medic teams to be deployed throughout the ship. We're as ready as we can be at this point."

"Major Prechitt?" Nathan stated, inviting the major to discuss his readiness.

"We are ready, Captain. I admit I would have preferred more time to conduct additional drills and training sorties, but my pilots had a lot of time in the simulators on Corinair while we were waiting for our spacecraft to be modified. During that time, we concentrated on fighter interception as well as attacking large warships."

"What about your deck teams?" Cameron asked. "Are they ready?"

"This is going to be a pretty straight-forward operation for the flight deck, Commander," Master Chief Montrose stated. "I do not expect a significant amount of recovery and re-launch. While it has been a long time since the Corinari have fought such a battle, history tells us that the battle will be measured in minutes, not hours."

"I hope history is correct, Master Chief," Nathan responded.

"How are we on supplies, Commander?"

"Fairly close to full loads. I've requested that we top off all fuel, life support, water, and other consumables, just in case. While I agree that the battle will most likely be short, we have no idea of the outcome. There may not be a resupply available afterward, so I'd prefer that we're fully stocked and ready for any contingency."

"Agreed."

"To that end, I've also asked that the Corinari send up some additional combat teams just in case. They might also prove useful if the Ta'Akar attempt to board us again."

"God, let's hope it doesn't come to that," Nathan

said, "not again."

"Let's hope. However, if it does, we will be ready to respond."

"Hell yes," Jessica agreed. "A couple dozen nukes and a ship full of Corinari spec-ops. Now that sounds like a party."

Nathan cast a cock-eyed grin Jessica's way as he continued.

"Major, any chance of getting additional air support from the Corinari ground bases?"

"There are only a handful of orbital intercept missiles left in operation," the major explained. "But their warheads were scavenged for use in our nuclear torpedoes. They were replaced with conventional warheads, but against a shielded Ta'Akar warship they would be of little use."

"What about fighters?" Nathan asked.

"There are at least one hundred interceptors left on various ground bases across the globe. However, they are currently outfitted for orbital interception only, so unless you can get the target into orbit over Corinair, neither will be of much use."

"Well, we're going to try and keep them away from Corinair, if possible," Nathan assured him. "They've taken enough of a beating."

Major Prechitt nodded his agreement as Nathan turned his attention toward Tug.

"Tug, what can you tell me about these ships?" Nathan asked.

"The Loranoi is one of the empire's newest patrol frigates. She is a significant advancement over the previous models, like the ones you faced in the Korak system. While she has no fighters, she does have four missile turrets placed fore and aft on her top and bottom sides. Each turret can fire up to eight missiles per load and can fire both high-speed short-range missiles as well as the slightly slower long-range type. She also has advanced sensors and weapons targeting systems, with multiple redundant arrays in order to maintain combat effectiveness even after taking several hits. We believe her design was in direct response to the original tactics of the Karuzari in which we targeted their weapons systems only in the hopes of capturing the ships relatively whole."

"What about guns?" Jessica asked.

"She has a significant number of rail guns as well," Tug answered. "However, they are remotely operated by individual gun crews located deeper inside the ship. This design was also in response to our earlier methods. We used to try to infect their weapons control systems."

"Nice," Jessica commented.

"It was never very effective, to be honest. It should be noted that their rail guns, while effective and capable of causing significant damage, are more for defense against fighters than for ship-to-ship actions. For that, they depend on their missile batteries, and they usually use them from a distance."

"How many missiles do they carry?"

"That is unknown," Tug admitted. "However, I have never heard of a frigate running out of missiles, if that tells you anything. They do have a weakness, however. Their missile batteries take several minutes to reload."

"That's not much of a weakness," Nathan observed, "not with four batteries."

"No, it is not."

Nathan leaned back in his chair, looking at the

faces of his staff as he considered their statements. "People, we are going to be outnumbered and outgunned. Our best, possibly our only hope is our jump drive and the element of surprise. To the best of our knowledge, the enemy ships that are about to arrive are completely unaware of the events that have transpired in this system over the last few months. If we're lucky, they'll come in without shields, expecting only fear and subservience from the Corinairans—no offense intended, Major."

"None taken, sir," Major Prechitt answered. "My people have cowered down to the Ta'Akar for more than three decades. In my opinion, the time for resistance is long overdue."

"Mine as well," Master Chief Montrose added.

"That's good to hear," Nathan admitted. "Not all of your political leaders seem to share in your sentiment, however."

"They are afraid," Master Chief Montrose stated without reservation. "That same fear is what led them to surrender to the Ta'Akar decades ago. With your help, we now have a chance to correct their mistakes."

Nathan took in a deep breath. "It is my intent to strike fast, strike hard, and strike without warning."

"Without declaring intent?" Major Prechitt wondered.

"Why give them cause to prepare?" Nathan defended.

"*I* do not disagree with you, sir," Major Prechitt explained. "However, I suspect that the Corinairan government will."

"He is correct, Captain," Tug agreed. "The Corinairans are quite rigid, both politically and in their interpretation and application of law. They will insist on making some sort of declaration prior to the commencement of hostilities."

"Well that's just dumb," Jessica commented.

"Not from the perspective of the Corinairan people, I suspect," Tug countered. "And this is their system, after all."

"Yes, but we do not want to lose the element of surprise," Nathan argued.

"You may not," Tug said. "As arrogant as they are, I would not expect a Ta'Akar nobleman in command of a warship to take any such declaration seriously. He will most likely respond with an arrogant threat of his own. If you attack at that moment, you may still have your element of surprise."

"And the Corinairan people will have their honor," Master Chief Montrose agreed.

"Very well," Nathan acquiesced, "but unless they immediately turn tail and run, I'm attacking. I'm not waiting around for the Prime Minister to grant his permission."

"I am confident the Ta'Akar will not 'turn tail' and run, Captain," Tug insisted. "This battle will take place, rest assured."

"I expect so, Tug," Nathan agreed. "Now, we've got about ten hours until the frigate arrives, and we still haven't confirmed the arrival time of the Wallach yet, so we have to assume that either ship could arrive at any moment. Meanwhile, I think we should check and recheck all systems, maybe even take the time to conduct more drills in order to better prepare the..."

"Captain, pardon me, sir," Master Chief Montrose interrupted, "but I disagree. The ship and the crew are ready, sir. Right now, they need two things; they need to rest, and they need to know that you believe they are ready. If you believe in them, they will believe in themselves. Stand them down as soon as we finish our replenishment. Let them rest. Let them mentally prepare for what lies ahead."

Nathan looked at the master chief, realizing he was right. He looked at Tug, who had become something of a mentor to him over the last few months, sort of like the commanding officer he had never really had. Tug nodded his agreement with the master chief. "Very well, Master Chief," Nathan agreed. "We'll stand down after the replenishment, but first we're moving the ship to Karuzara. I want the system to look helpless when the Ta'Akar arrive, and the sooner we go into hiding the better. We have no idea how deep in the system they will be when they come out of FTL, and I don't want our old light to give us away."

* * *

Nathan had always been a sound sleeper. Ever since he was a child, he had slept through the night, every night, without waking. Even in the academy, his roommate, Luis, had envied Nathan's ability to simply lie down, close his eyes, and drift away into blissful slumber.

Unfortunately, that had ended when he came to the Pentaurus cluster. These days, he was lucky if he slept even a few hours in a row. Occasionally, he would get a full eight hours, but never in a row, and never without waking at least once. He had tried everything to get back into his normal pattern of deep sleep: exercise, meditation, herbal teas, even white noise. None of them seemed to help. So it was no surprise that with the pending confrontation looming on the horizon that Nathan Scott, captain of the UES Aurora and leader of the Earth-Darvano Alliance, could not sleep.

Nathan sat up and swung his feet off the side of his bed, turning on the light on his night stand. He looked at the clock. It had only been thirty minutes since the last time he had checked. He had been trying to sleep for two hours now, and he was still wide awake. Resigning himself to the inevitable, he rose, went back into the main room, and pulled a bottle of water from the mini-fridge in his kitchenette.

The door buzzer sounded and Nathan walked to the entrance, turning on the main lights before opening the door. Standing in the corridor, looking as haggard as Nathan felt, was his chief engineer and friend, Vladimir. "You couldn't sleep either?" Nathan asked as Vladimir entered carrying a coffee pot and a couple mugs.

"I did not even try," Vladimir admitted. "I brought coffee, or at least what passes for coffee in this part of the galaxy. I knew you would not be sleeping."

"Thanks. How did you know?"

"You forget, Nathan; before you became captain, we shared a cabin together. It was not long, I know, but I know you better than you think. Besides, we are alike, you and I. If I were in your position, I would not be able to sleep either. Not possible."

Nathan sat down on the couch across from Vladimir and poured himself a cup of the dark liquid that the Corinairans had gotten them all addicted to over the past months. It wasn't coffee—it was more nutty and sweet—but it had the same effect, and that was what he needed right now.

"So how would you like to pass the time?" Vladimir asked. "We can a watch movie, or maybe a sporting event? I am sure there are many programs in the database that we have not yet seen." Vladimir could tell by Nathan's lack of enthusiasm that he was not in the mood for mindless diversions. "*Bozhe moi*, Nathan. You look like a little boy who was just told that he could not go outside and play." Still there was no reaction. "You are worried about the battle, *da*?"

"*Da*," Nathan responded, choosing to mimic his Russian friend as it usually irritated him to no end.

"What do you have to worry about? You are the mighty Na-Tan!"

"Funny."

"Seriously, Nathan, what is it?"

"Is it wrong to feel guilty?" Nathan asked.

"Guilty about what?"

"Guilty about wishing that someone else was captain. Wishing that I would've ended up on the Reliant working the D-watch like I'd planned, instead of facing down a couple of Ta'Akar warships on the other side of the Milky Way."

"Are you joking? Who would wish for your responsibilities? Certainly not me, my friend," Vladimir insisted. "Seriously, Nathan, only a crazy man would want this responsibility."

"Then I guess I'm not crazy because I sure as hell don't want it," Nathan admitted. It felt good to say it to someone, especially to himself.

"Of course, life never asks us what we want," Vladimir added as he sipped his coffee.

"Now you're starting to sound like Tug."

The door buzzer rang again.

"Expecting company?" Vladimir asked. "Hey, we should have a party, invite some of the Corinairan nurses over," Vladimir joked. "There are some really cute ones, I hear."

Nathan opened the door and found Commander Taylor standing there.

"Am I interrupting?" she asked.

"Not at all," Nathan said, opening the door to let her in.

"Not exactly the cute nurses, but good enough," Vladimir joked.

Cameron looked at Nathan as she entered, puzzlement on her face.

"We're having a meeting of the insomniacs," Nathan stated. "Care to join us?"

"Yeah, I guess I'm qualified enough," Cameron stated, taking a seat on the couch. "What are you guys talking about?" she asked. "If you're telling stories about women, I'm leaving," she warned.

"Nothing of the sort," Nathan assured her.

"Nathan was just whining about the pressures of being captain," Vladimir teased, receiving a dirty look from Nathan as a result.

"Really?" Cameron wondered, "because, you know, I'd be more than happy to take over for you."

"Careful what you wish for, Commander," Nathan warned.

"You see?" Vladimir said. "You could have given up command right there, but you did not."

"Oh, come on," Nathan protested as he sat down.

"And do you know why you did not?" Vladimir asked.

"Because I'd look like a wuss?"

"Because Nathan Scott always does the right thing."

"Which Nathan Scott are *you* talking about?" Cameron asked in jest.

"I don't *always* do the right thing," Nathan

protested.

"Yes, you do," Vladimir argued, "or at least you try to."

"That's a little more accurate," Cameron agreed.

"Okay, maybe sometimes you do not do the right thing," Vladimir admitted. "Maybe sometimes you do something stupid, but you always *try* to do the right thing. And *that* is what makes you a good man."

"A good man? A second ago you were calling me stupid," Nathan protested.

"I'm really beginning to like the direction this conversation is heading," Cameron announced, pouring herself a cup of Corinairan coffee.

"Okay, maybe stupid is the wrong word," Vladimir said. "My English is not always correct. I meant silly, *da*."

"So now I'm stupid and silly. Great." The door buzzed again. "Just in time," Nathan stated, rising to answer the door.

"Maybe it is the nurses this time," Vladimir joked.

"If it is, I swear I'm leaving," Cameron declared.

"Jess! Perfect, come on in," Nathan invited as he opened the door. "How did you know about our little get together?"

"I noticed all three of you gathered together on the personnel tracking system," she announced as she entered the room. "I figured it was either a party or a mutiny. Either way I figured I should check it out."

"Well, who's watching the bridge?" Nathan asked.

"I left Mister Hayes in charge," Jessica admitted.

"You left Josh in charge of the bridge?" Cameron asked. "Are you nuts?"

"We're holed up in the middle of an asteroid. What's he going to do?"

"But he's a civilian," Cameron pointed out.

"Jesus, Cam, relax," Jessica said. "I'm kidding. I left Ensign Yosef minding the store."

Nathan leaned back in his chair, listening to his friends banter back and forth mindlessly about one thing or another. After a few minutes, he realized that if he couldn't sleep, then spending a little time relaxing with friends was the next best thing.

* * *

"As soon as we exit, I want to jump away while we're still hidden behind Karuzara," Nathan instructed.

"Where would you like to jump to, sir?" Loki asked.

"Turn outward, away from Darvano," Nathan instructed. "We'll jump here," Nathan said, pointing to the system chart showing on Loki's console. "That should be just past the Wallach, assuming she's still inbound. It will also be far enough away that she won't see us until well after the engagement has started. We take a quick peek to get a fix on her position. Then, we immediately jump to the farside of Corinair, right into a high orbit behind her. That way, we'll come out around the planet and break orbit heading directly toward the frigate on her way to Corinair. If the Corinairans want to broadcast their declaration, they can do it while we're hidden on the backside of their world."

"Interesting strategy," Cameron admitted.

"We've been hidden inside Karuzara long enough that our image is already past them, so they don't know we're here. I want to keep it that way for as long as possible. As far as the Loranoi knows, they're headed toward a planet full of sheep."

"You're assuming that they didn't stop to take a deep scan of the system before entering," Jessica pointed out, "like we did before we charged into the Savoy system."

"That's not their M.O.," Nathan said. "But if they did we'll surely know about it, as they'll come in with their shields up and their guns blazing."

"Thirty seconds to open space, Captain," Loki reported.

"Very well."

"First jump plotted and locked, Captain," Loki added.

Nathan turned his head and glanced at Abby. Their eyes met for only a moment, but he knew that she was keeping an eye on the jump plots that the new interface was creating.

"Open space," Loki reported as the walls of the Karuzara exit tunnel fell away on the main view screen.

"All sensor feeds from Karuzara have been discontinued," Ensign Yosef reported. "All sensor data is now live."

"Turning to new course," Josh reported.

The stars on the view screen began to slide to port as the Aurora turned to starboard, followed by the nearby gas giant, Cleo, as it also slid into view along the uppermost portion of the view screen.

"All hands, stand by to jump," Abby announced.

"Jumping in three......two......one......jump," Loki announced.

The bridge filled with the blue-white light of the jump flash, which subsided a moment later.

"Jump complete," Loki reported.

"Tactical plot to main view screen," Nathan

ordered. He still found it extremely annoying that the standard view everyone seemed to expect was of nearby space, especially since ninety percent of what you saw was so far away it didn't matter.

The system plot appeared in a window in the middle of the forward view screen in a rectangular box superimposed over the image of space outside the ship. The map showed the Darvano system, as well as a light day outside the system. There were two tracks, one coming in from the left that represented the flight path of the Loranoi, and another coming in from the right that represented the last known path of the battleship Wallach.

"We are in position, one light day outside of Darvano, along the route from Juntor," Loki reported.

"Helm, come about on a heading for the backside of Corinair,"

"Aye, sir, coming about on new course for Corinair," Josh reported.

"Sensors, find that battleship," Nathan ordered Ensign Yosef.

"Aye, sir," Ensign Yosef answered.

"Mister Sheehan," Nathan said, "calculate a jump to high orbit over Corinair, and make sure we come out on the backside where the frigate can't see us."

"Yes, sir," Loki answered.

"With any luck, the Wallach has been delayed," Tug said quietly.

"I can't afford to bet on luck," Nathan replied, "not anymore."

"Contact," Ensign Yosef reported from the comm station. "Definitely faster than light, Captain. Calculating course and speed now."

Nathan looked at Tug. "See what I mean?"

"Speed is nine times light, on course for Darvano.

Based on size and similarities with Tug's earlier contact, I'd say it's the Wallach, sir."

"Calculate its arrival time at Darvano, Ensign."

"Based on course and speed, ETA to Darvano is thirty-two minutes, Captain."

"Tactical, mark that time and keep an eye on it for me," Nathan ordered.

"Aye, sir," Jessica answered.

"Whenever you're ready, Mister Sheehan," Nathan told Loki.

"All hands, prepare to jump," Loki announced ship-wide.

For a brief moment, Nathan thought about just changing course and jumping away. His ship was fully repaired and fully stocked. It would take at least one hundred jumps over a few months, but they would probably make it back to Earth in one piece. That was, after all, his primary mission.

Unfortunately, the time to cut and run was long past. Vladimir had been right about him all along; he always did try to do the right thing, at least *Captain* Scott tried. The old *Ensign* Scott, he wasn't too sure about.

"Jump plotted and locked, Captain," Loki reported.

"Execute."

"Jumping in three......two......one......jump."

The bridge filled with the blue-white jump flash again. When it cleared a moment later, the right side of the screen was filled with the image of the planet Corinair.

"Jump complete," Loki reported. "Now orbiting Corinair."

"How long until we peek our nose out far enough to be seen by that frigate?" Nathan asked.

"Twenty-two minutes, Captain," Ensign Yosef reported.

"How far out is the frigate?"

"We can't see the frigate right now, sir, but based on its last known course and speed it should be approximately twenty-five light minutes out," Ensign Yosef answered.

"Comms," Nathan began, "contact the Corinairans and tell them that if they intend to transmit any type of warning to that frigate, they'd better do it now, because when we come out from behind their planet, we're coming out shooting."

"Yes, sir," Naralena answered.

"Captain," Abby warned, "even if the Corinairans transmit a message immediately, there will not be enough time to receive a response before we come out from behind Corinair."

"We'll be jumping to just in front of them," Nathan answered. "They can transmit their response then if they so choose."

"And if they agree to stand down?"

"Seriously?" Jessica asked.

"I'm not really interested in their response," Nathan stated calmly.

For several moments, the bridge was relatively quiet. "They'd probably just say something pompous anyway," Jessica mumbled.

"Captain, there will be very little time between your initial contact with the Loranoi, and the arrival of the Wallach," Tug stated.

"He's right," Cameron agreed.

"Jess?" Nathan asked.

"About five or six minutes," Jessica answered from her post at the tactical station.

"Once the Wallach sees you jump, your element

of surprise will be lost on them," Tug continued. "If they witness your attack on the frigate, they may keep their shields tight, and your opportunity to jump inside them will be lost. If that happens, you may not be able to defeat her."

"I had considered that," Nathan stated.

"You must strike quickly and decisively," Tug insisted. "Cripple her on the first pass."

"That was my intention," Nathan added.

"Captain," Naralena began, "message from Corinair, sir."

"Go ahead," Nathan answered.

"Message reads '*Warning transmitted to Ta'Akar Frigate Loranoi as follows. The Darvano system declares its independence from the Ta'Akar Empire. Your ship is in violation of our sovereign space. You are hereby ordered to withdraw immediately or you will be fired upon. This shall be your only warning.*'"

"Damn," Jessica muttered. "That was straight to the point."

"It sure was," Nathan agreed.

"That message was *not* written by the Prime Minister," Cameron observed.

"Yeah, it's too direct," Nathan added.

"I suspect the Prime Minister of Corinair has handed the situation over to the Corinari at this point," Tug concluded.

"There is another message as well, sir," Naralena interrupted. "The second message is being transmitted on a secure channel from Corinari Command. It reads '*Aurora, attack any and all hostile forces at your discretion. Advise if assistance is needed, the Corinari are standing by. Good luck.*' The message was signed by General Valachin, sir."

"Typical," Tug stated. "The politicians satisfied

their obligation to the law, then handed the problem over to the military while they run and hide in their bunkers."

"Commander, shouldn't you be heading for flight-ops? We're about to set general quarters."

"Yes, sir." Cameron paused for a moment, staring at Nathan. He noticed her pause and turned to face her. "Good luck, Nathan."

Nathan recognized a vote of confidence from Cameron when he got one, which wasn't often, as best he could recall. "Thanks, Cam."

Cameron looked at Jessica and nodded to her as well before she left the bridge.

"I should get to my interceptor as well," Tug stated.

"Remember, Tug, as soon as we jump in, you get off the deck and jump away," Nathan said. "You're only going to have about twenty seconds."

"Do not concern yourself with me, Captain," Tug told him. "I can take care of myself. You have more than enough to worry about."

"Just don't jump too far; we may need you."

"I will remain close by," Tug promised. "Call and I will respond."

"Good luck," Nathan wished Tug as he headed for the exit.

"To us all," Tug bid on his way out.

"How long until we get line of sight on the Loranoi?"

"Five minutes," Loki answered.

"Very well." Nathan took in a deep breath and let it out slowly, clearing his mind as best he could. He was about to take the Aurora back into battle. Only this time, she was fully armed and fully crewed.

"Set general quarters, amber deck," Nathan

ordered.

"General quarters, amber deck, aye," Jessica answered.

Nathan moved to his chair, glancing at his watch and noting the time as he walked. As he took his seat, the warning klaxon sounded, and the lighting on the bridge took on a red tinge.

"*General quarters. General quarters. All hands, man your battle stations,*" the prerecorded voice announced ship-wide. Nathan knew that, all over the ship, every man and woman was moving into position in quick, orderly fashion. Every member of his crew knew where they were supposed to be and what they were supposed to do. They had practiced this many times over the past month, all in preparation for this moment.

"All compartments report general quarters manned and ready, Captain," Jessica reported. "Amber deck is set, the XO is in flight-ops, and the chief of the boat is in damage control."

Nathan looked at his watch again in surprise. "Thirty seconds?" he said, rotating his chair around to look at Jessica. "Is that even possible?"

"I suspect everyone was already *at* their battle stations," Jessica responded.

"Mister Sheehan, new jump plot. As soon as we get line of sight on the Loranoi, I want to jump to thirty seconds directly in front of her, based on our closure rate."

"Yes, sir," Loki answered.

"Tactical, load all forward tubes, nuclear with full yield, rig for snapshot, staggered firing."

"Loading all forward tubes, full nukes, rig for snapshot, staggered firing, aye," Jessica answered.

"Deploy all rail guns. We'll start with the forward

guns only."

"Yes, sir," Jessica answered.

"Helm, as soon as we fire our torpedoes, pitch down under the target and go to full power. As soon as your course is set below the target and you have a clear jump line, kill your burn and jump us one light minute forward."

"Yes, sir," Josh answered.

"Mister Sheehan, you're only going to have about twenty seconds to get us out of there before the nukes go off," Nathan warned.

"Understood, Captain," Loki answered.

"I'll get us pointed under," Josh insisted to Loki. "You just be sure you jump us in time."

"Jess, once those torpedoes are fired, I'll need a countdown of the last ten seconds of their flight."

"Understood," Jessica answered.

"Comms, tell the air boss that Tug should be sitting on the apron ready to launch in..."

"Three minutes, Captain," Loki answered.

"Three minutes," Nathan repeated to Naralena. "If he doesn't get off the deck immediately, he'll have to ride it out and take his chances with us."

"Yes, sir."

Nathan took another breath. "Comms, put me ship-wide."

"Ship-wide now," Naralena answered.

"Attention, crew of the Aurora. This is your captain. The Corinairan government has transmitted their declaration of independence from the Ta'Akar Empire. In a few moments, we will be backing those words up with our actions. We will be outnumbered and outgunned, but we will have the element of surprise, the jump drive, and the strength of the Corinari on our side. Perform your duties as you were trained, watch each other's backs, and we shall prevail. That is all." Nathan gestured for Naralena to kill the channel.

Nathan rotated around again, noticing Jessica's expression. "Just thought they should know what they're getting into."

Tug backed his interceptor out to the port corner of the Aurora's flight apron in preparation for launch. He made one final check of his systems and instruments before activating his comms.

"Aurora, Tug. Ready for launch."

"Tug, Aurora copies. Thirty seconds to jump."

"Understood."

"Attention, all hands. Stand by for jump," Abby announced.

"Twenty seconds to line of sight," Loki said.

"As soon as you get line of sight, start your jump plot," Nathan reminded Loki.

"I've already got the plot, Captain."

"That plot was based on an assumption of the target's position," Nathan warned. "If we're going to jump into the path of another vessel, we want to be damned sure of its actual course and speed, Mister Sheehan."

"Yes, sir, but even with line of sight, her track is still going to be fifteen minutes old."

"It's the best we can do," Nathan stated calmly. It was a risky move, and Nathan knew it. He would have preferred to make the sudden jump from much closer, and even with a greater distance between him and the frigate. But their torpedoes were unguided line of sight weapons, so they needed to jump in close enough to hit them before the frigate had a chance to take evasive action. Still, there was no way to know for sure. All they could do was make a guess based on the target's current course, speed, and deceleration. Since the target did not yet know they were headed for a trap, there was no reason for them to alter their approach from the standard pattern that the Ta'Akar had always used in the past.

"We have line of sight," Ensign Yosef announced. "Contact. Transferring plot to tactical."

"I have the contact," Jessica reported. "Takaran frigate. It's the Loranoi."

"Helm, break orbit and head for that frigate, full speed ahead."

"Breaking orbit and coming to intercept course, full speed ahead, aye," Josh answered.

"Start your jump plot, Mister Sheehan."

"Calculating jump," Loki answered

"Tactical, check the system for contacts," Nathan ordered.

"No other contacts, Captain," Jessica reported. "Other than the Loranoi and us, the system is clear. ETA to the Wallach's arrival is five minutes."

"Jump plotted and locked," Loki reported.

"All right, here we go people," Nathan announced. "Jump."

"All hands, jumping in three......two......one...... jump."

The brilliant blue-white flash of the Aurora's jump filled the cockpit of Tug's interceptor. A moment later it was gone and Tug fired his ascent thrusters at maximum power. His interceptor leapt off the Aurora's flight apron, and within a few seconds, he was above her topside line, looking forward. In the distance ahead of them, he could barely make out a small white dot, slightly larger than the background stars and more irregularly shaped. What made it stand out most, however, was that it was rapidly growing larger.

"Nathan you crazy bastard," Tug exclaimed as he pitched his nose up and fired his main engines, reaching for his jump drive control interface as he did so.

"Flight-ops reports interceptor is away," Naralena announced. "Incoming message from the Loranoi."

"Staggered snapshot, all forward tubes. Fire," Nathan ordered.

"Firing all forward tubes, staggered snapshot," Jessica reported.

"Hold the message," Nathan ordered Naralena.

"One fired," Jessica reported. "Two fired..."

"Interceptor has jumped away," Ensign Yosef reported.

"Three fired," Jessica continued. "Four fired. All torpedoes away!"

"Helm, pitch down! Loki next jump, one light minute forward," Nathan ordered.

"Torpedo impact in fifteen seconds," Jessica reported.

"Pitching down, aye," Josh acknowledged as he pitched the Aurora's nose down a few degrees in order to fly under the frigate that was now coming straight at them.

"Calculating new plot," Loki announced.

"Torpedo impact in ten seconds," Jessica announced.

"Sensors, are her shields up?" Nathan asked.

"No, sir," Ensign Yosef reported, "but they're charging their emitters now."

"It will take them a few seconds at least, Captain," Mister Willard advised from the electronic countermeasures station. "Our torpedoes still might beat their shields!"

At that point, Nathan knew that his rail gun rounds would not be fast enough to catch up to the torpedoes before they struck the Loranoi and detonated. Although some of them would probably be vaporized by the nuclear blast, the rest would strike an already damaged target. It might not make a difference, but Nathan knew he might not get another shot at the frigate, and he wanted to make this one count.

"Open fire, all forward rail guns!" Nathan ordered.

"Rail guns firing!" Jessica announced.

On the outside of the Aurora, on her forward section, the six forward-most rail guns opened fire. Burst of pale blue magnetic energy leapt off the rails as the quad guns spat forth a hail of fist-sized metal-alloy projectiles at a staggering rate.

"Five seconds to impact," Jessica reported from tactical.

"Jump plotted and locked," Loki announced from the navigators chair at the helm.

"No Count! Jump now!" Nathan ordered.

"Jumping!" Loki reported, the bridge instantly

flooding with blue-white light.

The Aurora disappeared in a flash of blue-white light as the four nuclear-armed torpedoes streaked toward the frigate. With only a few seconds notice, the Loranoi had no time to maneuver out of the way of the oncoming torpedoes and took all four of them right in her forward shields, which had barely come up to fifty percent charge when the first torpedo detonated in a blinding flash. Each of the remaining three torpedoes struck the exact same section of shielding at one second intervals, all detonating with the same brilliant flashes of light. The force of the four nuclear detonations was more than the Loranoi's forward shields could withstand, and all the shield emitters across her bow shorted and fused, making them inoperable. Only seconds after the last torpedo detonated, a hail of rail gun rounds drilled into the nose of the frigate, ripping her bow open in several places and causing numerous secondary explosions within the forward section of her hull.

"Jump complete," Loki reported.

"Helm, new course. Come sixty degrees to port," Nathan ordered.

"Coming hard to port, sixty degrees, aye," Josh answered.

"Mister Sheehan, as soon as Josh finishes his turn, plot another jump, one light minute out along the new course."

"Yes, sir."

"Damage report?"

"DCC reports no damage, Captain. The frigate

never got a shot off."

"Jess, load all tubes again, fore and aft this time, just in case."

"Loading all tubes," Jessica reported.

"How long until you finish your turn?" Nathan asked Josh.

"Fifteen seconds, sir."

"Comms, play the Loranoi's last message," Nathan ordered.

"Yes, sir." Naralena tapped her console and called up the recorded message. *"Your declaration is in direct violation of the terms of your surrender. If you denounce this declaration immediately, we will consider your unconditional surrender to the Ta'Akar Empire and spare your world. Failure to do so will result in the immediate unrestrained bombardment of all military and civilian targets..."*

"Turn it off," Nathan ordered.

"Well, I guess they weren't planning on withdrawing," Jessica cracked.

"Turn complete," Josh announced.

"Plotting next jump," Loki announced.

"Sensors, keep an eye on the target. I want a damage assessment as soon as possible."

"Yes, sir," Ensign Yosef acknowledged.

"How long until the Wallach arrives?" Nathan asked Jessica.

"Four minutes."

"Anything on sensors yet?" Nathan asked.

"I'm tracking the target now. Her light is old, so I just saw us launch torpedoes on her."

Nathan looked impatiently at Jessica again.

"Ain't relativity a bitch?" Jessica quipped.

"I'm seeing four good detonations, Captain," Ensign Yosef reported.

"Were her shields up?"

"Whoa. If they were, they went down awfully fast. I'm seeing secondary explosions in her bow. Looks like our rail guns tore her up."

"Outstanding."

"Jump plotted," Loki reported.

"Very well, Mister Sheehan. Jump the ship again."

"Yes, sir. Jumping in three......two......one...... jump."

The bridge filled with the jump flash again.

"Jump complete," Loki reported.

"Forty-five more degrees to port, Mister Hayes," Nathan ordered. "Then increase your altitude to match the Loranoi's altitude relative to the Darvano ecliptic."

"Aye, Captain. Coming forty-five degrees to port. Increasing altitude to match the target," Josh answered.

"New jump, Mister Sheehan. I want to be one hundred kilometers ahead of the target, and one hundred to her starboard. We're going to fly across her bow."

"Aye, sir," Loki answered.

"Jess, as we pass, I want to pummel her with rail guns."

"Recommend we roll over and put our topside toward the target, Captain," Jessica suggested, "That way we can get all our guns on her at once."

"You heard the lady, Josh."

"Got it, sir."

"Captain," Ensign Yosef reported, "for our rail guns to get through to her like that, her forward shields have to be completely down."

"If they are, a single nuke might finish her,"

Jessica added.

"Turn complete, altitude matched to target's altitude, sir," Josh reported.

"Plotting jump," Loki added.

"I don't want to use our nukes if we don't have to. We just used four, and for all we know, that might have been overkill. We've only got twenty left, and I have no idea if we're ever going to get anymore. Besides, if we can take her without too much damage we might be able to salvage some of her ordnance," he added. "And I have a feeling we're going to need it."

"Guns it is, then," Jessica agreed.

"Jump plotted," Loki reported.

"Execute jump," Nathan ordered. "Stand by to roll, Mister Hayes. Stand by all rail guns."

"Jumping in three......two......one......jump."

The bridge filled with the jump flash.

"Jump complete."

"Target is one hundred kilometers forward and one hundred to port. Cutting across her path quickly."

"Target is locking weapons on us," Mister Willard reported.

"Rolling forty-five to port," Josh announced.

"Can you jam her lock?" Nathan asked.

"Attempting to jam," Mister Willard replied.

"Open fire, all rail guns," Nathan ordered.

"Firing all rail guns," Jessica answered.

"Distance to target is seventy kilometers and closing fast," Ensign Yosef reported. "Her forward shields are gone, Captain. I'm seeing fried emitters all across her bow, also several hull breaches."

"She's firing," Jessica reported.

The ship rocked as the bridge filled with a red

flash.

"What the hell was that?" Nathan asked.

"Energy pulse cannon," Ensign Yosef answered. "She's still firing, but her weapons aren't tracking us properly, sir."

"Good work, Mister Willard," Nathan congratulated. "Damage report?"

"Checking," Jessica answered. "Minor damage to the port side, just forward of the aft torpedo tubes. That fancy coating the Karuzari applied helped."

"Fifty kilometers and closing," Ensign Yosef announced.

"Rail gun fire will reach the target in ten seconds," Jessica announced.

"Captain!" Ensign Yosef reported. "She's launched a comm-drone. It's headed out of the system."

"Course?"

"I'll give you three guesses," Jessica said.

"It's headed for Takara, Captain. It's accelerating rapidly.

"Comms, hail Tug," Nathan ordered. "Tactical, lock a full spread of missiles onto that comm-drone and fire!"

"Loading missiles, firing in five seconds!" Jessica reported.

"The frigate is starting to take hits from our rail guns," Ensign Yosef reported.

"Keep pounding her with our guns, Jess."

"Twenty-five kilometers and closing," Ensign Yosef reported.

"Missiles locked and loaded," Jessica announced. "Firing four!"

"I have Tug on comms, Captain," Naralena reported.

"Put him on," Nathan ordered as he watched the

missiles streak away from the Aurora on the main view screen. "Tug, are you in position to intercept that comm-drone before she goes to FTL?"

"*I am already at full power and turning to intercept,*" Tug reported. "*If the drone takes the time to accelerate to maximum subluminal velocity before it goes to FTL, I might be able to destroy it.*"

"Thirty seconds to missile impact," Jessica reported.

Nathan watched the tactical plot on the main view screen as the four missiles headed toward the accelerating comm-drone. The longer they could keep word of Corinair's rebellion a secret the more time they would have to build up their forces. That comm-drone could ruin everything.

"Comm-drone just went to FTL, Captain," Ensign Yosef reported.

"Damn it!" Nathan felt his heart sink.

"It was at half-light when it did so. Best guess is fifty times light."

"Tug," Nathan called, "did you hear that?"

"*Yes, Nathan. I tracked it as well.*"

"Can you catch it?"

"*I will do my best,*" Tug answered. "*but I do not have the capability to transmit the dropout signal.*"

"Do what you can," Nathan told Tug over the comms.

"Five kilometers," Ensign Yosef reported. "The frigate is taking heavy damage."

"Tug has jumped away, Captain," Jessica reported. "Sir, if Tug can't get that drone to drop out of FTL, how's he going to shoot it down?"

"He'll just have to make a guess at its position and fire blind," Nathan answered.

"Captain! New contact! Ninety degrees to

starboard, fourteen down," Ensign Yosef reported. "Transferring track to tactical."

"Got it," Jessica reported. "Pretty sure it's the Wallach. Range one hundred thousand kilometers and closing."

"Helm, hard to starboard and pitch down," Nathan ordered. "Put us on an intercept course for the Wallach."

"Aye, sir. Coming to starboard and pitching down," Josh answered.

"What about the frigate, sir?" Jessica asked.

"Can we fire a torpedo from the aft tubes?" Nathan asked.

"On our current trajectory, no, sir. And by the time we line up, she'll have enough room to take evasive if we do fire at her."

"Load four missiles and prepare to fire at the frigate."

"Aye, loading missiles and deploying battery," Jessica answered.

"The Wallach is raising shields and charging energy weapons, Captain," Ensign Yosef reported.

"She's joining the fight," Nathan muttered.

The ship vibrated and shook as it was struck by hundreds of small objects.

"We're taking rail gun fire from the Loranoi!" Jessica announced. "Damage to the number one heat exchanger."

"Helm, roll us back over so we don't take any more damage to the exchangers."

"Rolling," Josh announced. "We're passing the Loranoi's flight path now, Captain."

"Range from the Loranoi is five hundred meters," Jessica announced. "We're still taking fire, but it's hitting our undersides now. No significant damage reported."

"Turn will complete in thirty seconds, Captain," Josh reported.

"Bring the missile battery to bear on the Wallach," Nathan ordered. "We'll worry about the Loranoi later."

"Yes, sir," Jessica answered.

"Turn completed," Josh reported. "Now on intercept course with the Wallach."

"Missile battery ready, Captain," Jessica reported.

"Fire four and reload."

"Firing four," Jessica announced.

"Mister Sheehan, new jump," Nathan ordered. "I want to be five kilometers off the Wallach's starboard side."

"Plotting," Loki answered.

Four missiles shot out of their tubes on the face of the Aurora's missile battery. As soon as they cleared, the launch block tilted straight up and sat down against its base. Four more missiles slowly slid up into their respective launch tubes and locked into place. A moment later, the launch block rose back up and quickly tilted downward until it was level with the ship once again, pointed forward.

"Missiles reloaded," Jessica reported.

"Fire four more and reload," Nathan ordered.

"Firing four. Missiles away."

Nathan watched the forward view screen as the four missiles streaked overhead, disappearing into the blackness of space ahead of them.

"Range to target, ninety thousand kilometers

and closing."

"They're spinning up their point-defenses, Captain," Ensign Yosef announced.

"First round of missiles should reach their target in ten seconds," Jessica reported.

"Jump plotted," Loki stated.

"Very well. Stand by," Nathan told him. "Let's see what the missiles do first."

A wall of small explosions began to form about twenty kilometers away from the Wallach, directly between her and the incoming missiles from the Aurora. Within a few seconds, the wall had grown in both depth and density. One by one, the four missiles reached the wall and were torn apart by the shrapnel from the Wallach's fragmenting point-defense rounds.

"No joy, Captain. The Wallach's point-defenses are too good. She took the first four missiles down without breaking a sweat," Jessica reported.

"Anything you can do about their point-defenses, Mister Willard?" Nathan asked.

"No, sir. She is already jamming. Our missiles will not be able to lock on to her now. To the missiles' sensors, there is nothing out there."

"Second round of missiles has also been destroyed," Jessica reported.

"Update your jump plot," Nathan ordered. "Jess, stand by to fire all forward tubes. Same as before, full nuclear, staggered snapshots."

"Yes, sir," Jessica replied. "Setting one through four, full nukes, snapshots, staggered firing."

"Captain, I wouldn't recommend jumping through their point-defense screen," Abby warned.

"No choice, Doctor," Nathan responded.

"Jump plot updated," Loki reported.

"Execute jump," Nathan ordered.

The bridge again filled with the blue-white jump flash as the Aurora leapt forward more than ninety thousand kilometers in a single instant, coming to her new position five kilometers away from the second Takaran warship.

The entire ship shook violently as she came out of her jump. Sparks flew from one of the newly repaired consoles on the starboard side of the bridge, showering that side of the room and quickly filling the entire bridge with a pale, acrid smoke. Nathan held on tight to the arms of the command chair to keep from sliding out of his seat. Jessica nearly lost her balance, falling forward on to the tactical console.

"Shit!" Josh exclaimed, "What the hell was that?"

"Jump complete," Loki reported. The violent shaking subsided just as suddenly as it had begun.

"FIRE!" Nathan yelled, pointing at the starboard console between Mister Willard and Doctor Sorenson. Mister Willard immediately grabbed a nearby fire bottle and doused the burning console with a fire suppressant powder, quickly extinguishing the blaze.

"Range to target, five kilometers and closing fast!" Ensign Yosef reported.

"Damage reports coming in from all over the forward section," Jessica reported.

"Vent the bridge!" Nathan said as he coughed. He did not look at Abby, wanting to avoid the 'I-told-you-so' look that was undoubtedly adorning her face at the moment.

"The Wallach is firing!" Ensign Yosef reported. The entire ship shook as the Wallach's massive energy pulse cannons began to pound away at the forward most sections of the Aurora.

"Snapshot one through four!" Nathan ordered

"Firing one through four," Jessica reported. "One away. Two away. Three away. Four away."

"Helm, pitch down under her, full speed ahead. I want to blow past our torpedoes," Nathan ordered. The ship continued to shake from the Wallach's continuous barrage from her energy pulse cannons.

"Pitching down," Josh acknowledged. "Bringing the mains up to full power."

"Arm all aft tubes, snapshot, full nukes, simultaneously fired."

"Should I start another jump plot, sir?" Loki asked as he held onto the handrails along his console to steady himself.

"Negative, I want to dive under and shoot from the aft tubes as we come out the other side," Nathan explained. "As soon as we pass under her, plot an escape jump, one light minute ahead."

"Aye, sir," Loki answered. He turned his head to his right and looked at Josh, who looked about as scared as he felt.

"We're passing our torpedoes," Josh announced.

The image of their torpedoes as they rushed toward their target slid backward over their heads as the Aurora accelerated under and past them. The image of the Wallach grew quickly in the uppermost portion of the screen as it came rushing toward them. The screen continued to flash in brilliant reddish amber with each strike by the Wallach's energy pulse cannons.

"We are getting pounded," Josh exclaimed as the ship took another hit. The entire bridge seemed to shift to port as a result of the energy blasts.

"Ten seconds to first torpedo impact," Jessica reported.

The image of the Wallach slid over them on the spherical view screen that encompassed the front third of the bridge. As they passed under the enemy battleship, the incessant pounding from her energy pulse cannons subsided. But it was only for a moment as the bombardment continued as they came out the other side.

"Five seconds to impact," Jessica updated.

"Stand by to fire aft torpedoes," Nathan advised.

"Standing by," Jessica answered.

"Plotting escape jump," Loki reported as he struggled to plot the next jump with his right hand only. His left hand was holding firmly onto the side handrail along the left of his console to keep from being shaken out of his seat as the Wallach continued to pound them.

The bridge filled with light as the first torpedo struck the starboard side of the Wallach just after the Aurora passed under her.

"Torpedo impact!" Jessica reported. There were three more flashes of light that followed as the other three torpedoes also detonated.

"Range from target is five hundred meters and increasing," Ensign Yosef reported.

"Escape jump plotted and locked, Captain!"

"Fire aft torpedoes!" Nathan ordered.

"Five and six fired," Jessica reported. "Impact in five seconds!"

"Jump the ship!" Nathan ordered.

"Jumping!" Loki answered.

Blue-white light spilled out from the Aurora's various emitters as she accelerated away from the Wallach. In an instant, the light enveloped the entire ship and intensified into a brilliant flash of light, after which she was gone. A moment later, the two torpedoes she had fired from her stern tubes struck the Wallach's shields and detonated in a pair of blinding nuclear flashes.

"Jump complete," Loki reported. The shaking caused by the Wallach's barrage had ceased the moment they had jumped, leaving them in a sudden, eerie calm.

"Helm, come about to port, reciprocal heading," Nathan ordered. "As soon as you finish your turn, start decelerating and bring us back down to combat speed."

"Aye, sir. Coming about."

"Start your scans, Ensign," Nathan told Ensign Yosef. "I need a damage assessment on the Wallach."

"Yes, sir."

"Chief of the boat. Damage reports," Nathan called over his comm-set.

"*Lots of hull damage to our forward section, Captain,*" Master Chief Montrose reported over the comm-set from the damage control center. "*Several breaches in the outer hull, starboard side. No inner breaches. Number one heat exchange panel in the primaries is offline. Number two is damaged and working at half capacity. If we do not open up the bottom and bring the backup exchangers online, we will have to start shutting down non-essential items*" *very soon. I would not recommend another prolonged exchange, Captain,"* the master chief warned. *"You may not like the results."*

"What about casualties?" Nathan asked.

"Minor injuries at this point, sir. However, there were a few radiation burns from what little of the heavy stuff got through the hull from our nukes detonating. If the target had not been between us and those weapons, it would have been much worse. No deaths or serious injuries yet reported."

"Go ahead and open up the secondary exchangers, Master Chief," Nathan ordered over his comm-set. "We can't afford to take anything offline yet."

"Aye, sir."

"Captain, the Wallach's shields are still up, sir," Ensign Yosef reported.

"Damn. Did we at least weaken them?" Nathan asked.

"Marginally, sir."

"How marginally, Ensign? Would more nukes do the trick?"

"Very marginally, sir," Ensign Yosef admitted. "We could fire all our nukes and her shields would still hold. She's just got too many redundant emitters on her. When one goes, there's another four of them ready to take over."

"Even if we had enough nukes, we can't keep jumping in close to launch torpedoes at her," Jessica reminded him. "A few more passes like that last one and we're toast."

"We need to get her to launch her fighters so she'll be forced to extend her shields. Then, we can jump inside them and hit her hard," Nathan exclaimed.

"We could launch our fighters," Jessica suggested.

"The Wallach will not see our fighters as a threat,"

Mister Willard warned. "I doubt she will launch *her* fighters to defend against ours."

"What if we launch them against the Loranoi?" Nathan suggested. He turned back to Ensign Yosef at the sensor station on the left side of the bridge. "What shape is the Loranoi in right now?"

"One moment, sir," Ensign Yosef answered.

"Turn complete, Captain," Josh reported. "Decelerating."

"Very well," Nathan answered.

"Captain, the Loranoi's forward shields are still down, and her starboard shields are down to fifty percent. I suspect that our first attack took out enough emitters that her starboard shields are running on their last good ones," Ensign Yosef reported.

"What about her guns?" Nathan asked.

"She's still fully armed, Captain."

"If we send our fighters after the Loranoi, she'll cut them down before they even get close," Jessica observed, "and the Wallach probably knows that as well."

Nathan tapped his comm-set to open a channel. "XO, Captain."

"Captain, go for XO," Cameron responded over the comm-set.

"Commander, how many fighters can we launch simultaneously from our flight apron?"

"At least half of them, sir."

"Put twelve fighters on the apron, ready to launch. We'll jump them in close to the Loranoi. They'll need to launch quickly, straight up, just as fast as they can get off our deck, because we'll be jumping out again as quick as we can."

"Understood."

"Yosef will send them the damage assessments on the Loranoi. Tell them I want that ship rendered harmless as quick as possible."

"Yes, sir," Cameron answered. "What about the Wallach's fighters? Won't they come after them?"

"That's the idea, Commander. Have the rest of our fighters ready to launch through the tubes. We'll jump in and put them behind the Wallach's fighters as cover."

"Yes, sir. Give us five minutes to put the fighters on the apron."

Nathan tapped his comm-set again to close the channel. "Mister Sheehan, new jump plot. As soon as those fighters are ready, we're going to jump in close to the Loranoi, about five kilometers ahead of her," Nathan explained. "Once the fighters are clear, we'll pitch down again and jump away, one light minute forward, just like before."

"Understood, sir," Loki answered. "Plotting the first jump."

"Captain, suggest we roll over again as we pitch down," Jessica stated. "It will take us a few seconds to plot our escape jump and we need to protect our topsides from any more damage."

"Good idea," Nathan agreed. "Did you copy that, Josh?"

"Yes, sir," Josh answered. "Pitch and roll."

Major Prechitt was the first to roll out onto the Aurora's flight apron, having pulled into position on the port edge of the deck. One by one and as rapidly as possible, the other eleven fighters pulled into position, lined up in two rows of six, evenly spread out across the flight apron.

"Flight, Talon One. All birds are in position."

"Talon One, Flight copies. Stand by to launch."

"Talon One to all birds. Do not forget your auto-visor for the jump," Major Prechitt reminded his pilots as he dropped his own visor. The last thing he needed was a bunch of blind pilots.

"Jumping in three..." Loki's voice came across the comms in the major's helmet, *"...two......one...... jump."*

Blue-white light came spilling over the top of the entrance to the transfer airlocks and down onto the flight apron, moving quickly across the apron until it engulfed all six fighters. During that brief moment before the flash, Major Prechitt thought it looked like some ethereal river had overflowed its banks and was rushing toward them. An instant later, however, the light had flashed and it was gone.

"Jump complete," Loki announced over the comms.

"Talon flight! Launch! Launch! Launch!" Major Prechitt ordered his pilots.

All twelve fighters fired their ascent thrusters, causing them to jump up off the Aurora's flight deck simultaneously. It was a maneuver none of them had ever practiced together as a group, and the major was surprised that they were able to launch without knocking into one another.

The top of the Aurora's hull quickly dropped down and Major Prechitt could see forward beyond her. The Loranoi was still a few kilometers away and would not be visible for a few more seconds. As he fired his main engines, four jets of smoke shot out the back of the Aurora's missile battery as she launched a full round of missiles at the Loranoi in the distance. A moment later, the Aurora pitched down and away from the fighters and began to roll over. As his main engines came up to full power and they began accelerating away from the Aurora, he knew she was about to take a lot of rail gun fire, thus keeping most of it off of his flight of fighters.

"Talon One to all birds. Lock missiles and prepare to fire." He looked at his weapons display. The range to target indicator showed them at two kilometers and closing fast. "We fire at one kilometer," he ordered. There was a blue-white flash of light from below them as the Aurora jumped away again. He raised his auto visor in order to see better as his range came down to one kilometer. "Firing missiles!" he announced.

Two anti-ship missiles left the rails on the fighter's stubby wings, racing forward on tails of blue-tinged golden jets of burning gases. "Time to impact, ten seconds. Two through six will break left with me. Seven through twelve will break right and draw some fire."

"The Aurora scored big time!" one of his pilots reported. *"Her starboard shield is gone!"*

"Change in plans! All birds, fall in behind me, single file!" Major Prechitt ordered. "We all slide sideways along her unprotected starboard side. Target her guns on the first pass and her hull on the second. I want to open her up."

"Missile impacts! She is taking damage!" another pilot reported. With the fighters launching the anti-ship missiles from such short range, the frigate did not have the time to spin up her point-defense screen. Nearly every missile fired struck its target.

"Incoming fire! Check your shields!" Major Prechitt ordered. Outside his fighter, hundreds of rail gun rounds began striking his shields, creating little yellow-red explosions as the impact blew them apart and the shield robbed the projectiles of their deadly kinetic energy. Every impact drained his fully charged shields just a fraction, but continued passes with hundreds of impacts per pass would quickly result in complete shield failure. If that happened, he would become combat-ineffective and would have to stand off for several minutes while his shields recharged and reached full strength again. Unfortunately, in a few minutes this engagement would be over, one way or another.

The Loranoi quickly grew in size as Major Prechitt raced toward her. He adjusted his course slightly so he would slip past her starboard side at a range of only fifty meters. At that range, the frigate's rail guns would not be able to keep up with him as he shot past her. As odd as it seemed, that would be when he was in the least amount of danger.

Just as he was about to pass by the Loranoi, Major Prechitt killed his engines and swung his nose to starboard, opening fire with the mini-rail guns in his nose, applying slight forward thrust to counteract the reverse push of his rail guns. Hundreds of projectiles streamed out of his barrels, smashing violently into the side of the enemy frigate, carving a long line down her starboard side. He watched in fascination as his rounds smashed through already fried emitters, external conduits, hull plating, and even a few of the rail guns that were desperately trying to keep up with his fast moving fighter as it streaked past. His entire attack run only lasted two seconds and then he was aft of the frigate and beginning to take fire once more. He swung his nose back around to face the same direction his ship was traveling and kicked in his main engines, wanting to get away from the frigate's aft rail guns as quickly as possible.

One by one and in rapid succession, each of the fighters performed the same sideways strafing run along the unshielded starboard side of the enemy frigate. As each fighter passed by, more of the frigate's rail guns along her starboard side began to fail as they took damage. Finally, in a desperate attempt to protect herself, she started rolling over to bring one of her working energy shields in between herself and her attackers. As the frigate rolled, more of her undamaged guns were brought into action, eventually managing to destroy the last two Corinari fighters as they streaked past.

After two more jumps with turns in between, the Aurora was now sitting half a light minute astern of the Wallach and slightly to her starboard, the same side that faced the approaching Loranoi.

"The Wallach is extending her shields, Captain," Ensign Yosef reported.

"Stand by all rail guns," Nathan ordered.

"Rail guns are ready, sir," Jessica answered.

"Helm, roll us forty-five degrees to port and prepare to jump," Nathan ordered.

"Rolling to port," Josh answered.

"How close do you want us, Captain?" Loki asked.

"How far out are her shields extended, Kaylah?" Nathan asked Ensign Yosef.

"Five hundred meters, Captain," Ensign Yosef reported.

"Put us at three hundred meters, Mister Sheehan."

"Are you sure, sir?" Loki wondered. "That's awfully close."

"No, I'm not," Nathan admitted, "but do it anyway.

And make our speed so that we take from five to ten seconds to pass her. I don't think we can withstand her guns any longer than that."

"Do you want five or ten, sir?" Loki asked.

"Five."

"Plotting jump," Loki reported, shaking his head in disbelief.

"Comms, make sure flight-ops is ready to launch the rest of our fighters."

"Yes, sir," Naralena answered.

"The Wallach is launching fighters," Ensign Yosef reported.

"Mister Sheehan?" Nathan asked.

"One moment, sir," Loki answered.

"We don't have a moment, Loki. That's old light. They launched those fighters thirty seconds ago."

"I'm plotting a jump to within three hundred meters, sir. If it's all right with you I'd like to double-check my..."

"They're good!" Abby insisted.

"Jumping," Loki announced without hesitation.

The bridge flashed with blue-white light. The battleship Wallach suddenly appeared above them as the flash cleared.

"Jump complete!" Loki gasped.

"Open fire!" Nathan ordered.

"Firing all rail guns," Jessica announced.

All sixteen of the Aurora's rail guns began spewing forth their fist-sized, metal-alloy slugs, sending them streaming toward the Wallach as the Aurora slid past her. Before the first slugs to leave their barrels had reached their target, the Wallach opened fire with her own rail guns, firing slightly ahead of the target.

Enemy fighters launched out of the side of the Wallach, cutting directly across the path of the Aurora as she slid past the massive battleship, two of the fighters slamming into the Aurora's port side.

Nathan toppled forward, nearly landing on the helm's center console from the force of the impact. Jessica was slammed into the tactical console, and both Ensign Yosef and Mister Willard were knocked from their seats, falling forward.

"What the hell?" Nathan yelled.

"Two of their fighters launched right into our port side!" Jessica announced, grabbing her side and wincing in pain.

The ship continued to shake violently as the Wallach's rail guns sprayed them along their port side from fore to aft as they passed by.

"We're taking rail gun fire!" Jessica reported.

"Loki, get us out of here!" Nathan ordered.

"Escape Jump plotted!" Loki reported.

"Jump! Jump! Jump!" Nathan ordered.

The bridge again filled with the jump flash, open space and the usual background of stars filling the screen on all sides. The violent shaking instantly stopped as the jump completed.

"Jump complete!" Loki reported.

"Position?" Nathan requested.

"Thirty light seconds down range ahead of the Wallach, just past and above the Loranoi, sir," Loki reported.

"Captain! COB reports hull breaches along the port side!" Naralena announced.

"How bad?" Nathan asked.

"Aft maintenance shops are open to space. Port fighter alley was partially depressurized before they sealed it."

"Is the port alley still functional?"

"Yes, sir. COB reports the alley is intact and operational."

"Casualties?"

"Four dead, six missing, twelve wounded," Naralena reported.

"Very well," Nathan answered. "Notify the air boss. Green deck. Let's get those fighters launched before something else happens."

"Talon One Three, cat one, launching!" the voice announced over the pilot's helmet comms. The large door in front of him dropped into the floor with amazing speed. A moment later, the catapult fired. He held on to the handrails that ran along the sides of his cockpit lip as the launch catapult accelerated his fighter down the launch tube. Two seconds later, he was out the end of the launch tube. He let go the railings and grabbed his flight controls, switching off his auto-flight system and taking control.

"Talon One Three, airborne!" he announced as he fired his engines and began accelerating.

"Talon One Four, airborne!" he heard his wingman announce over his helmet comms. As he cleared the nose of the Aurora, he joined up with his wingman who had launched only a few seconds after him. Two more fighters launched at the same time on the other side of the ship, and he could see them moving closer to him to join up on his starboard side. "All right, we come about and take them head on. First group, break right, now, now, now," he ordered as

he started turning hard to starboard.

"Air boss reports all fighters away, Captain," Naralena announced.

"Very well," Nathan acknowledged.

"That last pass did a lot of damage to their starboard side, sir," Ensign Yosef reported.

"Any change in their shields?" Nathan asked, hoping for a miracle.

"No, sir."

"I should have put nukes into her when I had the chance," Nathan stated.

"When was that?" Jessica wondered aloud. "They only extended their shields five hundred meters. There was no way we could've turned to bring our tubes onto her. There just wasn't enough room."

"Yeah, you're right," Nathan admitted. "How many fighters did they launch?"

"Thirty-two, including the two that rammed into us," Jessica reported.

"How's the first group doing with the Loranoi?"

"First group is down to nine fighters. The Loranoi has taken heavy damage. All of her shields have failed and she's losing main power. It's just a matter of time, sir."

"Comms, tell flight-ops to call off the first group from their attack on the Loranoi. She's no longer a threat. Tell them to join up with the second group to deal with the Wallach's fighters."

"Yes, sir," Naralena answered.

"Why not finish her off?" Jessica asked. "If she's left alone, she might get her shields back online."

"If we finish her off, the Wallach no longer has

a reason to launch fighters. We need her to extend her shields again so that we can put some nukes into her."

"I do not think that will happen, sir," Mister Willard stated. "Ta'Akar captains do not usually put their own ships at risk to bail out another."

"You're kidding."

"No, sir, I am not."

"Our fighters have engaged the Wallach's fighters, sir," Ensign Yosef announced.

Cameron watched silently as the dogfight unfolded on the holographic tracking grid floating in the air in the middle of the Flight Operations Combat Information Center. Slightly elongated three-dimensional green triangles represented the Corinari fighters. Red ones represented the Ta'Akar fighters. The Corinari were dogged combatants. Working in pairs and with the assistance of their flight controllers on the Aurora, they were slowly carving away at the superior enemy numbers.

She couldn't help but be amazed at the professionalism of the Corinari pilots and technicians, especially considering that today was their first actual space combat in over thirty years. Although the average age of the Corinari was thirty-five, none but the most senior of their ranks had ever flown in any type of actual combat. She couldn't imagine the number of hours they must've spent in the simulators on Corinair in order to achieve the level of skill they displayed at the moment.

By comparison, the Ta'Akar pilots were quite inferior. Their tactics were scattered and their pilots appeared to be more interested in personal glory than in winning the engagement. She wondered how the Ta'Akar had managed to stay in power for so long, considering the embarrassing performance she was witnessing today.

In less than five minutes, the Corinari fighters had cut the enemy fighter strength in half. Now, with the Corinari's first group of fighters joining up, they had the upper hand. This dogfight would soon be over.

"Flight-ops reports fifteen kills so far, Captain," Naralena reported, "and the first group is just now joining the engagement."

"Captain, I'm picking up really high thermals from the Wallach," Ensign Yosef reported. "I think we might have damaged one of her heat exchange systems when we got inside her shields. I don't think she can still run everything at once. Not with that much heat showing."

"What does she have that uses the most power?" Nathan wondered.

"Her shields?" Jessica guessed.

"Probably," Nathan agreed.

"Her energy weapons," Mister Willard stated with assuredness.

"Most definitely," Nathan agreed. "I'd also bet her main propulsion produces a considerable amount of heat."

"She has to maneuver," Jessica stated. "Otherwise, all she can do is sit in one place and fire. You can't win a battle that way."

"Comms, send a message to the Wallach," Nathan said. "Tell them to withdraw or be destroyed."

"Are you kidding?" Jessica wondered aloud.

"They might be more damaged than we can tell. If they fall for it, they'll withdraw and our work is done for the day."

"But they'll be back, and with friends," Jessica pointed out.

"That's going to happen no matter what we do here today," Nathan stated. "It's only a matter of time."

"Helm, head toward the Wallach, standard combat speed."

"Aye, sir," Josh answered.

"Response coming in, sir," Naralena reported. "Message reads, 'You are in direct violation of the original terms of surrender. The Ta'Akar will now exercise our rights under article twelve, section twenty-two, subsection...'"

"What the hell?" Jessica interrupted.

"Thanks, we get the point," Nathan stated, relieving Naralena of the need to finish reading the message.

"Captain, the Wallach has changed course," Ensign Yosef reported. "They're headed for Corinair."

"ETA to Corinair?" Nathan asked

"Ten minutes," Ensign Yosef reported.

"Mister Sheehan, new jump plot. Put us between the Wallach and Corinair. Helm, adjust course for the jump. Tactical, load all forward tubes and prepare for snapshot, staggered, full nukes. Lock all missiles on her as well."

"She's still jamming, Captain," Mister Willard warned.

"Then point and shoot the damned things. I want all rail guns as well."

"Yes, sir," Jessica reported.

"Comms, warn the Corinairans."

"Yes, sir."

"Jump plotted, sir," Loki reported.

"Execute."

The bridge filled with the jump flash again.

"Jump complete, Captain," Loki reported.

"Helm, hard to port! Head straight for the Wallach. Be ready to dive under her on my order. Plot an escape jump, Mister Sheehan."

"Hard to port, aye," Josh answered.

"Flight-ops reports the Wallach's fighters have been eliminated," Naralena reported.

"Tell them to send the fighters back to finish the Loranoi," Nathan ordered. "I want that ship dead in space."

"Turn complete, Captain," Josh reported.

"Range to target, five kilometers," Loki reported.

"They should be firing their energy weapons by now," Nathan stated. "You may have been right about their heat exchangers, Ensign."

The ship began to shake violently. "We're taking rail gun fire," Jessica announced.

"Fire missiles," Nathan ordered.

"Missiles away," Jessica answered. On the main view screen, four missiles streaked over their heads, disappearing ahead of them as they sped toward the target that was still too far away for them to see.

"Range to target, three kilometers," Loki reported.

"Snapshot all forward tubes," Nathan ordered.

"Firing all forward tubes," Jessica answered.

"Helm, new course. Come down one degree. Take us under the target."

"Coming to new course, one degree down, aye," Josh answered.

"Plot me an escape jump, Mister Sheehan," Nathan stated.

"Missiles reloaded," Jessica reported.

"Fire again."

"Manually targeting," Jessica reported. "Missiles away."

"Jump plotted," Loki reported.

"Five seconds to torpedo impact," Jessica reported.

"Jump."

"Jumping."

The bridge again flashed with light as they jumped just beyond the enemy battleship.

"Jump complete," Loki reported. "We're thirty seconds down range, directly astern and slightly below the Wallach, sir."

"Helm, forty-five degrees to starboard. New jump. Take us one light minute forward along the new course as soon as you finish your turn."

"Aye, sir."

"What are you going to do?" Jessica asked.

"I'm going to hit them again, this time from their port side."

"Sir, we've only got ten torpedoes left," Jessica warned. "That's not going to do it."

"The Wallach will be entering orbit over Corinair in two minutes," Ensign Yosef announced.

Nathan was getting desperate. He looked around the room, looking for answers. "Doctor, would an object traveling at eighty percent the speed of light have enough kinetic energy to get through their shields?"

"Possibly," Abby said, "but it would have to be a big object."

"What about something the size of this ship?"

"You can't be serious," Jessica said.

"I'll put the crew off in escape pods," Nathan

said, "near Karuzara."

"There's no reason…"

"They're going to attack Corinair, Jess," Nathan insisted. "I can't let that happen, not again."

"With what?" Jessica protested. "They can't use their energy weapons, engines, and their shields at the same time. You saw it for yourself. And they can't use their rail guns on the surface from orbit. Their rounds would burn up in the atmosphere."

"They don't have to!" Nathan protested. "Don't you see? Once they're in orbit, they don't *need* to use their engines any longer. They can just continue circling the planet, blasting away from orbit with their energy weapons. Meanwhile, they'll fix their heat exchanger, and then what?"

"You can't sacrifice this ship," Jessica protested.

"But I can sacrifice the entire planet? No, I can't do that! I have a responsibility to that world!"

"You have a responsibility to our world first! Or have you forgotten that?"

Nathan was torn apart inside. He had already caused the loss of thousands of innocent lives on the surface of Corinair, and now he had to choose between sacrificing millions more lives there or millions of lives back on the Earth. He looked at Jessica, pleading in his eyes. He desperately wanted someone to tell him what to do. Anyone.

"Captain," Mister Willard said, "what about the comm-drone?"

"What?" Nathan asked, still facing Jessica.

"The comm-drone, sir."

"We sent Tug after it," he reminded him.

"No, sir, the other one—the one we were testing. It is still out there."

"They didn't work, remember?"

"They worked, sir. They just did not pick up the moving target soon enough. We just have to give it a better signal."

Nathan turned around slowly to face Mister Willard. "Like what?"

"The Yamaro's transponder, sir. It's still installed, isn't it?"

Nathan looked at Naralena. "Is it?"

"Yes, sir, it is," she answered.

"Captain, the Wallach has settled into orbit above Corinair," Ensign Yosef announced. "She's charging energy weapons."

"Where is the launch platform?"

"Right where we left it, sir," Mister Willard told him. "If I can get Lieutenant Commander Kamenetskiy to help me, I am sure we can alter the navigation code on the drone and tell it to steer toward the Yamaro's transponder signal."

"Will that work?" Nathan asked.

"I fail to see why it would not," Mister Willard assured him.

"Captain, how are we going to launch the drone?" Abby asked.

"Same way we did before," Nathan said. "We jump out and transmit the launch signal."

"No, that won't work," she warned, shaking her head. "You need time for the Yamaro's transponder signal to reach out far enough. The drone needs to pick up the signal early enough so that it still has time to alter its course to intercept the signal source."

"Why can't we just give it a delayed launch signal, tell it to jump a few minutes after we leave?"

"We are talking about an extremely small margin for error, Captain," Abby warned. "The Wallach is in orbit above the planet. If that signal is not in the exact perfect position, if that drone misses and slams into the planet at tens of times the speed of light, Corinair will die a much more violent death than at the hands of the Ta'Akar."

"The Wallach has opened fire on the planet, Captain," Ensign Yosef announced.

"Mister Willard, talk to the Cheng and get on that code," Nathan ordered.

"Right away, sir," Mister Willard promised.

"Comms, get me Corinari Command. I need to know the patrol schedule of the early warning jump shuttles. We're going to need one of them to jump out and launch the drone."

"Yes, sir."

"Captain, I cannot stress enough the risk that you are subjecting the planet to..." Abby started to repeat.

"I appreciate what you're saying, Doctor, but right now, people are dying by the hundreds with every energy blast the Wallach fires, and she'll just keep looping around the planet over and over again, firing away, until everyone on that world is dead. We've already seen them do it, both in Taroa and here. If we don't do something, right now, millions of Corinairans will surely die. This is the only chance they've got."

Nathan stared at Abby for several seconds, waiting for her to respond.

"I'll try to calculate an angle and launch window that will result in the least risk for the planet, Captain," she finally stated.

"Thank you, Doctor." Nathan took a deep breath. He finally had a plan.

"Captain," Naralena said. Her voice was weak, as

if something terrible had happened.

"What is it?"

"I cannot raise Corinari Command, sir."

"What?"

"Neither can flight-ops."

"Communication and control is always the first target," Jessica stated.

Nathan felt his heart sink. Without the patrol schedules, it could take them hours to locate one of the jump shuttles.

"Contact!" Ensign Yosef announced.

"Are you kidding me?" Nathan cried in desperation.

"A new contact just came into the system, about two light minutes out. Transferring track to tactical."

Jessica stared at her screen, tapping buttons on her console as she analyzed the new contact. "I've got it," she stated.

"Who is it?" Nathan asked, afraid of the answer.

Jessica's expression suddenly relaxed. "It's Tug, sir!"

"Oh, hell yes!" Nathan exclaimed. "Comms, tell him to get his ass over here."

"Multiple contacts coming up from the surface," Ensign Yosef announced.

"From where?" Nathan asked.

"From all over the planet, sir. They appear to be Corinari interceptors."

"They're going to attack the Wallach," Jessica said, astounded. "Don't they realize how hopeless that is?"

"They don't care," Nathan said. "They're refusing to go down without a fight."

* * *

"The Wallach will be coming around the far side in ten minutes," Nathan announced ship-wide. "According to our calculations, that will be the best moment to strike as it presents the least risk for the planet should the drone miss. We need to get this right the first time. If we don't, we'll have to wait another ninety minutes for the Wallach to complete another orbit and come back into position. Every time she makes an orbit, tens of thousands of Corinairans die. We cannot allow that to happen. We *will not* allow that to happen. I intend to put this ship in close proximity to the Wallach, directly in the path of the incoming drone in order to use the Yamaro's transponder to guide the drone to the target. We will jump out of the way at the absolute last second in order to ensure that the drone collides with the Wallach. That means we're going to have to take a lot of rail gun fire, and maybe even some energy weapons fire. So damage control parties will need to be on their toes, as well as medical." Nathan paused for a moment, trying to decide what else to say. "No captain could expect a better crew. It has been an honor to lead you all into battle. That is all."

Nathan looked around the bridge. Never had there been a quieter moment. He looked at the solemn faces of his crew. Each of them understood the risk, but each of them also understood what was at stake. What amazed him was that not one of them complained. Not one of them asked to leave. That's when he realized that Tug and Master Chief Montrose were right; the captain was someone that you were willing to follow into battle, even if you knew you would die doing so.

"Mister Sheehan," Nathan said, "jump us in."

Tug watched as the Aurora jumped away in a blue-white flash of light. She had only jumped a light minute away, jumping straight down into orbit, not more than five hundred meters ahead of the Wallach. By now, she would already be taking fire, even though it would take another minute for that fact to show up on Tug's sensors. He watched and waited, trying not to think about the astronomically long odds they were about to play. Even if every single thing went absolutely perfect, it might still fail. There were just that many unknowns involved. The only thing he was sure of was that the amount of energy that would be unleashed if the drone actually did impact the Wallach would far exceed any weapon ever known to have been invented or used in the history of humanity.

The history of humanity. Tug thought about that for a moment, wondering how history would judge their actions on this day. Would they call them heroes or madmen? It could go either way.

Eighty-seven seconds after the Aurora had jumped away, Tug picked up sensor readings indicating that they had engaged the Wallach in battle in orbit over Corinair. A few seconds later, he picked up the Yamaro's transponder signal being transmitted by the Aurora from her position in front of the Wallach. He now had five minutes and thirty-seven seconds in which to execute his part of the plan. He applied a small amount of forward thrust, just enough to set his ship in motion, and then pressed the jump button.

A moment later, as the flash cleared, Tug

picked up the comm-drone launch platform on his sensors. It was exactly where it was supposed to be, two hundred meters away from him. He began transmitting the update to the drone's navigational software that included the instructions for the drone to steer toward the Yamaro's transponder signal. With any luck, the Wallach's electronics jamming would not interfere with the transponder signal, since it was a 'friendly' signal, but there was no way they could know for sure. It had been another reason they had chosen to take their shot at this particular time, as the drone and the Wallach would be headed directly toward each other instead of the Wallach going across the drone's flight path. This moment not only decreased the likelihood of striking the planet, but it decreased the amount of course correction needed by the drone to stay on target right up to the moment of impact.

Tug's communications system beeped, indicating that the data transfer to the drone had been completed. He checked his mission clock and saw that the proper launch window was coming up in fifteen seconds. He spun his interceptor around and prepared for the chase. A few seconds later, the mission clock hit zero and he pressed the launch button.

The drone streaked past him a few seconds later. Tug fired his engines and brought them up to full power, the force pushing him back into his seat slightly despite his interceptor's inertial dampeners. He chased the drone, watching it continue to accelerate away from him. The comm-drones were extremely fast and could reach subluminal speeds of ninety percent the speed of light in as little as thirty minutes. Even if his ship could accelerate that fast, his inertial dampeners could not prevent his body from becoming a pile of sludge against the back of his seat.

For their purposes, however, a few times the speed of light would be enough. Even with the deceleration effects of the Wallach's multi-layered shielding, the amount of kinetic energy that the drone would be carrying upon impact would devastate the Wallach. The beauty of the plan was that, because the drone would be traveling faster than the speed of light, the Wallach would not even see it coming. About the only warning she would get would be when her shield emitters suddenly fried due to overload as the drone passed through the shield layers. They might actually see the drone for a split second before it struck their ship, a thought that Tug found intriguing.

Within a minute, the drone reached ten percent the speed of light. As it did so, it disappeared as its FTL fields engaged and the drone instantly jumped up to ten times the speed of light. Tug checked his sensors, ensuring that they had registered the exact speed of the drone and the time that it had gone to FTL. The Aurora would need the information for their part of the plan.

The Aurora vibrated and shook as she continued to take rail gun fire from the battleship Wallach not more than five hundred meters behind her.

"Keep it up, Josh," Nathan ordered. "The more we move around, the more she has to work to hit us."

"It doesn't look like they have to work hard enough, sir!" Josh responded as he jogged the ship from side to side and up and down.

"Missiles reloaded!" Jessica announced.

"Helm, steady her out for a moment. Fire when ready, Jess!"

Jessica waited for the ship to steady, adjusting the angle on the missile battery sitting on top of the Aurora until the aiming reticle was centered on the Wallach's live image in the target camera. "Firing!" she announced, pressing the launch button.

On the forward view screen, four more missiles streaked over their heads on their way to the Wallach. Nathan knew they weren't going to do any good, but at least it kept the enemy thinking they were invincible, which was fine with him.

"They're still firing their energy weapons at the planet, sir!" Ensign Yosef reported.

Nathan felt guilty for thinking it, but as long as the Wallach was firing her energy weapons at the planet, they weren't firing them at him. They could take a pounding from her rail guns for a while, as their hull had been designed for just that purpose. It was several layers thick, with specialized sections in between that greatly absorbed the kinetic energy the enemy's rail gun rounds carried. It would take several very lucky shots, all striking in the exact same spot and at the exact same angle, for one of those rounds to puncture their inner hull.

"Don't worry about that right now, Ensign," Nathan ordered. "You just keep your eye on that mission clock."

Of course, it wasn't only hull punctures they were worried about. There were a lot of things on the hull that could be damaged, and they had already lost several external systems. If it hadn't been for the constant jamming being performed by Mister

Willard, the Wallach would have gotten a much clearer targeting image and would have been able to take aim at specific components.

"Captain!" Abby shouted above the noise of rail gun rounds striking the hull and the various warnings and alarms going off all around the bridge. "We'll have a much better chance of hitting the Wallach if we can get her to turn and show us her profile."

"Not much chance of that!" Nathan told her. "No captain shows any more cross-section to an enemy than they have to."

"Contact!" Ensign Yosef reported.

"It's Tug, sir!" Naralena reported. "I am receiving a data transmission from him now."

"It's about time!" Nathan observed.

"Missiles reloaded," Jessica reported.

"Fire when ready," Nathan ordered.

"I've got the launch data," Ensign Yosef reported.

"Send a copy to Doctor Sorenson as well," Nathan ordered. "I want two brains as well as all our computers checking the math on this one."

"Missiles away!" Jessica reported. "We're down to seventy-five percent on our rail gun ammo."

"Why isn't she firing any missiles at us?" Nathan wondered.

"She doesn't need to," Jessica stated. "She's just harassing us, giving her rail gun operators some target practice. If she ever runs out of rail gun ammo, she might start lobbing missiles at us. Besides, she knows we can jump away if she does."

"Her captain's not as dumb as I'd hoped," Nathan stated.

"I have a solution, Captain!" Ensign Yosef announced. "Coming up on two minutes to impact.

Setting countdown clock."

"Abby?" Nathan called, turning her way.

"I concur!"

"Very well," Nathan agreed. "I just hope we can last two more minutes."

"Captain, can't we just turn our belly to him and take the shots?" Jessica asked.

"If we stop firing, he might think we're out of ammo and turn his energy weapon on us for a finishing blow," Nathan stated. "Mister Willard, what can he see of us through your jamming?"

"Nothing more than a silhouette, sir," Mister Willard explained. "He cannot see any more detail than that."

"I'll keep that as a last option," Nathan decided.

"Ninety seconds to impact!" Ensign Yosef announced.

Nathan tried not to think about the comm-drone that was streaking toward him at ten times the speed of light.

An alarm sounded on Abby's console. Red and orange lights began flashing on a drawing that represented the Aurora and all the jump field emitters that were placed about her hull. "Captain, I've got a hit on a primary junction on the power distribution system for the emitters!"

"What does that mean?" Nathan asked.

"It means I'm not sure if the system will compensate properly through the other nodes."

"Will it or won't it, Doc?" Nathan asked, shouting to be heard above the alarms as well as the sound of rail gun rounds as the sprayed across the top of the ship.

"I don't know! I did not design that part of the system; my father did!"

"Great! Can we pull out of the way manually?" Nathan asked.

"If we do, the drone may alter course to stay with us," Mister Willard warned.

"What if we just turn the transponder off and then try to move?"

"I don't know, Captain," Mister Willard admitted. "It may just track the ship itself, in which case it will still alter course to stay with us. The whole plan was based on the idea that we could jump out of the way at the last second!"

"One minute to impact!" Ensign Yosef announced.

"Do what you can to make sure the other nodes compensate, Doctor," Nathan ordered. "And pray that your father designed those compensation systems correctly."

"I will try, Captain," Abby promised, "but it would help if we did not take any more hits like that along our topside. The system can only compensate for so much before it will refuse to allow a jump to occur."

"Doctor, you have to override that particular fail safe. This ship has to jump!"

"If I do and the other nodes do not compensate for the damaged power pathways, some parts of the ship might not be included in the jump!"

"Yeah, I was trying not to think about that part!" Nathan admitted. "Josh, roll us over and show them our belly!"

"Rolling!" Josh announced as the ship began to roll, the stars on the main view screen rotating.

Nathan could hear and feel the vibrations of the Wallach's rail gun rounds as they walked from the top of his ship, around the port side, and across onto her reinforced underside. The shaking eased slightly, as did the noise, but both were still present.

"Thirty seconds to impact!" Ensign Yosef reported.

"Tell me you have our escape jump already plotted," Nathan said to Loki.

"Are you kidding?" Loki asked.

"Captain," Jessica called, "she's turning!"

"What?"

"The Wallach, she's yawing and rolling! I think she's trying to bring more guns on us!"

"She thinks we're out of ammo!" Nathan exclaimed.

"Twenty seconds to impact!"

"She's moving in closer as well!" Jessica added. "She's trying to move in for the kill!"

"I was wrong about that guy," Nathan mumbled. "He's a dumbass."

"Ten seconds to impact!" Ensign Yosef yelled.

"Mister Sheehan! Stand by to jump on my command!" Nathan ordered.

"Standing by to jump, aye!" Loki answered.

"Five......"

"Set forward view screen to the target!" Nathan ordered, wanting to take one last look at the ship he was about to destroy.

"Four......"

The main view screen switched over, showing a view of the Wallach as she approached. She was still a few hundred meters away.

"Three......"

"Magnify," Nathan ordered.

"Two......"

The image on the screen magnified once. The image of the Wallach now filled the screen.

"JUMP!"

Tug watched from his position just a few kilometers away in a higher orbit over Corinair. He could see neither ship from his position, but had all of his reconnaissance cameras trained on the event. On his main console, he had one of his cameras zoomed in on the Wallach's position. He saw the Aurora's jump flash, followed a moment later by a flash so intense he had to cover his eyes despite the auto-darkening capabilities of his helmet visor. It took several seconds for the flash to subside enough to actually see anything on his monitor. He zoomed out slightly in order to encompass the entire image of the explosion. The force of the drone's impact had ripped the massive battleship in half. The concussion and subsequent secondary explosions had then blasted her apart from the inside out sending fragments spinning off in all directions. The biggest debris field had shot out from the opposite side of the once great warship, the force of the impact causing the far side of the ship to spew outward. Those pieces would have enough velocity to leave orbit. They probably would have enough velocity to leave the entire system.

Tug wondered if pieces of the Wallach might be found thousands of light years away some time in the distant future. He wondered what the finders of such objects would think. Would they figure out what it was, where it came from, and how it was destroyed? Would they even know of the battle that took place here this day? If so, would they display their artifact in some private collection, or in a museum on some distant world?

His thoughts were interrupted by his helmet comm. *"Tug, Aurora. Do you copy?"* It was Naralena.

"Aurora, go for Tug," he answered.

"Tug, Aurora. Hold one."

Tug continued to watch his monitor as pieces of the Wallach began to burn up on the Corinairan atmosphere. *It must have been an incredible sight for them to behold,* he thought.

"Tug, Nathan. How does it look?"

Tug laughed. "Glorious, my friend. Glorious."

* * *

Nathan entered his ready room, thankful to finally have a moment alone. The bridge, in fact the entire ship, had been awash with congratulatory handshakes and pats on the back. He had thanked his bridge crew for their excellent work, and had waited for all his surviving fighters to be recovered before he set a course back to Karuzara. There were repairs to be made, and wounded to be tended. Unfortunately, Tug had been right; there were new dead to be buried.

He sat alone in his chair, his hands quivering, the adrenaline of the engagement still coursing through his veins. It would wear off soon—he was sure of this—and then he might finally sleep, from pure exhaustion if nothing else. It would not be from peace of mind, of that he could be sure. Although the losses among his crew had been few, thousands had surely died on Corinair. The Wallach had been allowed to make nearly a full orbit around the planet, bombarding the Corinairans with a near constant rain from her energy pulse cannons. It had been a difficult decision to wait to take their shot, but he had been left with no other choice. The risk of cracking the planet in half was too great. It had been better to sacrifice thousands to protect millions. At least that was what he would continue to tell himself.

The door buzzer sounded, breaking him from his guilt. He grasped his hands together to stop the quivering and tried as best he could to compose himself. "Enter," he called out.

The hatch opened and Cameron stepped into the room, closing the hatch behind her. "You look like hell," she commented upon seeing him.

"I feel like hell," he admitted. "It's probably just the adrenaline rush wearing off."

"You should be pleased with yourself right about now," she encouraged.

"I don't think so, Cam. I just allowed thousands of people to die on Corinair," he stated in hushed tones.

"But you saved millions by doing so."

"Did I save them," Nathan wondered, "or did I just postpone their deaths another day?"

"You can't look at it that way, Nathan, not if you expect to live with yourself in the end."

"Perhaps." Nathan leaned back in his chair, taking in a deep breath and changing the subject. "How many of our own did we lose?"

"Twelve dead, forty-seven injured, fourteen of them are serious."

"How many pilots?"

"Four did not return."

The hatch opened again, slowly, and Tug peeked inside. "Captain?"

"Tug, come in," Nathan said.

"Commander," Tug added, noticing Cameron as he entered.

"Nice work," Nathan congratulated.

"To you as well," Tug returned. "Your crew

performed admirably."

"Yes, they surely did," Nathan agreed. "By the way, in all the excitement, I forgot to ask you about the drone. Did you manage to catch it?"

"No, I did not," Tug admitted, his expression falling. "But I am afraid I have even more troubling news to report."

"What is it?" Nathan asked, noticing the dour expression on the face of his friend and mentor.

"I'm afraid Mister Dumar was correct in his conclusions, Nathan. That drone was traveling at well over five hundred times the speed of light. It will only take three days for it to reach Takara."

"Then it's true," Nathan said, his expression falling as well. "They've already started implementing the zero-point energy device."

"Yes. If we do not act quickly, soon it will be too late."

"Then we have to attack immediately," Cameron stated emphatically.

Both Nathan and Tug looked at Cameron with surprise. From the beginning, she had been against their involvement in the affairs of the Pentaurus cluster. She had never made any illusions to the contrary. Her sudden and enthusiastic endorsement was all Nathan needed.

"We will, Commander. We will."

53284717R00275

Made in the USA
San Bernardino, CA
11 September 2017